Praise for

HARRY SIDEBOTTOM

'Makes you feel as though you are there'

BETTANY HUGHES, *THE TIMES*

'Harry Sidebottom's epic tale starts with a chilling assassination and goes on, and up, from there'

MARY BEARD

'An amazing story of bloodlust, ruthless ambition and revenge'

KATE SAUNDERS, *THE TIMES*

'An extraordinarily vivid take on the ancient world. Think of *The Killing* crossed with Andy McNab crossed with Mary Beard, and you're there'

DAVID SEXTON, *EVENING STANDARD*

'Ancient Rome has long been a favourite destination for writers of historical military fiction. Much the best of them is Harry Sidebottom'

SUNDAY TIMES

'Swashbuckling as well as bloody, yet curiously plausible . . . a real gift for summoning up a sense of place'

TIMES LITERARY SUPPLEMENT

'The best sort of red-blooded historical fiction – solidly based on a profound understanding of what it meant to be alive in a particular time and place'

ANDREW TAYLOR

'Absorbing, rich in detail and brilliant'

THE TIMES

'Sidebottom's prose blazes with searing scholarship'

THE TIMES

'Superior fiction, with depth, authenticity and a sense of place'

TLS

'A storming triumph . . . wonderful fight scenes, deft literary touches and salty dialogue'

THE DAILY TELEGRAPH

'He has the touch of an exceptionally gifted story teller, drawing on prodigious learning'

TIMOTHY SEVERIN

THE
LAST
HOUR

THE
LAST
HOUR

HARRY SIDEBOTTOM

ZAFFRE

First published in Great Britain in 2018 by
ZAFFRE PUBLISHING
80–81 Wimpole St, London W1G 9RE
www.zaffrebooks.co.uk

This is a work of fiction. Names, places, events and
incidents are either the products of the author's
imagination or used fictitiously.

A CIP catalogue record for this book is
available from the British Library.

Hardback ISBN: 978-1-78576-421-9
Trade Paperback ISBN: 978-1-78576-422-6
Ebook ISBN: 978-1-78576-423-3

1 3 5 7 9 10 8 6 4 2

Typeset by IDSUK (Data Connection) Ltd
Printed and bound by Clays Ltd, St Ives Plc

MIX
Paper from
responsible sources
FSC
www.fsc.org   FSC® C018072

Zaffre Publishing is an imprint of Bonnier Zaffre,
a Bonnier Publishing company
www.bonnierzaffre.co.uk
www.bonnierpublishing.co.uk

Harry Sidebottom was brought up in racing stables in Newmarket where his father was a trainer. He took his Doctorate in Ancient History at Oxford University and has taught at various universities, including Oxford, where he lectures in Ancient History.

His first book *Ancient Warfare: A Very Short Introduction* was published in 2004 to critical acclaim and he has published numerous chapters in books, and articles and reviews in scholarly journals. His career as a novelist began with *Fire in the East*, the first of his six-novel Warrior of Rome series, which has sold over half a million copies worldwide. His next series, Throne of the Caesars, was equally acclaimed. *The Last Hour*, his tenth novel, introduces us once again to Marcus Clodius Ballista, hero of the Warrior of Rome books.

www.harrysidebottom.co.uk

To my aunt, Terry Bailey

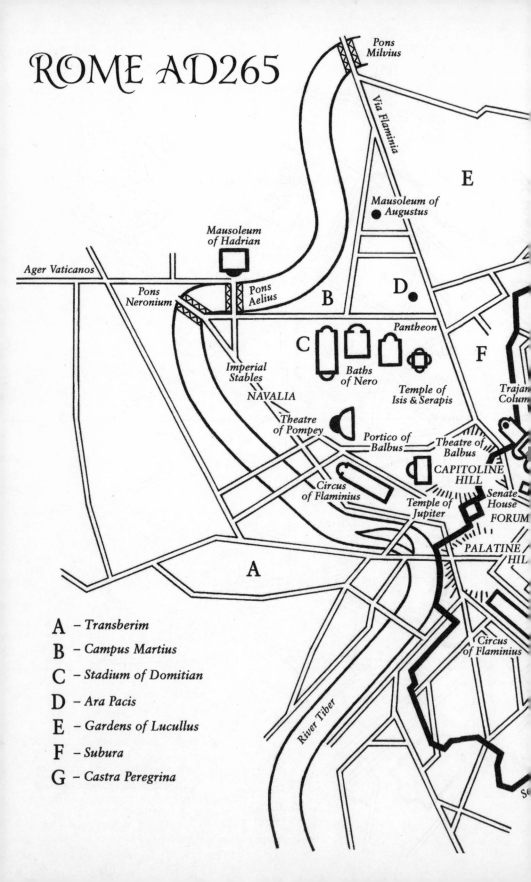

ROME AD265

Pons Milvius

Via Flaminia

E

Mausoleum of
● **Augustus**

Mausoleum
of Hadrian

Ager Vaticanos

Pons
Neronium

Pons
Aelius

B

D ●

Pantheon

C

Baths
of Nero

Temple of
Isis & Serapis

F

*Traja...
Colum...*

Imperial
Stables

NAVALIA

Theatre
of Pompey

Portico of
Balbus

Theatre of
Balbus

**CAPITOLINE
HILL**

Circus
of Flaminius

Temple of
Jupiter

Senate
House
FORUM

**PALATINE
HILL**

A

Circus
of Flaminius

River Tiber

S...

A – Transberim
B – Campus Martius
C – Stadium of Domitian
D – Ara Pacis
E – Gardens of Lucullus
F – Subura
G – Castra Peregrina

N

W E

S

QUIRINAL HILL

Pretorian Camp

VIMINAL
HILL

ESQUILINE HILL

Trajans Market

CARINAE

Trajans
Forum

Baths of
Trajans

Colosseum

Via
Sacra

Meta
Sudans

Temple of
Claudius

CAELIAN HILL

G

n Wall

Gardens of
Donabella

0   500m   1000m

PROLOGUE

The Mausoleum of Hadrian
The Day before the Kalends of April

'THE LAST HOUR.'

The dying man lay on the floor, propped against the wall, with both hands pressed to the wound in his stomach.

Ballista bent over him. 'The last hour of what?'

'Tomorrow. The last hour of daylight. They are going to kill the emperor when he leaves the Colosseum.'

A noise came from somewhere below them in the depths of the tomb.

Ballista went to the door, stepping carefully over the two corpses.

The sounds of boots, hobnails on stone, the clatter of weapons. Armed men down at the entrance of the Mausoleum. There were a lot of them. They were coming up the stairs.

Ballista went back into the room.

'Help me,' the injured man said.

Ballista slapped him across the face. 'Who?'

'They never said.'

Ballista hit him again.

'Please. I do not know.'

Ballista believed him.

'Don't leave me here.'

Ballista had killed the two knifemen when he had burst through the door, but he had been too late to save the informant. Still, he had found out the time and the place.

'Please.'

The mission had not failed, not if Ballista could get away. He stood up.

'They will kill me.'

Ballista moved to the door. The sounds were closer.

'You cannot leave me.'

No way down. He had to go up. Ballista turned left, and started up the stairs two at a time.

'You barbarian bastard!'

Ballista pounded up the stairs.

'Bastard!'

The corridor ran in a spiral through the heart of the enormous monument. Ballista had been here once before, many years ago, when he first came to the city. The view of Rome was good from the top. He remembered a roof garden up there, and a statue of the Emperor Hadrian in a chariot. The Allfather willing, there would be another passageway down.

The meeting had been a trap. Scarpio had sent him to meet the informant. He had insisted Ballista go alone. Had the Prefect of the City Watch known it was a trap? No time to think about that now. Work it out if he survived the next hour.

Ballista ran, holding his scabbard clear of his legs. Always upwards, always turning to the left. On and on, two steps at a time. As he ran under the light wells set in the ceiling, he flashed through insubstantial columns of bright air, then plunged back into the gloom.

His chest was beginning to hurt, his thigh and calf muscles complain. How far could it be to the top?

There were closed doors on the inner wall. He did not stop. If they gave onto chambers like the one that he had left, they would contain nothing but the ashes of long-dead members of imperial dynasties. They would offer no way down.

Raised voices, then a scream, echoed from below.

The men rushing up had found their friends, found the inform-ant. The deaths of the former would not please them. It made no difference that the latter would tell them about Ballista. The armed men would want them both dead, and there was nowhere else that Ballista could have gone but up towards the roof.

Another scream echoed up the long passageway, then ended abruptly.

Every breath hurt. Sweat was running off Ballista. Would the stairs ever end? It was like some infernal punishment in myth.

A final corner, and there was the door. *All the gods, let it be unlocked.*

The door opened outwards. Ballista closed it behind him, and leant against it as he fought to regain his breath. Forty-three winters on Middle Earth; too long for this exertion.

The roof garden was gently domed, like a low hill. It rose to where a plinth supported the more than life-sized statue of the Emperor Hadrian in a triumphal chariot drawn by four horses. The terrible storms of the last several days had passed, but the air smelt of rain. The stones underfoot were still wet.

There had to be another way down. Ballista pushed himself off the door, set off up the path to the top.

The sun was dipping towards the horizon. It cast long shadows from the cypress trees, dappled where they were festooned with vines or ivy. Less than an hour until darkness.

Ballista circled the base of the statuary. No door, no trapdoor. Nothing. There had to be another way down. A passageway for gar-deners, plants, servants. He looked around wildly.

Under the cypresses the garden was thickly planted with fruit trees and flower beds. Paths radiated out. There were hedges, potted plants, heavy garden furniture, small fountains, more statues. The service access would be carefully hidden. The elite did not want to see slaves when they were enjoying the views. There was no time to search.

Ballista thought of the light wells. No. Even if he could find one of them, it would be too narrow, offer no handholds. Another thought came to him. He took the path down to the east.

There was a thin wooden rail above a delicate and ornamental screen along the edge of the garden, with yet more statues at intervals. Ballista did not look at the city spread out beyond the river, barely glanced at the swollen waters of the Tiber at the foot of the monument. He gripped the sculpted marble leg of Antinous, the doomed boy, loved by Hadrian. A Roman might have been troubled by the association. As heir to the different world view of the north, such omens did not bother Ballista. He had a head for heights, and leant out as far as he dared over the rail.

The cladding of the Mausoleum was white marble. The blocks were so artfully fitted together that there was barely a discernible line where they joined. No hope of a finger hold. Seventy foot or more of smooth, sheer wall down to the base, after that ledge perhaps another forty foot down to the narrow embankment and the river. No way to climb down.

Ballista ran back to the head of the stairs, opened the door. The men were nearing the top. Their laboured ascent was loud. There was nothing else for it. Without any conscious thought, Ballista went through his own silent pre-battle ritual: right hand to the dagger on his right hip, pulled it an inch or so out of its sheath then snapped it back; left hand on the scabbard of his sword, right hand pulling the blade a couple of inches free before pushing it back; finally he touched the healing stone tied to the scabbard.

Allfather Woden, watch over your descendant. Do not let me disgrace my forefathers. If I am to die, let me die as one worthy of my ancestors.

Ballista took off his cloak and wound the thick material around his left forearm as a makeshift shield, arranging the folds so that about a foot was hanging down to catch and entangle the weapon of an opponent.

He did not want to die. There was too much to live for: his wife Julia, their sons Isangrim and Dernhelm, his closest friend Maximus. He pushed the thoughts away. There were no choices. Either fight his way through, or fall sword in hand. If he were to die, let it not be as a coward.

Ballista drew his sword with a flourish, like some martial vision imagined by a priest.

Do not think, just act.

He went back through the door, pulled it shut, and took his station behind the last corner of the stairs.

The men were near the top.

It was a pity the stairway was wide enough for two men to attack at once, three if they risked encumbering each other.

Heavy footfalls, grunts of effort, the rattle of weapons. They were almost upon him.

Sword down across his body, his back to the steps, Ballista stilled his breathing. Setting his boots close together, he balanced on the balls of his feet. *Just wait. Not long now. Wait.*

The noise of their approach thundered back off the walls, nearer and nearer, building to a crescendo.

Now!

He stepped out and swung the blade backhanded in one fluid motion.

The edge of the steel caught the first man full in the face. A spray of blood, hot and stinging Ballista's eyes. The others stopped, stunned by the attack as unexpected as an apparition.

Infernal gods, there are so many of them.

Ballista recovered his blade from the ruined face, and shoved the man down the stairs. The mortally injured man clawed at those on either side, collided with those behind. Densely packed, they all staggered back, clutching at each other, struggling not to fall.

'Kill him!' Further down the stairs someone was yelling.

Ballista advanced, thrust at a figure to his right. The man blocked with military precision, but gave ground anyway.

Ten, twelve, or more – Ballista could not see them all. The throng stretched around the curve, out of view.

'He is alone. Kill him!' The voice from below was high with emotion, but vaguely familiar.

Two men readied themselves. The others waited a few steps below. This was bad. They knew their business, and did not intend to get in each other's way. They were dressed in civilian clothes, but were equipped for the task. Each held a gladius. The short sword had gone out of fashion with the legions, but in a confined space was a nimbler weapon than the long blade Ballista carried.

The two glanced at one another, then rushed up. The one on the left aimed a cut at Ballista's legs. Ballista caught the blow with the hanging folds of his cloak, turned it across his front, dragged the man between him and the other assailant. Thrust, always thrust. The steel only needed to go in an inch or two to be fatal. The man tried to jerk back, but his momentum was against him. It was not a clean thrust. The tip of Ballista's blade scrapped up across the breastbone before plunging into the soft flesh of the throat.

Ballista withdrew his sword. More blood, spraying everywhere. The man collapsed against his colleague. Ballista dropped to one knee, and swung around the dying man at the uninjured one's thigh. Sometimes you could not thrust. It was like a butcher's cleaver chopping into a side of meat. The man howled, and went down. His sword clattered on the marble steps. He would not die, unless he bled to death, but he was out of the fight.

Now was the moment to attack. Break the resolve of the others, send them rushing back down the stairs.

Ballista descended, fast but careful. The steps were slick with blood. Sword out in front. Use the longer reach. He yelled a barbaric war cry of his youth. The sound roared from the stones of the arched passage, primeval and terrifying.

The men did not lose their nerve and flee pell-mell down the stairs. They barely flinched. Squat and purposeful, they had closed three across, no intervals now between the ranks. Crouching, swords to the fore, cloaks wrapped around their left arms, they had formed an impromptu warhedge. No novices, they knew what they were about.

Ballista feinted at the one to his left, then jabbed at the swordsman in the centre. The man parried. The one to the left closed the distance, thrust. The impact jarred up Ballista's arm. He felt the steel slice through the wadded material of his cloak, but not deep enough to reach his forearm. Quick as a snake, Ballista jabbed at his face. The man ducked under the blow, then retreated, two steps, then three. The other two in the front fell back with him. The rear ranks let them give ground. Ominously disciplined, the formation kept its defensive line.

This would not work. Quickly, while he had a moment of time, a little space, Ballista needed to come up with another plan.

'Finish him!' The same disembodied voice from below.

The hired killers looked at each other, but did not move.

Backwards, face to the enemy, Ballista went back up above the fallen men. He grabbed the wounded man by the scruff of his tunic, pulled him half up, got the blade across his neck.

'One step and your tent-mate dies.'

In the gloom, the eyes of the men below shifted from Ballista to each other, searching for who would take the initiative.

'I am going to the roof. If you follow, when the first man comes around the corner, I will cut your friend's throat.'

The men were silent, unmoving.

'I will take others with me. You were paid to kill, not to die.'

Ballista retreated, dragging the wounded man with him.

Those below did not move.

Out of sight, Ballista hauled his captive through the door. He left it open, to hear.

No sound of pursuit yet. It would not be long.

'Let me live.' The man spoke softly.

Ballista was looking around, thinking. He was almost out of options.

'I have a wife, children. I needed the money.'

Ballista pulled his head back. 'You chose the wrong employment.'

'I do not want to die.'

'Do not be afraid,' Ballista said. 'Death is nothing. A return to sleep.'

With a practised hand, Ballista cut his throat. He fell like a sacrificial animal.

Automatically, Ballista wiped his blade on the dead man's tunic. He had not believed his own words.

The half-remembered voice from below. 'Cowards! Get up there and kill the barbarian.'

Ballista had seen what he wanted. He sheathed his sword. As he nudged the door shut with his boot, he heard the sounds of a cautious approach.

A few paces away was a garden bench. It was a bulky, elaborate piece of ironwork, its acanthus leaves and lotus flowers designed to complement the foliage of the garden for those sitting at their ease.

Straining every muscle, groaning with the effort, Ballista dragged it to the door, wedged it against the boards. It would not hold long, just buy him a short time.

Panting like a dog after his effort, Ballista set off through the garden towards the side facing the river. There was only one option left. It was not good.

The fragile rail by the statue of Antinous snapped with one hefty kick. A couple more and it was gone. Shattering the fine latticework of the screen it had supported caused no delay.

Ballista stood on the edge of the void. The river was far below him. On the far side the city was spread out, like the backdrop of a theatre. Off to his left stood the great bulk of the Mausoleum of Augustus, its circular drum echoing the tomb on which he stood. Next to it were flat and green open parks, dotted here and there with isolated monuments. The northern Campus Martius was laid out by the emperors to give their subjects somewhere to stroll, to give the urban plebs a taste of life in the luxurious country villas of the elite. Only a haze of smoke from the cooking fires of the home-less spoilt the image of the leisured countryside transposed to the city: *rus in urbe* invaded by vagrants.

Directly ahead were the ordered monuments of the southern Campus Martius. Ballista's gaze followed the curve of the Stadium of Domitian to the Baths of Nero. Beyond them and to the right rose the Capitoline, crowned with the Temple of Jupiter, its gilded roof still glittering in the late sunshine. Behind the Capitoline, also catching the light, were the roofs of the Palatine, under which the emperor might be about to pass his last night on earth, unless Ballista could warn him.

Ballista brought his thoughts back to the matter in hand. The river, so very far below, was already in shadow. The waters of the Tiber were tawny. The spring melt in the Apennines and the recent days of rain had made it run high. Off to his right the final grain barge of the day was being towed to the warehouses. With the river in flood, it would have been a long, hard pull upriver; four days from the port, not the usual two or three. Just to his left the Pons Aelius was a thin, white line crossing the stream. Beyond the bridge, the last couple of rafts were being warped to the far bank. The nearer was laden with marble. On the further stood cattle, raised on the water meadows upriver. At this distance the cows looked as small as children's toys fashioned from lumps of clay and daubed with tan paint.

A muffled thumping from behind. They would have nothing but boots and fists and the pommels of their swords to break down the door. There was still a little time.

Ballista unwound the torn cloak from his left arm, let it fall on the damp earth. He took off his boots, then unbuckled his sword belt, and lifted the baldric over his head. He did not want the sword to fall into their hands. Battle-Sun was not just any sword. Forged in the dawn of time, it had passed down through generations of northern heroes until Heoden, king of the Harii, had given it to his foster-son Ballista. Briefly Ballista considered throwing it down into the river, but then he turned and looked for somewhere to hide the blade.

As he slid the scabbard under a clump of rhododendrons, the ornaments on the belts caught his eye. The embroidered wallet; money had never much concerned him. The Mural Crown, the original decoration awarded so many years ago for being the first man in the Roman army over the wall of an African town. The jewelled bird of prey that had travelled with him so much longer, down from the distant North, a gift from his mother. There was no time for sentimentality. If he survived, he could send a message asking his mother to send another.

The pounding was louder, more rhythmic, better organised.

Ballista went back to the edge. More than a hundred feet down to the river, perhaps as much as a hundred and fifty. Dangerous, not necessarily fatal. In his youth he had jumped from cliffs as high. But he had to clear the base of the Mausoleum and the narrow embankment.

The crack of splintering wood. A hoarse cheer.

Ballista took twelve long paces back from the lip. Far away was the dome of the Pantheon. Inconsequentially, he noticed it lined up perfectly with the Column of Trajan even further off.

Shouts. Men crashing through the shrubbery. Getting closer.

Do not think, just act.

Ballista forced himself to set off, put one foot in front of the other, gathering speed. A slight misjudgement. On the eleventh step he had to jump and leap out into the abyss.

CHAPTER 1

The City of the Dead

The Kalends of April

The Hours of Darkness

BALLISTA CLAWED AT THE AIR as he fell, clutching in panic for some imaginary purchase. The city and the river and the monument – without connection or reason – wheeled before his eyes.

Death Blinder do not let me die.

The dark river and the white embankment were rushing up. His limbs were flailing impotently.

Master yourself or die.

Ballista stopped thrashing, forced his arms across his chest, gripped his right wrist with his left hand. With a more than human effort, he leant back, brought his legs near together, slightly bent at the knee. His fall controlled, he plummeted feet first.

Allfather . . .

The water and the stones were surging up so fast. Had he jumped out far enough? Would he clear the bank? If not . . .

Be a man . . .

The pale brickwork was very close. Any second now would come the sickening impact, the snapping of bones, his body splattered like a crushed insect.

Then the wall of the embankment was flashing past, the river reaching for him.

Agony as he hit the water. White hot pain running up his legs, flaring in the small of his back, knocking the breath from him.

Driven down deep, his feet sank into mud. Sediment blossomed around him. He could see nothing. A surge of fear, as he thought he was held fast by the clinging sludge, then the current took him. The water cleared a little, and a moment later his head and back thumped against the masonry of the embankment.

Better to stay under until he was some distance from the Mausoleum. But there was no air in his lungs. He had to breath. There was light above him, light and air. Strong in the water, he struck out for the surface. The awful realisation dawned that the undertow had him. He could make no progress. Fear again rising, hard to control. His chest was crushed, on fire. The light getting no closer.

In the opaque murk of the river, he half saw the looming riverine wall. Twisting, he found the bricks with his feet. A convulsive shove, and this time he shot upwards.

Breaking the surface, Ballista gulped in the air, coughing and spluttering.

The great bulk of the Mausoleum was receding. Small figures, black against the sinking sun, were silhouetted at its top. Could they see him? The river was in deep shadow. Had he gone far enough?

Filling his lungs, Ballista slipped below the surface, and let the river take him.

The pain in his chest, and the bitter residue of fear, would not let him remain submerged for long.

Resurfacing, the Mausoleum was appreciably smaller. The figures were gone. Perhaps they were already rushing down to search the dockside.

The clouded waters surged against the retaining wall. He was being swept past the imperial gardens. There were empty jetties, and here and there the roofs of pavilions showed above the foliage. Downstream was a bridge, and through its arches Ballista could see a line of tall warehouses, and further off the ramshackle huts of fishermen. Beyond the bridge, there would be people. If he wanted to slip away unnoticed, to leave no trail for his pursuers, he had to get out now. With evening drawing in, the pleasure gardens should be deserted.

A jetty was approaching. Ballista started to swim. His back still ached, and the pain in his chest was undiminished. He put them out of his mind, and angled across the current. He was close, safety no more than a few strokes off, when the impersonal power of the river again seized him. For a few moments he struggled, before surrendering, and letting himself be rolled out towards midstream.

The Tiber in flood was notorious for the strength of its sudden eddies and whirlpools. To escape, good swimmer though he was, neither technique nor brute strength would serve. Ballista had to think, read the water, turn it to his advantage. No mortal could fight the god of the river and win.

There was another landing-stage: solid pillars and a ladder.

Ballista scanned the surface. Inshore the water was racing, bouncing back from the retaining wall, foaming through the uprights of the pier. Ahead floated the bloated carcass of a dog. It dipped, bobbed up again, and was drawn out, away from the bank. Perhaps the beginning of a whirlpool. Against all instinct, Ballista swam away from the shore.

In moments he felt his pace increase, as the turbulent waters carried him along. He was still going out as the dead dog turned, and was dragged back towards the quay. The stream pulled Ballista in its wake. A half remembered line of Stoicism: *A man is tied to his fate, like a dog to a cart.*

This would all be about timing. Ballista watched the cadaver. Fate was not immutable. Some five paces from the nearest pole of the landing-stage, the crosscurrent hit the dog, and sent it spinning downriver.

Not yet. Wait. The river was in turmoil where the currents collided. Fifteen paces, ten.

Ballista gathered all his strength.

Now! He launched himself into the maelstrom.

Three strokes, and the race pushed him sideways. Five strokes. The massive wooden pile just out of reach, the ladder just beyond. Summoning all his resolve, he drove towards them.

A desperate lunge, and his right hand found the upright. Coated in slime, it offered no grip. He was slipping, the water tugging at him. A mortal could not fight the father of waters.

A stinging pain, as the head of a projecting nail tore the palm of his hand. Regardless of the injury, he clutched the spike. The river was determined to tear him away. Somehow he hauled himself in, hugged the foul timber, got a leg around it.

The ladder was to his right, just too far to reach. One push, and he would be there. The water breaking over his shoulders, Ballista could not force himself to let go of his temporary sanctuary.

This was absurd. His courage could not fail him now. *Be a man.*

Still he did not move.

Do not think, just act.

He lunged at the ladder, grabbed one of its rungs. With a snap audible above the roaring water, it shifted. The whole thing threatened to give way. Spurred into action, Ballista swarmed up the slippery, unstable woodwork, and hauled himself onto the decking.

He lay for a moment, sucking in air, blinking at the sky. High up swallows banked and swooped. A promise of fair weather.

Rolling over, he crawled to one of the pillars, set his back against the wood.

If he could get to the pleasure gardens, he would be able to find somewhere to lay up. First, he needed to see if he could walk. It would take the knifemen some time to get down from the roof of the Mausoleum, and he had been carried quite a distance down-river. There was no time to waste, but he had a few moments respite. He began to check himself over, swiftly, yet with care and methodically. There was a nasty cut on his right palm. It would need washing and dressing. The river was filthy. Without a knife, he could not tear his tunic for a makeshift bandage. It would have to wait. His feet were now bare. They were livid, soon they would be covered with bruises. His legs and back ached. Flexing them proved that nothing was broken. His chest was another matter. Every movement brought a sharp stab of discomfort. Deliberately he took a deep, shuddering breath. The left side of his ribcage hurt, but the pain was not so intense as to indicate that any ribs were fractured. Most likely one or two were cracked, or that some of the muscles between them had been torn.

Using the pillar, he levered himself to his feet, then lent against it while a wave of nausea passed. The decking where he had sat was stained dark with the water oozing from his tunic and trousers.

Some atavistic sense for danger made him look upstream. A group of men not far from the Mausoleum, working their way downriver, still a couple of hundred paces off. At least twenty of them, they were searching the bank. They had not seen him yet.

At the end of the landing stage a paved path ran away into the gardens. To run would be to give himself away. If he acted naturally, at this distance, they might not realise it was him.

Ballista walked slowly down the jetty. He kept his left arm pressed to his ribs. Each step stung the soles of his feet. He moved out onto the towpath. Halfway across, he heard the shout.

Out of the corner of his eye, he saw the men break into a run.

Ballista set off like a hare.

In moments he was out of sight. The gardens stretched away on either side.

Should he go left or right? Away from them or double back? Behind him he could hear them baying like hounds.

Ballista ran left.

There was a walkway, but it was gravel, and his feet were bare. Ballista hurdled a low hedge, and took off across a lawn. There was a wide grove of trees ahead. The outliers were low fruit trees. He ducked down under the blossom, almost crawling, and emerged into an open space artfully designed to resemble a forest clearing. A tall figure stood in the centre, wearing a headdress of reeds and sporting an enormous erection. There were flowers at his feet. Priapus, carved in wood, served as both scarecrow and warning to evil-minded men who would desecrate this glade. Ballista went around the deity, and into the stand of tall trees beyond. These oaks had been ancient when the gardens had been laid out. Almost at once, he saw one with its lowest branch growing out near horizontal only a couple of feet above his head.

Ballista jumped, got both hands on the bough. His battered body complained as he scrambled up, the rough bark grazing his arms. From that branch he climbed to another, then one higher still. Finally he wedged himself where a huge limb formed an angle to the trunk.

Ballista was not sure how well he was hidden. A passage of Tacitus came to mind. Some battle, long ago in the northern forests. The Germans had taken refuge in the trees. The Roman soldiers had shot them down like sitting birds. Sometimes a Classical education brought little comfort. Yet there was a difference between a lone fugitive and a multitude. Most men, especially those bred in the city, never raised their eyes from the ground.

The passage of time slowed. The air was full of birdsong. Through the foliage, Ballista could see the rustic head of Priapus, the reeds stirring in the evening breeze. He waited. For nine nights and nine days the Allfather had hung from the Tree of Life. No one comforted him with bread, revived him with a drink from a horn. Nine days and nine nights, and the Allfather Woden had learned the secrets of the dead. Ballista waited.

The sunlight only touched the very tops of the oaks, and the evening chorus faded as the song birds sought their nests for the night.

Ballista heard the men coming: barked orders and guttural responses. They blundered through the fruit trees. Clearly they felt no need for discretion. Neither the City Watch nor the local police who conducted nocturnal patrols on the right bank of the Tiber concerned them.

Ballista saw three hairy, somewhat unkempt men walk out into the clearing. They were well spaced, fifteen paces or more apart, like beaters drawing a covert. They wore a motley array of clothes, one had shoulder-length hair, but the swords in their hands, the ornaments on their belts, and the way they moved, all proclaimed military service. One wiped the sweat from his forehead. There was a tattoo on his wrist. Too far to see which unit, but it was the final proof.

There was little undergrowth below the oaks, and the hunters stepped out quickly, scanning this way and that. One was heading straight for the tree in which Ballista had tried to conceal himself.

Stilling his breathing, Ballista watched the man. *Allfather, do not let him look up.*

The man stopped beneath the oak. He stretched, rolling the stiffness out of his neck, then looked to either side, waiting for the others to catch up: a trained soldier dressing the line.

Suddenly the man glanced up, as if aware he was observed.

Ballista shut his eyes.

The noise of men moving further off. From the base of the tree no sound.

Ballista peered down.

The soldier was rubbing his shoulders. A veteran on manoeuvre, with no immediate threat in sight, he waited stolidly.

A whistle, and the line moved on again.

Ballista did not move, hardly dared breathe.

Soon the noise of their passage diminished.

The centurions of few regular auxiliary units, and none in any legion, would tolerate such a slovenly turn out. Perhaps they were not soldiers, but deserters. The gods knew there were enough of them. Not all that long ago, back in the reign of Commodus, a man called Maternus had raised an army of them. He had terrorised Gaul and Spain, sacked whole towns, even tried to kill the emperor himself.

The sound of the hunters was lost in the sighing of the wind through the broad canopy of leaves. There was no telling how soon they would return. Ballista clambered down from his perch. His ribs and feet hurt. The cut on his palm throbbed. He needed to rest, but had to find somewhere more secure. Putting aside the pain and fatigue, he retraced his steps.

Coming out on the path through the gardens, he turned left, away from the river. The heat of the day was still in the smooth paving stones. It seemed to burn the tender soles of his feet.

Abruptly, the paving gave way to a track of beaten earth, and the gardens on either side ended. The land here was rough heath. The necks of dozens of half-buried amphorae protruded from the earth. Some had been dug up and broken. There was a scatter of white bones. It was a graveyard of the poor, one of the many that ringed Rome. Not of the destitute; they would be pitched into mass graves. Here the corpses of slaves, pulled from their narrow cells, would be brought by other servile members of their household, and the urban plebs would be carried in a cheap box. It stood right next to the shaded gardens, where the living and the affluent strolled and talked, and ate delicacies off silver plate. No wonder that the inhabitants of the eternal city held mixed feelings about the suburban areas. They were places of pleasure, of parks and pavilions, where you took your leisure. At the same time, they were where the city dumped its rubbish, deposited its dead, where the condemned were executed, and funeral pyres burned.

Ahead was a necropolis for the better off. Ballista had long got used to the Roman custom of fashioning tombs that resembled houses, and of building them together, as a city of the dead. There were two streets running away to the left. He turned into the second.

Never hide in a solitary structure. It would draw your pursuers like a magnet. But in one among many, you would have some warning, hear the search working towards you. Not all these tombs were tended. Ballista passed several with gaping doors. He stopped at the fourth or fifth that had been opened, one set back down a narrow passage.

Undesirables lurked in such surroundings; vagrants, down on their luck prostitutes and their clients, midnight hags in search of ingredients for their arts. If disturbed, they might raise the alarm. He was uncertain if he was in a condition to stop them.

He took a deep breath, causing a spasm of pain in his ribs. It would be as the Fates decreed.

Cautiously, he entered the tomb.

For a time he stood, braced for an outcry or attack, letting his eyes adjust to the darkness.

A smell of dust, of mould and faint decay. No movement in the still air. The tomb was empty.

Wearily he folded himself down to sit with his back to a wall, and thought what had brought him to this place, and of the man that he had left to die in the Mausoleum.

Scarpio, the Prefect of the City Watch, had said the informer would only talk to an individual. Ballista must go alone, and, as there was no knowing how far the conspiracy had spread, he must tell no one. The informer was an ex-slave and a thief. Pilfering from the changing room of the baths on the Caelian Hill, the day before, he had heard two men approaching, and had hidden. Only one of the men had spoken, but the eavesdropper claimed that he had caught every word.

Gallienus will leave the amphitheatre at the last hour. Once he is in the passageway, out of the imperial box, present your petition. While he is distracted, strike. Do not waste words, no prattling about liberty, strike quickly. Do not be afraid. The guards will not stop you. Remember we will all be there.

Ballista wondered how accurate the dialogue was. Even the great Thucydides had admitted that in the speeches in his *History* he could not always give the exact words, but instead would provide those appropriate. At least Ballista was sure the informant had done the latter.

The conspirators had not seen the spy, but, as they left, he had had a glimpse of their faces. Both were old and well-dressed. The silent one was bald, the talker had a face like a peasant. In a city of a million souls, it was not much to go on.

Now that Ballista was accustomed to the faint light in the tomb, he saw there were frescos on the walls and ceiling. In the gloom above his head was the glimmer of white horses pulling a chariot driven by a god. On the opposite wall a shepherd carried a sheep on his shoulders. More puzzling, on another wall a man who had fallen from a boat appeared to be about to be consumed by a sea monster, perhaps a whale. The hero of Lucian's *True Story* had been swallowed by a whale. The satire was an unlikely choice for a funeral monument.

Could it be Jonah and the whale? A story of the strange cult of the crucified god? Ballista had encountered Christians in the East. A sect of them had betrayed his defence of the town of Arete on the Euphrates. He had been given the unpleasant task of overseeing their persecution in Ephesus. They were spreading everywhere, seemingly even to here, the insalubrious and unhealthy *Ager Vaticanus*.

The light dimmed, and the paintings blended back into the walls. It was almost fully dark.

Tomorrow. The last hour of daylight. They are going to kill the emperor.

And only Ballista could save him.

CHAPTER 2

The Bridge of Nero

*C*UI BONO? WHO WOULD BENEFIT if Emperor Gallienus was killed?

Ballista sat in the dark, thinking.

Postumus, the pretender in the West, was the obvious choice. While Gallienus had wintered in Rome, his troops had been gathering on the plains of northern Italy. In four days Gallienus would leave to lead them over the Alps. Postumus had sent several envoys saying that he did not want to fight, that he would defend the Rhine from the barbarians, and was content with the provinces he ruled. They had been wasted journeys. While Gallienus lived, nothing could avert war. At the outset of his rebellion, five years before, Postumus had killed Gallienus' favourite son.

Ballista's legs ached. Gingerly he tried to stretch the stiffness out of them.

Postumus was far from the only candidate. Odenathus of Palmyra ruled Rome's eastern provinces, nominally in the name of Gallienus. Ballista knew Odenathus, and thought he harboured no greater ambitions. But those around the Palmyrene were another matter, especially his wife Zenobia. If Gallienus were assassinated, it might force Odenathus to make a bid for the throne.

Stretching was not helping. Ballista used the wall of the tomb to lever himself to his feet.

Here in Rome the senate had no love for Gallienus. Many of their number claimed to find the emperor's lifestyle offensive: the boys and girls, the drinking in arbours of flowers, the philosophy and poetry. More to the point, they resented being excluded from high military commands, and thought Gallienus did not treat them with the respect they deserved. Among the nobility there would be those who thought their lineage better qualified them to wear the purple.

Whoever was behind the plot, did they not realise the chaos that would ensue? If Gallienus was struck down, the intricate web of alliances that he had woven along the Danube would unravel. The barbarians – Goths, Alamanni, and Sarmatians – would pour over the river. They would bring fire and sword to the frontier, untold destruction to the peaceful, unarmed provinces to the South. Greece, the cradle of civilisation, would lie open. Athens would burn.

Ballista knew there was worse. When an emperor was murdered, those close to him would also die, their estates would be confiscated, their families hunted down. Political expediency and the need for funds to reward supporters of the new regime would result in a bloodbath.

Ballista was counted a friend of Gallienus. If he were executed, his family . . . He pushed the thought away, sought something else to occupy his mind.

Was Scarpio part of the conspiracy? The Prefect of the City Watch had prevailed on Ballista's loyalty, but had he sent him to his death? Scarpio had insisted Ballista go alone: time had been of the essence, who could tell how far the plot reached? No one at court could be trusted. Ballista had only met the prefect once before. Returning from the distant North, Ballista had been welcomed by Gallienus, had been seated at the emperor's right hand in the Circus. Scarpio, standing at the rear of the imperial box, had been one of those cursorily introduced. Although Ballista did not know the prefect, his reasoning had been cogent. It was possible that Scarpio had acted in good faith.

With geriatric slowness, Ballista walked through the darkness to the door.

A sudden noise outside made him freeze. The footsteps passed by the tomb.

His heart was pounding. He was in no condition for this: alone and unarmed, battered and in pain, barefoot with no money or friends, and on the wrong side of the river. His family came into his mind. No, he would not give way to despair. The thing was simple. He had to save Gallienus, and all would be well.

As youths they had grown up together, diplomatic hostages on the Palatine for the good behaviour of their fathers; the one a leading senator, the other a client king. Years later, serving in the East, Ballista had been forced to let himself be acclaimed as emperor. After a few days, he had stepped down. Even so, under most rulers such presumption would have led to the headsman's block. Gallienus had spared him, and subsequently entrusted him with important missions. Everything else aside, Ballista was honour-bound to save the emperor.

He needed a plan.

Turning, he began to pace, trying to walk off the hurt, order his fractured thoughts.

To the South was Transtiberim. The region was densely populated with immigrants from the East: Syrians, Jews, Armenians, even Parthians and Persians from beyond the frontier. They worshipped strange gods – *Hadad*, *Iaribol*, and *Malakabel* – Ballista had no friends among these people. Then there were the barracks of men seconded from the fleet at Ravenna. Ballista had never served with them. Again, there was no reason to expect their help. And there was a station of the City Watch, but given the circumstances they were best avoided.

He needed to cross the Tiber. Swimming was not an option. Some doctors recommended swimming the river as a cure for insomnia. With the Tiber in flood, it would bring a sleep from which there would be no waking. The river was not so fast that you could not row across. But he had nothing with which to pay his passage, and stealing a boat would raise an outcry. It would have to be a bridge. Most likely the knifemen from the Mausoleum would be watching them.

Ballista stopped by the door.

He had lived in Rome for years in his youth. The rhythms of the streets of the city were eternal, as familiar as his own heartbeat. If he was to slip across unnoticed, there was no better hour than now.

Part of him did not want to leave the tomb. *Be a man*, he told himself. There was no choice.

At first, as he made his way down through the graveyards and gardens towards the river, the streets were nearly deserted. A lone wagon passed, going in the other direction. It was stacked with unclaimed corpses. Every night the metropolis produced its harvest of paupers. Naked and waxy, they made their last journey to some mass burial pit. No headstone would mark their grave, no coin in the mouth would pay the ferryman.

The collectors of the dead did not speak to Ballista, and he did not acknowledge them. They lived outside the city, only allowed to enter to ply the trade that set them apart from humanity.

At a crossroads was a small fountain, water spilling from the mouth of a dragon. Ballista washed thoroughly. The cold water stung and partly opened the gash on his palm. He rinsed and pushed back his long hair. He doubted he looked any more respectable.

The noise reached him first, a murmur of many voices like the surf on a stony shore. It was punctuated with the sharp calls of different animals. Then came the smell. There was cut wood, fresh produce, and flowers, but also sweat and dung, both human and bestial.

The queue stretched back two hundred paces from the Bridge of Nero. There were herds of sheep and pigs and cattle, wagons full of timber and kindling, carts piled with roses and jasmine or laden with vegetables, in-season asparagus and artichokes. There were trussed chickens and loose dogs. All, apart from the latter, waiting their turn at the customs house.

This was the produce of local villas and market gardens brought in by road. The staples that fed the megalopolis – grain, oil, and wine – came by river. Some was floated downriver on rafts, but much more was towed against the current from the ports where it was offloaded having been shipped from abroad.

It was clear that Ballista had nothing to declare, and he was largely ignored as he walked up the line.

Ahead, a herd of nine or ten bullocks was playing up. An old man and a boy chased after the stamping, agitated beasts. No one helped them. Some of the onlookers scuttled away from the widespread horns; others laughed. As a child, Ballista had joined the thralls herding in his father's cattle.

Standing tall, arms outspread – now hallooing, now silent – he helped round them up, calm them, get them to a stand.

'We have nothing to pay you.' The old peasant had the ingrained suspicion of his sort.

'I want no coins, Grandfather.' Ballista addressed him with respect.

The peasant grunted, turned away in dismissal.

'A swallow of wine would be welcome.' Ballista nodded at the pack the man wore. 'Perhaps a bite of bread.'

The old man gestured Ballista to sit, and told the boy to watch the cattle. He sat next to Ballista on the kerb, put aside his stockman's cudgel, opened the sack, and passed a wineskin.

The wine was smooth and well watered, brought for refreshment not intoxication. There was only the one skin, and Ballista was careful not to drink too much.

A usurer came down the queue, offering rates for those who needed credit to pay the custom's dues. The old man jerked his head back to send him on his way.

'You have had a hard time.' The peasant handed over the heel of a loaf.

Ballista chewed, just sipping the wine to moisten the hard bread.

'I was robbed,' he said at length. 'Out by the fifth milestone.'

'They were fools.' The rustic nodded at Ballista's hand which held the wineskin.

On the third finger was the gold ring of an equestrian. Ballista had forgotten it was there.

'A god blinded them, or they were fools,' Ballista finished the bread, and gave back the wine.

The queue moved, and they got to their feet to drive the cattle forward.

They halted not more than fifty paces from the customs post. It was lit by torches. Ballista could see those at the front being divided. The livestock was corralled into pens to be counted for the Gate Tax. The vehicles remained in the road, their contents tallied for the Handle Tax. Ballista could see a squad of eight of the City Watch lounging against the parapet of the bridge. That was to be expected. Their equipment – axes, buckets, unlit torches – were scattered around their feet. The *Spartoli*, the Little Bucket Men, as they were known, did not look alert. Apart from the customs men, he could see no one else checking the multitude entering the city. No sign of the men from the Mausoleum.

'Where were you coming from?' The eyes of the old man were pale blue, bright in a face tanned and lined by a life out in the weather.

'I am a soldier, returning from a posting in Africa. Most of my money was lost at dice on the boat. I had to walk up from the port.'

'Now you have nothing, but that ring.' The peasant took a pull of wine. 'What will you do in the city?'

'My service is ended. My brothers in the emperor's German Guard will take care of me until my discharge pay comes through.'

'Your Latin is good, but I could tell you were a barbarian. You could not be anything else at that size, and with that fair hair and chalky skin.'

The peasant seemed to have accepted the story. *Crafty Odysseus*, Ballista thought, *cunning Loki*.

'Will you be going home to your people?' Now that they were talking, the attitude of the rustic was thawing.

The boy had sidled closer. 'Did you fight in any battles?'

The old man hefted his cudgel. 'Hold your tongue when your elders are talking.'

The boy backed off, not looking greatly abashed.

'Usually my brother comes on the drove. He has the fever. That is his son. Useless, a dreamer. His first time in the city. If I take my eye off him, they will rob him blind, fuck him up the arse, turn him into a bitch.'

Ballista was grateful that the talk had moved from his invented life story, and he encouraged the peasant to talk. 'You do not care for the city?'

'Care for it?' The rustic smacked his lips to avert evil. 'It is a shithole. You can smell it a mile off. You cannot breath for all that smoke. Those tenements towering over you, never a glimpse of the sun, a breath of fresh air. Streets ankle deep in shit and offal. People everywhere, pushing and shouting. Your best tunic gets ripped to shreds in the crush. You look down and your wallet is gone. No idea who did it. No one gives a fuck. You can hardly move, not hear yourself think in all that crush. Here is the great trunk of a fir tree swaying along on a wagon, another behind stacked high with pine logs, all about to topple on your head. If an axle snaps and a cartload of marble crashes down, what will be left of you? Who could identify bits of flesh and bone? Your flattened corpse vanishes along with your soul. Meanwhile, all unwitting, your wife at home is scouring dishes, blowing the fire to a glow, setting the soup to boil, filling up your oil flask, a pitcher of wine. A meal you will never eat. You are sitting by the Styx. No chance of a passage over, without so much as a copper stuck in your mouth.'

Like many unaccustomed to company, the rustic had a store of words when he found an audience.

'The beef has to be sold, but, if the gods were kind, I would not set foot in the city. My brother and me inherited our place from our father. Two huts, a byre, a barn, and an enclosure of palings for the calves. The vegetable garden is not large, but the home meadow grows a good deal of hay to put up. The pasturage is set in a valley, deep and shaded. Through the centre flows a quiet stream. The cows and calves can wade across with perfect ease. Abundant water, bubbling up clean and sweet from a spring nearby, and in the summer a breeze always blows through. Never a gadfly or any other pest. No wonder the cattle never range very far.'

'It sounds idyllic,' Ballista said.

The rustic gave him a sharp look. 'Better than this shithole, at any rate.'

At last it was their turn at the stock pens. A customs officer came over to talk to the old man. One of the City Watch glanced over. Ballista averted his face, hunching slightly to disguise his height.

'Carry on.' The customs man, wax tablet and stylus in hand, went ahead to open the gate of the stock pens.

Out of the corner of his eye, Ballista saw the watchman talking to his neighbour. *Allfather, let it be about the weather, some girl.*

Ballista moved to the far side of the herd.

With a call, and a clout of his cudgel, the rustic tried to urge the bullocks into motion. At first they stood, sullen and mulish.

The two watchmen were walking around, their shadows disjointed in the guttering torchlight.

Ballista did not look at them again. It might be nothing.

The old man shouted louder, used the cudgel again.

Hooves clopping on the paving, reluctantly the beasts began to trudge after the customs officer towards the gate.

A hand grasped Ballista's arm.

'Don't fight,' the watchman said. 'Marcus Clodius Ballista, you are under arrest.'

CHAPTER 3

The Quayside

'We've got him!'

The speaker gripped Ballista's left arm, while the second watchman was moving up behind him.

If Ballista was going to escape, it had to be now, while the rest of the squad were still on the bridge. The customs officer had not yet opened the gate of the stock pens, and the cattle remained in the way.

Without warning, Ballista spun, jerking at the waist. Ignoring the stab of pain in his own ribs, he brought his right elbow clubbing down into the face of the shorter man. The watchman released Ballista's arm, his hands going up to clutch his nose. Ballista's injury had robbed the blow of some of its force. The man did not go down, merely staggered away a step or two.

No time to finish him. Ballista kept turning. He glimpsed the old man and the boy, both open mouthed with surprise. The cattle, now stationary, were shifting uneasily.

The other watchman was fumbling to get the hilt of his sword free of his cloak. Ballista stepped close, aimed an identical blow. The City Watch might be under military discipline, but they were firemen by profession. A soldier trained in unarmed combat might have dived forward, taken the blow on his left shoulder or upper arm. The Bucketman did the opposite. Raising an ineffectual hand, he reared backwards. His chin came up like a novice boxer. Ballista's elbow, the weight of his body behind it, crashed into the exposed throat. This one went down, full length, the back of his head cracking on the pavement. He was unlikely to get up anytime soon.

The left hand of the first watchman was still pressed to the bridge of his nose, but he had his sword in the other. Behind him, across the broad backs of the bullocks, Ballista could see the other six men drawing their weapons, readying themselves for the fight. Very few men can move straight to violence without some moments of preparation or bluster.

'Drop the weapon,' Ballista said. 'Let me go.'

'Fucker!' The watchman lunged, the torchlight glittering on the naked steel.

Ballista stepped inside the thrust. He caught the man's wrist with one hand, his elbow with the other. Pivoting on his left foot, he brought his right knee up hard under his assailant's forearm. The watchman dropped the blade, but got Ballista around the throat with his free hand. Grappling, they stumbled back, almost on top of the man on the ground.

Resisting the urge to try to claw at the fingers choking him, Ballista punched the man in the stomach with his left, then threw a short right to the kidneys. The watchman released his hold. The breath wheezed out of him. But he was not done yet. His dagger was in his right hand.

Only a pace apart. If Ballista turned and ran, the dagger would find his back.

Ballista feinted to the right, the tip of the steel following, then sidestepped to the left, and kicked. His heel hit the man's right knee. Ballista heard a crack. Still the watchman did not fall. Instead he slashed the dagger in a wide arc. Ballista jumped backwards, the wicked steel hissing past. A fraction slower, half a hand closer, and it would have been over. His stomach sliced open, intestines sliding out, he would have been gasping out his life in the dirt.

The watchman came on again, limping, but undefeated. Some men, maddened by anger, no longer feel pain. This bucket man would be hard to stop. But it needed to be ended quickly. The others were off the bridge, approaching the restless bullocks. A clear head and quick thinking won more fights than brute strength. Ballista's advantage was mobility.

Ballista crouched, as if to charge, then set off to the man's right. Impeded by his knee, the watchman could not turn fast enough. Ballista launched a flying kick. Again his heel found its mark. A terrible splintering sound, like a door kicked open. The watchman screamed, crumpled to the floor, his right leg at an improbable angle.

Ballista picked himself up.

The rest of the squad were pushing past the first of the cattle.

'Sorry, Grandfather.' Ballista yanked the cudgel from the old man's hands.

Roaring, Ballista whacked the nearest bullock on the rump. The beast kicked and jumped, rolling its eyes. Ballista hit it again. The beast bellowed and charged. In a heartbeat, the rest of the herd broke into a veering, switching run towards the still closed stock pens. The customs officer hurdled the gate to safety. Turned by the rails, the bullocks swerved. Heads ducking, horns weaving, they thundered towards the bridge. Cornering, the back legs of one skidded out from under. It slid for a moment on its flank, then with a twist it was back on its feet. Another, baulked by a cart, tried to jump the obstacle. Its great weight sent the cart crashing over. Bundles of artichokes spilled across the roadway, to be pounded and thrown into the air by stamping hooves.

The squad of watchmen fled before the stampede. One, too slow, was bowled over. The beast stopped. Frisking, almost playful, it nudged the unfortunate along the ground, seeking to get its horns under to toss and gore.

Dropping the cudgel, Ballista turned and fled south along the embankment.

The quayside ran straight. To his left was the river, bulky grain barges moored for the night, lashed fast against the current. On his right ramps led up to tall detached warehouses. Within a few strides his damaged ribs were agony, each breath like a knife thrust. The tumult behind spurred him on.

The dock was near-deserted, just a few people someway downstream by the fishermen's huts. The path was cluttered with impedimenta of the working day. Ballista swerved around cranes and winches, coils of rope and iron stanchions. The black mouths of alleyways, firebreaks between the warehouses, flashed by on his right.

The pain in his chest was mounting, his breath coming in sobs. There was no way he could keep running. When a stack of barrels blocked the view from the customs post, Ballista ducked into one of the dark alleyways.

To protect the contents from damp, the floors of the warehouses were raised. There was a gap of several paces between the pillars, but the clearance was low, less than two feet. Ballista dropped to the ground. He was a big man. Painfully, shoulders scrapping against the boards, he wriggled backwards, feet first, into the pitch blackness under the building.

Ballista had always had a horror of confined spaces. Siege tunnels, catacombs and the like were anathema to him. Now he could sense the immense weight suspended above him, pressing down on his shoulders, waiting to crush him.

Years before, perhaps ten years now, at the siege of Arete, he had been forced to abandon a friend in a tunnel under the walls. It still haunted his dreams. Trapped in the dark, unable to move, waiting to die. Ballista could imagine no worse fate.

Boots thudding on the quayside broke his unhappy reverie. He crawled a little way forward. Shielding his face with his sleeves, fearing the pale glimmer might betray him, he peered out.

The watchmen paused. They had torches, and peered into the alleyway. There were five of them. Not enough to search each passage, they pressed on.

Ballista listened to them moving on to the next ally. Five watchmen. He had taken down two, the bullock a third. That accounted for all of them. There would still be customs men at their post, but they did not count. The bridge might be unguarded.

Marcus Clodius Ballista, you are under arrest. The watchman had known his name. That answered one question. The Prefect of the City Watch had issued orders for his arrest. Scarpio was part of the conspiracy against Gallienus. The meeting with the informant in the Mausoleum of Hadrian had been a trap. Kill two birds with one stone; the eavesdropper who threatened to expose the plot, and the loyal friend of the emperor.

The noise of the search was receding.

Scarpio could not order the men of the City Watch to kill Ballista. The bucketmen were not hired murderers. But once confined, Scarpio would find a way to ensure that Ballista did not leave alive.

A sword with a hairline, a coiled snake, the pillow talk of a bride; things not to trust. The sayings of his childhood came back to him. Scarpio would not be alone in the conspiracy. A Prefect of the City Watch could not hope to overthrow an emperor on his own. More powerful men must be involved. Ballista could trust no one.

There were no sounds now but those of the river; the suck of the water, the creak of mooring ropes, the click-click of lanyards against masts.

Using his fingers and toes, Ballista worked himself out of his hiding place. He got to his hands and knees, then hauled himself to his feet. The soles of his feet hurt, but as nothing compared with the left side of his chest. The Stoics said pain was an irrelevance. What did philosophers know?

Stumbling slightly, Ballista moved back to the end of the alley.

Nearby, the quayside was empty. Far off to the south, down among the huts of the fishermen, Ballista could see the yellow halos of the watchmen's torches. To the north, the torches were burning along the parapet of the bridge. They were at least two hundred paces away. He had run further than he had realised.

Cautiously, moving from shadow to shadow, flitting from crane to stanchion to barrel, Ballista began to work his way back towards the bridge. It came as second nature to him to move quiet and unseen in the dark, using every scrap of cover. As a boy, following the custom of the North, he had been fostered with another tribe. The Harii were famed night fighters; even the historian Tacitus had known of them. Ever since his time in their halls, Ballista had worn black clothes. It was useful now, as it had been so many times before.

Halfway there. Concentrating on his craft made the discomfort recede. His spirits were lifting. After what had happened, there was no hope of crossing the bridge unnoticed. But, with no goods to declare, he was beyond the remit of customs. Even unarmed and in his weakened state, should an officer or two try to detain him, he thought that he could deal with them. Customs men were not fighters. They might be reluctant to intervene. Certainly they would have seen what he had done to the watchmen. Once over the river,

Ballista could vanish into the metropolis. The Palatine was no great distance. There was plenty of time to reach the emperor.

His fond imaginings sank like a stone when he saw the men on the bridge. They were marching from the city. There were twenty, thirty, and more of them. They carried torches, and the buckets hanging from the axes over their shoulders betrayed their trade. Ballista could not remember the location of the nearest barracks of the City Watch. It made no difference. Scarpio had his men out in numbers.

Ballista watched from behind a ramp leading up to the door of a warehouse. After a few moments, he turned, and slipped into the nearest alleyway. The wall to his right was buttressed with brick columns. He slid from the shelter of one to another. The warehouses here stood two deep from the docks. A street ran between them, parallel to the quayside, with another beyond which was fronted with more buildings, indistinct in the darkness. He would move away from the river, then work his way north, coming back to the Tiber upstream at the Aelian Bridge by the Mausoleum of Hadrian.

He felt a stab of pain as his bare foot trod on the shards of a broken amphora. Silently cursing himself, he brushed the sharp terracotta from his sole. The alley was strewn with rubbish. The stench of cat piss overlaid the smell of grain and chaff. He went on more carefully, eyes down, watching where he put his feet in the ambient light.

By the last buttress, he halted, and took stock. The first street was quiet and empty, but now there were lights on the one further away, beyond the second row of warehouses. In itself that was not alarming. They were close to the tenements of Transtiberim. The buildings fronting the street might be dwellings or bars or brothels. But the torches were not moving. They were not held by men trudging home or out seeking nocturnal pleasures. The ones that he could see were spaced a few paces apart. In the guttering torchlight, was the glitter of swords and axes. Ballista looked north. There were more armed men on the road that led to the bridge. Scarpio had acted quickly, and with thoroughness. The Prefect of the City Watch had thrown a cordon around the area.

Ballista stepped back, and rested his back against the buttress. He needed somewhere to go to ground. All warehouses shared the same construction: a myriad of small chambers opening off a central courtyard, and internal stairs to identical levels above. These big warehouses were built on three or four levels. Openings for ventilation connected the chambers, and made the interior into a rabbit warren. Judging by the smell, these buildings were granaries. From childhood games in his father's barns, Ballista knew that sacks of grain could be shifted to make ideal hiding places.

Yet by their nature warehouses contained valuables. They were designed to keep out thieves. The few external windows were narrow, shuttered, and situated far above the ground. The walls were smooth brick, unscalable. There were only two doors, one in each of the end walls. They were solid, locked and bolted. There would be a night-watchman, perhaps more than one, in every warehouse. Apart from the doors, there was no entrance.

Ballista looked back to the river, where the black waters rolled. Pinpricks of light showed on the far bank. So close, yet as distant as Bactria or the fabled Isles of the Blessed. From the other side a walk of half an hour, and he would reach Gallienus in the Imperial Palace. From the Palatine less than an hour would bring him to the Bronze Gate in the south-east of Rome. There, in the House of Volcatius, his household would be settling in for the night. Having bathed and dined, his two sons, and Julia, his wife, would be preparing for bed. Most likely the four northern warriors of his hearth-troop, his bodyguards as the Romans considered them, would be playing dice. Maximus and Tarchon, Rikiar the Vandal and Grim the Lame would be sharing a drink, flirting with the maids. The warriors had not wanted to let him go alone. They had given him the sword-oath, were his sworn men. Ballista had ordered them to stay. True to his word to the Prefect of the City Watch, Ballista had not told them where he was going, only that he would not be back until late. He had implied that it was a thing of no danger. All unaware, his household would not miss him for hours.

He thought of his sons. In some ways they had grown to be very different. Isangrim would turn thirteen on the Kalends of the next month. He was tall for his age, quiet and given to introspection. Dernhelm was just six, would not be seven until November. He had a slighter build, and was always talking, always in motion. Both had inherited their father's pale skin and fair hair. Like all Roman citizens they had three names. Although their first two were impeccably Roman – Marcus Clodius – Julia had objected to the final names. Men descended on their mother's side from consuls should not sound as if they were barbarians. Through the frigid disapproval, and the outright arguments, Ballista had insisted. His sons must know their paternal heritage. They were as much diplomatic hostages as Ballista himself. A turn of the stars, a shift in the tide of imperial politics, and either might be sent to the distant North as an imperial-sponsored candidate for the throne of the Himlings of Hedinsey. Given his own recent visit to the lands of his ancestors, Ballista doubted that all their countrymen would welcome his sons to the shores of the Suebian Sea.

Looking back, the differences over the naming of their children had been nothing, a passing squall in an otherwise happy marriage. Something had changed, perhaps five years before, when they were in the East. Julia had changed. Before their silences had been companionable. Afterwards they seemed to hold a secret. Julia had become withdrawn, as if locking him out of a part of her existence. Discreet inquiries, prompted by jealousy, had revealed no evidence of another man. Often Ballista thought that it must be his fault. He had had an affair. But that was after things were different, and he doubted that Julia knew. In any case, outside the babbling of a few philosophers, no Roman wife would be brought up to expect sexual fidelity from her husband. It was his own sterner northern morality that objected.

He wondered how they would get the news of his death. If the plot against Gallienus failed, there would be an inquiry. If the Prefect of the City Watch managed to distance himself from the failed coup, he would describe it as a terrible mistake. Scarpio would weep crocodile tears. The noble Ballista was killed resisting arrest or trying to escape; a tragic case of mistaken identity. If the prefect was implicated, the truth would come out in the cellars of the Palace under pincers and claws wielded by the skilled hands of men without compassion.

If the emperor was assassinated, troops hammering on the doors of the House of Volcatius would be the only warning the household would receive. Rough men, lamplight shining on leather and steel, harsh voices calling for the family of the *traitor*. Maximus and Tarchon would not stand aside, nor would Rikiar or Grim. The former two considered that they owed Ballista their lives. They would pay that debt trying to protect his family. Yet numbers would tell, and when they were dead . . .

It was all his fault. Three years he had been away. Three years since he had parted from his family on the quayside at Ephesus. It was less than a month since he had returned to Rome. If he had still been abroad, his family would not be in danger. His friendship with Gallienus would have been immaterial. He would have been out of sight, somewhere beyond the frontiers, and out of mind. If he had not sent a fast message ahead by the imperial posting service, summoning his wife and sons to meet him in Rome, they would still be in Sicily. Even if he were killed, the distance might have saved them.

Ballista gazed down the length of the alleyway at the river. The dark waters looked almost inviting. Better that than being hauled from a futile hiding place under this warehouse, dragged out like a rat from its nest, then quietly butchered. He had always been strong in the water. Perhaps it was not impossible to brave the flood, and reach the far shore. Perhaps some god might carry him across.

CHAPTER 4

The Warehouses

'OPEN IN THE NAME OF the city watch!'
The shout carried through the night.

Ballista levered himself off the brickwork. Watching where he put his feet, he made his way back to the end of the alley. Stooping, covering his face with his forearm, careful to make no sudden movement, he peered around the corner.

Neither the torches upstream nor those away from the river had moved. To the south, the line of the City Watch had moved up, and blocked the street at the last pair of warehouses. Men hammered on the doors.

So that was how they would draw the covert; one line of beaters driving the quarry into the waiting cordon. It was a pity. If they had all set off at once, in the confusion of the darkness, a gap might have opened through which their prey could have escaped. The Prefect of the City Watch was quite the huntsman. If it was Scarpio in charge here. It had not been the prefect urging the men on at the Mausoleum. Having met Scarpio just once, Ballista would still have recognised his disembodied voice. The voice he had heard from down below was someone else's, and, of course, the figures coming up the stairs had not been the firemen of the City Watch but hired killers.

One of the doors opened. A nightwatchman came out. The City Watch pushed past him, hardly glancing at the figure in the hooded cloak, carrying the crook and shuttered lamp of his profession. The bucketmen were going to search each pair of warehouses as they worked their methodical way north. These granaries were not as huge as the Galban warehouses downstream on the other side of the river, but they were still substantial. They must contain dozens of chambers. There were five pairs of warehouses between the searchers and Ballista. He still had some time.

'Open in the name of the City Watch!'

The other door finally opened. The City Watch, intent on their task, again put down the buckets and axes with which they fought fires, and drew the swords they used to detain malefactors. They brushed aside the hooded figure who emerged from the granary.

Ballista slipped back into his malodorous lair. *Cowards! Kill the barbarian!* Ballista turned over in his mind the shouts which had echoed up the Mausoleum. Recognition swam just below the surface. A voice accustomed to command, yet not cultured. A junior officer, perhaps a centurion, risen from the ranks? The knifemen themselves had served in the army. Ballista knew that voice, but it was like trying to grasp the fleeting remnants of a dream. He put the speculation aside.

The river surged past, its surface bright and shining in the starlight. There was no other way. If he could find something to help him stay afloat. There were barrels stacked on the quayside. But he had to get across to the far bank. Clinging to the hoops of a barrel, he could not swim. He would be at the mercy of the flood. Tiber Island was not far downstream. Even if he could make landfall there, it was only halfway across. The bridges from the island to the city would be guarded. He needed to get beyond the cordon of the City Watch, reach the huts of the fishermen, somehow get his hands on a boat.

'Open for the City Watch!'

Searching in numbers, the bucketmen were making good time. Ballista heard the firemen beating on the next pair of doors, and inspiration struck.

Bent over, scuttling like a vagrant in the gloom, he searched among the rubbish littering the alley. Smashed amphorae, broken roof tiles, a mouldering pile of unwanted sacks, other fouler detritus. It was very dark in the firebreak between the tall granaries. At last his hands found something more useful. A half-brick. Wherever there were buildings, inexplicably there were always discarded half-bricks.

Which door to choose? The street away from the river was clear; you could look from one end to the other. Along the quayside there were cranes, barrels, stanchions, all sorts of things blocking the line of sight. It was an easy decision.

Before committing himself, he paused in the mouth of the alley-way, checking both directions. A hundred paces or so upstream, the torches still burned along the bridge. By their light, in the gaps between the lumber of the dock, he could see the City Watch. They lolled on the rails of the stock pens, secure in their numbers. To the south, four warehouses down, there were fewer in view. Most would be combing through the building.

Despite the pain in his ribs, the stiffness in his back, Ballista stood up straight. Anything furtive would give him away. A deep breath – catching in his chest – and he walked purposefully out onto the quayside. There was no immediate outcry. He turned north, and went up the ramp to the door of the warehouse.

With the half-brick, he rapped on the boards.

'Open in the name of the City Watch.'

Nothing happened. Out of the corner of his eye, he could see the men up by the bridge. He had never felt more exposed.

Again he knocked on the door. 'City Watch, open up!' He forced himself to call louder this time.

Now there were faint noises from inside the building.

Downstream, one of the firemen was pointing him out to his colleagues. *Allfather, let them take me for an overzealous one of their own.* Don't let it occur to them that the fugitive might be standing brazenly in the open. Don't let them notice that his feet were bare.

The sounds behind the door were getting louder; echoing footsteps, muffled talking. *At least two men, damn them to Hades.*

'Who is there?' The voice was sullen and welcoming.

'The City Watch.' Despite his apprehension, Ballista made his words loud and peremptory. The watchmen had the right to enter any premises in the City.

As the first bolt could be heard being drawn, another voice came from inside. 'All they ever want is to come in from the weather, drink our wine, stink the place out with the tallow of their torches.'

A second bolt scraped free. Ballista stared at the boards, willing them to work quicker. At any moment a shout might ring out down the quayside, or someone might come to investigate.

The sound of a key in the lock, tumblers turning. *Infernal gods, get a move on.* Finally there were grunts of effort, and the noise of a bar being lifted.

The door opened inward, little more than a crack. A thin face, half hidden by a hood, peered out.

Ballista put his shoulder to the door, and pushed passed the man into the cavernous interior.

'You are not . . .'

Ballista swung the half-brick. Completely unsuspecting, the man had no time to defend himself. The blow struck him on the temple. There was a sickening thud. The man's head snapped sideways, and his legs gave way. Dropping the half-brick, Ballista caught the unconscious man as he fell. In the light of a hanging lamp, the other nightwatchman stood open-handed, mouth hanging slack. The unexpected violence had rooted him to the spot. Ballista lowered his victim to the floor, and pushed the door shut with his foot. The other man, gradually comprehending what his eyes saw, hesitated. Would he run or fight? He turned and ran. Ballista was after him in a moment.

The second nightwatchman only had a couple of paces start. Ballista hurled himself forward, tackling the man around the thighs. They both thumped down onto the wooden boards, skidded along the floor. Chaff and spilt grain grazed Ballista's elbows. He felt a splinter or raised nail tear his right shin.

Releasing his hold, Ballista scrambled to his hands and knees. Beneath him, the man at once was half up, boots fighting for purchase as he tried to resume his flight. Ballista punched him hard in the kidneys. The man exhaled in pain, but continued to rise. Ballista brought his weight down, his knees landing in the small of the man's back. This time the man stayed down. Ballista got up, stood over him. The man was curled into a foetal position, whimpering in agony.

'Don't make a sound.'

Ballista went back to the door, pulled it open, glanced both ways. Torches still burned up at the bridge, others downstream. The dockside nearby was still dark and empty. No one was coming. No one seemed to have noticed. He shut the door again, shot home two of the bolts. He considered the key and the bar, but given what he planned to do, left them unlocked.

The second nightwatchman started to crawl away as he returned.

'Take off your cloak, belt, and boots.'

'Don't hurt me.' The man sat still, looking up at him, eyes frightened.

'Do as I say, and you will soon be out of here. Take off your things.'

Painfully the man shrugged off the cloak, and began to fumble with the buckle of his belt.

Suddenly Ballista realised there was something he had overlooked in his plan. 'Where is the key to the other door?'

'In the lock, the second one on the ring.'

As the man removed his belt, Ballista went and took the keys.

'You have killed poor old Marcus. He never did anyone any harm.'

'Keep going.' Ballista came and crouched over the unmoving body. There was a gash on his head, a nasty swelling, blood seeping through his hair.

'We haven't got any money on us.'

'Don't talk.' Ballista touched a finger to the man's neck. There was a pulse, and he was still breathing, if shallowly. Ballista unbuckled the belt of the prone figure, shifted the dead weight to slide it free.

'All this for some old clothes.'

'Your friend will live.' Ballista had seen men in similar cases never come round, but he wanted the conscious nightwatchman cooperative. 'Now your boots.'

The man tugged at his boots. 'I think you have broken my back.'

'You can move. It is just bruised.'

When the boots were off, Ballista took the two belts and tied the nightwatchman's arms behind his back with one, secured his legs with the other. Then he sat next to him almost companionably, and tried to tug on the boots. They were far too small.

'Do not make a sound until they come to rescue you.'

A look of cunning came over the nightwatchman's face. 'You will not get away with it.'

'Perhaps not, but if you do not stop talking, you will not be leaving here alive.' Ballista got up, and went to wrestle the boots off the unconscious man.

'They crucify your sort. Your only chance is to run now.'

'Enough talk.' Ballista looked across hard-eyed. 'I have already killed three men tonight. One more will not weigh heavily on my conscience.'

That made the nightwatchman fall silent.

The new boots were too tight as well, but Ballista managed to get them on. They would soon pinch and blister his already tender feet, but he had to wear them for a time if his plan had any chance of working.

Ballista stood, and put on the cloak. He went back to the door, took down one of the lanterns hanging there, and picked up a crook.

'Make a sound, and I will return and kill you. I do not want to, but that is the way things are.'

The nightwatchman said nothing.

'You understand?'

The man grunted.

Ballista walked deeper into the warehouse.

When he came out into the central courtyard, it seemed very bright after the corridor. In the starlight, the inner walls of the granary stretched up far above his head. By day the arcades would be full of noise and bustle – merchants talking, overseers shouting, stevedores and porters whistling and joking, inured to the weight of the endless sacks of grain they carried – but now the warehouse was as quiet as the grave.

The heels of Ballista's boots clicked on the pavement as he crossed the shadowed, blue-white expanse. The partly shuttered lantern in his hand emitted just a thin beam of yellow light.

The colonnade on the far side, which led to the door which opened away from the river, was in deep shade. Ballista heard nothing as he walked into the darkness, but he sensed a movement in the still air. Automatically he dropped into a crouch. Something hit him hard across the shoulders. The force knocked him to his knees. The things he carried clattered to the floor.

Ballista heard his assailant regain his balance, gather himself for another blow. He rolled away. He saw a dark, bulky shape. Something heavy swished down, and cracked onto the flagstones, where his head had been a moment earlier.

Ballista kicked out. The man leapt back.

The beam of Ballista's overturned lantern shone away from them, but there was enough light for Ballista to make out the cloaked figure holding a cudgel. *Hades, there had been a third nightwatchman.* That accounted for the crafty look on the other one's face.

Stooping, the man righted the lantern.

In the moment's grace, Ballista scrambled to his feet.

The man advanced.

The wall of the passageway was at Ballista's back.

The man jabbed with the club. Ballista sidestepped. The wood smacked into the brickwork. Ballista was cornered, but there was an open doorway off to the left. He ducked into it, and immediately realised his mistake.

A big, gloomy storeroom, filled with sacks of grain, piled two high. No other door, just a ventilation window to the next room, high up. The light dimmed almost to nothing. The man was blocking the entrance. Without hesitation, Ballista climbed up the cliff of sacks. The man was hard on his heels. The grain shifted and gave under Ballista's boots. The neck of one of the sacks split open as he floundered to the window. The man was close behind. No time to wrench open the woodwork. Ballista turned to fight. His right foot slipped between two sacks. He wrenched his leg, and went sprawling on his back.

'Got you, you fucker.'

The cudgel was at his chest. The homely smell of harvested corn was strong in his nostrils.

The man drew back the cudgel.

Trying to push himself up, Ballista's hand sank into loose grain.

The man tensed himself to strike.

Ballista closed his fist, and threw the handful of wheat.

Instinctively, the man flinched as the grains flicked up from the darkness into his face.

Ballista hooked his free leg around the nightwatchman's ankle, twisted, and the man went down.

With no more thought than a cornered beast, Ballista swarmed up and over him. His hands found the other's throat. The man clawed at Ballista's wrists, scratched at his face, sharp nails seeking his eyes. Ballista had the longer reach. He leant back, face averted, his grip unbroken. With all his strength, Ballista throttled the man, strong fingers deep in his flesh, crushing his windpipe, choking out the fragile life.

Time slowed. It was as if they had been locked in this macabre embrace forever. Then – a final convulsion – and it was over.

Ballista collapsed on top of the corpse, panting like a man spent by the act of love. The stench of the man's loosened bowels tainted the sweet smell of the wheat. There was a horrible intimacy to killing with bare hands.

Ballista rolled off his victim. The fresh scratches on his forearms and face smarted, and his shoulders throbbed. The pain in his ribs had returned, sharp and insistent.

Fighting off a childish desire to crawl away and hide, Ballista clambered down from the piled sacks, limped out of the storeroom, and retrieved his lantern and crook, and after a few moments search, the keys.

'Titus.' A voice was calling through the quiet warehouse.

Ballista retraced his steps.

'Titus, is that you?' At the sound of approaching footfalls, the bound nightwatchman dropped his voice to a whisper.

'Unfortunately for you, no,' Ballista said.

'What have you done with him?'

'Titus is finished.'

The man's eyes were wide with fear.

'I warned you what would happen if you made a noise.' Ballista hefted the crook. Yet somehow he could not do it, could not beat to death a bound, helpless man.

'One more sound, and you will be waiting with him by the Styx. You will not get a second reprieve. Not another sound.'

Ballista knew he was blustering. Any more words, and the night-watchman would realise too. He turned, and went back the way he had come.

There were no empty sacks in the storeroom where the corpse of Titus was sprawled. Ballista opened two of the full ones. The knots were tight, and the twine was rough and cut into his fingers. Laboriously, he heaved them up, and emptied the grain out onto the floor. Kneeling in a cloud of dust, he poured most of the oil from the lantern on the corner of one. When he was satisfied that the sackcloth was soaked with the inflammable liquid, he arranged it between some full sacks, where he could feel a draft on his hands.

Ballista felt no guilt about Titus' body. The Romans often gave their dead to the pyre.

Standing, Ballista applied the flame. The material caught immediately. He placed the second empty sack over the burning one. Blue tongues of fire licked up through the sacking.

At the door of the warehouse, Ballista inserted one of the keys into the lock. He turned it, but the tumblers did not move. He jiggled it. Nothing. He pushed the key further in, then not so far.

Still nothing. He tried turning it the other way. The lock remained obstinately closed.

Tendrils of smoke were coiling out from the storeroom.

It must be the other key on the ring. Inserting it brought no better result.

Now the smoke was rolling out, billowing up to the ceiling.

Feverishly working the key, Ballista cursed himself. Why had he not thought to unlock the door first? He was a fool.

The smoke now was hanging lower, catching in his throat. He could hear the crackle of the flames. The grain was tinder dry. The whole building could go up at any moment.

Ballista leant against the door, desperately fumbling with the key, and then – above the noise of the fire, above his own harsh breathing – heard the most wonderful sound. The tumblers clicked open.

Shooting back the two bolts presented no problem, but then there was the bar. Belatedly Ballista saw the sheer size of the thing. Solid metal, slotted into a pair of L shaped hooks, it was designed to be lifted by two men. By all the gods, he was the biggest fool that had ever walked the earth.

Coughing, almost blinded by the thick smoke, he seized one end of the bar, and heaved. The monstrous band of iron lifted; a finger, two, then half a hand's breadth. Just a fraction more, and he could slide it out. But the weight was too great. He had to let go. The metal clanged back down into the retaining hooks.

The roar of the fire was deafening, like some malignant daemon. Its baleful light flickered in the corridor. Ballista had to get out now. Planting his feet wide, bending his knees, he summoned every ounce of strength. Again the bar raised. Not quite far enough to slide it out. He would not be defeated. One last effort. Almost to the tipping point. And then, with a rasp of metal on metal, it went.

The clatter of the bar on the floor ringing in his ears, Ballista wrenched the door open, and stumbled, choking, half-retching into the night.

'Fire!' Ballista tried to shout, but he could not.

He staggered down the ramp, and across the street. Clouds of smoke, backlit by the inferno, roiled out in his wake.

The City Watch were by the next warehouse.

'Fire!' Ballista doubled up, racked with coughing.

True to their training, the firemen grabbed their buckets and axes, and ran pell-mell to the conflagration. Their cordon was broken, all thought of the fugitive forgotten.

Bent over, Ballista pulled the hood of his cloak over his head.

Officers of the Watch were shouting orders, getting their men into action, calling for ladders and pumps.

Ignored amid the furious activity, Ballista moved to slip away down the street. He had gone no more than a dozen steps, when one of the Watch grabbed his arm.

'Are you the nightwatchman?'

It was easy to feign another coughing fit. Ballista kept his head down, obscured by the hood.

'Marcus and the others are still in there. They are at the river end. You have to get them out.'

The Bucketman told him to stay where he was, and rushed to find an officer.

As soon as he was unobserved, Ballista moved off. He went past the next warehouse, and left into the alleyway which ran down to the river beyond. Coming out on the quayside, he turned right away from the fire and towards Transtiberim. Behind him the firemen were already busy wielding their axes to break down the door of the warehouse. As if summoned out of thin air, idlers come to gawp at the disaster were filling the dockside. In moments Ballista was beyond the crowd, safely out of sight.

Downstream of the granaries was the Quinctian Meadow, named for Quinctius Cincinnatus. It was here, back in the mists of time, that the Roman hero had been summoned from his ploughing to become dictator and save the republic, and it was here, to his oxen and back-breaking labour, that he had returned on laying down his exalted office. Although buildings had long since covered the meadow, the association with frugality and hard work remained. The riverfront of the district was lined with the huts of poor fishermen.

Ballista walked into the darkness between the jumble of clapboard dwellings. There were few people about. He could smell the river and mud, damp ropes and tar, wet stone and fish.

On the opposite bank of the Tiber was the *navalia*, and Ballista's gaze travelled over the pitched roofs of the ship sheds. Under the tallest, he knew, was preserved the flagship of a long dead Macedonian King. The *navalia* was a curious complex, put to more than one use. Originally the home of the Roman fleet, for centuries now it had been a naval museum. Yet, apart from such things as the ship of Aeneas, it also housed animals destined for the games and certain hostages from beyond the frontiers. The latter were as much exhibits as the dusty war galleys or the savage tigers or long-lashed ostriches.

Ballista did not know what hostages were confined there now. They might include men from the far North. Yet it was of no account. One or two individuals would be of little help this night. There were northern warriors in Rome, a thousand of them, all armed. Among the emperor's German bodyguard would be men who would follow Ballista as a member of the Woden-born Himling dynasty. But those not on duty around Gallienus were quartered in the Gardens of Dolabella to the south-east of Rome. They might as well still be on the Rhine or the shores of the Suebian Sea.

As a youth Ballista had not been confined in the *navalia*. His father's diplomatic importance, and the Roman citizenship that

Ballista had been granted for his role in assassinating Emperor Maximinus Thrax, led to Ballista being housed in the Palace itself. There on the Palatine he had been educated at the imperial school. His companions had been the sons of leading senators and the governors of armed provinces, each one guaranteeing the loyalty of his father, as Ballista guaranteed the loyalty of his.

It had been a bad time. Ballista could never forget the day that the centurion arrived at the hall of his father, and announced that the emperor demanded one of his sons as a hostage. It had been years before Ballista could understand, let alone forgive his father's choice. His schoolfellows had not harmed or even insulted him. Such behaviour was beneath their dignity, and anyway they were too closely watched. But they had treated him with silent contempt and ostracised him. Gallienus had been one of the few that ever spoke to him. For the first time, Ballista had been lonely. There on the Palatine, he had realised something important about the Romans. For all their philosophers' fine orations about free speech and liberty – the things they claimed set them apart from every other people – the Romans, at least those from good families, could not say aloud what they thought. Ballista had learned to guard his tongue. The habit had become ingrained.

Yet it had not all been bad. He had been young, and he had money; both that sent by his father, and an allowance from the imperial treasury. When he could escape from the school, he had explored the city: the drinking holes and gambling dens and brothels. Although he liked reading, he had never been destined for an ascetic or philosophical life. The chariot racing in the Circus had been his especial delight. He had felt safe enough in his wanderings through the teaming city, for Calgacus had always been at his side.

Calgacus had seemed old to Ballista. Yet, looking back, he could not have been. Ugly, sharp tongued and querulous, Calgacus was a

Caledonian slave assigned to the young Ballista by his father. *Been wiping your arse since you were a baby*, as Calgacus frequently liked to say. After the Palatine, when Ballista entered imperial service, Calgacus had accompanied him on all his postings. Together they had journeyed to Africa and Hibernia, fought on the Danube and in the East. Always there, always complaining – *working my fingers to the fucking bone* – Calgacus had been one of the very few people after his exile to whom Ballista could speak openly. Ballista had loved Calgacus.

Two years before, out on the Steppe, Calgacus had been killed. It had been Ballista's fault. The murderer was Hippothous, the Greek. Ballista had appointed Hippothous his secretary, brought him into his *familia*. Ballista had failed to see the Greek's madness. Ballista had failed to save his friend. He had given chase, but Hippothous had got away.

Ballista had made no vows to the gods – his record with oaths was not good – but he would not rest until Calgacus was avenged.

First, of course, he had to live through tonight.

CHAPTER 5

The Tiber

IN THE DARKEST SHADOW OF AN ALLEY, Ballista sat with his hood drawn up, and his hands and feet tucked out of sight. The dockside was quiet. Perhaps, with the river running so fast, many of the fishermen had gone to watch the fire. Certainly crowds had streamed up from Transtiberim, past Ballista's hiding place, to view the spectacle. The City Watch had summoned ladders and pumps. They were aiming water on the neighbouring warehouses. Torsion artillery had been brought up ready to tear down buildings and create a firebreak. Yet so far they had managed to confine the conflagration just to the original granary. Even so, the fire had lit the night sky purple. The air smelt strangely homely, of burning wood and toasted grain.

A few night fishermen were busy preparing to go out. Ballista had selected one. He was not proud of his reasoning. The man's boat was at a distance from the others that were being readied. The man was old. If necessary, Ballista could overpower him, and take his boat before anyone could intervene. The thinking was both dishonourable and inept. Having grown up on the shores of the Suebian Sea, handling a small boat under oars was second nature to Ballista. Of course he could row to the opposite shore, but the whole point was to do so discreetly.

The old fisherman was working in his hut. The door was open, and his endeavours lit by a single candle. He was checking and repairing his nets. It was not just the candle that proclaimed his poverty. Ballista could see that every time he found that a weight was missing, he replaced it with a pot shard. In some he must have bored a hole, as he strung them on to the net. Others he tied. In the latter he must have scratched grooves, and smoothed the sharp edges, so they would not cut the cords.

The scene summoned up a vivid memory. Last spring, a waterfront bar in the remote town of Olbia, off the Black Sea. Another aged fisherman outside stringing nets. Ballista had been drinking with Maximus and Tarchon. He remembered that the wine had a cloying taste of elderflower. Another friend had been with them; Castricius, the strange, little Roman officer. They had been unhappy, grieving for the murdered Calgacus. Some off-duty soldiers had been drinking with some whores. The afternoon had ended in a fight. Two of the soldiers had died. One of the whores had got her nose broken. A sordid, violent afternoon, but Ballista not been alone. He had been embraced in the companionship of his friends. He pushed away the loneliness that threatened to unman his resolve.

Twice the old man got up and carried nets to where his boat sat on the slipway. Both times Ballista prepared to approach him, but the fisherman returned to his hut. Ballista remained in cover, studying him. He was balding, with a stubby beard, his face haggard. His stained tunic hung loose from an emaciated frame. The veins on his neck were dilated, stood out like whipcord. When he walked, it was obvious that his back was hunched.

There was a market in Rome dedicated to selling deformed slaves. The rich liked to keep them as pets. At drinking parties they brought out hunchbacks, dwarfs, cripples, grossly obese women, as part of the entertainment. It was rumoured that cruel fathers mutilated young children for profit. It was not just the living. The homes and gardens of the wealthy often boasted finely sculpted and expensive statues of the grotesque. It was a common belief that such unfortunates attracted the evil eye, that they would deflect any malice or envy from their owners. Ballista also had heard it argued that the practice was to provoke philosophical thought; a demonstration that the body was nothing, that true beauty resided only in the soul. Somehow, he suspected that many had less elevated motives, that the twisted and wasted bodies of their ornaments and playthings simply made them feel superior. Perhaps, at heart, the malformed were nothing but a source of cruel amusement.

The old man got up again. This time, along with a net, he carried a lantern.

Ballista emerged from the alley, and walked over.

The aged fisherman gave him a sharp look, but did not seem unduly alarmed.

'Are you going out tonight, Grandfather?'

'The fish do not catch themselves,' the old man said. 'A man has to eat.'

Ballista nodded, as if weighing some serious thing.

'A lot of the Syrians down in Transtiberim don't eat fish.' The fisherman grinned. He had few teeth. 'Thank the gods – the native gods of Rome – that is one of their eastern customs that has not spread. Not like their fucking crucified god.'

'Christians to the lion,' Ballista said.

'Christians to the lion.' The fisherman repeated the traditional phrase.

The old man clambered on the boat to hang the lantern from the sternpost. 'The markets will open at dawn. By the third hour, if the gods are willing, I will have some coins in my wallet, and bread on the table.'

'I was wondering, Grandfather, if you would take me over to the other side?'

'I may be ill-favoured, but do you see a three-headed dog?' The old man wheezed with amusement at his own joke. 'Do I look like Charon, the fucking ferryman?'

Ballista said nothing.

'Why not use a bridge?'

'I will pay you more than the obol Charon receives.'

'Why would you do that?' There was a crafty look on his face.

Ballista decided a fragment of the truth might help. 'The City Watch are after me.'

The words provoked another bout of senile mirth. 'I know. They were round here, asking for a man of your description: a huge, pale barbarian from the north with long hair, speaks good Latin, can pass himself off as one of us – as if! Dangerous, they said you were.'

Ballista tensed, ready to seize the boat, whatever it took.

'They never said what they wanted you for.'

Ballista relaxed a little. But this was going on too long. He needed to be away across the water.

A sudden look of suspicion crossed the fisherman's face. 'Not something to do with the fire, is it?' A hooked knife for gutting fish appeared as if by magic in his hand. 'No, wait. The bucketmen were round hunting you before the fire.'

'Not the fire, gods no. Nothing more dangerous in the city than fire.'

The old man had not put down the knife. Ballista measured the distances and angles between himself on the slipway and the fisherman in the boat.

'Tell what you did, and I will think about it.' The knife was still out.

This was getting more like the *Odyssey* all the time. Ballista hunted for a suitable story.

'No confession, no ferry,' the old man cackled. 'In case you haven't noticed, I have got a knife. And one shout and the Terentius twins down the way will be here. Nasty bastards, they are.'

Speechless, Ballista let his shoulders drop, like a sullen donkey with too heavy a load.

'I don't think you've got all night.'

Ballista mumbled something inaudible.

'Speak up.'

'I had just got my hand on it, when the dog started barking, the door burst open, and there was her husband.' Ballista opened his cloak, to show the various cuts and bruises on his limbs.

'Gave you a hiding, he did.' The old man sounded pleased.

'He had two slaves with him.'

'Been within his rights to kill you. I don't hold with adultery.'

A fisherman with old-fashioned morality. That was not good. Crafty Odysseus himself might have had trouble talking his way out of this.

'It wasn't like that.' Ballista was thinking fast. 'The bitch told me she was a widow. I had to jump out of the window, leave my wallet, leave everything of value.'

The old man looked a fraction less stern.

'The whole thing was set up.' Ballista pressed on. 'Never should have trusted the Syrian bitch.'

No longer the stern arbiter of sexual mores, the fisherman laughed. 'Lucky he and his slaves didn't fuck you up the arse while they were robbing you.'

'So you will take me?'

'Wait. You said he got your wallet. No payment, and you can wander this shore like a lost soul until the City Watch take you.'

Ballista pulled the gold ring from his finger, reached up, and handed it over.

The old man bit it with one of his scarce teeth. 'A northern barbarian with the gold ring of an equestrian, eh? Equestrian or not, you been slumming it in Transtiberim, and got caught with your britches down. All right, put your shoulder to the stern, and run her out. We'll have you on the other side in no time.'

The keel lifted from the ramp, Ballista hauled himself aboard, and the current caught the boat. The fisherman was skilful. At first he let the river rush them downstream, close in to the bank. Then, with a few deft sweeps, he angled them into an eddy that pulled them out into the stream, and swung them around, so that the prow pointed into the flow. Now the old man set to with a will; long, powerful strokes combating the force of the river. In the blackness, water creamed down the sides of the boat. Although he appeared emaciated, working in perfect rhythm, as if one with the vessel, the aged rower edged them across with little leeway.

'Where do you want me to set you off?'

'Near the stables would be good.'

It dawned on Ballista that the old man's bent back was not congenital, but the result of a lifetime of this labour.

Secure in the hands of the fisherman, Ballista stretched his aching body, and looked around.

On the west bank, the warehouse still burned brightly. The roof had gone. Every now and then a muffled thump could be heard over the water, as a store of grain exploded. Once there was a thunderous crash as an internal wall collapsed. Little black figures capered in front of the flames, like some strange sect's vision of infernal damnation.

Ballista hoped the two nightwatchmen had been rescued. He thought of the one that he had killed. At least the man had a magnificent funeral pyre. That was heartless. The nightwatchman had only being doing his job, but Ballista felt little guilt. When he was young, he would have done. Life had not changed him for the better.

To break the chain of thought, Ballista looked away at the dark water.

'Tiber, the river most dear to heaven,' he said. The line of Virgil surfacing from his schooldays.

The fisherman spat over the gunnels. 'Kindly old Father Tiber saving the twins, snagging their little wicker basket in the roots of a fig tree, delivering the founder to the foot of the Palatine. People talk all sorts of bollocks about the river.'

He rowed in silence for a time, as if meditating, then spoke.

'Only fools who don't know the river praise it. They drone on about how the Tiber supplies their needs, gives them work, flushes the city clean. Once a year you see the vestals come. Watched by the good and the great, they throw a few handfuls of dust into the water. Young idiots swim in it. Greek doctors make invalids stand in the shallows. You hear gluttons in the market waxing lyrical on the taste of its fish. *Our* fish, they say, nothing tastes like *our* fish caught between the bridges.'

He shook his head at the folly of the world.

'The river is foul and cruel. The sewers pump it full of offal and shit. The fish gorge on the filth, stuff themselves with it. I catch them all right – no one does it better – but you wouldn't find me eating one of the fuckers. Suicides jump off the bridges. Murderers throw in the corpses of their victims. The number of men I've seen floating face down, guts all bloated, stinking, ready to burst. Cats, dogs, cattle, any animals you care to name – dead in the water. I saw a camel once. All those boards of senators, appointed by the emperor himself, for the *care of the riverbanks*, what good to they do? They put up a lot of inscriptions in their own honour, but how often does the river rise, flood the city? Honest folk – young and old, babes in arms – swept to their deaths, or crushed when the waters undermine their tenement, bring the whole lot down on their heads. The whole city stinking for a month or more, and then comes the sickness. The corpse carriers working all night, every night, those that catch it being added to the cart. But you know the worst of it?'

'No,' Ballista said, knowing he would be told.

'All the shit that flows up the river. Syrians, Jews, Cappadocians, all sorts of sly little easterners, jabbering in their nasty languages, worshipping their weird gods, doing decent Romans out of work, corrupting our ways. No chance of decency or virtue with those fuckers loose in the city. No wonder the empire is going to the dogs; revolts, barbarian invasions, the emperor's own father a captive, the Persian king using him as a mounting block.'

A new type of divine punishment, Ballista thought, to be trapped for eternity in a small rowing boat with a homespun, xenophobic philosopher.

'Romulus welcomed foreigners into his city,' Ballista said.

The old man again spat over the side. 'That was then, this is now.'

'Times change,' Ballista said.

The fisherman grunted. 'You northerners are not too bad, if you can be kept from drinking and fighting.'

'No one accuses us of cunning,' Ballista said.

The old man laughed. 'Too true. Know yourself. That is what the oracle said, *know yourself*. Nearly there now.'

He brought the boat bumping in against a set of stone steps, held it fast to an iron ring.

'I'll hang on to your ring for a couple of days, if you want to buy it back. You know where to find me.'

'I know where to find you.'

Ballista clambered out. Every inch of him was hurting. His ribs had stiffened, and every movement again brought a stab of pain.

The fisherman raised a hand in valediction, and pushed off.

A man consumed by such vitriolic bitterness could not be trusted. Quite likely he would keep the ring, and raise the alarm in the hope of a reward. He needed watching.

Ballista was bone tired, and tempted just to sit down on the damp steps. But the City Watch patrolled this side of the river too. He walked up to the embankment, and leant against a corner where a street ran inland. From here he could see the river, and three avenues of approach. A fundamental rule of warfare was to ensure you had a line of retreat.

The old fisherman did not rush to raise the alarm. He skulled the boat out a way, then lit the lamp, and waited. When he thought the light would have attracted fish, he stood. The boat drifted downstream. With the dexterity of endless repetition, he cast a net. In the gloom, the water flecked white where it landed. The weights on the sides sank. After a few moments, he hauled it in with smooth motions. Fish flapped in its coils. He tipped them into the bottom of the boat.

Cast your net onto the waters. Ballista could not remember where the line was from. Was it a Christian saying? What was the result? Would a beneficent god provide? Probably only if you had faith.

The old man had shifted to another spot, but continued his fishing.

Ballista still watched the man, but his mind moved elsewhere. To get to Gallienus, he had to safely negotiate the streets of Rome. With both the City Watch and the knifemen from the Mausoleum searching for him, he could not blunder about like a peasant newly arrived from the backwoods. His route needed planning with care. He knew parts of the city like he knew the back of his hand: his objective, the Palatine, and away to the south-east, the Gardens of Dolabella,, and the area around the House of Volcatius, where his family waited. The Praetorian Camp, and parts of the Campus Martius, were familiar. As a youth, he had spent much time hanging around here, at the stables of the Circus Factions, where he had got the fisherman to drop him. The problem was the sheer size of Rome. Certain districts were familiar, but he found it hard to stitch them together into a coherent whole.

Of course he had seen the famous map. It was in the Forum of Peace. He closed his eyes, and imagined a visit. He walked along the portico, the flower beds to his left, the pink marble columns and the statues on his right. He went into the office of the Prefect of the City, and there on the right hand wall was the map. Immense and detailed, the river running through it, like cursive script. The buildings were picked out with red paint against the marble. The map was claimed to show every temple and warehouse, street and alleyway, shop, courtyard, baths, and residence in the city. All to no purpose. It was too immense, too detailed, set too high to study. The map was utterly unusable.

And it was upside down. South was at the top. It did not fit Ballista's mental map of the world. When he had travelled south as a hostage, he had gone *down* into the empire. Arbitrary though they were, the things you grew up with – say reading from left to right – became the correct and natural way, the only acceptable way. Perhaps that would not be a thought welcomed by the old fisherman.

This was getting him nowhere. Ballista opened his eyes, checked that no one was approaching, and picked out where the old man on the river was fishing. He needed to concentrate, find a simple path, stick to well known landmarks.

If he struck inland, across the southern end of the Campus Martius, he should find the Theatre of Balbus, reach the Forum of Trajan, and so from there to the Palatine. As he ran through the itinerary, he realised its impossibility.

The headquarters of the City Watch was in a portico opening off the Theatre of Balbus. Scarpio would not have to hunt for him, Ballista would have delivered himself up, neatly wrapped, like a present at New Year. Even if he got past the Theatre of Balbus, or went another way, after dark the Forum and paths up to the Palatine would be almost deserted. Both Scarpio and the leader of the knifemen at the Mausoleum must know where he would be headed. The handful of approaches to the Palace would be closely watched. Alone, at night, Ballista would be intercepted before he got to Gallienus. He needed help, men at his back.

Who could he trust? Maximus and Tarchon, of course, Grim and Rikiar as well, but they were out of reach at the House of Volcatius. The German Guard were further away still in the Gardens of Dolabella. His own former secretary, Demetrius, was now intimate with Gallienus, and thus already in the Palace. Over long years of service, Ballista had become friends with several fellow army officers. Castricius, Aurelian and Rutilus were with the forces gathered around Milan. Tacitus was on his estates somewhere up near the Danube. Ballista cudgelled his brain: a reliable army officer stationed in Rome, preferably one of the *protectores*, Gallienus' trusted inner circle.

The broad, ruddy face of Volusianus, the senior Praetorian Prefect, suddenly came to mind. The ex-trooper Volusianus had risen from the ranks by courage, discipline, and steadfast loyalty to Gallienus and his father. Volusianus was a proper soldier. The prefect would be in his quarters in the Praetorian Camp, and that was in the opposite direction from the Palatine.

Ballista levered himself off the wall, and set off north, following the dark river.

CHAPTER 6

The Field of Mars
The Stadium of Domitian

BALLISTA MOVED NORTH, the great shining river rolling through the darkness on his left. In the main he kept to the embankment, just cutting a block inland every now and then, not to leave a straight trail. There were not many people about. The air here was full of the scent of hay and straw and the warm, sweet smell of horses and their droppings. He passed between the shuttered stables of two of the racing factions: the Whites, the favoured team of his youth, and that of the Greens, where the mad Emperor Caligula had often dined and slept, and built a stall of marble and a manger of ivory for his favourite stallion.

He knowledge of this district was good, the areas he intended to traverse less so. His vague plan was to head up to the ornamental parkland at the top of the Field of Mars, turn east, cross the Gardens of Lucullus, and so reach the camp of the praetorians. By the time he reached the horses' exercise track called the Trigarium, he realised that he must make a detour. The boots which he had taken from the nightwatchman were too small. They had blistered his already tender feet. Every step was painful. He was limping. It could draw attention, and soon he would be unable to walk. He needed new boots – a weapon would be good – and he must have money. He needed a whore. Where there were whores, there were clients and pimps, and they carried coins. Money could buy you anything in Rome: advancement, divorce, the death of a rival; certainly a blade and a pair of boots.

Away from the river, the southern end of the Field of Mars was studded with temples and theatres and bath houses. Respectable by day, after dark they were the playground of the raffish. Since the reign of Alexander Severus, the baths remained open at night. Men and women bathed naked in the soft light of the lamps. Masseurs kneaded and oiled bare flesh. Wine was drunk by the amphora. *An incitement to vice*, thundered philosophers and other stern moralists. Outside, the arcades of the monumental buildings sheltered prostitutes of both sexes and all types, none more than the Stadium of Domitian.

Ballista turned into a street running away from the river, and, at once, recognised his mistake. Two blocks away a patrol of the City Watch were heading towards him. Otherwise the street was almost deserted. To turn back was to invite suspicion. Ballista quickened his pace, forced himself not to limp. When they were still about fifty paces off, he turned left into the first side street. It was long and empty. His footfall echoed from the walls. If he ran, they would hear, almost certainly chase. He glanced back from under his hood. The bucketmen had turned in after him.

Ignoring every instinct to flee, he tried to walk as fast as could still seem natural.

The City Watch followed. Their axes and buckets and sword belts rattled and banged. He had seen that there were eight of them. How many usually constituted a patrol? Ballista had no idea.

He turned into another street, somewhat wider, and completely empty. On either side were the blank walls and locked doors of imposing buildings set back in gardens. The walls were scalable, but almost certainly there would be guard dogs. Ballista muttered a prayer.

The gods did not listen. All too soon he heard the tramp and clangour of the patrol behind him. There were side streets. Ballista took one at random. This time, as soon as he was out of sight, he broke into a run.

'After him!' someone shouted.

The street opened into a small square with a fountain in the centre. Three alleys led off the square. Two stretched away into the darkness, while the other ran just a few paces before ending in closed gates, in front of which stood an empty cart. Only a fool would trap himself in such a place. Yet sometimes it was best to hide in plain sight. Ballista vaulted up into the cart, and hunkered down in its bed.

The cart smelt strongly of onions. Through a crack in the boards, Ballista saw the City Watch clatter into the square, come to a halt, swearing. One of them, a big fellow, overweight and already panting, went to the fountain, and started to drink from his cupped hands.

'Gaius, get back here.' The speaker was evidently the leader.

'How do you know it was him?' Gaius sounded put out.

'He ran.'

'Scarpio didn't even know if he was on this side of the river. Be a busy night if we try and arrest every man in a hooded cloak who does not want to talk to the City Watch.'

'Stop your moaning. You three go with Gaius. The rest with me. Meet up in the square of the Dolphin. Gaius, get your fat arse moving. No stopping for a drink or a pie.'

Ballista stayed still, listening to the sounds of them moving away. So, the old fisherman had not reported him. His heart lifted. The City Watch had lost his tracks back by the warehouses in Transtiberim. If they did not know his whereabouts, neither would the swordsmen from the Mausoleum. Surely both would expect him to make straight for the Palatine. The way to the Praetorian Camp should not be guarded. Once he had talked to Volusianus, and found an escort of praetorians, neither Scarpio nor whichever man to whom the hired killers answered would have a hope of stopping him reaching the emperor. Within an hour of Gallienus being informed, Scarpio would be in the cellars of the Palace. Once the imperial torturers got to work with the pincers and claws, Scarpio would soon confess the names of his fellow conspirators. In stories men bit off their own tongues rather than implicate others. In the awful agonies of reality – twisted in pain, reeking of their own blood and urine – anyone, no matter how strong or how resolute, would give up his closest friends, his own father or beloved son.

Once he had seen the emperor, Ballista would take a horse from the imperial stables, and he could be at the House of Volcatius in no time. His family would be safe. As soon as the conspirators had been detained, he would petition Gallienus for permission to retire to their house in Sicily. In the first flush of gratitude, Gallienus would not refuse. Then they would all be safe – Julia, his sons, Maximus and Tarchon – all safe in that beautiful provincial backwater; out of sight and out of mind, far from the dangers of Rome, the court and the army. For a moment he was transported to the terraced garden outside the villa, high on the slopes of Tauromenium, looking down on the Bay of Naxos.

This was no time for bucolic daydreams. He needed to concentrate, have his wits about him. If he failed, they would all die.

Ballista clambered down from the cart. *Gods below, these boots pinch and hurt.*

Slowly and carefully, Ballista doubled back the way he had come. The tall buildings blocked his view of the moon. But the night was still young. There was more than enough time. When he thought that he had put enough distance between himself and the patrol, he began to try to work his way eastwards. In open country his sense of direction never failed him. It was different here in Rome, at the bottom of canyon-like streets, with the stars out of sight.

Eventually he emerged onto a broad thoroughfare. A few groups of men strolled its length. Some passed wineskins or amphorae from hand to hand. At the end of the street the graceful arches of the Stadium of Domitian reared into the sky, their pale marble gleaming in the moonlight. At night many of the arches on the ground floor were occupied by prostitutes. Some had an improvised curtain, the rest relied on the shadows for a modicum of privacy. Business was moderately brisk. There was nothing furtive about the clients as they came and went. Other men, hard faced and brutal, stood about. Sometimes they spoke to each other, or went to collect money from the girls they pimped.

Ballista ambled along, as casually as his blistered feet allowed. A beggar sat on the other side of the street. He was neither old nor young, barefoot, but clean enough, and, although thin, did not appear to be starving. Propped at his feet was a slate with a crude drawing of a shipwreck. Ballista went and sat next to him.

'Health and great joy.'

'Fuck off, this is my pitch.'

'You mistake me. I am thinking of having a girl.'

The vagrant looked at him with silent suspicion.

'You got any use for a pair of boots?' Ballista tugged the horrible things off, the relief blissful. 'Too small for me. If they don't fit you either, you can sell them.'

'You drunk?'

'No.'

'You are a strange one.' The beggar took the boots anyway. 'Name, race, free or slave?'

Ballista chuckled. 'Spend a lot of time in court, do you?'

'That is how I got here. What is your occupation?'

'Onion seller.'

'That explains the smell.'

'Any new girls here?'

The beggar was trying on the boots. 'They brought down a tasty little Christian earlier. Condemned to the brothels, dragged her over to the third booth, the one with the two bruisers outside. Naked as the day she was born, about fourteen, lovely little tits and arse. Virgin, so they said. If I had any coins, I wouldn't mind being one of the first to plough her delta.'

'No one stops a man buying what is openly for sale.' Ballista wanted to keep the beggar talking. The City Watch and the knifemen were looking for a man on his own. Hide in plain sight. 'No one prohibits anyone from going along the public road.'

'Too true, my friend, and a whore will do all the things your wife won't.'

Ballista nodded, as if struck by the sagacity of the words, but all the time his gaze was moving over the Stadium and the arches.

The mendicant was warming to his theme. 'Try to get your wife to suck your cock, take it from behind, leave the lamp on so you can see what you are getting.'

Some of the arches, Ballista noted, were more out of the way than others.

'As for mounting up, so she can do the work . . .'

To forestall the enumeration of every sexual position and foible, Ballista pointed at the picture of a shipwreck the by the beggar's feet. 'That what happened to you?'

'Indeed. I coursed over the great sea with swift-sailed craft, reached many far-off lands. I did not peddle fripperies, luxuries which corrupt, but sold goods which people could use. My honesty was praised everywhere – Ostia, Carthage, Piraeus.'

How was it that even a Roman reduced to the meanest condition could talk about himself as if the hero of an epic poem? Ballista thought it might stem from learning to read and write from Virgil's *Aeneid*.

'Always paid my taxes, straightforward in my dealings with everyone, would always help a man if I could.'

One of the arches was isolated, the two on either side empty, just the one pimp nearby.

'Then my ship went down in the Hollows of Euboea, all the cargo lost. There was a court case.'

A client left the arch that Ballista was watching.

'What good are the laws, when money rules? A poor man has no chance.'

It was time to act.

'A judgement in court is nothing but a public sale. The aristocrat who sits on the jury casts his vote according to who pays him. That was the end which the Fates had spun for me at my birth.'

'Tell you what,' Ballista interrupted, getting to his feet, 'when I come out, I will give you some coins for a girl or a meal.'

Lost in self-pity, the beggar ignored Ballista's words. 'All judges hand down decisions for a price ...'. He continued to chunter, as Ballista walked away. 'Togate vultures, every one of them.'

Ballista pushed through the curtain and into a makeshift cubicle lit by a cheap lamp.

The whore was pulling on her toga, preparing to leave. 'Always time for a handsome man.' Her smile did not touch her eyes. 'Even if he does smell of onions.'

'Take off your clothes.' Ballista shrugged off his cloak.

'Eager, aren't you?' She began to unwind the folds of the heavy material. 'I like a man who knows what he wants, doesn't hang about wanting to talk.'

The cheap clay of the lamp was moulded with a relief of a woman copulating with a swan; Leda and Jupiter. It was an unlikely location for the King of the gods to take his pleasure.

'All of them.'

She let her tunic fall to the ground, and stood naked, tilting a hip, and thrusting out her breasts. She was not young, and time had not been too kind to her.

'Like what you see?' she said. 'Now the money.'

'That is not going to happen.'

'What? You think you're getting it for free? You off your head? One word and Marcus will cut off your balls.'

'Call him in.' Ballista crowded over her. 'Speak naturally.'

'Marcus!'

The pimp was sharp. Distrust was inherent in his profession, or perhaps he had detected something in her tone. He came through the curtain, knife already in hand.

'A problem?' His eyes were on Ballista.

'Fucker, does not want to pay.'

The pimp glanced at the whore. Ballista stepped forward, seized the wrist of the pimp's hand which held the knife, jerked the man forward, off balance.

'What the . . .'

With his right hand, Ballista gripped the pimp's elbow. He brought his knee hard up into underside of the man's forearm. There was a sickening crack, like breaking the carcass of a chicken. The pimp yelped in pain, dropped the knife, and curled to the ground, clutching his shattered arm.

The whore started for the curtain. Ballista dragged her back by her hair, pushed her back into a corner. He picked up the knife.

'Not a sound,' Ballista said. 'This does not have to end in tragedy.'

The pimp stopped whimpering and looked up at him. 'You are dead, you fucker.'

'We all are in the long run. Now, you're the one with the broken arm, and I'm the one with the knife.'

'Fucker.'

Ballista passed the knife close to the pimp's face. 'Let me be very clear about this. If you do exactly what I tell you, nothing worse will happen. Choose another path, and you will both be dead.'

Ballista gestured the whore forward. 'Take off his boots and belt.'

As she did as she was told, Ballista moved to stand between them and the curtain.

Her breasts swung as she bent to the tasks. Ballista felt an unwanted stab of lust. The beast was never far below the surface of man.

'Throw them over, and get back in the corner.'

The knife in his teeth, Ballista tugged on the boots, and buckled the belt. The former were little bigger than the previous pair, but from the latter hung a heavy purse of coins. Scooping up the whore's toga, Ballista tucked it under his left arm, and brandished the knife with his free hand.

'You know the beggar with the picture on the far side of the street.'

They looked at him with utter hatred.

'He is the lookout for my gang. Don't call or come out before he leaves, or my boys will come and finish the job.'

No doubt both were vicious, but Ballista was uncomfortable with his actions.

'Remember, I don't want to hurt you.'

The whore spat. 'That is what they all say who like to give you a beating, enjoy causing pain.'

'Then do not give me the excuse.'

'They will crucify you.'

'But neither you or your pimp would be alive to see me on the cross. Quiet as mice, and you will live.'

Ballista sheathed the knife, and turned and left.

Outside, the normality of the night struck Ballista as bizarre; clients and idlers came and went, the other pimps stood around.

'Enjoy yourself?' The beggar grinned. 'What about what you said?'

Ballista tipped about half the coins – some of reasonably high denomination – into the outstretched palm.

'May the gods smile on you.' The beggar was grinning. 'Now to have a go on that little Christian.'

'If I were you, I would leave.'

'Why? Even stern old Cato thought a man could go to a brothel, as long as he did not make it his home.'

'When I have gone, it would be in your best interest to leave soon after.'

'Of course, whatever you say.' A look compounded of cunning and lust betrayed the vagrant's words.

'Never in the future say that I didn't warn you.' Ballista walked away without looking back.

CHAPTER 7

The Field of Mars
The Portico of Balbus

S CARPIO SAT AT HIS DESK, in the office of the Prefect of the City
Watch, wondering how it had come to this.

Always strive to be the best. Perhaps poetry learned in childhood
lay at the root of it all. The example of Achilles in Homer – *always
strive to be the best* – dunned in by a schoolmaster, with endless
repetition and liberal use of the whip. Only with maturity came the
realisation that ambition was both a vice and a virtue. It had not
ended well for Achilles. His companion and lover slaughtered, maddened and alone, he was doomed to die young. Even after crossing
the great divide, he had known no peace. His shade had demanded
the sacrifice of an innocent young woman, had torn another girl
limb from limb.

The office in the Portico which led off the Theatre of Balbus
gleamed with affluence and success. Antique Corinthian bronzes
shone in the gentle lamplight. An original painting by Apelles
graced one wall. The desk was cedar with legs of marble. The scent
of the wood pervaded the room.

Scarpio had come a long way. He was born in Apulia, on an estate
that was little more than a smallholding. Hard work, skilled book-
keeping and an appearance of unswerving loyalty had underwritten
his rise. His father had only just possessed the property qualifica-
tion of an equestrian, the second rank in society that allowed his son
a career in the service of the emperor. The assiduous cultivation of

more affluent relatives and their connections had produced Scarpio's first appointment, the command of an auxiliary Cohort in distant Britain. After that he had served all over the empire; tribune in a legion on the Danube, prefect of auxiliary cavalry in the East, financial posts in Gaul and Spain and Africa. A good marriage to a plain woman had brought a substantial dowry and familial links to men in the senate. Finally he had secured a major prefecture, command of the City Watch in Rome. In an equestrian career only the Praetorian Prefect and the Prefect of Egypt ranked higher.

A lifetime of service and loyalty to his superiors and to Rome, and now it was all at risk. Indeed, in many ways, it was the latter quality that had put him in this terrible position. Sometimes Scarpio wished that he had never left the little town of Lupiae in the heel of Italy. There was much to recommend the life of a country landowner; ease and comfort, a book of poetry and a jug of wine, the companionship of neighbours, and the respect of the local townsfolk. Nothing more troubling than a sudden downpour or some cattle trampling the wheat. If he had never set out to sail on the greater seas of imperial service, he would never have been this frightened, and his life would not hang by a thread.

A voice from behind the curtain. 'Your visitor, sir.'

'Show him in.' Attempting to act normally, Scarpio shuffled some documents on his desk.

A tall, broad man entered, flanked by two of the City Watch, his face hidden beneath a hooded cloak.

Scarpio got to his feet. 'You may leave us. We do not wish to be disturbed.'

The watchmen saluted, and withdrew.

Scarpio respectfully waited to be addressed.

Instead, the big man turned and looked out through the curtain, then let it fall back into place.

'Can you trust those two not to eavesdrop?' he said.

'As far as we can trust anyone.'

The visitor pushed back the hood. His face was lined and weather-beaten. It would not have looked out of place behind a plough. 'A drink would be good.'

Scarpio hastened to get two goblets.

'Not too much water.' The man remained standing, looking around, seemingly impassive.

'How is Sempronius?' Scarpio wanted to postpone the conversation that he knew would come.

'The *tortoise*, always use the codenames. Even when you think we are alone.'

Scarpio, handing over the drink, did not reply.

'You are mouse and I am the peasant.' The man sat down. The chair creaked under his weight.

Scarpio nodded, accepting the reproof.

'Our bald friend the tortoise is as nervous as ever.'

Scarpio took a drink. It nearly caught in his throat. 'He lacks the stomach for these stakes. We should never have approached him.'

The peasant took a swig. 'You know that we need him, or someone like him. He is from a senatorial family, and the rest of us are not. Gallienus has to be killed by a senator. Then all the senate will acclaim the assassin a hero, and rush to elect him emperor. If one of us strikes the blow, half of the senators will look to Postumus, and the rest will wrangle for months. The safety of the empire demands a smooth transition of power.'

Scarpio nodded.

'Yes, the tortoise is an anxious old woman, but tonight his fears are well founded.'

Here it comes, Scarpio thought. He sat back behind his desk, feeling as if his limbs had been unstrung.

'Where is Ballista?'

'We think he has crossed the river.'

'Think or know?'

'Two brothers have just reported that they saw a fisherman ferry over a man fitting his description.'

'What does the fisherman say?'

'He denies it.'

'Have you questioned him?'

'Yes, but my men are firemen, not the *frumentarii*. I can't order them to torture him. They are searching his shack and boat.'

The peasant ran his hand over the stubble on his chin. It was getting late, he needed another shave. When he spoke, his voice was mild. 'This is your fault. You insisted that Ballista went to the Mausoleum.'

Scarpio felt his heart hammering in his chest. 'You said yourself that Ballista would not join us, would never desert Gallienus. If he would not stand aside, he had to be eliminated.'

'No, I said that he should have been got out of the way, sent home to Sicily. You wanted him dead.'

Scarpio's hand was trembling. He put down his drink. 'It was not me who let him escape from the Mausoleum. If you and those thugs of . . .' He checked himself, remembering the code. 'If those thugs of the ferret had done what they are paid to do, Ballista would be with the informant at the bottom of the Tiber.'

Quite deliberately, the peasant tipped some of his wine on the floor, on Scarpio's exquisite Persian rug. 'That is not going back in the glass. You take my meaning?'

As shocked as if he had been slapped, Scarpio stared at the ruined carpet. It was hard to accept the casual lack of propriety and respect.

'What is done is done,' the peasant continued. 'Yet since he escaped, you have failed to catch him.'

'But . . .' Fear and guilt and anger over his rug were beginning to stoke Scarpio's indignation. 'But the ferret's men have not caught him either.'

'You have seven thousand men. The ferret has a couple of hundred.'

What about you? Scarpio was tempted to throw the criticism back. *Since the Mausoleum, you have done nothing. You have many men under your command, but you claim that if they were employed to search for Ballista, then for certain Gallienus would be informed. For all your excuses, you have not got your hands dirty. Are you keeping your distance, hoping to find a way out if it all goes wrong?*

Not daring to say anything of the sort, Scarpio spluttered excuses. 'The ferret's men are trained for this work. Mine put out fires, arrest pickpockets. The City Watch aren't spies. They don't track and fight savage barbarian warriors.'

'You have a point.' The peasant was unflappable. No wonder the old bastard had risen so high, Scarpio thought, mastering his resentment.

'Ballista is a hard man to stop,' the peasant continued. 'I know him from years ago, and you do not. You must never underestimate him because he is a barbarian. Yet he is just one man. You can still catch him. You must catch him, and you must kill him. If he gets to the emperor, Gallienus will believe everything he says, and, once the torturers have finished with us all, our heads will be decorating pikes outside the city gates.'

The peasant drained his drink, got up, pulled his hood back over his head.

Scarpio stood.

'I will see myself out,' the peasant said. 'Do not fail.'

As the curtain closed Scarpio slumped down in his seat. He could not take his eyes off the stained rug. The peasant had come here – the headquarters of a senior prefect – and deliberately humiliated him. How dare the jumped-up bastard?

Scarpio should call someone to take the carpet away, try to salvage it. He did nothing. *This is your fault.* What, in the name of all the gods, had he been thinking? Why had he argued that Ballista should go to the Mausoleum? He had only met the man once. *To kill two birds with one stone.* That argument was specious. The motive had been personal. It stemmed from that one fateful meeting in the imperial box at the Circus Maximus. The disgusting spectacle of the great, hulking barbarian sitting in the place of honour at the right hand of Gallienus. The debased fool of an emperor flattering and fawning on the hairy northerner returned from his native woods. Romans of high rank, men of *dignitas*, consigned to the rear seats. Gallienus had fleetingly introduced Scarpio to Ballista. The barbarian had glanced back, barely bothered to speak. Ballista had dismissed Scarpio as beneath his attention.

When I get my hands on you, Scarpio thought, *I will have your attention. When the knife peels the skin from your flesh, you will learn your place. Before you die, you will know what the Fates hold for your wife and sons.*

CHAPTER 8

The Field of Mars
The Camp of the Immigrants

A MIST HUNG LOW OVER THE NORTHERN Campus Martius. Mingled with the smoke of innumerable cook fires, it screened the camp of the immigrants. The smell gave the location away; a compound of wood smoke and faeces, unwashed humanity and rotten food.

Suddenly, Ballista was in the belly of the beast. In the wan moonlight, the squat huts and lean-tos slumped against each other at crazy angles. They were built of river mud and reeds, scavenged blankets and stolen timber. Their roofs were held down by half-bricks and rocks. The narrow alleys formed a maze that Ariadne's thread could not have unravelled. But for the first time tonight, Ballista could see the moon and the stars. The six Pleiades shone high above, the seventh sister, as ever, hidden from all but the keenest eye.

Ballista worked his way north and east. He went carefully. Awnings and washing lines overhead, guy ropes and rubbish underfoot, impeded his progress. There were no adults in the lanes. Only hushed voices, chinks of light and furtive movements behind tattered curtains betrayed their presence. Twice he stumbled across roaming packs of feral children; no sooner seen than squealing and gone.

Every summer the authorities sent in the City Watch to tear down the shanty, disperse its inhabitants. Every summer the political will failed, and the task was left half done. By the autumn

the dispossessed had drifted back. By the close of the sailing season they had been joined by thousands of newcomers washed in
from across the Mediterranean by poverty and the illusory promise of the eternal city. Not all in the camp were from overseas.
Every year illness or injury, a turn of the stars or a run of bad luck,
reduced many Romans to homelessness. Some went to live under
the bridges; more preferred the camp.

There were specific laws against erecting huts and lean-tos on the
Field of Mars. The penalty was eternal exile. Enforcement was well
beyond the capabilities of the authorities. Was it Aristotle who had
said that a law which could not be enforced was no law at all?

Ballista stopped to take his bearings. He lined the Scorpion
up with the Pleiades. Perhaps, like Merope, the seventh sister, he
should hide his face in shame. No doubt the pimp and his whore
were bad people. Yet he had visited unprovoked violence on them,
had taken much of what little they possessed. He was strong,
they were weak. Only the conscience of a Sophist or lawyer could
believe that might was right, and that self-interest was of more
account than justice.

Rounding a corner, the way was blocked by four men. They
were tall. In the ambient light their faces had the pallor of the
bellies of fish.

'Health and great joy,' Ballista said.

They did not move, but stood, hands on the hilts of knives. Their
air of menace was palpable and deliberate.

'You are out late,' one of them said. His accent marked him as
from the north, one of the provinces by the Rhine, maybe a Batavian
or Frisian.

'I have to meet someone at dawn out by the Milvian Bridge.'

'Better to go by the Via Flaminia. It is not safe for a man on his
own wandering through the camp at night.'

'I have been in bad places before.' Ballista smiled, trying to defuse what he feared was coming.

'What are you carrying?' The speaker obviously was the leader.

'A toga, a few coins, my knife, and twenty-five years experience in the army.'

One of them went to flank Ballista. Shifting slightly, Ballista stopped him, filling the passageway with his broad shoulders.

The leader stepped close in front of Ballista. The man's face was bulbous, lumpy. It looked like tallow that had melted and been pinched into shape by an unskilled Prometheus. No doubt a physiognomist would have read in it a dark past and an evil future.

'Where are you from?' The leader's breath reeked of garlic, fish sauce, and the fumes of stale wine. These men ate better than most in the camp. The money that paid for this food would not be honestly gained.

'I move about.'

'Where were you born?'

'Beyond the frontier, by the shores of the Suebian Sea.'

'You look like you can handle yourself,' the leader said.

'If it is necessary.'

The leader grinned. 'Come and have a drink.'

'Until I have been to the Milvian Bridge, I have few coins.'

'The drink is on us. You might be just the sort of man we need.'

Thessalian persuasion, Ballista thought. *Necessity disguised as choice.*

Their lair was not far. A straggling compound of huts, animal pens, and a corral for seven or eight horses and mules, surrounded a yard of beaten earth with a fire burning under a tree in the centre. Another half dozen men sat around the fire.

Ballista squatted down next to the leader. A wine sack passed from hand to hand.

'What is your name, stranger?'

Ballista thought fast.

'Publius Licinius Vandrad.'

The names fitted Ballista's story. The first two would have been taken from the reigning emperor when the veteran was granted citizenship on discharge from the auxiliaries, the last a birth name from *barbaricum*.

The leader nodded. 'I am Diomedes.'

Many Batavians and the like took ridiculously inappropriate Greek and Roman names.

Two slatternly looking women brought out olives, flatbread, and cheese.

Ballista was hungry, and ate.

'What do you think of Egyptians?'

'I never served there.'

Diomedes laughed. 'You don't have to go there, half the scum from the Nile are here now. A gang of them has settled on the other side of the camp; probably to be near the big Temple of Isis.'

'You see them everywhere,' another said, 'dressed all in linen, carrying about lit lamps in broad daylight. Some of their priests walk about with their heads all covered with the mask of a dog.'

'They do say they worship strange gods,' Ballista said. 'Monstrosities with the heads of birds and crocodiles.' Feigned prejudice might establish some pretend bond with these men. He could not fight his way out against ten of them.

'That is not the worst of it,' Diomedes said. 'Each of them is convinced that only the god *he* worships deserves to be recognised. It is not just our gods they deny, they hate each other's. There were two towns out there, one worshipped dogs and the other fishes. They set to at a festival: faces bashed to jelly, features knocked out of true, cheeks split wide to expose the bone. Yet because there were no corpses to trample, they regarded the whole thing as mere horseplay. So they picked up stones, some got hold of swords. One poor bastard got captured. They tore him apart with their bare hands, and ate him piece by piece, all raw.'

All around the fire shook their heads at such barbarity. Ballista recognised the story as a garbled version of one of the *Satires* of Juvenal.

'And now they are bringing their filthy foreign ways here,' Diomedes continued. 'They are happy to eat people, but will they touch honest mutton or lamb? To eat onions or leeks is some sort of outrage.'

Another of the gang appeared from a rickety shelter in the corner of the yard. He roped the door shut behind him, and walked over looking pleased with himself.

'Good time?' The others were smiling with complicity.

'She said she had never had better.'

'My turn.' An ugly brute got up. 'Show her what a real man can do.'

The rest chortled, their faces, lit from below by the fire, daemonic.

Ballista looked up at the green boughs of the tree. They seemed incongruous, vitiated by the squalor of the surroundings.

Diomedes touched his arm. Leaning forward, he adopted a conspiratorial air. 'We have got a good thing going here. All the drinking dens and whores in the camp give us our due. The rag pickers and rubbish sorters need our license. The City Watch don't bother us, not since we paid off the local station.'

'Many thousands in the camp,' Ballista said. 'Business must be good.'

Diomedes shrugged. 'Has been for a couple of years. But now we've got a problem.'

'The Egyptians?'

'Knew you were quick, as soon as I saw you. The dog worshippers are running their own whores, trying to get the others to pay them a cut, muscling in on all our clients. The other day one honest man told them to fuck off. He went off along the bank looking for what had washed up, never came back. Got a wife and son; loved that boy he did, would never have deserted him.'

Ballista took a drink, and said nothing.

'Lot of Egyptians there are. We got twenty good boys, all handy with a knife or a cudgel. But it seems to me a man like you, experienced with a sword, not afraid to use it, could help tip things our way.'

'Some say money is the root of all evil,' Ballista smiled. 'What do I get?'

'Share and share alike with us. Four shares for me, two for Titus and Marcus, my legates, one for everyone else. Join us, swear the oath, and I reckon a double share for you would be fitting.'

'A good offer,' Ballista said, 'but I don't like to rush into things.'

Diomedes gave him a sharp look. Ballista knew that he would only walk out of this with this bandit leader's permission. Odds of ten or more to one were no odds at all. To get away called for a change of tack.

'But it is a good offer. I have a debt to collect at the Milvian Bridge. When I return, I will swear the oath.'

There was applause around the campfire, not all of it wholehearted. Some would be resentful that an incomer should be awarded twice their share of the profits.

Diomedes, however, clapped him on the shoulder. 'We northerners must stick together, eh? The rest of the boys will get used to you. Tell you what, it is hours until dawn. When Marcus has finished, why don't you enjoy the woman we've got over there?'

'That is kind, but I was with a whore just now in the Stadium of Domitian. I am not as young as I was, maybe tomorrow.'

One of the bandits guffawed. 'Wont be no good to you tomorrow.'

Diomedes' waxy face was ill suited for showing emotion, but his eyes glittered with malicious glee. 'The wife of one of the Egyptians chose a bad path this morning. But we are civilised men. When she has paid for her lodging, we will send her back to her husband.' Diomedes grinned, showing little pointed teeth, like those of a rat. 'Send her back piece by piece – I was thinking of starting with her nose.'

Ballista felt sick, the wine he had drunk turned to vinegar in the back of his throat.

'Or maybe her ears. Perhaps the Egyptians will eat her morsel by morsel.'

The mist still lay close to the ground. If anything, it had thickened, spectral tendrils coiling through flowerbeds, shrubs, and the lowest branches of trees. Yet, looking up, the stars were clear. North of the camp the parkland of the Campus Martius, apart from isolated monuments, resembled open countryside. The tall obelisk erected by Emperor Augustus at the centre of his now defunct sundial loomed above the fog. Taking it as a bearing, although he could see but a few paces around himself, Ballista had no difficulty navigating his course north and east.

Send her back piece by piece. The cruelty of men was infinite. Some philosophers held that there had once been a bucolic golden age, a time before possessions and cities and power had corrupted mankind. For others savagery was innate, only laws and civilisation restraining the beast in man. Some of both persuasions thought that in the fullness of time the sins of humanity provoked the gods to bring down fire and flood, to wipe the slate clean in a cataclysm of destruction.

Send her back piece by piece. It was nothing to do with Ballista. He was not Hercules, set on this earth to punish the wicked, to vanquish evil. When he reached Volusianus, the prefect could send a squad of praetorians. If they moved swiftly, they might be in time to rescue the unfortunate woman. Ballista could not be distracted. If he did not reach Gallienus, his own wife would die. Most likely Julia would be tortured, almost certainly raped, before she was killed. The end would not be kinder for Isangrim and Dernhelm. Lust ignited by the boys' beauty, their brutal killers would not be swayed by their innocence and youth. What did an unknown Egyptian woman weigh in the scales against Ballista's own family? Her fate was not his concern.

Ballista judged that soon he would strike the Via Flaminia, which ran across his route. He was tired, the effects of the wine dying out of him. His whole body ached, and his ribs hurt. The new boots fitted better, but his feet were lacerated. He should rest before crossing the road, and setting off into the Gardens of Lucullus.

Without warning, a wooden fence emerged out of the mist on his left. It encircled a pit. Ballista knew it at once. He had been to the Altar of Peace before. Long ago it had been a central piece of imperial propaganda. At some point the land around had been raised, and now, half hidden in the earth, it had become no more than picnic destination for idlers and a curiosity for provincials and those of an antiquarian disposition. No one would be drawn to it on a foggy night.

The gate to the fence was chained, but it was low. Ballista tossed over the rolled toga, and climbed after. He stumbled down the incline. The south wall of the monument rose above him. If it had once been painted, centuries of weather had stripped it back to the bare marble. The half-remembered reliefs shimmered in the mist: intricate sculpted foliage – acanthus and lotus flowers – topped by a formal procession of men in togas and women in dignified costume. There were four children. One, with the long hair of a barbarian, clutched the trailing hem of a stern-looking Roman's clothes. A matron placed her hand reassuringly on the boy's head. As a youth, the image had saddened Ballista. It had evoked a care and love that had been absent from his life as a young hostage in an alien city.

He went around to the western side, and climbed the steps to the entrance. Above his head Aeneas prepared to sacrifice a pig, and the she-wolf suckled Romulus and Remus. Inside, Ballista settled his back to the wall, took off his boots, and spread the toga over himself as a blanket.

Send her back piece by piece. He tried to get the woman out of his mind. His thoughts were broken, they came and went unbidden. Pius Aeneas doing his duty to his family and the gods. The terrible crack of the pimp's broken arm. His howl of pain. A beast offering kindness to helpless babies. A woman in the dark, men grunting on top of her. Had they told her what awaited? That refinement of cruelty might appeal to Diomedes. The Egyptian was nothing to Ballista.

But, as Diomedes had said, it was hours until dawn.

Ballista shrugged off the toga, painfully pulled on his boots, and levered himself to his feet. He draped the toga around his shoulders, as if a cloak.

Once Calgacus had said that there was nothing worse for a man than waking up and wondering who he was.

'As you said, it is hours until dawn.'

Diomedes slapped Ballista on the back. 'And what better way to pass the time than with a drink and good company.'

The rest of the brigands were less effusive.

'Your lookout was sleeping,' said Ballista.

'Useless bastard.' Diomedes turned to one of his men. 'Get out there, and kick his arse. Those Egyptians must suspect that we have their bitch.' He gestured to one of the serving women to bring more wine.

'Not for me,' Ballista said. 'I will need my wits about me. Actually, I thought a woman might sharpen me, before what has to be done on the Milvian Bridge.'

'Knows you are coming does he, your *friend*?'

'Not exactly. But I know that *he* is coming.'

'Only what you share with your friends is yours forever,' Diomedes said. 'Might go easier if a few of us came along.'

'This partakes of the personal. You might call it a debt of honour. One last thing I need to do on my own, before I join your brotherhood.'

Diomedes' face was unreadable, like a badly made effigy. It was odd that men who were strangers to honour might still respect its name.

'As for sharing,' Ballista made himself sound convivial, 'is anyone with the Egyptian woman?'

'Worn us out, she has. Was thinking it was near time, but help yourself, before we cut her.'

Ballista untied the knots that secured the hut. The door was solid, no doubt stolen from a building site or merchant's yard. The shelter itself was flimsy, knocked together out of mismatched scraps of wood. There were no windows. The interior was lit by a clay lamp. It stank of wine and sweat and copulation. The woman lay on a pallet of soiled straw, naked. Her throat, breasts and thighs were mottled from slaps and covered in scratches and bites. She did not look at Ballista, but stared at the ceiling. Ballista latched the door behind him.

Her eyes remained fixed on the rafters as Ballista sat on what passed for a bed. She neither flinched nor reacted in any way when he leant over her.

'Do not make a sound.'

She did not respond, her gaze still fixed, perhaps on something that was not there.

Ballista wondered if her suffering had unhinged her mind. Against his will, Ballista noted the shape of her breasts, the big, flat nipples. The philosophers who said the beast was innate were right.

'I have come to get you out,' he whispered.

She looked at him, seemingly uncomprehending.

'When I return, do not scream, be ready to run.'

Finally she spoke. 'Did Horus send you?'

'No.' He had no idea if Horus was her husband or a deity.

'Then why?'

'I am not sure myself.'

Ballista waited for a time, but, when he went back to the fire, was still greeted with the inevitable ribaldry about the brevity of his visit.

'I need a piss.' He stretched, like a man whose back ached after vigorous activity.

'Over there, the midden is beyond the horse lines.'

Perhaps the Allfather did watch over his descendants, the Woden-born. The corral was central to his plan.

Ballista ambled off into the gloom. The horses shifted as he went past. One whickered, and came over. He spoke softly to it over the fence, bringing his face close, his breath in its nostrils.

The smell guided him towards the dung heap at the rear.

'You the newcomer?' The sentry had been concealed by some bales of hay and straw. No, the Allfather was not one of those gods who often intervened, even for their distant progeny. Nothing in life was ever easy.

'Vandrad.' Ballista put out his right hand. The lookout grasped it. Ballista moved close, as if to embrace him, and punched the knife in his left hand down into the side of the man's neck. The sentry grunted, sounding more surprised than in pain. Still clasping the man's hand, Ballista swung him around, got his left hand over his mouth, and used his weight to bear him to the ground. The sentry thrashed – the fingers of his left hand clawing at the hilt of the blade protruding from his neck – then lay still.

Ballista retrieved the knife, and slipped through the rails into the corral. Quietly he moved through the horses to the wicket gate that faced the yard. Although he could clearly see the men drinking, with luck, the glare of the fire around which they sat should have robbed them of their night vision. As he sawed through the rope that held the gate, a horse came and nuzzled his face.

Ballista opened the gate a fraction, then moved behind the herd. The horses were restless now; either they could smell the blood of the sentry, or they sensed the tension in the man in their midst.

Taking several deep breaths, Ballista readied himself. He would have to move quickly now. *Do not think, just act.*

'Egyptians!' Yelling, he slapped the rump of the nearest beast. 'The Egyptians are here!'

The horse jumped and lashed out. Its hooves missed Ballista's head by a hand's breadth. He whacked it again. The horse thundered forward, chesting the gate wide open and bursting out into the yard. Where one horse runs, all the others will follow. In moments the entire herd were tearing out. They crashed around the confined space, overturning cooking pots and jugs of wine, scattering the half drunk bandits.

'Egyptians!' The bandits had taken up the cry, as they dodged the flying horses. 'Get the weapons!'

Ballista vaulted the rails, and ran to the rear of the hut. Inserting the blade into the chink between two ill joined planks, he prised one free. Nails popped out of rotten wood. The clamour from the yard covered a couple of hefty kicks, which snapped another piece of thin timber.

The woman sat, hugging herself on the straw.

'Come on!'

She made no move.

Ballista reached in through the hole, grabbed an arm, and hauled her bodily out. She collapsed in a heap in the alley. Ballista pushed himself half through the gap, and flicked the oil lamp onto the bedding.

'Now run!' He yanked the woman to her feet.

He had planned his escape when he had worked his way back to the lair. On some of the junctions he had carved an arrow. They had a start. Ballista had seen the chaos a loose horse could cause in an army camp at night, let alone seven or eight among a rabble of drunk brigands. To begin with, Diomedes' men would not be looking for them, not until they found the dead sentry or realised that the woman was gone. Even then they would not know which direction they had fled. But the woman was in no condition to run. They had gone no great distance when she fell. There was no hope of her getting up.

Ballista knew that they had to get clear of the camp. There were voices shouting not far away. Soon the whole place would be in uproar. The slum dwellers were afraid of Diomedes. They would lead the bandit to the fugitives. If Ballista could get them both to the open parkland, with the fog, he was confident that he could lose any pursuit. Even with a semi-comatose woman, his training by the Harii night fighters could render them invisible.

First he had to get there. He pulled the woman upright, wound the material of the toga around her. Then, grunting with the effort, slung her over his shoulder, like a badly rolled carpet. There was no question of running, but grimly he put one foot in front of another.

This was going to be a long night.

CHAPTER 9

The Gardens of Lucullus

'I'M NOT WEARING THAT.'

Ballista was beginning to regret that the Egyptian woman had recovered the power of speech. 'Why not?'

'Only prostitutes wear the toga.'

'Would you look less like a prostitute naked?'

The woman took this with an ill grace. 'Turn away. It is not fitting for a married woman to be seen by anyone other than her husband, and then only on the wedding night.'

Not pointing out that it was somewhat late for such decorum, Ballista turned his back. As he listened to the rustling of her arranging the folds of the voluminous garment, he thought that the woman displayed remarkably little gratitude to him for preventing her mutilation, almost certainly saving her life. Horus, for he turned out to be her husband, could not have an easy domestic life.

Once they had got clear of the Camp of the Immigrants, Ballista had set her down. With the toga wrapped around her like a blanket, he had led her through the foggy parkland back to the Altar of Peace. She had tottered at first, but did not complain, and had seemed to gain strength with every step towards safety. Apart from some shouts drifting from far off through the mist, there had been no evidence of any pursuit.

Judging by the silence that her dressing must be complete, Ballista turned to face her again. Despite the scratches on her face, and the bites on her throat, she looked as imperious as any of the sculpted matrons on the frieze outside.

'All you have to do is follow the Via Flaminia, turn off when you see the Temple of Isis, and then you can find your way home.'

'Impossible.'

'Why?'

She regarded him as if were a slow child, or his wits were addled. 'Do you think Diomedes and his brutes will be sitting quietly around their campfire? You killed one of the gang. Worse, you robbed them of their revenge, made them look foolish. Diomedes has to catch both of us, or he will lose the respect of his men. If that happens, they will turn on him. The next night or two, he will get a knife in his back.'

Ballista said nothing.

'Where would I go, except to my husband? Where will Diomedes have his thugs searching? If I fall into their hands again, what do you think they will do?'

It was annoying that she was right.

'You must take me with you.'

'No.'

'You can send me back when it is day.'

'No.' In retrospect, leaving her to her fate might have been a better option. Women got raped and murdered all the time in Rome, although perhaps less often mutilated. Ballista hunted around for another plan.

'Do you have a house?' she said.

'Yes.'

'Then I can stay in the women's quarters until dawn.'

'I am not going there.'

'Then you must take me where you are going.'

Ballista had a better idea. 'The other side of the Via Flaminia is the seventh region. The station house of the City Watch is just down the road towards the city. Go there, report what has happened. The Watch will arrest Diomedes and his gang. They can reunite you with your husband.' And the Watch will be drawn away from the seventh region, Ballista thought.

'You will take me there.'

'No.'

'Because they would put you under arrest. No wonder Diomedes thought you would make a useful member of his band. You are nothing but a criminal, like them.'

'Gratitude is not a virtue in Egypt?'

Her shoulders trembled. She was trying not to cry.

Ballista wondered if her prickly intransigence might be some form of defence against the horrors that she had experienced. He could not abandon her. Sometimes you have to admit defeat.

'I am going to the Praetorian Camp. It is not that far. When we get there, the prefect can send a squad to deal with Diomedes. I am sure that Volusianus can detail some guardsmen to take you home.'

She seemed to accept this.

'Come with me, keep quiet, and do not lag behind.'

The mist was lifting, but the Via Flaminia was empty. Ballista could see south as far as where the aqueduct of the Aqua Virgo straddled the street. Not a soul was about. Like thieves in the night, they slipped across into the shade of the Gardens of Lucullus.

The great villa of Lucullus lay to the north. Ballista intended to skirt well to the south. The Gardens were not a place he would visit unless driven by necessity. For all their beauty, they had a dark past. In the reign of Claudius, they had been owned by a man called Asiaticus. The emperor's wife, Messalina, had coveted them. She had brought about the death of Asiaticus. Possession of the gardens had done her no good. With a terrible irony, it had been there she had waited for the executioners sent by her husband's minions.

There was a more prosaic reason for Ballista to seek to avoid the gardens. The imperial treasury had sold the gardens to the patrician family of the Acilii Glabriones. A scion of that noble house had died serving under Ballista in the east. The family believed that Ballista had abandoned the young man to his fate. The Acilii Glabriones did not forget or forgive. Nothing good would happen should Ballista fall into their hands.

The western side of the gardens were terraced up the slopes of the Pinician Hill. Gravel paths meandered between ornamental steps. Ballista did not take them, instead striking out across lawns and through copses of trees. It was not long before the Egyptian woman complained.

Ballista halted in the deep gloom under a grove of cypresses. 'There are others hunting us than Diomedes' gang,' he said.

'Who?'

'The City Watch, and . . .'

'And?'

'Some ex-soldiers. I do not know who has hired them.' Ballista smiled. 'Are you still sure that you would not be better off alone?'

'Get me to the Praetorian camp, and we need never see each other again.'

The latter would be no bad thing, Ballista thought. Although he had to admire her resilience. He wondered how Julia would have coped under the circumstances. He tried to push out the ghastly thought. But once framed, it would not be banished. Years before he had shared a boat out of Ephesus with a group of Christians. One of their endless, strange debates there had been on the subject. One speaker had held that if there had been violence or force then no shame attached to the woman, that a virgin remained intact. Another vehemently disagreed; a woman could always throw herself into a river, or find some other way to take her own life, if defilement was inevitable. Suicide was a sin, but God would be merciful. The followers of the crucified god were much concerned with suicide and virginity. Yet ordinary Romans, worshippers of the traditional gods, always had the example of Lucretia. Raped by the son of the tyrant, she steadfastly determined to end her life, despite all the arguments and entreaties of husband and family. Whatever gods were given credence, the world was a harsh place for women.

An easterly breeze was getting up. The fog dispersed, although fragments still lingered in hollows. The wind hissed, sibilant through the foliage, creaked boughs together. Small nocturnal creatures scuttled away. The moon cast deep shadows across their way. The woman crowded close at Ballista's back. Walking at night in the country, even in this crafted and tamed imitation, was profoundly alien and unsettling for a town dweller.

Ballista was in his element, his senses sharpened. Barefoot, the woman was not making too much noise. He was aware of everything around them, and he detected a presence before registering what had alerted him.

Halting, he gestured the woman to silence. There was a faint tang of wood smoke on the air. No one should be kindling fire in the gardens at night. Ballista stilled his breathing, probing the darkness. Up ahead, slightly to the left, was there an indistinct murmur, like a man muttering to himself?

'Stay here.'

'No.'

'I will return quickly. Do not make a sound.'

Leaving the woman unhappily huddled under a tree, Ballista moved at a tangent to the sounds. The years with the Harii served him well. Using every scrap of cover, and the shadows cast by the moon from passing clouds, he ghosted through the gardens. Soon he saw a glimmer of light on the lower leaves of a cypress. There must be a fire underneath. If you wanted a fire to remain undetected in the dark, you should never kindle it under the boughs of trees which could reflect its light. Not looking directly at the shimmering leaves, the better to preserve his night vision, he crept closer.

Now exercising every ounce of caution, he took care with every step. Placing just the outside of each foot, he felt for any twigs which might snap, or stones which could turn, before letting his weight come down. When he found a point of vantage, he hunkered down, letting the raking shadows break his outline.

The low fire burned by a freshly dug trench. A man – long bearded, hairy, and unkempt – stood over them. A young boy, no more than seven or eight, lay on the ground, asleep or unconscious. His chest was rising and falling. He was not dead. The man was chanting softly, with the cadence of a prayer: *Aion, Iao, Kmephis.* The individual words were meaningless, but the overall intent was clear. No wonder the man had sought this remote place. Ballista smiled, perhaps here was an answer to the problem of the Egyptian woman.

There were three bowls on the ground. One by one, the man tipped the contents of each into the trench. *Iaeo, Aee, Chphuris.* He moulded a cake of dough into something resembling a man. On its head he fixed a crown of laurel and fennel. Satisfied with his handiwork, the doll also was thrown into the pit.

Suddenly the man produced a sword. An old legionary *gladius*, Ballista noted. The man flourished the blade over the child. Ballista was but fifteen paces away. He half rose, tensing himself to run. Still reciting the supposed words of power, the man turned the sword on himself. Without hesitation, he slit the skin of his left forearm. Ballista saw the blood running black in the moonlight.

Oblivious to pain, the man picked up a branch of laurel. With precise, even fussy, movements he wiped the blood onto the leaves, then tossed the branch into the fire. Stooping, the man whispered into the child's ear. The boy did not stir. The man tried to pull him to his feet. The child was a dead weight, and the man let him slump back down.

Some way off, Ballista heard a large animal moving through the brush, disturbing the undergrowth, cracking twigs. A deer or a dog, there would be both roaming the gardens.

Aamasi, Nouthi, Merope. The man was chanting louder, working himself up into a frenzy. Brandishing the sword, he leapt over the fire. Long hair streaming, three times he jumped the flames. The child stirred. Bending, the man pulled the boy up. The child's eyes opened, blinked without focus.

'Tell me what I seek to know.'

The boy did not speak, but swayed, and looked as he might fall. The man held his shoulders.

The animal was getting nearer. Most likely a dog; a deer would not approach people.

'As I have summoned you, I command you to tell me.'

Deep in the trance, when the child spoke, it was in an unnatural deep, guttural voice.

'Another will come, the sun-sent, dreadful lion, breathing fire.'

The child's words were Greek, in a rough, broken hexameter.

'Fame will attend him; perfect, unblemished, and awesome, he will rule the Romans, and the Persians will be cast down.'

The man broke the flow of strange poetry. 'Tell me what I seek to know.'

The boy paused, frowning, before taking up his thread. 'When the ruler of the mighty Romans will be of the third number, he will be clad as a woman, but have the nature of a wolf, which tears the gentle sheep. On the Ausonian plains, the sons of Ares, men inured to violence, will ring him around. He will be smitten by gleaming iron, betrayed by his companions.'

'Murderer!' The Egyptian woman burst into the circle of light. The man stood, rooted to the spot. She hurled herself at him. Heedless of the sword, she raked her nails down his face. Ineffectually, he reeled away, tried to cover himself.

Ballista got up. Too late. In an instant the boy had snapped out of his abstraction, and was running. Ballista could not catch him and deal with the man.

Vaulting the trench and the fire, Ballista reached the struggling pair. He wrenched the hilt of the sword from the man's grip. The blade went spinning into the darkness.

'He was going to kill that innocent little boy,' the woman yelled.

Pushing her away, Ballista got a firm grip on the front of the man's ragged tunic.

'He was going to sacrifice that child,' the woman spat.

'Get this whore off me,' the hedgerow mage pleaded. 'I would never harm anyone.'

'I am not a whore, necromancer.'

'Nothing like that.' There were livid scratches down his cheeks. 'My art looks to the heavens, frequents with the gods, devotes itself to all that is good and helpful to man.'

'Lying bastard!' The woman surged forward.

Ballista shoved her back with his free hand. 'Stay there,' he said.

'Thank you, sir.' The magician wiped his scoured face. 'You know that the boy was in a trance. He would not be hurt. I have done nothing wrong.'

'Nothing wrong?' Ballista shook him slightly. 'You think that the authorities would take that view of meddling in forbidden things?'

'A philosophic inquiry.'

'Into the death of the emperor?' Ballista gave him another shake, harder, like a dog with a rat.

'You are mistaken.'

'I have served in the East. There are men peddling Sibylline oracles in every market place over there.'

'I would never . . .'

'The ruler of the Romans will be of the third number? Alpha, beta, gamma. Our emperor's name begins with the third letter of the alphabet. You think that Gallienus will see your nocturnal activities as philosophic inquiry?'

The mage rallied. 'And a vagabond like you has his ear?'

'My name is Marcus Clodius Ballista. You may have heard of me.'

'The barbarian who dared take the purple,' the man's words trailed off.

'And who was pardoned by his childhood friend, our emperor.'

'Ballista?' The Egyptian woman sounded incredulous.

'Not now.' Ballista pulled the man almost up off his feet, bringing his face very close to his own. 'Who paid you?'

'They will kill me.' The mage's eyes were wild with fear.

'You might not tell me, but do you think you can keep silent in the cellars of the Palace?'

'Please . . .'

'On the rack, as they get busy with the pincers and the claws?'

The man was sobbing.

'Of course, it does not have to end that way. No one need know.'

'Anything, just don't make me tell you their names.'

'Instead of agony and a drawn-out death, you could end this night at home.' Watchful, in case the wizard tried to bolt, Ballista let go of the man's tunic, and unlaced the wallet from his own belt. 'Safe at home, with a fat purse of coins.'

'What do you want me to do?' Despite his desperation, the mage was suspicious.

'You know the district of the Bronze Gate?'

'In the south-east?'

'Take this woman there. Ask for the house of Volcatius. Tell my wife that I want her to give you coins to match those in this wallet. She will look after the woman. In the house is a Hibernian called Maximus. Easy to recognise, the end of his nose is missing. Tell him to meet me at the Praetorian Camp.'

The man nodded.

'And tell him to bring Tarchon the Suanian.'

'I am not going with this creature,' the Egyptian woman said.

'You wanted to shelter in my house. Now you can. You will be safe there.'

Ballista handed the wallet to the mage.

'He is a magician,' she said.

Ballista sighed. 'You are an Egyptian, you should be used to such things.'

'But . . .'

'If you come with me, things may take a turn for the worse. This will be a long night. If you go with him, in the morning my wife can arrange for you to be restored to your husband.'

Although still dubious, the woman seemed to acquiesce.

'What shall I tell those who hired me?' The mage sounded plaintive.

'Tell them what the boy said. You know it is what they want to hear.'

CHAPTER 10

The Praetorian Camp

T HE VIA TIBURTINA WAS FULL OF MOVEMENT. All through the
hours of darkness, carts trundled into the city piled with
local produce; wine and food, forage and bedding for animals.
Heavy wagons were laden with builders' materials; stacked bricks
and tiles, swaying baulks of timber. Herders drove in beasts for
slaughter. Most of the vehicles leaving were empty, but one or
two enterprising hauliers had acquired a load for the return journey; imported luxuries for country villas, or cheap gewgaws and
mass-manufactured goods for thrifty peasants. The carts taking
out night soil were given a wide berth by the rest of the road
users.

Rome, it was said, was a city that never slept. Watching from the
shelter of an alleyway, Ballista could see the truth of the complaint.
Men shouted, animals bellowed and bleated, wagons creaked, and
their weighty, iron-rimmed wheels groaned and shrieked along
and over the deep ruts ground into the stones by generations of
their predecessors. If you lived on a main thoroughfare, like the Via
Tiburtina, sleep would be near unobtainable.

It would be easy enough to hitch a ride on an empty cart. A lone
driver might welcome the company. But it would be too exposed.
From his place of concealment, Ballista had already seen a squad of
the City Watch marching out from the centre. It was not far to the

Praetorian Camp, and the night was not half run. He settled to wait for the right company to join.

His gaze idly followed a cart topped with hay. Ballista wondered how far the mage and the Egyptian woman had got towards the House of Volcatius. Judging by the moon, they had been gone about an hour. The district of the Bronze Gate lay away from the Campus Martius. No one outside the immigrants' camp was hunting them. They could go openly, make good time. Of course, it was possible that the magician would abandon her, slink off into the night. But, on balance, greed should keep him honest; the promise of more coins would outweigh any inconvenience. And, as Ballista could attest, the Egyptian woman was hard to shake off. Even if the hedge wizard vanished, most likely the indomitable woman would reach the house on her own.

He hoped that the sudden arrival would not scare Julia and the boys too much. No one ever pounded on the doors of a shuttered house in the dead of night for a trivial or pleasant reason. Maximus and Tarchon were there, Grim and Rikiar as well. If not very drunk, they would be competent and reassuring. Ballista wished that he had thought to pass the message for Maximus and Tarchon to come to the Praetorian Camp armed, to bring his mailshirt and a sword. Yet they were veterans, and had served with him for years. They would feel unclothed without weapons. *Allfather, it would be good to have them at my side.* Ballista was not sure that he had ever felt so alone.

An insidious fear struck him. With Maximus and Tarchon gone, would Grim and Rikiar be able to guard his family? He pushed the thought away. They were skilled warriors. The doors would be bolted. The porter was reliable and carried a cudgel. There were several tough slaves in the household, an arsenal of weapons in the building. In any case, surely the conspirators would not come for them until they knew Gallienus was dead.

He will be smitten by gleaming iron, betrayed by his companions. The magician must have suggested the words to the boy before putting him into a trance. But who had commissioned the hedge wizard? Anyone inquiring into the death of the emperor wanted that event to come about, and soon. Gallienus was in the prime of life, a natural death was unlikely. *Smitten by gleaming iron.* This summer Gallienus would take the field against Postumus in Gaul. Death on the battlefield would have been the obvious prophesy. *Betrayed by his companions.* Treachery had struck down many emperors. No one knew that better than Ballista; he had killed two of them with his own hands. It was better to forget the last moments of Maximinus the Thracian and the odious pretender Quietus. A predicted assassination might be welcome to the employers of the mage, but it did not mean that they were part of the conspiracy uncovered in the Mausoleum. There were always plots against the life of the emperor. There were so many that long ago the Emperor Domitian had complained that no one believed in their reality until the ruler was struck down.

Another will come, the sun-sent, dreadful lion . . . he will rule the Romans, and the Persians will be cast down. The words could only refer to Odenathus, Lord of Palmyra. The prophet would seek to tell what his listeners wanted to hear. The men who had consulted the mage must favour those in the court of Odenathus who would bid for the whole empire. Such high politics traditionally was the preserve of senators. The senate chaffed under the rule of Gallienus. Excluded from military commands, not shown the respect their dignity demanded, many senators would welcome an alternative. If he came to the throne, Odenathus, most likely, would remain in the East, giving the senate a free hand in the West.

Was the location of the magic rites significant? The Gardens of Lucullus were owned by the Acilii Glabriones. There was no more prestigious family in the senate. At least two of them were in the imperial entourage. One of them was well known to Ballista. Vain, proud, and headstrong, Gaius Acilius Glabrio had served under Ballista in the East. Nothing was beyond the ambition of the young patrician. Gaius blamed Ballista for the death of his brother at the siege of Arete. Sending Ballista to his death in the Mausoleum of Hadrian would have given Gaius nothing but pleasure.

This was leading nowhere. The problem with unravelling conspiracies was that, once you had started, the thread never ran out. More and more plotters joined the ranks on the most slender and spurious grounds. Quite likely the words uttered by the boy in his trance were no better than gibberish. The mage was a charlatan, his clients no more than fools indulging in a dangerous fantasy.

Above the rumble of traffic came music and a high, wild keening. The funeral cortege could be heard before it was seen. The carters pulled their vehicles over to the kerb, and herdsmen chivvied animals to the side of the road. The Via Tiburtina was still.

First came the torchbearers, flames sawing aloft in the breeze. The musicians followed, puffing their cheeks, as they blew doleful notes from flute and trumpet. The deceased had been well-to-do. There were a dozen hired mourning women. They shrieked and wailed, tearing their clothes, raking their faces and breasts until the blood ran.

As the dead man came into view, the bystanders were quiet. Some muttered a prayer – *may the earth lie lightly on him* – others put thumb between fingers or smacked their lips to avert evil.

The bier was carried by eight strong men. These *vespilliones*, professional handlers of the dead, wore the black tunics and colourful caps of their profession. The corpse lay under an awning embroidered with the moon and stars. The dead man was clad in a snow-white toga, his face powdered as white as the material. Slaves carried incense burners behind the bier, but, as it passed, the sickening waft of decay was strong in Ballista's nostrils.

The family – the widow, three children, others of less obvious relationship – headed a long train of mourners. All wore dark clothes, the men unshaven, the women with loose, unkempt hair. A few had tipped dirt in their hair.

The rear was brought up by a gaggle of men and women wearing the cap of liberty. Freed by his will, despite their master's death bringing them their life's ambition, they managed an air of suitable sadness.

Ballista walked out from his alleyway, and joined the cortège. He worked his way through the newly created freedmen and women to stand at the back of those who had either known liberty all their lives, or whose manumission lay further in the past. Here, among those whose connection to the dead was not the closest, he should not be obviously out of place. His long, dishevelled hair and dark cloak were fitting. The latter was voluminous enough to disguise the outline of the sword that he had taken from the mage.

His neighbours talked softly. 'Poor old Chrysanthus. Nice man – only the other day he stopped me in the street. We're just so many walking bags of wind. We're worse than flies – at least they have got some strength in them.'

'Let's think of the living,' another said. 'He got what he deserved. He lived an honest life, and he died an honest death. What has he got to complain about? He started out in life without a coin to his name. He was ready to pick up anything from a dung heap, even if he had to use his teeth. Everything he touched turned to gold, regular Midas, he was.'

'Call me a Cynic,' said a third. 'He had a foul mouth, and too much lip. He wasn't a man, he was just trouble.'

The dead had much to complain about, Ballista thought, given Roman views on the afterlife. The souls of the dead who were not properly buried, who lacked a coin to pay the ferryman, would wander for eternity in misery. Those, like Chrysanthus here, for whom the living had made proper provision, faced a stern judge in the underworld. The wicked – murderers, adulterers, oath-breakers, hoarders of money, and the like – were condemned to Tartarus, a place of fire and whips and screaming. There was no appeal, and no end to the sentence. The rest were bound for Hades, the gloomy meadow of asphodel, ringed by black poplars, and lit by dark stars. There they would gibber, and flit like bats, sentient enough to resent and envy the living, but beyond joy, pleasure, or contentment. Only a handful of the just would make the journey to the West, to the Elysian Fields or the Islands of the Blessed.

Better by far to belong to one of those sects that held that death was the end. For them life was nothing but unceasing atoms moving in the void, without purpose or design. The soul was so fragile, composed of such minute particles, that it dissolved with the last breath.

Julia had been brought up in an Epicurean household, and genuinely believed that death was nothing but a return to sleep. Ballista would have liked to share her equanimity, but for him the fear of the underworld was equalled by the fear of nothingness. He still clung to the tales of his childhood. If he died in battle, fighting to the last, not turning his back like a coward, like a *nithing*, the

Shield-maidens might carry him to the hall of his ancestor. There he would pass countless years at the side of Woden-Allfather, feasting and warm, companions to hand, until the final battle, and the death of gods and man.

Thoughts of childhood summoned Calgacus. The old man had been a Caledonian. Ballista had never asked what Calgacus thought lay beyond the great divide. As a child it had not occurred to him, and when a man there had always seemed to be time. Now he knew that one of the terrible tragedies of losing a loved one was the unasked questions, the lost stories.

The procession had reached Ballista's destination. To the left of the road the buildings fell back to reveal the parade ground of the Praetorian Camp. Ballista stepped out of the cortege, and let the freedmen pass. One or two glanced at him, and he sat on the curb, making as if to remove a stone from his boot.

When the funeral party was gone, the Via Tiburtina came back to life. Carters cracked whips, beasts plodded forward, and the endlessly repeated nocturnal supply of the metropolis resumed.

Ballista leant against the corner of the last building, everything about him suggesting a weary traveller snatching a moment's rest. Across the beaten earth was the camp, its tall brick walls, crenulations, towers and solid gates sharp in the moonlight. Ordinary people kept away from the camp. When Ballista had first come to Rome, there had been fighting here; a pitched battle, as the citizens had tried to storm the symbol of their oppression. They had failed, and the praetorians had issued out, sword in hand, and burned swathes of the city.

Half a century or so before, the camp had been the scene of perhaps the most shameful moment in Rome's long history. After the murder of the Emperor Pertinax, two senators had stood at the base of the walls, and bid for the throne. Gesticulating, indicating on their fingers the sums that they would pay for the purple, each had tried to win over the praetorians.

The praetorians existed to protect the emperor, but they had a dishonourable record of betraying and murdering the men to whom they had given their oath. Hated by the plebs, they were despised by ordinary soldiers. Overpaid and pampered, decked out in elaborate military finery more suitable to the stage, every time they had faced the legions in battle, the praetorians had been beaten, had surrendered or turned tail and fled.

Ballista shared the common soldiers' contempt, and the citizens' mistrust. But now he must put his life in their hands. The praetorians were commanded by two prefects. Volusianus was the senior, a man called Censorinus his subordinate. Thank the gods that the latter had been ordered to lead a detachment of the Guard to Milan to join the field army gathering to fight Postumus on the other side of the Alps. Censorinus was known to Ballista from the East. A sly, underhand officer, steeped in deceit, Censorinus had survived and prospered in the civil wars and through changes of regime by timely treachery and desertion.

Volusianus, who had remained in Rome, was a very different man from his colleague. Like Cincinnatus, in the myth, summoned from the plough to serve Rome, Volusianus had left his father's smallholding somewhere in the backwoods of Italy, and enlisted as a common trooper. Courage, native intelligence, and loyalty had secured an extraordinary career. When Gallienus had formed the *protectores*, that mixture of bodyguard and college of senior officers, Volusianus had been the first man admitted to the elite band who were allowed to bear arms in the presence of the emperor. Recently Volusianus had distinguished himself against the barbarian horde of the Alamanni at Milan, and against the forces of Postumus in the Alps. Volusianus was a man upon whom Ballista could rely.

Ballista set off across the parade ground. The dust puffed up under his boots. A gull screamed overhead. It was strange walking in the open, in the blue-white night. He angled towards the main gate, where torches flared.

'Halt!'

The torchlight gleamed on the chased and polished armour and the unsheathed blades of the eight praetorians.

Ballista halted, and opened his cloak to show the sword and knife in his belt.

'State your name and business.'

Four of the praetorians came forward, and surrounded him.

'Marcus Clodius Ballista, and I have come to see Lucius Petronius Taurus Volusianus.'

'Is the prefect expecting an armed barbarian in the middle of the night?'

'Volusianus will see me.'

The centurion nodded to his men. 'Take his weapons, and search him.'

Ballista held his arms out as they took the blades, patted him down.

'Take me to Volusianus.'

'Open the gate.' The centurion gave the command over his shoulder, then turned back to Ballista. 'The Praetorian Prefect is at the Palace, but the gods have guided your steps here. The Prefect of the City Watch has issued an order for your arrest.'

Ringed by armed men, there was nothing to be done.

'You two take him to the cells. You get down to the Theatre of Balbus, and tell Scarpio that we have the man he is looking for.'

'This way.' The praetorian did not manhandle Ballista, but made an almost courtly gesture.

The gate clanged shut behind them.

Ballista knew that he had to make his move before they reached the cells. Once locked in, there would be no escape.

'Sorry about this, sir. We all know your war record.'

The other praetorian nodded. 'Must be a mistake, but they are saying you killed some men over in Transtiberim, set fire to a warehouse.'

Ballista stumbled. The guard on his left put out a hand to steady him. Ballista punched him hard in the stomach. The second guardsman turned, his weapon in no sort of position. Ballista kicked him in the balls. Thank the gods the praetorians spent their time on ceremonial duties or bullying civilians, not fighting.

The steps up to the southern wall walk were not far. With both men down, Ballista ran.

'Guards!' One of the praetorians had got to his knees, and found his voice. 'The prisoner is getting away.'

Ballista took the steps two at a time.

A squad of praetorians was tumbling out of a guardhouse, tugging on their equipment.

There was a man on the wall walk. In the gloom, he had not seen Ballista, and was peering down in puzzlement at the commotion in the yard. Ballista bounded to the top of the steps. As the praetorian spun around, Ballista tackled him, shoulder into midriff. The guardsmen crashed onto his back. Landing half on top of him, with an open hand, Ballista cracked his head back onto the flagstones.

'Up there! On the wall! Get him!'

The wall was too high to jump from. Outside, the Via Tiburtina ran at its foot. As ever there were wagons: one loaded with amphorae, another with barrels, a third piled with sides of meat.

The guards were clattering up the steps.

Ballista moved along the fighting platform, desperately scanning the road. A cart laden with roof tiles, a flock of sheep. There, at last, a wagon full of hay. Ballista climbed up onto the crenulations. The guards were pounding along the wall walk towards him. Just a moment longer.

The wagon was below. Ballista jumped.

A moment later he landed on his back in the soft hay.

'What the . . .' The driver twisted around. 'Where the fuck . . .'

Ballista scrambled up and seized him by the scruff of the neck.

'My apologies.' Ballista heaved the man off the side.

'Stop the bastard!' The praetorians above were shouting. They were unwilling to make the jump in full armour. Ballista did not blame them.

Grabbing the reins, Ballista shook them up. Yelling, he flicked them across the rumps of the two dray horses. Startled by the unfamiliar urging, the horses bolted. A moment's delay, and the traces yanked the cart after them so fast that Ballista was almost propelled off the seat, back into the hay.

The shepherd ahead dived for cover, and his flock scattered, bleating in distress.

The horses, wild eyed, whipped into a frenzy, raced down the road.

In moments they would overrun the cart with the roof tiles.

There was a narrow street to the left. Standing, Ballista hauled hard on the reins. The horses responded. The turn was far too tight. The cart was skidding. Ballista felt it begin to tip. He hurled himself over the trailing edge. Rolling on the paving stones, the breath knocked out of his body, he heard the crash.

Levering himself to his feet, fighting to get air into his chest, he saw the carnage. The shattered cart lay on its side, loose timbers scattered on the paving slabs, blocking the street. The horses, dragged by the traces, were struggling to get back on their legs. Although cut and grazed, thankfully neither seemed badly injured.

The onlookers were frozen, petrified with shock.

'Stop him!'

No one responded to the praetorians' command.

Ballista swarmed over the broken vehicle, dodged a couple of sheep, and dived down the narrow street leading off the via Tiburtina.

Once again, he was running.

CHAPTER 11

The Subura
The Tenements

BALLISTA WALKED DOWN INTO THE SUBURA. The chaos that he had left behind him at the Praetorian Camp had delayed any pursuit. As far as he could tell, no one had managed to follow him. It seemed that he got clean away, but now he needed somewhere to get off the streets, somewhere out of sight to decide what to do next. There was no better place to go to ground than in the twisting alleyways and crowded buildings of the subura. There were inns and lodging houses. It was late, if they were bolted for the night there would be drinking dens and brothels. He had given the pimp's wallet to the magician, and had lost his sword and knife at the Praetorian Camp, but there were always ways to get money. And Ballista knew from his youth that in the subura money could buy most things, no questions asked.

He turned off the main thoroughfare. The peeling walls and damp brickwork of tall tenements closed around him. Wedged in the low ground between the slopes of the Viminal and Esquiline Hills, the subura was a plebeian district. The poor lived in crumbling apartments, built so close together it was said that neighbours on the upper floors could shake hands from one balcony to another across the alleyways. The dilapidated structures tottered upwards in defiance of imperial building regulations. Their inhabitants were crammed together, often whole families in one room, under leaking roofs, behind ill-fitting doors. Most of the tenements only had one door at street level. They were death traps, and the threats of sudden collapse or fire could never be far from the thoughts of their occupants.

Poets condemned the subura as a sink of depravity, the haunt of criminals and whores. Like most poetry, it had an element of truth, but did not capture the complete reality. The subura was home to many tradesmen – blacksmiths, bootmakers, workers in wool – as well as myriad shopkeepers. Among the latter were those who sold not basic provisions, but delicacies and finery. The most exquisite fish sauce and the softest linen were to be bought in the subura. And amid the plebeian dwellings and workshops were houses of the rich. In the main, the Roman elite made their homes high on the seven hills, for the views, and to catch the breeze, breathe cleaner air. But some had their houses down in the subura. Back in the days of the free republic, it might have been to exhibit fellowship with the common man, to garner votes. Now, under the emperors, the choice probably was dictated by cheaper property prices, or a delight in having rakish pleasures on their doorstep.

The pavement under Ballista's feet was wet and foul. Shards of broken terracotta crunched under his boots. With no access to plumbing, the occupants of the tenements emptied their chamber pots down into the streets. If the vessel was cracked, it was tossed out after. Neither the ordure nor its stench need trouble the rich who visited or lived here. Most times they would be carried from their doorsteps in covered litters, scented with precious fragrances.

Ballista came out into a tiny square. There was a water trough in the middle. He scooped a palmful of water, and sniffed suspiciously, before bathing his tired eyes. Repeated legal pronouncements against fouling drinking fountains were proof of the practice. Houses, statues, tombs; in a city with a million inhabitants, men relieved themselves everywhere, with scant regard for privacy.

Laughter and shouts, jarring and moronic in their intoxication, echoed from one of the alleys. Where there were drunks, there was likely to be a bar.

A few steps down the passageway, Ballista realised his error. Four revellers, and two prostitutes, were weaving after the guttering torch held by a linkboy. Too late to turn back, Ballista stepped aside to let them pass.

The revellers stopped, the whores clinging to them, tittering. Together, deliberately, they blocked the alleyway. The boy held up the torch.

'Where have *you* sprung from?' The speaker was young and well spoken. His garland of rose petals had slipped down almost over one eye.

Avoiding eye contact, Ballista looked at the building opposite.

'Ugh, what a smell – beans and sour wine. I know your sort, no better than a Jew. You've been round with some cobbler-crony, scoffing a boiled sheep's head and a dish of spring leeks.'

The stucco on the wall was discoloured and patchy, as if it had mange.

'Where's your pitch? What synagogue do you doss in?'

The others guffawed.

Ballista knew their sort; young and rich, slumming it in the sub-ura, out to beat up a passer-by for fun.

'What? Nothing to say for yourself?'

Ballista eased his back off the wall, noting where each member of the party stood; the linkboy on the right, the talker in front, the companion backing him entwined with a whore, the other two revellers and the final whore clumped on the left.

'Speak up, or I'll kick your teeth in!'

Ballista spoke quietly. 'This does not need to end badly.'

'It will for you, you insolent fucker.' The man reached out to grab him. Ballista yanked the torch out of the boy's hand, and thrust it into his assailant's face. Screaming, the man reeled back, collided with his friend and the whore.

The nearest reveller on the left hurled himself forward. Ballista brought the torch down on his head like a club. The first blow drove him to his knees. On the second, the haft of the torch snapped.

The linkboy was on Ballista's back, fingers clawing at his eyes. Dropping his right shoulder, Ballista rolled him off. As he landed, Ballista kicked him in the back of the head. The youth went down, making no effort to soften his fall.

The other man on the left had a knife. Ballista gave him no time to think. Feinting to the right brought the knife after him. Ballista gripped his wrist, tugged him off balance, and twisted the arm until he heard it break. The man crumpled into the gutter.

Three down, two standing, one of them hurt. Both the whores were running. One was yelling for help.

The two revellers still on their feet stood irresolute, befuddled by drink, and the suddenness and scale of the violence.

'Get the City Watch!' One of the whores was shouting.

Ballista picked up the knife.

The man with the burnt face was moaning, swaying slightly.

'The Watch! Call the Watch!' The whore was shouting as she ran.

The man he had beaten with the torch was trying to rise. Ballista kicked him in the ribs. He went down again. With precision, Ballista stamped on the side of his head. Get a man on the ground, Maximus had once said, and you can give him some leather in your own sweet time.

'That is enough.' The uninjured reveller held out his hands in supplication.

Ballista brandished the knife, herding the two together.

'For the love of the gods, don't kill us.'

'On your knees!' When they were slow to move, Ballista encouraged them with the knife close to their faces.

'It was only a bit of fun.' The young drunk sounded as if he might burst into tears.

'Give me your wallets.'

Fumbling in haste, they unlaced them, gave them up.

'And those of your friends.'

Still on their knees, they did his bidding.

'Now, face down.'

Fastidious, even in their terror, they tried to prostrate themselves as if the filth might somehow not stain their clothes.

Not that far off, Ballista heard hobnailed boots thudding on paving stones, men shouting, the shrill voice of the whore. She had found the City Watch. It was more than time to leave.

In a district notorious for loose living, it was proving strangely difficult to find a bar or a whorehouse. There was row after row of hermetically sealed shops and workplaces. Butchers and perfumeries, flower sellers and fullers, every kind of trade, each identified by a painted sign for the illiterates who made up the majority of their clientele. The pervading stench, and the large jars outside for collecting the urine of passers-by, made the sign pointless for the establishments where clothes were cleaned.

The streets were deserted. Faint sounds – a snatch of song, a burst of laughter, a sudden shout – drifted from the mouths of passageways. Now and then a dog barked. Sometimes it was answered, and briefly the night was full of angry yapping. Ballista wondered what hour it was. The towering buildings blocked the moon and the stars. The bakers were not working yet, so perhaps just past midnight.

If so, by the civic calendar, the Kalends of April had begun. It was no surprise that the poor, lacking fancy water clocks, or any other method of accurately measuring time in the hours of darkness, reckoned that the days changed at sunset. Either way, it was the first day of April. Unless Ballista could intervene, by the end of the day the emperor would be dead.

Disorientated in the labyrinth of the subura, Ballista took streets and alleyways at random. To be lost in the heart of a city was always unsettling. For some reason a passage of Thucydides came into his mind. Three hundred Thebans, trapped and lost in the hostile city of Plataea, fleeing through the darkness and mud of a wet, moonless night. Women and children yelling, hurling tiles and stones from the roofs. Armed men hunting them down. The Thebans blundering to their fate. Not an auspicious thought.

Ballista tried another alleyway. This one had no shops. There were rickety balconies above, but at ground level were just the blank walls and closed doors of tenements. Further down was a rectangle of yellow light. One of the doors was ajar. A man stood outside pissing into the gutter. Penis in one hand, a cudgel in the other, the man obviously was the doorkeeper for the block.

Ballista walked slowly and openly towards him.

'Health and great joy,' Ballista said.

'And to you.' The words were polite, but the tone grudging.

'I am lost, looking for a lodging house.'

The janitor pulled up his britches, adjusted himself. 'You won't find one open at this time of night.'

'I have money, are any rooms empty in your block?'

The man snorted. 'You are not from around here.'

Ballista fished a large denomination coin from one of the wallets that he had taken from the revellers. 'How about a space under the stairs?'

'A lot of counterfeit coins down here.'

Ballista handed it over. The man held it up to the light, studied it close, then bit it.

'That sort of money, you could buy something better,' the door-keeper said at length. 'If it was not the middle of the night.'

Ballista got out another coin. 'This one is yours too, if you keep quiet. Anyone asks, you have not seen me.'

'City Watch after you, are they? Or is it some householder or wayfarer you have robbed?'

'A misunderstanding.'

'What sort of *misunderstanding*?'

'I was set upon by some rich youths. Gave as good as I got. Think they might have their servants out after me.'

'Cocky young bastards.' The man spat. 'Always causing trouble, think they can do what they like to ordinary citizens. The bucket-men never arrest the likes of them, but you or me throw a pot out in the street, and they break the door down – *Open in the name of the City Watch!* – kick the shit out of you in front of your wife and children, in front of all your neighbours, drag you off in chains.'

'Quiet as the grave, then?' Ballista gave him the second coin.

'Fetching and carrying is for old women. I know how to keep my words locked behind my teeth. You will have to go up two flights; the lower floors are already full.'

Retying the wallet, Ballista adjusted the knife in his belt, just to let the man see he had a weapon.

'I will be gone early. Would you wake me an hour before dawn?'

'*Conticinium*, it is; when the cocks have stopped crowing, but men are still asleep.'

Few surroundings could be more be more depressing than the interior of a cheap subura tenement. Unless you were habituated to them, the mingled smells of damp and mould, of dirt and squalor, were choking. Over everything was the reek of boiled cabbage and stale cooking oil. As all tenants ignored the prohibition on kindling fires and cooking, it was a marvel that conflagrations did not break out more often.

There were no windows in the stairwell. The janitor had lent Ballista a tiny clay lamp. The oil it burned was rank, giving off more smoke than illumination. Its wan light revealed stained and cracked walls. As Ballista trudged up the uneven stairs, huddled shapes grunted and shifted under the flights. A child peered out from around its sleeping mother.

The landing on the second floor was empty. Two closed doors, flimsy looking and sagging on their hinges, led to apartments. The higher you climbed a tenement, the less salubrious the accommodation. At the top, on the sixth or seventh floor, were garrets, only fit for rats, right up under the tiles.

The space under the next set of steps was unpleasantly stained, with a malodour of urine and other people's copulation. A beggar could not be a chooser. Ballista folded himself into its narrow confines. He rolled his cloak as a pillow, and put his knife next to it. The doorkeeper had seen the wallets on his belt, and he might not be the only one in the building tempted to rob a sleeping man.

Pinching out the lamp, Ballista tried to get comfortable. His legs were too long for the space, and he had to stick them out into the corridor. Sleep was hard to imagine. In the near total dark, he turned over what had happened at the Praetorian Camp. Informed by Scarpio that the City Watch had orders for his arrest, of course the praetorians had tried to detain him. Volusianus had not been there. Was the Praetorian Prefect aware of the charges? If he was, no doubt he would be surprised. Long ago Volusianus and Ballista had served together at Spoletium, the battle which had brought Gallienus and his father Valerian to the throne. Yet the events of the night gave credence to the charges of incendiarism and murder. Ballista would not be the first soldier to run amok in the city. A life of violence could produce unlooked-for results. It was the duty of the Praetorian Prefect to help keep order on the streets of Rome. The actions of his men did not have to imply that Volusianus was privy to the conspiracy. The prefect was on the Palatine, at the side of Gallienus. Neither could be reached tonight.

Ballista fidgeted, but comfort eluded him. Gallienus and his entourage would not leave the Palace for the Colosseum until the third hour of daylight. They would go by the public streets, but once on the move they would be ringed by guards. Some emperors had been more amenable, but Gallienus did not care to be bothered by petitioners when crossing the city. Ballista had heard him cite the example of Mark Antony. Bothered by requests, Antony had stopped, smiled amiably, gathered the written petitions in the folds of his toga, and then thrown them all in the Tiber. At least Gallienus did not have his guards thrash those who dared approach him, as had some tyrants. When he reached the Colosseum itself, security would be tight. An emperor might show himself to his subjects at the Games, even banter with them through a herald, but without authorisation no one could get near to the imperial box.

It had to be before Gallienus left the Palace. As with the custom's post at the bridge, Ballista would try to use the rhythm of the Roman day. At dawn, hundreds, sometimes thousands, of citizens thronged the narrow ways up to the Palatine, crowded the great vestibule and the reception area before the gates. Ostensibly all went merely to pay their respects, but every one hoped to catch the eye of the emperor, to receive some favour or gift. If he could lose himself in the multitude, slip past the praetorians, and get to the Palace, he could bribe a door-man to take a message to Demetrius. The Greek youth, Ballista's one time secretary, was an imperial favourite and would be able to secure him access to Gallienus. Whatever people said about the habits of the emperor, Ballista knew that in a crisis Gallienus shrugged off his air of indolence, and acted like lightning.

A few words, and the emperor would be saved. A few words and Ballista's family would live. But could he get past the guards? Tall and broad, with shoulder-length fair hair, he stood out in a Roman crowd, every inch the northern barbarian.

Ballista's eyes had grown accustomed to the ambient light that filtered up the stairs from the doorman's lamp. The lime wash on the walls had a pale, scabrous glow. He needed to disguise his appearance. He had no change of clothes, and there was nothing to be done about his height or build. But his hair was another matter. Even with the hood of his cloak up, it showed. He crawled out from his refuge, sat sprawled on the floor, and picked up the knife.

Gathering his locks in his left hand, he paused. This was harder than he had thought. Among his own people long hair was a mark of noble birth. His dynasty were as often known as the long-haired Himlings, as the Woden-born. In all his years in the empire, wearing his hair to his shoulders was one aspect of his identity that he had never compromised. He answered to different names, spoke other languages, but never had he cut his hair short like a slave, like a *nithing*.

This was ridiculous. His vanity counted for nothing against what was at stake. He sawed at his hair. It was harder to do, and took longer than he expected. Eventually, surrounded by cuttings, it was done. With no reflection, he had could not tell what it looked like. Probably terrible, rough and sticking out in clumps, but it was shorter. Somewhere on the way down to the Forum in the morning he could buy a hat. Stooping, his appearance would be somewhat altered.

Ballista crept back under the stairs. Keeping the knife where he could reach it, he struggled to find some way of lying that was not intolerable. How many hours until *conticinium*? Sleep was impossible.

The body of the woman under him was soft and warm. She was eager, but someone was knocking on the door of the bedroom. Why must they disturb his pleasure?

The knocking was louder, someone was shouting.

Ballista jerked awake.

'All right, all right. Hold your horses, I am coming.' The voice of the doorkeeper came up the stairs.

Ballista slid out from his lair. Every bone in his body ached.

Bolts were being drawn, chains undone.

Ballista tucked the knife in his belt, then tried to stretch the stiffness out of his limbs. His ribs hurt like Tartarus.

'Open in the name of the City Watch!'

The words made Ballista's heart jump in his chest.

'I have opened.' The doorkeeper said truculently. 'What do you want? Lost one of your buckets?'

'Less of your lip. A fugitive was reported coming in here an hour or so ago.'

'Isn't no one come in here. See for yourself door was bolted.'

'Aiding a bandit is a capital offence. Want to be nailed on the cross next to him?'

'Don't know nothing about it.'

Ballista moved along the landing to the rear of the building.

'On your head be it. We are going to search the block. How many floors?'

'Seven. You'll be here until dawn.'

Ballista stood in front of the door to the rear apartment.

'How many residents?'

'Only the gods know.'

'You are not . . .' The rest of the watchman's words were lost as the remainder of his squad clattered through the door. In a moment their noise was augmented by the wailing of a child, and a woman shouting.

Ballista judged the distance as best he could in the near darkness, and kicked the door. The landlord having gone to the least expense, it flew open, almost flying off its hinges. Drawing his knife, Ballista stepped carefully into the room. In the gloom, he could just make out a woman. She sat up from a low bed, and yelled. 'Thief! Marcus!'

A movement alerted Ballista to the man. He had something in his hand, probably a blade.

'Calm, my friend,' Ballista said.

'Fucker.' The man edged closer. It was definitely a knife, a long kitchen knife.

'Whoa,' Ballista spoke as if he were soothing a horse.

The man stopped.

Behind him, Ballista could hear the City Watch pounding up the first flight of stairs.

'I am not here to rob you.' An idea struck Ballista. To save time, he cut the thongs that secured one of the wallets to his belt. He tossed it over. In the dark the man missed the catch. The wallet fell to the floorboards with a heavy chink.

'Do you have a balcony?'

The man pointed to a curtain.

The City Watch had reached the bottom of the second flight.

Ballista drew back the curtain. The balcony was narrow and sagging, and looked as if might part company from the wall with a gust of wind. It creaked ominously as Ballista stepped out. Thirty foot or more down to the ground. Too far not to be injured.

The sound of the City Watch was louder.

There were balconies on the tenement on the other side of the lane. They were at least ten foot away. So much for neighbours shaking hands across the divide.

Ballista tucked the knife back in his belt, and taking a plant pot from the rail, carefully placed it on the floor. This was not the moment to worry about a few herbs. He climbed precariously onto the rail. It gave a little under his weight.

'Where is he?' The City Watch were at the entrance to the apartment.

Aiming for the first floor balcony below on the other tenement, Ballista jumped.

The awful sensation of falling was replaced by the pain of the impact. He landed on top of the rail and screen. They shattered, and he rolled onto the balcony, amid pieces of rotten wood.

'Down there!' Someone was shouting.

As he groggily tried to get up, something hit Ballista across the shoulders. An old woman was wielding a broom.

'Get off, Grandmother.'

Not mollified, she continued to belabour him.

Ballista crawled to the edge, gripped the floor, and swung himself over feet first.

The ground beneath his dangling boots was no more than fifteen feet away. He was readying himself for the drop when the broom cracked down on his knuckles. His grip broken, he fell.

He hit the pavement hard. His left ankle turned as he sprawled. The white-hot agony suggested it was broken. He lay, curled, clutching the injury.

A plant pot shattered near his head. A shard nicked his ear. Fighting down the nausea induced by the pain, somehow he got up. He could put barely any weight on the damaged ankle. It was twisted, not broken.

'After him!'

The City Watch were crowded onto the balcony. A centurion was shouting. His men looked dubiously at the drop. One picked up another pot, and hurled it down. It did not miss by much.

Inspired, the others bent to find more missiles.

Stumbling and half hopping, Ballista lurched off into the night, pursued by a hail of shattering terracotta.

CHAPTER 12

The Subura
The House of Prayer

A BAR, AT LONG LAST A BAR that was not closed. The shutters were drawn across, but a narrow entrance was left open. Light and the murmur of conversation spilled out into the street. Ballista did not go in straight away, but hobbled past, and, squatting down, watched from the shadows opposite.

He rubbed his ankle. It was sore, but nothing worse. Injuries to that joint were strange. At first the pain was so intense that you were sure the tendons were torn, the bones broken, but then very quickly it faded, and you discovered that the ankle would support your weight. The tight boots that Ballista wore might have helped.

A man came out of the bar. He stood in the opening, saying his farewells to those out of sight inside. Ballista hoped that the bar was not about to shut. His valedictions concluded, the man walked down the street. As he drew near, he gave Ballista a sharp look. Deciding that the huddled figure was no threat, perhaps just a vagrant – the gods knew, there were enough in the city – he walked away without another glance.

Ballista did not know where he was within the subura. After falling from the balcony, his sole intention had been to put as much distance as possible between him and the tenement where he had been so nearly trapped. By the time the City Watch could make it down to street level, and rounded the block to the alleyway at the rear of the building, Ballista would have been long gone. He had not run into any patrols of the City Watch since. The subura was an enormous rabbit warren. It could be flooded with soldiers, and they would be swallowed in the intricate, unplanned maze.

The swordsmen at the Mausoleum of Hadrian had been soldiers. Had it really been only a few hours since that encounter? Everything about them – the way they carried themselves, their disciplined movements, the tattoo he had glimpsed – proclaimed years under the eagles. Their down-at-heel scruffiness argued against current service in a legion or regular auxiliary unit. He could not remember how many there had been – gods below, he was tired – perhaps twenty. Not a great number. They could not be everywhere. There had been no sign of them since, but he was sure that they would not have given up the search.

Ballista needed to get off the streets. He stood. The ankle was not too bad. In the light from the doorway, on the wall next to the shutter, he could see a painted drinking vessel, and a sign that read *Salvius*. Perhaps barkeepers took professional names like prostitutes or actors. It was time to test if the *hospitality* of the establishment lived up to its owner's name.

Ballista paused on the threshold, squinting in the brighter light.

On his appearance, all conversation ceased.

Ballista took stock of his surroundings. An L-shaped bar; a lone drinker to the right, two on the left, a couple more at a table towards the rear of the room, next to some stairs to an upper floor, and a corridor right at the back, which was partly screened by a curtain. None of the drinkers belonged to the City Watch, and none had a military bearing. Ballista walked to the bar, took a place to the right of the corner.

'Health and great joy, stranger.' The innkeeper wore the high-belted leather apron of his trade.

'Health and great joy.'

'What can I get you?'

'Wine, half and half with water.'

'The average wine, or the better stuff?'

'The better.'

As the innkeeper busied himself, the others remained silent. Not catching anyone's eye, Ballista scanned the room. There was a mirror facing him behind the bar. It was tarnished, but he could see the doorway at his back. The right hand wall of the bar was lined with racks of amphorae. A rail ran above them, hung with ancient, tough looking hams and some strings of garlic.

A slatternly girl emerged from the corridor at the back with a plate of bread and olives and oil, which she gave to the two men at the table. They grunted their thanks, began to eat, and resumed a low, weary-sounding conversation. By the cloaks and broad-brimmed hats beside them, they were travellers, at this hour of the night, most likely waggoneers or drovers. The other men continued to regard the newcomer in silence.

'Here you are.' The innkeeper put a jug and a glass on the chipped counter.

'My thanks.' Ballista opened one of the three wallets on his belt. He took out a coin at random. It was gold, far too high a denomination. It had the attention of the men at the bar.

'The dice have been kind tonight.' Ballista spoke with the over-careful precision of a man in his cups. 'A jug of the good stuff for every man here, and one for yourself.'

'That is generous. Isn't it, boys?'

Prompted by the barkeeper, the men at the bar muttered their thanks. The two at the table expressed their gratitude in the archaic formalities of the countryside.

'What about me, big man?' The girl was at his side.

'You too, sweetness.'

She was pretty.

'You want some company?'

Ballista smiled. 'After a drink or two, that might be good.'

She lingered. There was calculation in her eyes – hard-learned rules for self-preservation, a lifetime of hard choices.

The barkeeper brought the change. Ballista shovelled it back into the wallet with the unconcern of a drink-taken gambler up on his luck.

'The man will call you if he wants,' said the barkeeper.

Dismissed, the girl drifted off up the stairs.

'Hot little piece,' the barkeeper said. 'Isn't she, boys?'

The three at the bar nodded.

'Bought her down in Ostia, straight off the boat from Syria. Hot, but lazy. Needs a belt across her arse now and then.'

Ballista inclined his head, as if the barkeeper had said something important and profound. He had no desire for a girl, but some time in a room up the stairs offered greater privacy.

'Like I was saying about the pickled fish.' The man on Ballista's left was talking to his companion, but loud enough for all to hear. 'The owner could not work out where they were going.'

The barman went and leant against the counter by the speaker.

'He locked the kitchen, no one but him could get in, yet every night more of them were gone. So one night, he hides in the corner.'

The man paused for dramatic effect.

'And you know what he saw?'

No one hazarded a guess.

'In the dead of night, he hears something coming up the latrine. Then he sees a tentacle, then another. It's a fucking great octopus, what lives down there.'

'Well – its his own fault for connecting his latrine to the sewers,' the other man said. 'Any fool knows all sorts of horrors live down there. What is more: every time the Tiber floods, the sewer backs up, and your house is full of shit.'

'You're right there, my friend. A fucking waste of money. Throw your shit in the street, like everyone else.'

'Talking about wasting money, what about the colossal statue of himself our *beloved* emperor is having built up on the Esquiline?'

The barkeeper tipped his head slightly towards Ballista.

The speaker looked over. 'You are no *frumentarius*.' He turned back to his listeners. 'Any fool knows they pick men from the army who will blend into a crowd for the imperial spies. They don't pick a hulking great barbarian, twice the size of anyone else, covered in scratches like something wild has been at him, with hair like a badly reaped field of stubble.' He glanced at Ballista. 'No offense, friend.'

'None taken.'

'As I was saying, the statue has to be twice the size of the one down by the Colosseum, big enough so a child can climb right up inside the spear it's holding.'

The barman spoke. 'They say he wants a chariot and horses built to match now.'

The speaker ignored the comment. 'He has lost all the western provinces to Postumus, in the East this Arab Odenathus only pretends to follow his orders, and what does Gallienus do? Empties the treasury trying to found Plato's Republic up in the Apennines, that's what he does. A city of philosophers; what the fuck use is that?'

They were quiet for a moment, pondering imperial folly.

'And now, what's more, he has taken to wearing a dress.'

'A dress?' Ballista put down his drink. 'I saw Gallienus in the Circus about a month ago; he was wearing normal clothes.'

'Not all the time, he doesn't, look at this.' The man hunted through his coins. 'Bugger, Salvius, you got one of them?'

The barman got down the takings from a box on the shelves with the amphorae. Finding what he wanted, he tossed the coin over to Ballista.

On one side of the coin was a figure that looked like Gallienus dressed as the goddess Demeter, wearing her crown of corn. The inscription read Gallienae Augustae.

'He has a sister, Galliena, lives in Africa,' Ballista said.

'Has she got a beard?'

Ballista held the coin up to the light hanging above the bar. The figure had a beard. He could think of nothing to say.

'I want that back.'

Ballista handed the coin over. 'Where is the latrine?'

'Out back, down the corridor.'

As soon as he went through the curtain, Ballista could smell the latrine. The foul cubicle had no door. The dim light from a tiny lamp in the corridor revealed a wooden seat over a hole, and a large amphora. Ballista unbuckled his belt, eased down his britches, and pissed into the amphora.

The officials in charge of the mint chose the images and words on imperial coins, but they were shown to the emperor for approval.

From the other end of the corridor came the sound of the curtain being drawn back. Another customer wanted to use the latrine.

What had Gallienus been thinking when he passed that extraordinary coin type? Perhaps he had not bothered to look at the thing. There were many demands on his time.

The light from the corridor was blocked. The two talkative drinkers crowded Ballista's back. The point of a knife touched the side of his throat.

'Where did a barbarian like you steal all that money?' The man's breath was hot on the back of Ballista's neck.

'Told you, won it at dice.'

'Hand it over.'

Ballista adjusted his britches, buckled his belt.

'Hand the fucker over.' The knife pricked a little deeper, just nicked the flesh.

Ballista weighed his options. They were not good. Best give them the three wallets.

'He has seen our faces,' the other drinker said. 'Just do him.'

So that was how it was. This was not a good place to die.

'I won't say anything.' Buying time, Ballista fumbled with the laces of one of the wallets. If he threw himself backwards, he would get cut, but perhaps not fatally.

'No one move,' a previously unheard voice said. 'Kill the barbarian, and your friend here dies.' It had to be the man who had been drinking on his own on the right of the bar.

The pressure of the knife eased. Ballista could sense its owner's indecision.

'Tell you what, boys, there is more than enough for everyone.' Ballista removed a wallet from his belt, passed it back over his shoulder. The man took it, and removed the knife from Ballista's throat.

Ballista turned, and stood next to the man who had been about to kill him. Out in the corridor, posed like a scene from the amphitheatre, the quiet man had a blade pressed to the stomach of the other would be robber.

'No harm done,' Ballista said. 'Just a mistake.'

'Tell him to get that knife out of my guts.'

Instead Ballista drew his own weapon. 'Now we have all got steel in our hands. In a small space like this, at least two of us are going to die, all of us are going to get badly cut.'

'Like you said, just a mistake.'

'Exactly, so we are going to leave. You two follow in a moment. Then, when we have left the bar, you can buy yourselves a few drinks. How does that sound?'

'Good.'

'Yes, I thought so.'

Ballista went first down the corridor, the quiet man walking backwards, covering them both.

Back in the bar, the travellers had gone. The girl was nowhere in sight. Only the barkeeper remained. He stayed behind his counter, a hefty cudgel in his hands. He watched in silence as Ballista and his unforeseen saviour walked out into the night.

'You are not what I expected,' Ballista said.

'I am a great disappointment to my brothers,' the man said.

They had talked on the way down. Ballista could not have been more surprised at the identity of the man who had saved him.

'We are here.'

A shabby door at the end of an alley; not a tenement, a small house. The man rapped on the door in a rhythm, evidently a code. The door opened.

'Is he one of us?' The doorkeeper was suspicious.

'No, he is not.'

'Have you taken leave of your senses?'

'Let us in, or do you want to continue the debate in the street.'

The doorkeeper shut the door behind them. 'Are you drunk?'

'Perhaps a little,' Ballista's rescuer said. 'Is charity not a virtue?'

'Are we not told to fear our neighbours, our own families, lest they denounce us?'

'This is Marcus Clodius Ballista, the high official who saved our brothers and sisters in Ephesus. He had been set upon by robbers. They intended to murder him. I offered him sanctuary.'

An elderly man appeared in the hallway. Long-bearded, he looked like a follower of one of the more respectable schools of philosophy. Obviously he had heard every word. The other two deferred to him. 'You acted as a good Samaritan,' he said to the man from the bar. Then he addressed himself to Ballista. 'You are welcome, but, until the Eucharist is over, you must remain with those who listen by the door.'

There were three men and two women left standing in the vestibule with Ballista. They kept apart from him, and did not speak.

Ballista could see into the room used for their worship. There were rows of benches, and a low table at the front, but no altar or fire or statues; none of the apparatus of traditional religion. On the wall behind where the bearded elder had taken his stand there was a painting of a man with a sheep on his shoulders. On the other wall that Ballista could see was a picture of a man carrying a bed.

Ballista had run a terrible risk in Ephesus. The Emperor Valerian had ordered him to eradicate the followers of the crucified god from the city. Ballista very quickly had been sickened by the tortures and hideous executions, but also by the insane zealotry of some of the sect: *I am a Christian, and I want to die.* Manufacturing a riot, he had used it as an excuse to suspend his investigations. When leaving, he had smuggled the Christians already arrested from the gaol. As a persecutor, he had learned much about their sect. He knew that the man pictured with the sheep was the epiphany of their god, and the one carrying the bed was Lazarus raised from the dead by the wonder worker Chrestus.

'The Lord be with you,' the elder intoned.

'And with your spirit,' the rest replied.

There were Christians everywhere these days. It was no more than an accident of politics and war. There had always been sporadic, local persecutions. The crops failed, or a plague descended, and the mob shouted *Christians to the Lion*! The Governor executed a few adherents of the sect, employing inventive methods and exemplary cruelty, all under the approving gaze of the populace, and order was restored. Just over a decade ago, the Emperor Decius had ordered that all inhabitants of the empire should sacrifice to the traditional gods in public. A few years later, Valerian had decreed the universal persecution, which had sent Ballista to Ephesus. Decius had been cut down by the Goths, the first emperor to die in battle against barbarians. The fate of Valerian had been worse. Captured by the Persians, it was said that when the Sassanid king wished to go out riding that he used the aged emperor as a living mounting block. The Christians had exulted in what they saw as proofs of the vengeance of their god. It had given others pause for thought; perhaps there was some power in this strange, new god from the East.

'Take, eat; this is my body, which shall be broken for you.'

The old man held a plate of flat bread.

'This is my blood, which is shed for you; when you do this, you make my remembrance.'

The congregation, at least two dozen, moved forward. The elder placed his hands on the head of each that ate a morsel of bread and sipped the wine.

Those who partook of this simulacrum of a meal were of all conditions, Ballista noted. There were cobblers, laundry workers, illiterate labourers, one or two whose fine clothes showed higher status. There were men and women, free and slave, all indiscriminately mixed. Their very heterogeneity was a threat to the social order.

' ... through whom be glory and honour to you, to the Father and the Son, with the Holy Spirit, in your holy Church, both now and to the ages of ages.'

The service at an end, the worshippers slipped away, in ones and twos, into the night. Ballista's saviour departed without a word.

'Come.' The elder took Ballista's arm, and led him into a parlour.

'Eat.' A more normal meal was set out. There was bread, cheese and honey, although milk to drink, not wine.

The old man smiled indulgently as Ballista ate. 'You see, we are much maligned. There is no cannibalism or incest.'

Ballista politely finished a mouthful before replying. 'Why do you meet in the dark, like conspirators? Gallienus countermanded the decrees of his father for your persecution.'

'It is for our safety.' The hands of the elder fluttered, as he sought the right words. 'Imperial policy is not immutable. Even you pagans consider Gallienus . . . inconstant.'

'You do not dispute the authority of the emperor?'

'Our Lord bade us render unto Caesar the things that are Caesar's. We will not fight for the emperor, but we offer prayers for his success.'

'But you deny the gods?'

'It is better to die than to worship stones. He who sacrifices to the gods, and not to God, shall be destroyed.'

'Then the persecutions will come again.' Ballista felt that he had to try to explain the inevitable doom these Christians were bringing on their own heads. 'The Romans believe their empire rests on the *Pax Deorum*. If they do right by the gods, the gods will hold their hands over them, secure their rule. If the Romans let atheists like you insult their gods, the gods will desert Rome.'

'Life is good, but the life that we long for is better.' The old man sounded serene. 'It is far worse to burn after death.'

Ballista said nothing.

'To those who deny the Lord shall be given eternal punishment. The unquenchable and unending fire awaits them. No sleep will give them rest, no night soothe them, no death deliver them.'

The old man put his hand on Ballista's knee, looked at him full of solicitude. 'One of those you delivered from Ephesus, Aulus Valerius Festus, said that he had hoped to convert you.'

'He did try.'

'You are not Roman; their superstitions are not yours.'

Ballista did not want to offend the Christian. He needed this sanctuary. 'My wife follows Epicurus, and holds that death is the end, nothing but a return to sleep. If she is mistaken, then, according to the *superstitions* of my people, if I die well, I will live in the hall of my ancestor, Woden-Allfather; at least until the death of men and gods.'

The elder made the sign of the cross. 'If you acknowledge Christ, repent your sins, you will sit at his side for eternity.'

Ballista shook his head. 'The Greek historian Herodotus wrote that, everywhere, custom is king.'

The old man looked sad, then brightened. 'The scholar Origen said that those unbelievers in authority who help the faithful might not be irrevocably damned to hell, that the prayers of the faithful might rescue them. We will pray for you, Marcus Clodius Ballista, and you are safe under this roof until dawn.'

CHAPTER 13

The Esquiline Hill
The Carinae
Conticinium

*C*ONTICINIUM, WHEN THE COCKS had stopped crowing, but most men were still asleep, the still time of the false dawn, when it was no longer night, but not yet day. The senator, Gaius Sempronius Dalmaticus, had been up for some time, working on his correspondence. A report from the factor of his estate in Calabria, a request from a client to represent him in the courts, a letter from a young friend studying in Athens; mundane stuff in which it was difficult to feign interest in front of his secretary.

Appearances must be maintained, nothing could appear out of the ordinary. Sempronius always rose early and dealt with his correspondence. To do so was the right thing. Pliny the Younger had always got up before dawn to work. Sempronius had recently reread Pliny's *Letters*. They were an admirable guide to a senatorial life conducted according to the precepts of duty and dignity. The Emperor Marcus Aurelius also had shunned sleep, and by lamplight dealt with affairs both of culture and the state.

Sempronius sent away his secretary, and summoned his barber. His wife had suggested that, given his straitened financial circumstances, keeping a slave-barber was an unnecessary expense. Surely he could be shaved at the baths in the afternoon; it was not as if his bald head called for an elaborate coiffure. Sempronius had dismissed the idea. In the old days, a wife would not have uttered such words, would have better known her place. Anyway, after today there would be no lack of funds.

The barber drew the curtains. The light was gathering, but the slave arranged the lamp with the tools of his trade: the mirror, bowl of water, crescent-shaped razor, and tweezers. Sempronius, submitting himself to the process, gazed out of the window.

High, dappled clouds against a pigeon-grey sky held the promise of a fine day. Had the circumstances been different, it would have been an enjoyable day. A litter would carry him from the opulent district of the Carinae to the Palatine, and the stately formalities of the emperor's levee. He would process as a member of the imperial entourage down to the Colosseum, take his place in the perfumed shade of the royal box. They would catch the latter part of the morning's beast fights. They were promised ostriches, and, a rare beast indeed, a hippopotamus. Over a fine luncheon, they would witness the elaborate executions of those guilty of the foulest crimes. A notorious bandit from Asia had been condemned to castrate himself, like Attis, the oriental god from Pessinous. Given his origins, the punishment was apt, although, as he might survive, some held it too lenient. The afternoon would bring the gladiators, several hundred pairs. Sempronius had always favoured the myrmillones – solid and employing good Roman sword and shield – over flighty retarii, or foreign-sounding fighters like the Thracians or Gauls. A fine day's entertainment, but Sempronius knew it would bring him neither pleasure nor diversion. Not with what would happen at the end.

As the barber plucked his eyebrows, Sempronius mulled over the deaths of emperors. A few, a very few, had lived out their natural course; Augustus, the first emperor, Vespasian, the Divine Marcus Aurelius. One or two had fallen in battle; Decius against the Goths, Albinus in a civil war. Some, like Nero or Otho, had been forced to suicide. Yet many more had met a sudden end at the hands of others, often those close to them. Claudius was poisoned by his wife, Commodus strangled in his bath by a member of his household. Any number had been cut down by the soldiers. The corpse of Heliogabalus had been stuffed into a sewer. Sempronius could not recall any killed by their successor in person. Unless, of course, the rumour was true that Caligula pressed the pillow down over the face of Tiberius. Caligula was not a good precedent.

When the barber had finished his painful ministrations, Sempronius called for his valet. He shrugged off the tunic in which he had slept, and stood naked before the old retainer. With the respectful silence of long service, the valet slipped a new, clean tunic over the head of his master. Its broad purple stripe marked out its wearer as one of the six hundred richest, most elevated men in the empire; a senator of Rome.

'A visitor, sir,' said a voice beyond the curtains.

'Show him in.' Sempronius gestured for his valet to continue dressing him.

'Health and great joy, Gaius Sempronius Dalmaticus.'

'Health and great joy, Cecropius.' It was beneath a man who had been Consul to use the full three names of such an officer. Sempronius waved a hand for Cecropius to take a chair.

The valet brought out a gleaming white toga. The heavy wool was draped first over Sempronius' left shoulder, wrapped round under his right arm, then back over his left shoulder. The valet moved slowly, arranging the folds and swags, stepping back, head on one side, to study the hang and effect of the garment.

Cecropius waited, any impatience or irritation hidden, except perhaps for the way his fingers flexed on the hilt of his sword.

Born a goat boy, somewhere on the other side of the Adriatic, in the wilds of Dalmatia, Cecropius had risen from the barracks, up through the army, and now commanded a unit of cavalry. Gallienus had granted him equestrian status, and admitted him to the *protectores*. Sempronius loathed Cecropius and his sort. The *protectores* were a typical innovation of Gallienus. It was said the emperor had been inspired by the hearth-troops that surrounded barbarian warlords in the forests of Germania. Almost all originally common soldiers, uneducated and boorish, the *protectores* swaggered about, lording it over their betters. Allowed to bear arms within the sacred borders of Rome, in the houses of senators, even in the imperial presence itself, the *protectores* were little better than barbarians themselves.

Satisfied at last, the valet laced the elaborate shoes which only senators were allowed to wear, and then withdrew. Sempronius gave orders to be left alone with his guest.

'Would you care for some wine?'

'Too early.'

Cecropius' hair was suspiciously blonde. Perhaps, Sempronius thought, he copied the fashion of the emperor, and had it dyed. Gallienus had gold dust sprinkled in his artfully curled locks.

'Are you ready?' There was a note of insolence in the tone of Cecropius.

'Have they caught the barbarian?' Sempronius was annoyed that he sounded both petulant and frightened.

'No,' Cecropius said. 'He was last seen in the subura; jumped off the second floor balcony of a tenement. Hard man to kill, it seems. He escaped.'

'But the subura is . . .'

'Just at the foot of this hill.' Cecropius waved a hand, perhaps in reassurance, possibly with contempt. 'Don't worry, Ballista does not know who you are. With the City Watch chasing him, he must have realised that the *mouse* is part of the conspiracy. Having seen the men at the Mausoleum, he may have worked out the identity of the *ferret*. The man he murdered at the top of the monument may have talked. But there is no possibility that he knows the rest of us. Anyway, he is not coming here. His aim is to reach Gallienus.'

'And if he does, what then?'

'We all die, but it will not come to that. The Palatine is sealed tighter than a vestal's cunt.'

Sempronius tried not to show surprise or distaste at the crudity. 'But why do I have to strike the blow?' Again, he sounded like a scared child.

'We have been through this many times.' Cecropius spoke with exaggerated patience. 'The peasant is right. If Gallienus is not killed by a senator, half the senate will acclaim Postumus, the rest will quarrel among themselves, a few might even turn to Odenathus. It would be chaos. The civil wars will continue, we would be no better off, the empire no more secure.'

'If it has to be a senator, why not the peasant himself?'

Cecropius actually laughed. 'It has to be a senator of a more conventional background. Would *you* accept the peasant as emperor? He gave himself that nickname for a reason.'

'What about Tacitus? His family have been in the Curia for generations.'

'He is away on the Danube.'

'Conveniently.'

'Tacitus left before this *undertaking* was finalised.'

'How do I know that he is with us at all? You name all these *protectores* – Tacitus and Aurelian and Heraclian – none of them are here in Rome. What proof do I have they even know of our plans?'

'What proof would you have? Do you expect them to put it in writing, affix their seal? The friends of Catiline did, and the executioner strangled them.'

Sempronius was silent. He had not expected Cecropius to have heard of Catiline and his conspiracy. Surely this unlettered soldier had not read Cicero or Sallust? In his surprise, he did not take in the first words of what Cecropius was now saying.

' ... only some of them, to approach any more would have run too many risks, but rest assured all the *protectores* will welcome the end of Gallienus. Day by day the empire totters. In the West, Postumus must be crushed. In the East, Odenathus has to be brought to heel, the Persians defeated, the prestige of Rome restored. We are surrounded by war. The army cries out for men and money, proper leadership, old-fashioned Roman discipline and virtue. And Gallienus passes his time with mime artists and whores, wearing women's clothes. He empties the treasuries to build a gigantic statue here on the Esquiline, an enormous portico on the Campus Martius, a city full of philosophers in the Apennines. No wonder Postumus despises us, and barbarians like Odenathus and the Sassanid King mock our power. You know they say Shapur makes the old emperor kneel in the dirt, puts his boot on Valerian's shoulders when he mounts his horse. Poor old Valerian, to have a son like Gallienus, who makes no move to save him. Poor Rome, to have sunk so low.'

Cecropius took a deep breath. 'Everything is ready. The moment is propitious. You will be searched when you go into the presence of the emperor, but in the imperial box the peasant will pass you a weapon. Wait until Gallienus leaves. Hand him your petition when he is out in the private corridor that runs up to the Palatine. While he reads it, strike. Don't waste your breath on words, just strike.

The guards there will not intervene. We will all be with you. You must strike the first blow, but we will help finish him. As soon as Gallienus is dead, we will escort you to the Palace. Nothing will go wrong. Have no fear.'

Once Cecropius had gone, Sempronius went out into the atrium. At the rear, all the slaves were waiting by the household shrine, as they did every morning. Quintus, his surviving son, dutifully stood with them. The old ways were important to Sempronius. After all these years his eldest son's absence from the ceremony still hurt. Not a day passed that he did not mourn the boy. Quintus was a weak thing compared with his dead brother.

The slaves – bowing, blowing kisses from their fingertips – bade him a formal good day. Another absence caused merely irritation. Once again his wife had not appeared. She would be finishing her toilette, criticising her maids, slapping and pinching them. Sempronius' marriage had always brought her servants even more unpleasantness than it brought himself.

Sempronius stood in front of the shrine. He looked at the painted *genius* of the household. Toga-clad and dignified, his mirror image, it stared back. The *genius* was flanked by the two *lares*. Their short tunics flared as they danced, wine jugs and drinking vessels in hand. A long snake coiled across the bottom of the painting. In front a fire burned on the altar.

Have no fear. Typical impudence from the likes of Cecropius. An ancestor had won Sempronius' family the cognomen Dalmaticus by killing thousands of Cecropius' barbaric antecedents. If Cecropius and the other *protectores* thought they were getting an emperor who would be no more than a figurehead, they would quickly learn their mistake. The key was the emperor's German bodyguard. When an emperor was dead, the barbarians accepted the fact, easily shifted their allegiance to his successor. But while the emperor was alive, they honoured their word, and were unshakably loyal. Which was much more than one could say of the Praetorian Guard. It explained why the attempt on Gallienus' life must be made in the secret corridor of the Colosseum, after the Germans in the imperial box had handed the duty of guarding the emperor over to the praetorians. It was a sad indictment of contemporary Roman morality.

Sempronius had his plans in place. This coming evening, no sooner than Gallienus was dead, and Sempronius had reached the Palace, he would summon the Germans and administer their oath. Once they had given their word, Sempronius could rely upon them. His first command would be to order the execution of the *protectores* in the conspiracy. *Have no fear.* The *peasant*, the *ferret*, the *mouse*, and Cecropius – the *rider*, as he was styled among the plotters – would barely have time to register fear, let alone savour their transitory triumph.

The coup would cleanse the Augean stables of the court and the army. The *protectores* would be abolished. The equestrian officers who had clawed their way up from the mire of the barracks would be dismissed. Senators of good standing would again hold high military commands. Sempronius had sounded out some here in Rome. On the plains of northern Italy, Acilius Glabrio and Nummius Faustinianus were with the army, and poised to act. That no senator to whom he had spoken had betrayed him proved both their hatred of Gallienus and their commitment to the cause embodied by Sempronius himself.

The reign of Sempronius Augustus would be a return to the ways of the ancestors. Once again the *mos maiorum* would be respected.

The emperor would attend the senate, show due deference, draw his councillors from its number. When he took the field, his armies would be commanded by senators of traditional families, men shaped by generations of their forefathers' duty and service to the *res publica*. Sempronius would not rule like some oriental despot, but conduct himself as a first among equals. Sempronius was steeped in history. Its examples were ever before his eyes. Trajan, Antoninus Pius and Marcus Aurelius would be his models. Emperors who ruled not for themselves, but for the good of others. Sempronius' eldest son would have made a fine ruler. But he was dead. Weak and profligate, Quintus did not have it in him. When it came time for Sempronius to join his elder son in Hades, like the good emperors of old, he would designate as his heir the best man that could be found among the senate. Sempronius Augustus would haul Rome back from this age of iron and rust. Perhaps the times were too debased, and the gods too far, to return to an age of gold, but it was not too late to recreate one of silver.

Sempronius prepared to sacrifice. He pulled the folds of his toga over his head. The flute player struck up, and those assembled placed their right hands on their chests.

Only one aspect of his plans troubled Sempronius. Were all the officers named by Cecropius really part of the conspiracy? The Dalmatian had been careful to refer to those in Rome only by their epithets – the peasant, mouse, and ferret – even though Sempronius was well aware of their identity, had indeed met them all. But Cecropius had bandied openly the names of supposed fellow plotters who were away or with the army. Did they actually have any involvement with the plot?

Sempronius had instructed Acilius Glabrio to take whatever measures were necessary to secure the allegiance of the army.

Acilius Glabrio was not a man given to reflection. He had won the Battle of Circesium by leading a direct charge into the heart of the Persian enemy. Acilius Glabrio would act decisively. Sempronius would not lie to himself. He had signed the death warrant of Heraclian and Aurelian, most likely Tacitus as well. All three of whom might be innocent.

The attendant handed Sempronius a plate containing scraps of food. Anything that fell to the floor in the dining room should be offered to the *lares*.

As Sempronius gave the morsels to the flames on the altar, an awful idea swam up into his thoughts, like a monster rising from the depths. What if there was no plot at all? Last year Postumus had tried to suborn one of the *protectores*. The officer had remained loyal. The agent of Postumus had been caught. At the hands of the imperial torturers, he had revealed all that he knew. Gallienus had used the information to induce treachery among the high command of Postumus.

For all that he might choose to dress as a woman, defile his person with acts best left unnamed, Gallienus had sat the throne for more than a decade. He had survived numerous plots, had learned how to negotiate the currents of treachery. What if this *conspiracy* was nothing of the sort? What if Gallienus had manufactured the entire thing? Could it be designed to bring his domestic enemies into the open, to have them removed before he took the field against the forces of Postumus? The *protectores* who had approached Sempronius owed everything to Gallienus. The cellars of the Palace – the rack and the claws – made Sempronius shudder. Before it came to that, like most senators, Sempronius wore a ring containing poison. Before he betrayed his friends, before he betrayed himself, he would take his life like a Roman of old.

Like a Roman of old. Cato, Thrasea Paetus, Seneca; the annals of the senate were replete with men of courage who had taken the only road to freedom open in the face of imperial tyranny.

Like a Roman of old, Sempronius put aside his fears. Intoning a prayer, he took a saucer of wine, and gave it to the gods of his household. Gallienus was a drunk, a spendthrift. The *protectores* had enough reasons to want the emperor dead. Keep his nerve, and by nightfall, Sempronius would wear the purple.

CHAPTER 14

The Roman Forum
The Hours of Light

THE SUN WAS ABOUT TO RISE. The Pythagorean stood stock still in the middle of the street. The crowd gave him a wide berth. Some stopped to watch. Long-bearded, with hair to his shoulders, the Pythagorean began to hum, attuning himself to the coming day. His white linen tunic almost seemed to glow in the gloom, and somehow it might be easy to believe that the otherworldly figure was communing with the gods.

The first rays of sunlight caught the gilded roof of the Temple of Jupiter Optimus Maximus high on the Capitoline.

The Pythagorean raised his arms in prayer.

'Gods, may justice prevail.' His voice was strong, and carried well. The Attic Greek in which he spoke indicated education, and a wealthy background.

'May the laws not be broken.' This was no hedgerow philosopher, no ranting Cynic, railing against the established order. 'Gods, grant me what I deserve. If you count me among the worthy, send me blessings. If you rank me among the wicked, send the opposite. I shall not blame the gods, if, because of my own demerit, I am judged deserving of evil.'

The Pythagorean, and those who ringed him, were an island of stillness in the flow of people going down to the Forum.

'The gods, as they are beneficent, if they find anyone unscarred by vice, they crown him, not with gold, but blessings. They give him happiness and a sound mind. But if they find a man branded and foul with sin, they will expose him, and hand him over to the direst of punishments in this world and the next.'

Several of those who had paused to watch put their fingertips to their lips, and blew a kiss to this man touched with divinity.

'Gods, bestow on me whatever I deserve.'

The man standing next to Ballista at the side of the street snorted. 'He is the one that lives in the portico of the Temple of Saturn. Always begging.'

Ballista said nothing.

The man – a butcher by his stained apron – was not discouraged. 'Claims we shouldn't eat meat or touch a drop of wine.'

Ballista still did not respond.

'Charlatan!' The man shouted at the Pythagorean. 'What you deserve is flogging.'

Some of those around the Pythagorean looked over balefully. The last thing Ballista wanted was for this to escalate into a public disturbance.

'Do an honest day's work, and the gods might reward you.' The critic was not to be silenced. 'The gods themselves partake of the sacrifices, the bones and the fat. Set yourself up above the gods, do you?'

Some of the audience put their thumbs between their fingers to avert evil.

Ballista edged away.

'I will pray for you,' the Pythagorean said, with a tone of insufferable sanctity.

'Fuck you!' the butcher shouted. 'Trying to do a man out of his livelihood.'

The crowd was thickening, as passers-by inevitably were drawn to the prospect of an entertaining fight, but Ballista had got clear.

The *Via Fornicata* was the main thoroughfare out of the subura towards the Forum. It was narrow, and hedged with buildings of all kinds – all except *fornices*, the very arches that its name implied. Already the tradesmen – cobblers, barbers, cloak makers, and wool workers – were opening their shutters. Some were spreading their wares on the pavement, further constricting the passage. Ballista let himself be jostled along. He was tired. He had slept for a time, but badly. In his dreams he had been led out to the cross for execution. He had tried to demand the headsman's block, the death of a Roman citizen. The soldiers – rough, unshaven, like the men at the Mausoleum – had laughed. He might hang there for days, they had said, like his ancestor. As the nails were hammered through flesh and sinew, the pain had jerked him awake. The dream signified nothing. What else was to be expected if you slept under the roof of Christians?

Their talk may have disturbed his brief rest, but the followers of Chrestus had done well by him. In the still-time, they had washed him – the elder himself on his knees, bathing Ballista's grimy feet – and dressed his various wounds. They had trimmed his hair into something less wild, and given him a clean white tunic. When Ballista had told them where he was going, although with no mention of why, they had produced a spotless, if threadbare, toga. Ballista had buckled on his belt with his money under the toga, but left the knife behind. At the door, the elder had pressed his own staff into his hand. Despite Ballista's insistence, they had refused any payment.

There was much to admire about these Christians. Above all there was their alms giving and charity. They gave to those outside their own number, to pagans and Jews, to men who under other circumstances would revile them, perhaps call for their execution. Although it provoked the suspicion of the Roman authorities, they welcomed all into their gathering. They had no set prejudice against those of barbarian birth. All were equal in the sight of their god. The Christian afterlife gave hope of a better world to come to those offered little or nothing by this one. It was easy to see the comfort given to slaves and the poor, to women constrained and often brutalised by husbands or the world at large.

Yet there was the terrible arrogance of the followers of Chrestus. How could anyone believe that only his god existed, that those worshipped since time immemorial by thousands of others were no more than inanimate marble, or, much worse, were evil daemons? It defied all logic that a beneficent and all powerful deity would not have foreseen the problem of salvation for those born before his epiphany, before the birth of Chrestus. And there was their juvenile idealism. *Thou shalt not kill* was a workable creed for an obscure sect with no temporal power, but could never be maintained by those who sat on the throne of the Caesars. Not, Ballista thought, that any Caesar would ever take to worshipping the crucified god.

The subura left behind, Ballista walked passed the Temple of Minerva, and down the street known as the Potters' Quarter to come into the Forum by the Senate House. He moved slowly; to do otherwise clad in a toga would look odd. He wished he had a hat or hood, but, again, no one ever wore headgear with a toga.

The Forum was even more crowded than usual. The courts would not open for a couple of hours, but already many litigants and orators and jurors were about. They were shaking hands, talking, seeking influence or bribes, or just diversion. Gaggles of sightseers from the provinces meandered through the throng, gawping and exclaiming at the monuments. Local guides, self-styled experts on antiquity, hung about them offering their services. To those visitors foolish enough to hand over some coins, they told an exotic mixture of half-remembered stories and anything they thought

would entertain or shock. Flocks of the less enterprising indigen-
ous inhabitants were settling in the various porticos to idle away
the day with games of dice and aimless gossip. It was the Kalends
and, in addition to the regular denizens of the Forum, the money-
lenders were out in force. The interest on loans was due on the first
day of the month, and by nightfall the Column of Maenius, over by
the Arch of Septimius Severus, would be thick with notices posted
denouncing defaulters.

Ballista turned left, and went up the steps to the Portico of the
Aemilian Basilica. He leant against a column. From there he could
see out across the Forum. Once this had been the political heart of
the free republic. In the Senate House, the Conscript Fathers had
debated war and peace. There in the hallowed Curia, Cato had thundered that *Carthage must be destroyed*. Outside, from the rostra,
magistrates had faced the assemblies of the people, had employed
all the wiles of rhetoric to sway the voters to their way of thinking,
to induce them to pass or reject legislation. From that speakers'
platform, studded with the rams of captured warships that gave it
its name, Cicero had denounced Mark Antony as an enemy of the
republic.

The republic had been the perfect constitution, so had argued
the historian Polybius. All the elements held in balance – the consuls embodying the monarchic, the senate the aristocratic, and
the assemblies the democratic – it was unchanging, and would
never fall, not until the gods sent fire and flood from heaven, and
destroyed the world. Polybius had been wrong. The republic had
contained the seeds of its own downfall from the start. Driven ever
outwards by the desire of senators for military glory, the empire
had become too vast to be governed by the institutions of a city
state. Huge wars demanded not annual magistrates, but generals
holding power for years on end over sweeping territories. The gap

between the winners and the losers of the senatorial competition opened so wide as to destroy all pretences of equality. Ultimately, in a welter of civil war and proscription, a sole victor emerged. The bloodstained dynast Octavian reinvented himself as Augustus, the paternal and benign emperor, and power migrated from the Forum up to the Palatine.

'And over there,' the voice of a guide interrupted Ballista's thoughts, 'that stain is the very blood of the Emperor Heliogabalus, hacked to pieces by the mob. You all remember his foul vices . . .'

As far as Ballista could recall, the perverse youth had met his end in the Praetorian Camp at the hands of the guard.

'You see the column by the arch, the one with no statue? When his house was demolished the senator Maenius insisted one column be left, so that his descendants could view the games held in the Forum from the top.'

Ballista stopped listening to the nonsense, and looked across the Forum up to the Palatine. Since Romulus built his hut there, the hill had been the preserve of the homes of the good and the great. Now it was reserved solely for the imperial Palace. There were three main approaches: the bridge from the Capitoline, the ramp that started just outside the Forum by the Pool of Juturna, and the walkway which began further along the Via Sacra by the Arch of Titus. There were other entrances, but they were private, and closely guarded. Ballista considered his options. All three of the public ways would be thronged with men heading up to pay their respects to the emperor at his morning salutation. Perhaps the busiest would be the path from the Arch of Titus. Of course there would be praetorians there as elsewhere, searching everyone for concealed weapons, but they would be near overwhelmed by the numbers. Respectable in a toga, with no blade to catch their attention, Ballista might slip through.

Ballista left the shelter of the portico, angled across to the Arch of Augustus, and out of the Forum. Rubbing shoulders with Sarmatians and Arabs, Jews and Aethiopians, as well as Romans, he walked down the Via Sacra.

He had passed the House of the Vestals and was by the Markets of Vespasian when he saw the helmets of the City Watch over the heads of the multitude. A squad of eight were heading towards him. They were scanning the crowd, but did not seem to have seen him so far. Hunching his shoulders, leaning forward to conceal his height, he went into the next opening of the markets.

The long, dark corridor smelt of spices and papyri and leather.

Behind him, he heard the distinctive hobnailed tread of the soldiers following into the market.

'Tell your future from your dreams?'

Ballista stopped. The dream diviner must have a good clientele. Most of his sort practised their art on street corners or on the pavements of marketplaces. This one could afford a small cubicle with a curtain.

The City Watch had not spotted him yet, but they were getting closer.

'The gods give us all foreknowledge in our sleep, but only a skilled practitioner can unravel their true meaning.'

Ballista almost bundled him into the cell, and drew the curtain behind them.

Unruffled by the eagerness of this client, the dream diviner announced his tariff. Ballista did not bargain, but fished out some coins from under his toga.

'Sit, and tell me your dream.'

There was no other way out. Ballista was unarmed, except for a staff. There were eight of them. If the City Watch pulled back the curtain, it was the end.

'Do not be reticent. A man cannot be blamed for his dreams.'

The clatter of military accoutrements was getting louder.

'I have heard all manner of things: men who dream of having sex with their mothers, with their sons and daughters, with animals and statues.'

Distracted, Ballista told the dream of the cross and the soldiers. He spoke in Greek, somehow imagining the City Watch would expect him to talk in Latin.

'Are you rich?'

They were right outside.

'What?'

'Are you a wealthy man?'

'No.'

They had stopped.

'That is good. Crucifixion signifies harm for rich men, since the crucified are stripped naked, and lose their flesh.'

The soldiers were not moving.

'But for a poor man it is auspicious. A crucified man is raised high, and substance is sufficient to feed many birds.'

The soldiers were talking outside the curtain. Ballista could not make out the words over the voice of the dream diviner.

'Such dreams signify honour and wealth. Are you a seafarer?'

'No.'

At last – Ballista hardly dared believe the evidence of his ears – they were leaving.

'A pity. For the cross, like a ship, is made of wood, and a mast resembles a cross.'

The sounds were receding. They were heading deeper into the markets.

'Where was the cross?'

'I do not remember.'

'The location can be important. In Greece a man dreamt that he was crucified in front of the Temple of Zeus . . .'

Ballista got up.

'For a bachelor, the dream means marriage, for the connection between the victim and the cross is a bond, but it will not be an easy one.'

Ballista peeped out of the curtain.

' . . . a cross prevents a man from setting his feet on the ground.'

The City Watch turned a corner, and were lost to sight.

'There is much more I can tell you.'

Ballista tossed him another coin. 'Forget you ever saw me.'

A steady stream of petitioners trudged up from the Arch of Titus towards the Palace. Sure enough, where the path narrowed at the Arch of Domitian ahead, Praetorians were taking their names, patting them down, confiscating fruit knives and styluses. Ballista stepped off the concourse into the portico of the temple on his left. It would be best to wait for a dense throng to come up from the Via Sacra.

Inconsequentially, it struck Ballista that he did not know to which deity the temple was dedicated. The huge edifice had been ordered by Heliogabalus for the black stone that he worshipped. When Heliogabalus was killed, his god had been evicted. The perverted youth was haunting Ballista today. Heliogabalus had been the very worst of emperors – degenerate, profligate and effeminate. Obsessed with his oriental god, after the civil war that won him the throne, he had never gone near the army. It was the weakness of the empire that anyone could become emperor. A vote by the senate and the new man or boy – no matter how unfitted for the position, no matter that he had murdered his way to power, or been clad in the purple by the schemes of devious courtiers – was as legitimate as his predecessor. It would never happen among Ballista's people.

The ruler of the Angles had to be of the blood of the Himlings. He had to be a warrior of proven worth, a leader of men.

Despite the talk in the bar last night, Ballista knew that Gallienus was a leader of men. Had he not led the cavalry charge that had shattered the horde of the Alamanni on the plains outside Milan? When the Persians captured his father, as revolts flared in many provinces, against all odds, Gallienus had held the empire together. Only last year, high in the Alps, he had defeated the forces of the pretender Postumus. Certainly Gallienus had ever distracted himself with drink and sex and philosophy. But, like Mark Antony, when duty called, he cast off his indolence and pleasures. Even now, in three days' time, he would set out to take the field, cross the mountains, and bring Gaul and the West back under his authority.

Ballista had faith in the friend of his youth who had risen to be Augustus. And yet the gossip of the bar troubled him. It was a truism that power corrupted. No matter how the Romans sought to disguise the reality, dress it up with talk of a first among equals, the fact remained that the emperor was an autocrat. His will was law. To his subjects he was either the gods' vicegerent on earth or he himself was a god; his power was untrammelled. Such power might change a man. Gallienus had been emperor for more than a decade.

'By order of his sacred majesty, Gallienus Augustus,' a herald proclaimed as walked down from the Arch, 'let no one who knows himself a law breaker come to pay his respects to the emperor, lest he be discovered, and receive capital punishment.'

A large party of equestrians were climbing the hill. The narrow purple stripes of their tunics shone in the early morning sunshine. Ballista slipped out, and joined the rear of their group.

The equestrians were talking about the Games in the Colosseum. Crescens the retarius had been induced to come out of retirement. He would be matched against Iaculator the myrmillo. Then there was the hippopotamus. What a spectacle, and there would be gifts. Say what you like about Gallienus, he had never been parsimonious. Ballista envied them their innocent chatter and anticipated pleasure.

They came to a halt. The praetorians were working fast, but there was a queue. There were at least a dozen guardsmen, in undress uniform: helmeted, with sheathed sword and dagger, but in tunics, without armour. They were overseen by a centurion, his belt resplendent with awards for valour. But it was another who caught Ballista's attention.

In the shadow of the arch, just behind the centurion, stood another soldier. This was no praetorian. His sword belt had no decorations, and he wore no helmet. He was more smartly turned out, but in every other respect like the men at the Mausoleum. Although they had been searched by the guardsmen, the soldier scrutinised every-one who passed under the arch. As if aware that he was observed, he glanced up. The soldier looked straight at Ballista, and recognition dawned on his face.

Turning away, downhill, Ballista was faced by a solid phalanx of men.

'There he is!' The shout was that of one accustomed to carry across the parade ground.

'Excuse me.' Ballista pushed between the first of those waiting. They looked surprised, but did not try to hinder him.

'Stop that man!'

Ballista shoved through the crowd. A man tried to catch his arm. Ballista shrugged him off.

'It is Ballista! There is a warrant for his arrest!'

Ballista hefted his staff. Those in front of him shied away. Ballista plunged into the space. But the crush was too great. The gap closed. He could make no headway. Over his shoulder, he could see the soldier and half a dozen guardsmen thrusting into the crowd.

'In the name of the emperor, clear the way!' Ballista's invocation of the commander of thirty legions had its effect. The crowd parted. No one ever wanted to stand against an imperial order.

'Stop that man! He is a murderer!'

At the soldier's shout, someone grabbed Ballista.

'Not me, you fool.' Ballista pushed him away. 'The man down there.' Ballista pointed towards the bottom of the path, in the general direction of the Arch of Titus.

Confused, the bystanders shuffled aside. In moments Ballista was clear of the worst of the press. Both staff and toga were impediments. He dropped the one, and unwound the other as he ran. The folds of the toga spooled out behind him on the pavement as he sprinted down the hill.

At the bottom, he risked a look back. The soldiers also were clear of the crush. No more than fifty paces behind, they were hot on his heels, intent on his capture.

Ballista turned left, retracing his steps toward the Forum. There were pedestrians in the Via Sacra. They promenaded in ones and twos, or small groups. Not slackening his pace, Ballista swerved around them. The sounds of pursuit at his back spurred him on. An unencumbered man in fear of his life should outrun soldiers burdened with weapons.

Emerging from the shade of the Arch of Augustus, Ballista was forced to skid to a halt. The Forum was packed. Everywhere men stood talking, or threaded their way slowly through the mass. The only open area was a little ahead, where the ringing of bells warned the multitude to draw back to let a religious procession pass on its stately progress. Not hesitating, Ballista launched himself into the teeming humanity. Sidestepping, folding his body into what spaces offered, using elbows and shoulders, he bored his way after the procession.

'Stop him!' The yells of the soldiers were lost in the calls of hawkers, the sound of the bells of the devotees of the deity, snatches of song and bursts of laughter, the general hubbub of thousands.

Ballista had almost reached the procession when he tripped and went sprawling. Two men solicitously aided him to his feet.

'Are you hurt?'

'No, I am fine.' His knees and the palms of his hands were grazed. The cut on his right hand had opened again, and the ankle he had twisted when he jumped from the balcony in the subura was throbbing.

'You took a nasty fall. Let us help you.'

'No, really. It is nothing.' *Allfather*. His ankle hurt.

The soldiers were breasting the crush, twenty paces away, no more.

Ballista thrust aside his would-be helpers.

'Health and great joy,' one called out after him, laughing.

A final titanic effort – civility abandoned, men staggering in his wake, cursing his back – and Ballista hobbled up to the rear of the worshippers. Most were women, but a few were men. He did not look totally out of place. No one questioned his presence.

In the meteor tail of devotees that followed the priestesses, Ballista was ushered across the Forum without check or halt. Looking back, he saw the soldiers trapped in the throng, like Laocoon and his children in the coils of the serpents. Injured ankle or not, they would never catch him.

The traditional gods still had power. Ballista remembered that it was the Kalends of April, the day the golden necklaces were taken from the statue of Vesta. The goddess was washed, her ornaments restored, and roses were placed at her feet. Now the vestal virgins would take the faded blooms to the Tiber, give them to the tawny waters to bear away.

At the far end of the Forum, near the Mamertine Prison, Ballista slipped from the procession, and set off north. As he walked, the pain in his ankle receded.

The great courtyard of the Forum of Trajan was as good a place as any to take stock. There were people about – slaves awaiting manumission, scholars heading to the library, the usual groups of sightseers – but there was room to move. Ballista leant against a column, by the apse on the western side. From there he could keep an eye on the main entrance.

There was no chance of getting into the Palace unaided. The praetorians had orders for his arrest. They were not the only ones watching for him. The cordon around Gallienus would be equally unbreachable as he processed to the Colosseum, and while he was watching the Games. Ballista would not get to the emperor without help. Where could he turn? The first hour of daylight had not yet run its course. The assassins would strike at sunset. There was time to walk to the house of Volcatius, and return with Maximus and Tarchon. If they were still away searching for him at the Praetorian Camp, Rikiar the Vandal and Grim the Lame, the other warriors who had followed him from the North, would be in his house-hold. But what good would it bring? With a couple of barbarians he would not be able to force his way into the imperial presence. Greater numbers would be no better. There was no point in going yet further afield to the camp of the emperor's German bodyguard.

Who else could he trust? Of course, there was Demetrius. But the Greek boy would be with Gallienus in the Palace. The rest of Ballista's friends were not in Rome. Tacitus was on his estates by the Danube, the other officers – Castricius, Rutilus and Aurelian – were with the army outside Milan. Ballista cudgelled his thoughts. If only he was not so tired.

A poem by Ovid came into his mind; not the words, but the import. It had been written in exile. As the poet could not make his way to the Palatine, his little book would have to make its way alone. A message – Ballista needed to find someone who could take a warning to Gallienus. But who? Ballista was on cordial enough terms with two or three senators. They might have invited him to dinner, but could he trust them? Gallienus had banned their order from military command. Would they run a risk to save the emperor? Might they not prefer to see him dead? Perhaps they were part of the conspiracy?

Who could he find to act as a messenger? It had to be a man of status. Someone hired from the street would not be admitted into the imperial presence. Julia had a cousin in Rome. Decimus Gallicanus had a house up on the Esquiline. It was no distance. But the young equestrian was far from a man of action. At times the noise of a symposium appeared to frighten the bookish youth.

Something in the scene before Ballista was not right. Abandoning his speculations, he scanned those in the courtyard. Over there, by the entrance – two men, civilian clothes, but military bearing. They were moving slowly out into the open space. They walked side by side. The eyes of one quartered to the left, the other to the right. They reminded Ballista of huntsmen drawing a covert, or army scouts searching for the enemy.

CHAPTER 15

The Forum of Trajan

THE TWO MEN WERE SOLDIERS, without question. They might wear dark tunics and civilian sandals, and carry no swords, but their every movement betrayed them. There was a measure, almost a swagger, in their tread. As he went along, one even twirled the strap end of his belt. Service under the eagles moulded a man, made him walk as if he feared no one, would beat to the ground anyone who stood in his way. If, like Ballista, you had spent the greater part of your life in the camps, it did not matter how they were dressed; you would never fail to recognise their type. He had known them at the Mausoleum, and he knew them now.

They were soldiers, and they were looking for someone. They advanced slowly, shoulder to shoulder, almost marching. Each scrutinised just his side of the Forum. It spoke of discipline and orders.

Ballista could see no others, neither behind them at the entrance to the Forum, nor coming down the western aisle in which he stood. He had no doubt that he could slip past these two, and in any case there were other ways out of the Forum. But it was always better to know the location of your enemy. Ballista remained where he was, leaning against a column.

The raking early morning sunshine played on green and yellow marble columns, dazzled from the white marble pavement. It threw long, black shadows ahead of the soldiers. This was a place of joy, where newly freed slaves wore the cap of liberty, where debtors saw their records burnt. The dark shapes of the soldiers were interlopers. It was a wonder that no one else who was milling about registered their incongruous air of menace. But, apart from Ballista, no one else was looking.

As they drew near, Ballista moved around the base of the column, so it blocked their line of sight. It was like a child's game of hide and seek, only with deadly intent.

Sure enough, they went by without spotting him. Intent on their task, at no point did they so much as glance back.

Ballista watched them go. They were dwarfed by their surroundings. Above the soaring columns larger-than-life statues of Dacian prisoners in white marble gazed down with resigned faces. From between the barbarians, busts of former emperors and empresses regarded everything with the detachment of the divine. Highest of all, etched against the sky, were the standards of the legions with which Trajan had conquered Dacia.

The soldiers halted at the foot of the steps that led up to the Ulpian Basilica at the north end of the Forum. They stopped to confer. Perhaps their orders had been unclear, or it could be that they were overwhelmed by the magnitude of their task. Soldiers always complain. How were just two of them expected to search the whole of the Forum? What about the basilica? Were they meant to search that too? And the libraries and the temple beyond? There were hundreds of people, all these slaves and freedmen, all these foreigners wandering about. How, by all the gods, were they expected to find one man? The description said he was tall and fair. Lots of men were tall, half the foreigners here were from the north. Hercules' hairy arse, this was hopeless.

At length, they finished their discussion. They split up, and set off, with the same steady, arrogant stride, towards the aisles that flanked the Forum. Most likely they had decided to give the basilica a miss and work their way back to the entrance.

Ballista moved quickly. A group of freedmen were walking down the aisle, coming back from the basilica. There were four of them escorting a fifth, who wore the cap of liberty. They were laughing and joking, embracing each other.

'I give you joy of your freedom,' Ballista said.

'Health and great joy to you, sir.'

The soldier had entered the far end of the aisle. Ballista had no time to waste.

'Last night in a dream Asclepius told me to come to this colonnade, and give money to the first man that I met who had just been manumitted.'

The newly freed slave beamed.

Ballista reached for his money. There was only a single wallet at his belt. What? Think about the missing one later. He took out the highest denomination coin that he could find.

'The god instructed me to ask the man to whom I gave the money for his cap of liberty.'

The freedman looked dubious. The cap was a powerful symbol, something for which he would have longed for years.

'Indulge me, I have not been well, citizen.' Ballista used the title deliberately.

The ex-slave eyed the gold in Ballista's palm. 'The gods must be obeyed,' he said. Everyone knew invalids were superstitious, and that the god of healing sent strange dreams. 'The clothes are not the man.'

The exchange was made.

'May Asclepius cure you.'

Ballista walked with them, indulging in small talk. Nothing of what was said registered. They were strolling, and, even at his deliberate step, the soldier was overhauling them. Thank the gods, he never looked further than those immediately around him.

When they came to where the curtain screened the great western apse, Ballista said farewell, and slipped inside. The soldier was some fifty paces off, peering at everyone that he passed.

Behind the hangings, in incense-pervaded gloom, a magistrate was holding court. With the litigants, the attendants, and a few spectators, there were twenty or so in the apse. Ballista took a place on a bench in the middle, jamming the soft cap down over his distinctive fair hair, slouched to disguise his height.

The soldier would check the courtroom. Ballista was unarmed, but the soldier would have no more than a knife. Ballista must deal with him before his companion could cross the Forum. There would be a commotion. Others might appear. Cross those bridges if he came to them.

Where had the second wallet gone? It must have been when he tripped in the Roman Forum. At least the thieves had not got both. By the hefty chink of the wallet still on his belt, he still had money enough. Perhaps a god had smiled on Ballista.

The water clock was running out, and the accuser brought his speech to a close.

In literature, court cases were exciting. The declamations of Ballista's schooling were full of pirates, exiles and murderers, of adultery, incest and rape. In reality they almost always turned out to be about money. This one seemed to concern a codicil to a will.

The defendant was droning on about his own good character. Witnesses – men themselves of respectable standing and unimpeachable virtue – would be summoned to testify to the truth of his statements.

The light changed as the curtain was pulled back. Ballista sensed the newcomer standing there, surveying the room. Time's arrow was arrested in its flight. The drip of the water clock was loud. Some of the audience shifted to look around. The defendant faltered in his oration.

'Enter the court, or leave.' The magistrate barely glanced up.

The heavy material fell back, and the defence resumed.

Ballista got up, and sidled out as inconspicuously as possible.

The soldier's back receded down the aisle.

Once again sheltered by a column, it took Ballista only a moment to pick out the other soldier, working his way in tandem down the opposite colonnade. Two men could not begin to search a busy complex the size of the Forum of Trajan. Whoever the hunters were, there were not enough of them to search a city the size of Rome.

When they reached the far end, they came together again, and stood conferring by the gate. Soon enough, after a final look around, they left.

As soon as they were gone, Ballista turned away, and walked to the basilica. Inside was a forest of columns. Yellow and grey, two stories high, they towered over the assembled throng. This also was a place of good omen. Here, from time to time, in carefully staged pageants, emperors would appear in their majesty. From their throne, godlike and philanthropic, they would distribute gifts to their loyal subjects, donatives to mark anniversaries and victories. Some of the latter were real, others invented when it was felt loyalty needed bolstering with hard currency. In the Hall of Liberty, off to the left, slaves won their freedom, and by granting it their masters proved their magnanimity to themselves and to the world.

Although there must be at least a hundred waiting, both servile and free, the vastness of the basilica made it seem almost untenanted. Ballista crossed the floor, his boots treading on intricate patterns of purple, yellow, red and black marble. Shipped from the furthest reaches of the empire – Numidia, Phrygia and Egypt – the stones asserted the universal dominion of Rome.

Taking one of the doors at the back, Ballista came out into the courtyard dominated by Trajan's Column. He turned left, and went into the imperial library devoted to Latin literature.

The attendant at the entrance gave him an odd look. Ballista pulled off the cap. A disguise which worked in one place drew attention in another. Why indeed would a slave just given liberty rush to consult a book?

Ballista went up to the second floor. He knew the library well from his youth. Its smell of cedar wood and papyrus and dust reminded him of leisure and safety, of losing himself in other worlds.

Surreptitiously stuffing the cap into a bookcase, he took a seat on the gallery that overlooked the column. A man had to be somewhere, and a library was not an obvious refuge for a fugitive. He was as safe here as anywhere. There were copies of Trajan's *Commentaries* on the tables, as there had been half a lifetime ago, when Ballista was young. He picked up one of them, unrolled it. To blend in, a man in a library should be reading or writing. Sarmizegethusa, Blandiana, Germisara, the litany of Dacian place names, and the dry prose could not hold his attention. He looked out of the window.

Trajan's Column had always puzzled Ballista. The great spiral of relief sculpture pictured the emperor's *Commentaries* of the campaigns. Yet, despite its artistry, the visual narrative was unreadable.

If you stood at the bottom, and looked up, no matter how sharp your eyesight, no matter how you craned your neck, you could not really make out the figures at the top. From where Ballista sat on the second floor, he could not see those at the base. And there was no way to follow the story as it wound around the column.

Ballista studied the side which faced him. Romans marched in order, they crossed bridges, built camps, defeated Dacians. Trajan was depicted at strategic points. Larger than the other figures, possessed of a god-like calm, he oversaw everything, but never himself had to fight. The message was evident: resistance was futile; Rome would always win; like a deity, the emperor was everywhere.

Long ago Ballista had attended a lecture here. The sophist had proposed a different reading. It had hinged on the barbarian allies who were pictured fighting for Rome. A foreigner viewing the column, the sophist had argued, would take an aspirational message. He would identify with an ascent from hostile savage to Roman ally, and from there on to regular auxiliary soldier, and finally to citizen legionary. *Why not*, Ballista thought, *on that logic, from legionary to officer, and on to senator, or even emperor?*

Ballista gazed at Dacians fighting courageously to the death, at men committing suicide rather than submitting, and – right at the top – at men, women and children fleeing their burning homes. As the historian Tacitus wrote, the Romans create a desert, and they call it peace. Some barbarians always would choose to become refugees, to lose everything before they lost their freedom.

To think in such a way, Ballista knew, would brand him in Roman eyes as an irredeemable barbarian, beneath rational thought, incapable of understanding the benefits of civilization and Roman rule, little better than an animal. Ballista knew that it was not true. After all these years in the empire, he was part Roman. No longer totally welcome in his homeland, yet still not fully accepted in the imperium, he was between two worlds, he stood out in both. For sure, here in Rome, he stood out physically. He needed to alter his appearance.

'Marcus?' The upper-class drawl was familiar.

'Is that you?' At least Julia's cousin had used his *praenomen*, and not called him Ballista.

'Health and great joy, Decimus.' There were people at the desks, some moving through the shelves; best if this was cut short.

'You look different.'

Not different enough, Ballista thought.

'What has happened to your hair? A society beauty would have paid a fortune for your long, blonde locks.'

'What are you doing here, Decimus?'

The young equestrian made a self-deprecating gesture. 'Oh, you know, still writing. Would you like to hear my latest poem?'

Before Ballista could frame a polite refusal, think of a way to extricate himself, his wife's relative began to recite.

Grey Time moves silently, and creeping on
Steals the voices of articulate humans

'Now I had trouble with the next lines.'

Obscure himself, he hides illustrious men
And brings to light men who have been obscure.

The recitation was drawing attention. One or two scholars were looking up from their scrolls with irritation.

'You see the play on obscurity?'

O unforeseen finish of men's lives,
Who daily always advance towards the dark.

An idea occurred to Ballista. This chance meeting could be turned to advantage.

'I think the ending works well.'

'Decimus ...'

'It is one of a cycle on mortality—'

'Decimus.' Ballista got up, took his arm, and led him to a secluded alcove. 'Are you alone?'

'Yes, but—'

Ballista held up a hand to silence him. 'Have you got writing materials?'

'My secretary has, you remember Felix? I set him free last year. Were you at the party? No, of course, you were away.'

'Would you get them?'

'Of course, let me call him.'

'No, please bring them yourself. I do not want anyone to know that I am here.'

Decimus rolled his eyes. 'How deliciously mysterious. Not an affair? Should I help you? What would Julia say?'

'Please.'

'A moment.' Decimus walked off, throwing an arch look over his shoulder, like an actor in a mime.

Julia's cousin was a harmless innocent. His life consisted of a round of dinner parties and recitations, nothing more dangerous than the occasional trip to a rowdy theatre. It was wrong to involve him. Ballista would put him in as little danger as possible. Although ignorance might prove no protection.

'Here we are.'

'I need you to take a message for me.'

'So I gathered.' Decimus smiled. 'At least tell me her name.'

'It is not a woman.'

'Not a boy?'

'No, not a boy.'

'I am consumed by curiosity.'

Ballista opened the wooden block. He hesitated, the stylus poised over the smooth wax. There was no time for style or amplitude, and no point in subterfuge. He shielded the diptych from Decimus with his back, and wrote, his practised hand impressing the characters quickly but with clarity.

Ballista send greetings to Gallienus Augustus.

There is a plot to assassinate you as you leave the imperial box of the Colosseum at sunset today. Scarpio, the Prefect of the City Watch, is part of the conspiracy. There are others, I do not know who, but they must be close to you. One is bald, another is said to look like a peasant.

Take all precautions. Trust no one, except the German Guard.

The bearer of this message knows nothing. I will try and come to you.

Ballista shut the diptych, snapped the hinges closed.

'Decimus, do not read this.'

'My dear, I am the soul of discretion.'

'Take this to the Palace. In the vestibule ask for Demetrius the secretary. Tell him that it must reach the emperor.'

There was a look of horror on the equestrian's face. 'The Palace? Marcus, I want nothing to do with the Court. It is far too dangerous. You know I never go near the Palatine. We have estates in Gaul. Some of our relatives are with Postumus. It is not safe. I really do not know . . .'

Ballista gripped his shoulders, looked into his eyes. 'You know nothing. You will be safe. Just deliver the message to Demetrius. He will do the rest. Hand it to the Greek boy, and leave.'

'But . . .' Decimus stumbled over his words, as he sought a way out. 'An affair is one thing, but . . .'

Ballista held him tight. 'Decimus, as you love your cousin, do this thing for her.'

'Well, if I must. Just hand over the message, and leave?'

'Just hand over the message, and leave.'

Ballista released him.

'What did happen to your hair?'

'Another time. Please, just go.'

CHAPTER 16

The Markets of Trajan

THE STREET CHILD WAS SITTING on the pavement.

'Do you want to earn some coins?'

The boy looked at Ballista with suspicion, his eyes too knowing for his years.

'I am going into that barbershop.' Ballista got out a bronze coin. 'Let me know if you see the City Watch coming this way, or anyone else who looks suspicious. Keep an eye out for any soldiers trying to pass themselves off as civilians. There are two more coins for you, when I leave.'

The child smiled. Under the dirt and the deprivation, he was beautiful. 'I knew you were up to no good, as soon as I saw you.'

'I value my privacy.'

'But I thought you were after something else with me. Tell you what, five more coins and you can meet my sister. Nice and private up in her room.'

'That would be delightful, but perhaps another time.'

Ballista had walked past the barbershop twice already. It opened directly off the walkway, and there did not appear to be another way out, but there was a flight of stairs up to the next level of shops a few paces deeper into the labyrinth of the market.

'Be with you in a moment, sir. Do take a seat.'

The shop smelt of lotions and singed hair. Apart from the barber and his client, there was a young assistant, and two elderly men playing dice. Ballista sat on a bench from where he could see the urchin squatting outside.

On the wall behind the barber hung the main tools of his trade; the curling irons, combs, scissors and razors. Ancillary items – perfumes, creams, dyes, patches, the latter all too often required – were arranged on a shelf.

'Do you think your boy could go and buy some things for me while I wait?'

'Of course, sir. He would be delighted.'

'A small flask of wine for me, and another for these gentlemen here.'

The old idlers muttered their thanks. That was civil of him, indeed.

Ballista handed over some money, then added that he had lost his knife, and needed another; a decent-sized blade, something that could cut twine, not a little fruit knife.

When the assistant had left, Ballista closed his eyes. He wanted a real blade, but, if he intended to pass for a civilian, it was better that he had not asked the boy to buy him one. It was illegal for any except the military to carry a sword in Rome. It was not technically against the law to carry a sword for hunting or self-defence. But opportunities for hunting might be considered limited in the metropolis, and admitting that you needed a weapon to defend yourself raised difficult questions.

Ballista was tired. The sounds of the street were muted. The client must have asked to have his hair cut in silence. There was only the click, click of the dice, and the occasional murmur and grunt of the players.

Julia's cousin had given his word, but would he go to the Palatine? Decimus had looked terrified. He might be a dandy – a poet, not a man of action, he had never done military service – but he was not a fool. To take a secret message to the emperor was not something that anyone would undertake lightly. The closed writing block could contain nothing except a denunciation. *This man is a traitor.* Decimus must be wondering why Ballista could not deliver it himself. Even if Decimus plucked up his courage, did not find some excuse to delay, or abandon the unwelcome task, it was far from certain that the message would reach the emperor. Demetrius had access to Gallienus. The Greek youth was not just an imperial secretary, but a former lover of the emperor. Gallienus always had shown consideration to those who had shared his bed. Yet the approaches to the Palatine were closely watched. The message might never reach Demetrius. If Julia's cousin was intercepted carrying the message, neither Scarpio, nor the unknown knifemen from the Mausoleum, would believe that he did not know its contents. Ballista did not want the torture and death of Decimus on his conscience. Enough bad things weighed on that sensibility already.

The room and the street outside seemed very distant. Ballista's head felt light, his thoughts swimming away, until just one remained. He could not rely on Decimus. Somehow he would still have to warn Gallienus himself.

Ballista snapped awake when the assistant returned. Despite everything, he must have fallen asleep. He was more tired than he had realised. It was not merely lack of sleep. He had seen soldiers so fast asleep before battle that they could hardly be roused, even with a kick. A retreat into fatigue deadened fear seemed in a way to remove a man from danger.

The boy handed Ballista the knife, with some change, and distributed the two flasks.

Ballista tucked the knife in his belt, and took a swig of wine. It was strong, flavoured with resin, surprisingly good.

The barber was brushing down his customer. 'Let me sweep the floor, sir, and I will be ready for you.'

Ballista stretched, and looked outside. The urchin was still watching the entrance to the market. Ballista went and sat on the stool.

'What can I do for you, sir?'

'Shave my head.'

One of the geriatric dice players laughed. 'You thinking of joining an eastern cult? A bald head won't be enough. To be one of the Galloi, you have to have your balls off.'

'Don't mind old Gnaeus, sir. Always thought himself a comedian.' The barber spread a napkin over Ballista's shoulders. 'Shave it is, sir. The face too?'

'Leave the stubble.'

The assistant brought a bowl of hot water from the brazier at the back of the shop.

'Take care, Barber, I don't want to end up looking like a man married to a bad tempered woman with sharp nails.'

'Have no fear, sir. I have been doing this all my life, man and boy. Any little nicks, and we have plenty of spider's webs soaked in oil and vinegar.'

The barber arranged a warm and damp towel over Ballista's head. 'Those stories are all the wrong way around. Men who cannot control their wives blame their barber. Not that it is easy to keep any woman in her place.'

The whetstone and the razor were produced. The barber spat on the former, and set to putting an edge on the steel. 'You see all those tombstones boasting the dead woman's virtues. *She was chaste and modest, frugal and sober, good natured and hard working; first to rise from her bed, and last to return.* Maybe back in the day, back when Hannibal was at the gates. Perhaps back then poverty kept women chaste, hard work and little sleep kept them honest, put callouses on their hands.'

The towel was removed, and the barber made the first pass with the razor.

'But now they sit around all day, won't take a turn at the loom. If you don't put a lock on the storeroom, they will drink all your wine, spend all your hard-earned savings. If you try and stop them, they give you what for, answer back, try and scratch your eyes out. Blessed relief it was when my wife died.'

'Had her carried to the pyre on a shield, he did.' Gnaeus had looked up from his game. 'You know why?' The old man was laughing so much he could hardly get the answer out. 'Because she always liked a battle.'

Ballista hoped that the barber, given what he was doing, did not join in the senile hilarity.

'At a woman's funeral, a stranger asks, "Who is resting here?"' Gnaeus was enjoying himself. '"I am," says the widower, "now I have got some peace."'

'That is enough, Gnaeus. That joke was old when Nestor was a boy. The gentleman does not want to hear you prattling on.'

The barber was taking his time with the shaving. That was good. The street boy was still watching outside. There was no particular hurry.

'And as for their superstitions. My old woman was always running off to some cult or other.' Evidently the barber preferred his own monologues to his friend's witticisms. 'If it wasn't bad enough with Cybele and the rest of those eastern mysteries, now there are those fucking Christians. Who knows what they get up to? I heard they meet in a shuttered room, just the one light, and they tie a dog to the lampstand. They throw in a piece of meat, the dog pulls over the lamp, out goes the light, and then they can all fuck each other in the dark; brothers and sisters, fathers and daughters, no one any the wiser.'

The barber gestured for the assistant to wet Ballista's head again.

'You married, sir?'

'No.' Even Odysseus had not denied that he had a wife. Once you started to lie, it got easier. Perhaps after a time, it became second nature.

'Those Jews are no better with women ...'

Ballista stopped listening to the litany of misogyny and religious prejudice. He wondered what had happened when Maximus and Tarchon had reached the Praetorian Camp last night. They were hard men, they could look after themselves. But he had thought the same about Calgacus. When this was over, he would not rest until he found Hippothous. He would scour the empire. One day, maybe not soon, but one day, he would find Hippothous, and then he would revenge Calgacus, or die in the attempt. But first he must save the emperor. If Gallienus died ... Ballista would not think about Julia and his sons.

'What does a woman care when she is drunk? She drains the cup of undiluted wine, the room spins, the lights blur, and she opens her legs for anyone. Every one of them is a whore at heart.'

'They can't help it.' The other dice player spoke for the first time. 'It is bad for their health not to get fucked. If the womb is dry, it contracts, gives them pain. A good fuck heats the blood, helps the menses flow.'

The barber shook his head. 'Spurius here fancies himself a doctor.'

'He would never make a doctor,' Gnaeus said. 'For one thing, he is not Greek, and for another, not all his patients might die.'

'Laugh all you like,' Spurius said, 'but if they don't get it, they go off their heads. Some of them throw themselves down wells.'

'Worst of all is if you try to educate them.' This was his shop, and the barber intended to control the conversation. 'As soon as you sit down to dinner, she is weighing the merits of Homer and Virgil, blaming Aeneas for the suicide of Dido. An avalanche of words, like pans and pots being beaten. No one can get in a word, not even an auctioneer, or another woman. If you do get to speak, she will correct your grammar.'

With a flourish, the barber removed the napkin, and produced a mirror. 'See, sir, not so much as a scratch.'

Ballista stared at the apparition in the mirror. His scalp was very white, with pink blotches where the razor had scraped too close. He was unconvinced by the efficacy of the disguise. The reflection still looked like him, but with no hair.

As he paid the barber – *By the gods, the profession was a licence to coin money* – he saw a movement outside. The urchin had got to his feet, and was coming to the shop.

'Not in here, you don't, you thieving little bastard.'

The boy ignored the barber. 'They are coming,' he said to Ballista.

There would be no delay before the disguise was put to the test.

'What about my money?'

Without looking, Ballista gave the boy a couple of coins.

'You really should have gone to see my sister.'

The barber and his cronies looked expectant. They sensed entertainment, something which might provide gossip for months. Trying to exhibit no haste, Ballista bade them good day, squared his shoulders, and left.

A troop of eight of the City Watch were at the entrance out on the street. Axes on shoulders, buckets in hand, they entered the market. It could be just routine, a check that no one had infringed the fire regulations. Ballista turned left, away from them. The concourse was busy with shoppers. It was difficult to walk normally, as if he did not have a care.

'Stop! You with the shaved head, stop!'

Ballista kept walking. The disguise had failed at the first test.

'Halt, in the name of the emperor!'

Ballista ran, sidestepping shoppers, using his shoulders and weight to force his way through.

The calls of hawkers gave way to shouts. The confined space filled with cries of alarm from those strolling, peremptory commands from those in pursuit. At the foot of the stairs, Ballista glanced back. The City Watch were blundering down the concourse. They were impeded by their reluctance to abandon their equipment; every lost bucket or axe would come out of their pay. Shifting from foot to foot, starting for gaps, then swerving as they closed, they seemed reluctant to knock citizens to the ground. Each collision with a shopper and misstep into each other's way allowed Ballista to leave them further behind.

Ballista took the wide stairs two at a time. Emerging onto the next level of shops, he saw another stairwell opposite. Without pause, he hurled himself across. These stairs were dark, lit just by occasional light wells. They were narrow, the bare bricks on either side nearly brushing his shoulders. Halfway up, they turned, and Ballista collided with a man coming down. Picking himself up, without a word, Ballista scrambled over the prone, expostulating figure and resumed his ascent.

The stairs seemed to go on forever. All Ballista could hear was his own ragged, panting breathing, the thud of his boots. Suddenly he was out on the highest level. Here the shops were splashed with colour. Shafts of sunlight angled down from between the arches that spanned the open roof. He turned left, ran back towards where the entrance to the market was way below. There was only a handful of shoppers this high up. Some of them stopped, and stared as he raced past. Others studiously ignored him as being none of their concern.

In moments he was at the other end of the arcade. The gods had been kind. As he had hoped, there was a matching staircase at this end. It was very dark going out of the sunlight. Ballista crept down, going fast, but trying to step softly, fighting to control his laboured breathing. If the gods continued to smile on him, he could get down these stairs while the City Watch laboured up the others. If he could come out behind them, he should be able to slip out of the markets into the street.

A clatter of hobnail boots echoed up the passageway, around the corner, and ended his tender hopes. At least two of the Watch were coming up. As silently as he could, Ballista retraced his steps to the top.

Dazzled by the bright light, Ballista looked around wildly. There was nowhere else to go but the roof. He could see no way up. Ballista burst into the nearest shop. A small cubicle, stairs to a platform, where the shopkeeper probably slept. No other doors, no access to the roof. Ballista grabbed the merchant by the front of his tunic.

'How do you get on the roof?'

The man goggled at him, surprised beyond speech.

Ballista shook him. 'The roof?'

The merchant pointed, and stammered there was a ladder next door.

The City Watch still had not reached this level, but the sounds of their approach were loud; yells, curses, the rattle of weapons.

The adjoining shop was a clothes seller. The proprietor was showing a woman a robe. Ballista pushed them out of the way. The woman screamed as she fell. A ladder at the rear of the shop, a trap-door at the top. Ballista swarmed up the rungs, put his shoulder to the wooden boards, and climbed out onto the flat roof.

He was on the roof of the markets nearest the Forum of Trajan. Forcing himself to be calm, he stood still. His eyes roved over the surrounding buildings, measuring and judging the rooftops. There must be a way to escape. Nothing offered towards the Forum, just a sheer drop to the Via Bibracte. It had to be towards the Quirinal Hill. Across the markets, over the neighbouring offices and tenements. There must be a way down over there.

The arches that spanned the hall of the upper market were no more than two feet wide. Ballista went to the closest. No reason to fall, but best not to look down. Carefully, arms held out on either side for balance, he stepped onto the impromptu bridge.

The thump of the trapdoor opening made him look around. The helmet of a watchman appeared. The sudden movement had unbalanced Ballista. He swayed precariously, arms flailing.

'There! After him!'

Before he had fully recovered, Ballista started to run. One false step would send him cartwheeling down into the arcade. The narrow stones seemed to stretch to eternity. Off balance, he could feel himself starting to topple forward. Just as his boots went from under him, he staggered and half fell onto the opposite roof.

The roof was strung with washing lines, divided by low walls. Picking himself up, Ballista set off. Ducking under flapping garments, hurdling the walls, he glanced back. One by one, like creatures in a fable, the City Watch were edging across the arch after him. They had got rid of their buckets and axes. Firemen as much as soldiers, the bastards were used to scaling buildings. No praetorian would have made that crossing.

Having cleared the last wall, Ballista slackened his pace. With each hand he snatched a small cloth from the next washing line. As he ran, he twirled them around his hands. Behind him the watchmen were crashing through the clotheslines.

The roof ended in a drop taller than a man down to another flat roof. No time to lower himself – Ballista jumped. He landed on both feet and rolled forward onto his hands, tumbling to dispel the force. The cloths protected his palms from the rough plaster.

As he got to his feet, a cat, sunning itself, hissed and darted away. Ballista envied its assurance in its aerial domain.

This roof ended in a blank wall. Eight or nine feet above was the gutter of a taller, sloping roof. Ballista adjusted the cloths so they were wrapped around his palms, leaving his fingers free. Then he ran as fast as he could, and jumped. Banking on the wall with his right boot, he hooked his forearms over the gutter. There was a loud crack. He swung his left leg up onto the roof. The gutter shifted. Somehow he fought his way onto the tiles, before the gutter gave way, and smashed into a thousand shards on the roof below.

The incline was gentle, and, clasping the edges of the tiles, Ballista scrambled up to the ridgeline. On his knees, one either side, he looked back. There were six of the City Watch still in the chase. Perhaps the others were guarding the buckets and axes. Better that than going for help, or raising the alarm. The watchmen were boosting each other up onto the tiles. These were men inured to heights. They had no intention of abandoning the pursuit.

Like a monkey, running on hands and feet, Ballista went along the line of the ridge. A loose tile slipped out from under his left boot. A surge of pain in his damaged ankle. He thumped flat on his face, had to grab the apex of the roof before he started to slide. Infernal gods, his ankle hurt. *Not now, of all times.*

The watchmen were following, cautious, but relentless; some fifty paces behind.

Pain was an irrelevance. He forced himself up. If he were to save Julia and his sons, he had to get off this roof. Limping, he pushed on.

Ballista had not been able to see this far from the roof of the market. He had been sure that there would be a roof garden, or a skylight, perhaps some lower buildings by which to descend. There was nothing, just the expanse of red tiles. A couple of cross roofs ran out to the left. But they ended at a street, and the Via Bibracte still lay below the slope to his right.

At the end of the roof, Ballista skidded to a halt. There was an adjoining building below. Some forty feet below. No way down. *Do not panic. Just think.* The Via Bibracte was wide, too wide to jump. It had to be the other street.

Ballista set off the way he had come.

The leading man of the Watch shouted in exultation.

Ballista reached the first cross roof. He scuttled along it to the end. The street was a narrow ravine. The pavement perhaps seventy feet down. There was no convenient balcony or column, let alone a ladder. But the opposite building was set lower. A gap of say five or six paces, a fall of maybe fifteen feet.

Ballista stood, and turned. The City Watch were at the other end of the jutting-out ridge. One foot either side of the apex, Ballista walked towards them.

'That is it, there is no way down.'

Counting each step, Ballista did not reply.

'Give yourself up.'

Ballista stopped, facing them. The sky was very blue. Gulls screamed up here above the city.

The nearest watchman held out his hand, as if encouraging a nervous horse to come.

Ballista turned. He took a deep breath.

Woden Allfather, do not let the ankle betray me. Do not think, just act.

'Don't be a madman!'

Ballista started to run.

Five paces, six. The chasm getting closer. Nine, ten, and jump.

The vertiginous plunge ended in a sickening impact. Ballista's midriff hit the edge of the roof. The breath punched out of his chest, he scrabbled for a hold. He was slipping. His boots could find no purchase on the wall. He grabbed a tile. It came away, went spinning out into the abyss. The next tile also gave. Another moment, and he would be gone. He thrust his right hand down into the hole. His fingers curled around a batten. He hung, suspended. His own weight tearing at his arm, threatening to pull his shoulder out of its joint. Ripping away another tile, he got his other hand on a beam. Straining every sinew, he hauled himself up onto the roof.

Ballista lay, not daring to move. Angry shouts rose from the street below. Falling tiles were a constant danger in Rome.

He could not stay here. When he tried to move, he found that his arms and legs were shaking, his muscles rigid, locked with fear. *Do not think, just act. Get off this roof.*

Spreadeagled, belly to the tiles, Ballista inched up the slope. At the top, he hung over the ridge.

One of the City Watch was taking off his helmet.

'Don't do it.' Ballista tried to shout, but his voice was little more than a croak.

The man did not respond.

'Don't be a fool. You have done your duty.'

Now the watchman looked at him. 'There is a big reward on you.'

'Not enough to die for.'

'A man has to make his way in this world.'

The other watchmen were trying to talk him out of it, holding his arms. He shrugged them off, gestured them out of his way.

Ballista had to stop him. 'This will end in tragedy. Think of your wife.'

The watchman actually smiled. 'Not married. When I have the money, I can get any wife, anything I want.'

'One of us will die.'

'If it is you, I still get the reward.'

The watchman turned and paced out his run.

Ballista watched in horror as he set off.

Like a ghastly enactment of the myth of Icarus, the man fell through the air.

Ballista was sliding down before the man hit the roof. He had landed in the same place as Ballista. Like Ballista, only his arms and chest were on the roof, his legs dangling out into the precipice. As Ballista reached him, the watchman got a grip on the exposed woodwork.

Face contorted with effort, the man started to pull himself up.

Ballista could not do this. *Allfather, why did you not make him fall?* That was the thought of a *nithing*, a coward. Ballista thought of Julia, of his sons. He stamped his boot down on the man's hand. He heard the knuckles break.

Hanging by his one good hand, the man did not fall. As his useless hand scrabbled at the roof, he looked up at Ballista.

'Help me.'

'You made your choice.'

Ballista brought his boot down on the other hand.

CHAPTER 17

The Street of the Sandal Makers

GETTING OFF THE ROOF WAS EASY, compared with what had happened before. Ballista found a light well on the far side of the ridge. He levered the frame loose with his knife, and kicked the wood and glass to pieces. Despite the noise, no one came out onto the uppermost landing. Wriggling through, he avoided as far as possible the remaining shards of jagged glass. Ballista hung full length from his hands for a moment, then dropped down.

Getting back to his feet, he took care brushing the slivers of glass off his clothes. He was not cut, and the tunic was only a little torn. He unwound the strips of material from his hands. Still no one appeared. Ballista made his way down the several flights of stairs. There was no sign of a caretaker on the ground floor. Perhaps the sounds of violent destruction and heavy boots cautioned the inhabitants to remain behind bolted doors.

Ballista emerged two streets from the Markets of Trajan. There was no time to waste, but he hesitated in the doorway. The subura was close, and he could go to ground there. But that was where they would search, and hiding in that maze would not get him to the emperor, or save his family. He turned right, away from the slums.

Merchants selling the same goods often congregated in certain streets; jewellers along the Via Sacra, perfume sellers in the Vicus

Tuscus. But such merchants tended to cater for expensive tastes in luxury items. For the ease of local residents in a city the sheer size of Rome, most streets contained a heterogeneous mixture of traders, side by side without theme, selling all manner of merchandise. Ballista walked past butchers, cobblers, bakers and vintners. It was not until he was opposite the rear wall of the Forum of Augustus that he came across a shop selling clothes.

Before entering, he checked his money. So far he had lost several wallets, and spent freely from this one. The young man he had taken it from last night had been rich, but the coins were getting depleted. Still, there were enough for Ballista's present purpose, and later, if he needed more, he had a knife, so could always get another wallet. Perhaps life in the army had conditioned him for taking whatever he wanted without payment. Once a man on trial had been asked why he had become a bandit. In reply he had asked why his questioner had become Praetorian Prefect. Some held that all power amounted to little more than theft. Certainly it was an accusation that had often been levelled at the Roman empire.

The shopkeeper had none of the hauteur of those whose main trade was with the nobility. Ballista bought a blue tunic, a hooded Gallic cloak in dark green – one of those from which the Emperor Caracalla had acquired his nickname – and a broad-brimmed travelling hat, all new. He changed in the shop, and told the merchant that he could keep his old tunic; either repair and launder the garment, and add it to his stock, or sell the thing to a ragman. When he asked for nothing off the bill, his generosity was praised fulsomely. Ballista looked himself over in the mirror. By now the City Watch would be hunting a man with a shaven head in a grimy white tunic. In the distorted reflection, Ballista saw a man wearing immaculate apparel of different colours, and whose lack of hair could be hidden in two ways. He settled for the hat, pulling the brim low.

'May the gods hold their hands over you, sir.'

'And over you.'

When Ballista left, immediately a press of people forced him back against the wall.

'Make way for the Lady Iunia Fadilla.'

Three burly Aethiopians were clearing a path for a litter carried by eight more slaves.

Ballista waited quietly. The streets were still crowded, even though by this time some fifty thousand or more Romans would be crammed inside the Colosseum.

The progress of the litter was stately. Its occupants not to be jostled by any unseemly haste. Ballista knew of this Iunia Fadilla from his wife. It was one of Julia's favourite stories, a contemporary example of the underappreciated resources of women. As a descendant of Marcus Aurelius, Iunia had been married off to the vicious son of the Emperor Maximinius the Thracian. Iunia had run away from her husband's brutality. Somehow, in disguise, and almost alone, this delicate, imperial princess had made her way across the high country of Dalmatia in the midst of a civil war to reach the Adriatic and safety. It was hard to see anything of the beautiful, wild girl that had shown such daring, and braved such dangers, in the plump matron who reclined on embroidered cushions talking to a younger woman, who might well be her daughter.

Apparently, much later, Iunia had wed a dull, wealthy senator called Toxotius. Ballista did not condemn her life of quiet conjugal affluence and ease. It was all he wanted for himself.

The litter passed, and the crowd thinned as it spread again across the street. Ballista remained stock still, like Socrates struck by some philosophic speculation. The house of Decimus was not far, up on the Esquiline. As the husband of the master's cousin, the door would be open to Ballista. He could go there, and wait the return of Decimus from the Palatine. No, it would not do. If anything it would put Decimus in greater danger. And, of course, Ballista could not rely on the message that he had given Decimus reaching the emperor.

Ballista looked up at the sky above the great, blank wall of the back of the Forum of Augustus. He could not see the sun, but judged it to be about the end of the third hour of the day. By now Gallienus would have left the Palace, would be on his way to the Games. Perhaps he had already arrived. Ballista would have to go to the Colosseum. Somehow he must come up with a plan to gain access to the imperial box. There were less than nine hours left. Ballista needed somewhere quiet and secure to think.

The idea came fully formed, as if put into his mind by a god. The Baths of Trajan opened early. Thousands of people would be bathing, taking massages, listening to lectures and recitals, or just eating and talking. There could be no better place to lay low, and plan his next move. Almost with a spring in his step, he set off.

There had not been a cobbler on the Street of the Sandal Makers in living memory. The pedestrians here wore good shoes, and were well dressed. Most were customers of the booksellers that lined the street. Ballista had spent much time here in his youth.

Down the street children played around a man who was singing. Ballista stopped, and pretended to study some scrolls set out on the pavement. He looked back the way he had come. There was nothing out of the ordinary.

Not far now. Past the Forum of Peace and the Temple of Venus and Rome, up the steps to the Esquiline, and a short walk would bring him to the Baths of Trajan. Once there, he would be overlooking the Colosseum, no distance from his goal. He could blend in with those taking their leisure, and plot how on earth he would get into the amphitheatre, let alone the imperial box.

The children's laughter and cries were louder. They had a sharp and mocking edge. Now and then one of the children would dart forward, and spit at the singer.

Sabarbath, Sabarbathiuoth. The man's song was tuneless, its words without meaning.

A passer-by stopped, and put his thumb between his fingers to ward off evil.

Someone threw a stone. It hit the singer on the shoulder, and he stumbled. *Sabarbioneth.* His eyes unfocused, he continued to sing.

'Poor Lucius.' The passer-by addressed Ballista. 'He was a stone-mason, as sane as the next man. One day he was standing outside a tavern, when a black dog stood in front of him and yawned. Lucius yawned too, he could not help himself. The dog vanished, and the daemon leapt down Lucius' throat. His family paid for an exor-cism. It did not work, and they threw him out. Now he wanders the streets.'

Sabarbaphai. The madman and his cruel entourage went on towards the subura.

Watching them go, something struck Ballista as wrong. Those on the street either looked at the demented stonemason, or went about their business, studiously ignoring his passage. Except one short man whose eyes were fixed on Ballista. Realising his atten-tion was noticed, the man quickly turned away, and hurried into a bookshop.

Ballista waited. The man did not come out. For sure he was not a member of the City Watch, and nothing about him spoke of service in the military. His thin, ratty appearance did not suggest a love of books.

Then again, many bibliophiles were down at heel. People liked to browse. It might be nothing, a casual meeting of eyes misinterpreted. If this went on much longer, Ballista thought, he might end up as mad as the stonemason.

Striding out, although not so fast as to draw comment, Ballista came level with the Forum of Peace. On the other side of the street was an eating house with a painting of a lyre on its sign. Ballista went in, and found a seat from which he could watch the street. He ordered some bread and cheese, and a jug of well-watered wine. Before the food arrived, he saw the seedy little man.

A little too casually, his follower glanced into the Lyre as he passed.

Ballista took a drink, eyes on the street. People went to and fro. None of them were out of the ordinary, except for a priest of the goddess Isis, clad in linen robes, and wearing a mask over his face fashioned like the head of a dog. It was really no wonder people like Diomedes and the brigands on the Campus Martius saw them as alien.

All too soon, sure enough the short man retraced his steps, again peering into the eating house.

Ballista ate his food quickly, paid up, and went to the doorway. The little man was some way off to the right, leafing through some papyri. Ballista waited until a group of fashionably dressed young men blocked the little man's view of the eating house, and walked away.

As Ballista neared the statue of Apollo Sandaliarius, the street was crowded. He ducked behind the base of the statue.

A moment later the now familiar figure hustled past. Not being tall, the shabby man bobbed from side to side, trying to see around those in front.

Making sure that he was not observed, Ballista marched into the nearest bookshop.

'Health and great joy, sir.'

'And to you.'

Apart from the bookseller, there were two customers. The latter were in close conversation towards the rear of the shop.

'Are you looking for anything in particular?'

Ballista took off his hat. 'The *Encomium on Hair* by Dio of Prusa would be fitting.'

The bookseller smiled. 'One of his minor works, I am afraid that I do not have it. But I do have a copy of his *Trojan Oration*, on clean papyrus, in a fine hand.'

'If I may, I will see what catches my eye.'

'Of course, sir.'

The short man had not reappeared, and Ballista edged away from the door.

'You may be just the man we are looking for, good sir.'

The two customers wore elegant Greek mantles over spotless tunics. The one who had spoken sported a neat, trimmed beard, and short hair. His powerful physique was evidently the result of hard training. The other was more slender, with artfully curled hair. He was clean-shaven, and his cheeks showed the trace of cosmetics.

'My handsome friend here,' the bearded one continued, 'is from Corinth, and that city, notorious for the beauty and skill of its courtesans, is the cause of his obsession with women. You note how he employs curling tongs and depilation to make himself attractive to them.'

The Corinthian laughed. 'Whereas this hirsute man of Sparta is a devotee of the wrestling grounds, although only to watch the boys oiled and naked. To put an end to our contentious and inconclusive quibbling over which love is better, we would debate the issue in an orderly way. We need a man of culture and learning to act as judge.'

'You, sir,' the Spartan said, 'demonstrated such attributes just now with your witty reference to that Dio whose eloquence won him the title of the Golden-mouthed.'

'Forgive me,' Ballista said, 'I have little time.'

The Spartan took Ballista's arm in a manly grip. 'We will keep our speeches short. There is a back room for privacy, and I am sure that our host will offer us refreshments.'

Beware Greeks bringing gifts, Ballista thought. But among his people there was another saying, never look a gift horse in the mouth.

The door of the back room shut behind them. As they settled themselves on couches, the bookseller bustled about, ordering one of his slave boys to bring them olives, while himself pouring wine. These Greeks were valued customers indeed.

'You should draw lots to decide who should speak first.'

They did as Ballista had suggested, and the Corinthian won.

'Aphrodite, help my advocacy. You, goddess of love, plead the cause of womankind.' The Corinthian pushed some ringlets from his forehead. 'The love of man for woman is natural and ordained by the gods. Aphrodite herself imbued both sexes with desire for the other. The intercourse of man and woman preserves humanity by an undying succession.'

Over his years in the empire Ballista had listened, not always willingly, to the speeches of many Sophists. The words flowed over him. It was a lesson of office to appear attentive, while the mind moved elsewhere. By the time that this was over, the shifty little man should be long gone. Rome was full of informers. There must have been a proclamation. Most likely it had included a description. Either the new garments and headgear had not provided an adequate transformation, or the short man had already known Ballista. The latter was quite possible. Ballista had commanded armies, served on the imperial council. On his return from the North, he had appeared beside Gallienus at the Circus. If it was the former, there was little to be done. Ballista could think of no better disguise.

'Gradually the passing years degenerated to the lowest depths of hedonism, and cut out strange paths to enjoyment. Luxury transgressed the laws of nature. The same sex entered the same bed. Sowing his seed on barren rocks, it brought a little pleasure to the one at the cost of great disgrace to the other.'

Ballista had never fully understood Roman attitudes to sex. As far as he could see, a Roman could penetrate anyone, man or woman, boy or girl, and he incurred no shame. A member of the elite got into trouble if caught bedding the wife or daughter of another member of the elite, but beyond that almost anything seemed to go. Yet should a male ever play the role of a woman, just once allow himself to be the receiver, he was disgraced for the rest of his life. It accounted for the contempt in which freedmen were held. Once they had been slaves, and thus almost certainly would have submitted to the desires of their master.

'From maidenhood to middle age a woman is a pleasant armful for a man to embrace. Even if her beauty is past its prime, as Euripides said, "With a wiser tongue experience speaks than does the young." The intercourse of man with woman brings mutual pleasure. Unless we heed the judgement of Tiresias – that mortal who had been both sexes by turn – and say that the enjoyment of a woman is twice that of a man. Finally, as even the most dedicated pederast must admit, a woman may be used like a boy, opening up two paths to pleasure.'

No sooner had the Corinthian stopped, than the man of Sparta began speaking.

'Aphrodite, be propitious, for I am here to honour your son, Eros. Marriage is a remedy invented to ensure the perpetuity of man, but the love of boys is a noble duty enjoined by a philosophic spirit. As long as life was a daily struggle for existence, men were content to limit themselves to necessities. Once pressing needs were at an end, we were released from the shackles of necessity.'

Was necessity a hard master, or nothing but a convenient excuse? Ballista saw the watchman falling, an Icarus with burnt wings. *Help me.* He heard the knuckles break under his boot. He watched the second, fatal fall, heard the sickening impact, saw the shattered body on the pavement, and listened again to the outcry of those down on the street. Ballista had killed many men. He had killed his own half-brother. That had not left this horror. None of the victims had been so helpless. Never had there been that cold, inhuman calculation. There were rituals of expiation. Ballista would hold to necessity. Let the shade of the watchman haunt his sleeping and waking hours, let the Furies rise from Hades and hound his every step. Ballista would accept it all, but he would save his family. No one and nothing would stop him.

'If one were to see women rise in the morning from last night's bed, one would think them uglier than those beasts whose name it is inauspicious to mention early in the day. They need powders and unguents, jars full of dentifrices and contrivances, legions of maids, skilled hairdressers, Indian gems and Red Sea pearls, to cease to resemble monkeys.'

Ballista felt a great desire to leave. The trivial and precious concerns of these effete Greeks were sickening. The informer would have long since quit the street.

'But a boy rises at dawn, washes the sleep from his eyes, pins on a simple mantle, and leaves his father's hearth.'

It was time for Ballista to be gone. He needed peace to think.

'Next comes the glistening wrestling school. Under the midday sun his developing body is covered in dust. A quick bath and a sober meal, and a return to his books, before the evening ends, and he sleeps the sweeter for his exertions. Who would not fall in love with such a youth?'

Would this ever stop?

'This love is pure and beautiful, for the lover is driven, not by lust, but a philosophic attraction to the beautiful and virtuous. The boy repays this love with affection, and, if he chooses, satisfies the desire of his lover by some means that does not taint his own virtue.'

It took Ballista a moment to realise that the oration had ended. They were both waiting for his verdict. The Spartan was leaning forward, gazing into his eyes, a hand on his knee. *Beware the Greeks bringing gifts*. At home among the Angles, the practices advocated by the Spartan would have seen him drowned in a swamp. Deeds of shame should be buried out of the sight of man, stamped down, trodden deep.

This was no place to cause offense. Ballista had lived too long among foreigners to think only the ways of his own ancestors could be right. He reined in his thoughts. Something tactful to say, something enigmatic, which favoured neither side, and he could be on his way. A couplet of Homer came to mind.

A man who never sleeps could rake in double wages,
One for herding cattle, one for pasturing fleecy sheep.

He left them nodding sagely at each other as if they actually understood what it meant.

CHAPTER 18

The Baths of Trajan

BALLISTA HAD FORGOTTEN the festival of Venus. On the Kalends of April the pools of the public baths were reserved for women. After he had left the bookshop, he had taken a roundabout route, up to the Esquiline, then through backstreets behind the Temple of Tellus and the Baths of Titus. It was not until he reached the side entrance to the Baths of Trajan, and saw the crowd of women, that he remembered. They were of every age and class; girls and matrons in respectable long robes, prostitutes in the toga that showed their occupation. Inside all marks of status would be discarded. They would bathe naked. The haughtiest wife of a Consul would join with the lowest whore from the subura in offering a pinch of incense to Fortuna Virilis, that the goddess might hide any blemish on her body from the sight of men.

The festival made little difference. The rest of the vast complex was open to men. Ballista had not intended to bathe anyway. Being naked would not help, if he had to leave in a hurry.

Walking through the formal gardens to the main buildings, Ballista passed by the famous sculpture of Laocoon and his sons. The Trojan prince had objected to bringing the wooden horse into the walls. Athena had sent two great sea serpents. Caught in their coils, Laocoon had been crushed to death, along with his blameless sons. The gods were cruel. The innocent would be punished with the guilty. It was not a message a man in Ballista's position could be expected to find encouraging.

Going through a side door, Ballista came out into a palaestra. There were only a few men playing ball in the exercise ground. Ballista went over to a statue hung with green boughs and garlanded with roses, and pretended to read its inscription. A semi-circular auditorium opened off the palaestra. Attendants and slaves with satchels of books sat outside. Through the columns of the open wall, their masters could be seen strolling to their places on the benches. It was a good-sized audience. Some well known philosopher or sophist was going to declaim.

Ballista took a seat on the lowest tier, at one end. From there he could keep an eye on the palaestra, and, if necessary, slip out without much fuss. He took off his hat, and closed his eyes. The buzz of conversation was soporific. Once again fatigue threatened to overcome him. He rubbed his eyes, pinched the bridge of his nose. On his travels, he should have found an apothecary, and purchased a compound of natron and chalcanthite. It was said a single sniff banished tiredness. The magician from the Gardens of Lucullus no doubt would have recommended wearing the dried head of a bat as an amulet, or spooning up a drink with its wings. Too much of the latter, and apparently you never slept again. There was no end to the superstitions of men.

Like kicking on a weary horse, Ballista forced his mind back along the right path. Last night he had failed to reach the Praetorian Prefect. This morning he had failed to reach the emperor. Before sunset he had to get into the Colosseum, and somehow gain entrance to the imperial box.

There was a network of tunnels under the amphitheatre. One of the entrances was outside in the Ludus Magnus. If he could talk his way into the gladiatorial school . . . Ballista dismissed the strategy. The last thing he wanted was to come out onto the floor of the arena. There had to be corridors leading up into the building itself, but Ballista did not know them, and they would be securely guarded. The authorities would hardly leave avenues of escape open to reluctant combatants and wild beasts.

There was no longer any doubt in Ballista's mind, but that he needed help to reach the emperor. That help had to come from an officer or official with access, someone who could order the guards to let him pass. If not the Praetorian Prefect, then whom?

There was the *Princeps Peregrinorum*. Ballista did not like the thought. No one in his right mind sought out the head of the *frumentarii*. Their innocuous name suggested something to do with grain distribution or army rations. It fooled no one. Across the whole empire they were known, feared and hated for what they really were – the emperor's secret service, his spies and assassins. At least they were known collectively. They were a special unit of soldiers, its members transferred out of other units, with their base on the Caelian Hill. Individually, they were seldom known at all. One of their duties was to dress as civilians, and eavesdrop on those suspected of disloyalty. In the normal course of things, Ballista would not consider going to their camp. Few went into their camp willingly, and many of those who did were never heard of again.

Ballista yawned. The title of the commander of the *frumentarii* meant Leader of the Strangers. The man was called Rufinus. Ballista had never met him, and had no desire to meet him. Now necessity demanded that Ballista make his way to the Caelian Hill, make his acquaintance, and try to enlist his support. At least the Caelian was not far, and, given his unsavoury occupation, the Leader of the Strangers should be predisposed to believe the existence of a conspiracy.

The murmur of conversation faded as the speaker took the floor. He wore no tunic, just a cloak. The almost rustic simplicity of his dress combined with his long hair and beard proclaimed him a philosopher. The staff and wallet that he carried might indicate he was a Cynic, although the symbols were apposite to any sect, and the magnificent location argued against an adherence to the teachings of Diogenes. As soon as he started speaking in the fine Attic Greek of Plato and Demosthenes, it was obvious that he was an educated man, and no ranting dog-philosopher from the street corner.

'Words addressed to private persons pertain to those men alone, or to but a few others. But words addressed to kings are like public prayers or imprecations. Should I report the words that I spoke to the emperor as if they were a matter of no consequence?'

Ballista wondered what gave these hairy Greek intellectuals – unkempt philosophers and groomed sophists alike – the confidence to dare to lecture the ruler of Rome, and what induced every emperor to sit and listen? At heart, it must be politics. On the estimation of the Greeks themselves, a people had no history when they lacked autonomy. The Greeks could not escape the fact that they were ruled by Rome, but that subservience might be made more bearable if the foreign ruler was seen in public heeding the advice of his Greek subjects. For the Romans it might be more than conciliating the most vocal of the races in their dominion. By listening attentively to these interminable orations, the emperor exhibited his commitment to free speech and liberty. And it was *libertas* that the Romans judged made the emperor different from an oriental despot or a barbarian warlord.

As the philosopher got into his stride recounting the words of wisdom with which he had regaled the emperor, a late arrival joined the audience on the far side from Ballista.

'A king is a king because he chooses virtue. Because he has virtue, both his subjects and the gods love him. Because he is loved by men and gods alike, there will be no plots against him, and his rule will last the length of his natural life.'

The newcomer was muscular and squat, clad in the plain tunic of a working man. He looked an unlikely devotee of political philosophy.

'But if the ruler turns to vice, then he is no king, but has become a tyrant. A tyrant rules not for the common good, but for his own advantage and pleasure. Such a one is hated on earth and in the heavens. His subjects will conspire and rise up against him, and the gods will make haste to cast him from the throne, and trample him underfoot.'

A king is a king because he has virtue. Did Gallienus still possess that quality? Dressing as a woman, squandering money with both hands, did he still rule for others, and not for his own pleasure? Did Gallienus still deserve to be emperor? Ballista did not have the liberty to entertain the treasonous question. He had no choice but to preserve Gallienus on the throne. Ballista owed his life to the emperor. And as well as honour, there was pragmatism. If Ballista failed to save Gallienus, he himself would die soon after, and so would his whole family. If the emperor was assassinated, everyone Ballista loved would be put to the sword.

The late arrival stretched, and looked around at the other members of the audience. His gaze passed over Ballista, then darted back, before sliding quickly away. When he appeared to give his attention back to the philosopher, Ballista got up and left.

On the far side of the palaestra, Ballista glanced back. The man was following. Angling across the exercise ground, he was walking normally, but trying to keep the statue between him and his quarry. Ballista went into the baths, and turned to his right.

The columns of the luxurious ante chamber of the caldarium soared high to where arches sprung across the vault. The room was bright with light shining through the expanse of glass in the tall windows. It was warm next to the hot baths. An attendant approached deferentially.

'My apologies, master, but the pools are reserved for women on the Kalends of April.'

'You know the service corridors under the baths?'

'Yes, master.'

'The ones that run outside to the cisterns?'

'The public are not allowed down there, master.'

'Show me the way.'

A moment's indecision – the slave was reluctant to contravene the rules of the baths, but long subservience had taught him the dangers of disobeying the command of a free man. A slave should not wait for a master's hand. Either way, he might get a beating.

'Follow me, master.'

A discreet door was hidden by a panel. The man from the lecture was not in sight.

The corridor was plastered, its steps led steeply down. At the bottom it divided into two. The light dimmed as the figure of a man blocked the top. Before Ballista could stop him, the slave darted away. Not stopping to think, Ballista gave chase. Above him, he heard heavy boots thumping down the stairs.

The corridors were dark and stifling, full of smoke and steam. Only occasional holes in the low ceiling let in any light, or offered an inadequate ventilation. The narrow bare-brick passageways turned left and right, went up and down flights of steps. Other tunnels opened off at right angles. It was hard to breath in this subterranean maze. The sweat poured off Ballista as he pursued the sounds of the vanishing slave. He ran past naked slaves feeding furnaces set in the walls, brushed past others lugging wood.

In a deserted place, where four passages met, Ballista pulled up, panting. The slave had got away. Only the gods knew what had happened to the man from the auditorium. Eerie, disjointed noises – shouts, snatches of conversations, sudden footfalls, and bursts of mournful songs – echoed from the four gloomy openings.

Bent double, Ballista struggled to fill his lungs. Under the cloak, his tunic was stuck to his body. Down here it was like Tartarus, or a Christian vision of hell. Did the women bathing in the light and scented air above give a thought to the sufferings of those labouring in this infernal region beneath their feet? If they did, would they care?

Ballista was lost. There was no point in blundering about blindly. He could wander down here for days. *Find a slave, and make him lead the way out of this horrible nether world.* Ballista straightened up, and unsheathed his knife. He held it under the folds of his cloak. Best not to alarm or scare off whoever he found before he could reveal what he wanted.

Taking a corridor at random, he set off. It was hard to see through the darkness and swirling smoke. He moved slowly, senses alert. At every turning and opening, he stopped, and listened. The tunnels seemed unnaturally empty. There was nothing but crumbling bricks, choking smog, and distant noises. At a fork, the glow of a fire flickered from a passageway. Ballista went into the opening. Where there was a furnace, there would be slaves.

A disturbance in the atmosphere behind him. Ballista crouched and spun half round. The blade scythed just over his head. Sparks flashed where it scraped down the brickwork. The momentum of the blow drove the assailant into Ballista. They grappled, pressed together. The man's knife arm was trapped between them. Ballista could not get his weapon free from his cloak. They staggered like drunks.

The fingers of the man's free hand clawed at Ballista's face, nails seeking his eyes. Ballista pulled away. The man recovered his knife. Before he could use it, Ballista lunged forward. Arching his body, Ballista head-butted him. A sharp crack, a grunt of pain as the nose broke.

As the man reeled back, Ballista got his blade free from the clinging material.

Both dropped into a fighting stance. Feet balanced, knives out, each waited. The corridor was too narrow for manoeuvre. No room to sidestep. Face to face, like gladiators chained together.

Not taking his eyes off the man, Ballista unclasped his cloak, let it hang from his left hand.

'Been looking for you for all night.' The man spoke in the Latin of the camps.

Feinting with his knife, Ballista flicked the trailing cloak up at the man's face.

The man did not flinch. Instead he caught the leading edge neatly in his left hand. The cloak was stretched taught between them.

'You killed my friends at the Mausoleum.'

Without warning, the man tugged the cloak towards him. Yanked forward, off balance, Ballista threw himself to his right. His back thumped against the wall. The impact knocked his own knife from his hand. Ballista twisted away. Too slow, white hot pain as the blade slashed along his ribs.

Ballista crumpled. The blood was running hot down his chest. Go down now, and he was dead. The man drew back for the killing blow. Ballista surged up and into him. He drove him across the corridor. Using all his weight and strength, he hammered the man face first into the opposite wall. The breath wheezed out of his opponent. Ballista got hold of his hair, pulled his head back, then smashed it into the wall. A clatter as his opponent's knife fell to the floor.

As Ballista went to beat the man's face into the bricks again, his left leg was whipped out from under him. Ballista went sprawling. This fellow knew how to wrestle.

Groggily, the man shuffled towards where his knife glinted in the half light.

Feet slipping, Ballista used the wall to lever himself up. His chest hurt like Hades.

The man put out an arm to steady himself as he bent to pick up the knife. There was a dark smear on the wall where his face had been.

Three running, staggering steps, and Ballista hurled himself onto the man's back. The man collapsed under him. Ballista's weight came down through his knees into the small of the man's back. A scream of pure agony.

The man was a fighter. Despite the pain, his hand scrabbled towards the knife. Ballista flicked the blade away down the corridor.

'Who sent you?' It was hard to get the words out through the hurt. The foul air was catching in Ballista's throat.

The man did not reply.

'Who?' Ballista gripped the back of his head, punched his face into the ground.

Still nothing.

From the distance came the sounds of men approaching.

'Tell me, and I might let you live.'

'Fuck you.'

'Not a good answer.'

Again and again, Ballista beat the ruined face into the stones.

'Over there!' A disembodied shout from the labyrinth.

Slaves approaching, lots of them. There was no time to explain this away.

Ballista clambered to his feet, snatched up his cloak and one of the daggers, and lurched into the smoke in the opposite direction.

CHAPTER 19

The Colosseum

T HE PEASANT TOOK A SIP OF heavily watered wine. He wanted to keep his wits about him. At the front of the imperial box, the emperor evidently had no such qualms. Gallienus never drank more than one glass of the same wine, but through the morning his cup had been refilled again and again with Falernian and Caecuban, Lesbian and Chian; with wines from fine vineyards across the empire. It was a recipe for early inebriation and a powerful hangover, and that was all to the good.

Shifting the scabbard of his sword, the peasant stretched, and looked around the box. At the rear stood a rank of German guardsmen. Tall, with long braided hair and gold rings on their arms, they stood immobile and impassive. The peasant had fought alongside them, and against their kinsmen in the forests of the North. Fierce and strong, they made terrible enemies. The gods willing, everything should be over before they could intervene.

Off to one side the vestal virgins sat, quiet and decorous. The peasant considered he had the desires natural to a man. Yet the virgin priestesses had never aroused in him the prurient lust they inspired in many. Touch one of them, and you would find yourself out there on the floor of the arena. If a vestal broke her vows, she was entombed alive. Their presence made no difference to the plan.

Around the peasant were those with the title of *amicus* of the emperor. Most of these imperial *friends* wore the snowy toga and broad purple stripe of a senator. No more than half a dozen were in the undress uniform which denoted that its wearer was a member of the *protectores*. Apart from the praetorians, the only citizens permitted to be armed in the company of the emperor were the small group of officers admitted to the exalted ranks of the *protectores*. The peasant was careful not to catch the eye of either Scarpio or Cecropius, but he smiled reassuringly at the senator Sempronius. The latter was sweating, as well he might. It was only midday. There were hours to wait, but the peasant had already passed him the knife.

Looking at the seats reserved for the imperial family at the front of the box, the peasant felt a mixture of irritation and anxiety. The empress Salonina was not in attendance. Apparently she had preferred to go to a lecture by a philosopher called Plotinus. Men could not control their women these days. The peasant would not have his wife running off to be corrupted by the theories of Plato, or any other hairy charlatan. Women did not need education. Salonina did not matter. Of more concern was the absence of both Gallienus' half-brother and his youngest son. This evening they would have to be hunted down, and quickly. So would Salonina, although that was less pressing – what could a woman do?

Gallienus threw back his head and laughed. Even in the shade of the awnings, the emperor's hair shone. Every morning, after he had taken his draft of preventative poisons, Gallienus had his hair sprinkled with gold dust. Lacking his wife, the emperor had brought his mistress. With one hand he held his glass, with the other he pawed her. It would have been unseemly, even if she had not been a barbarian. The peasant was fully aware of her diplomatic importance. The daughter of the king of the Marcomanni, as a hostage in Rome, she helped secure the frontier on the upper Danube. It would be best if she were not harmed when Gallienus was struck down.

A burst of music brought the peasant's attention back to the arena. From a trapdoor in the middle appeared a man dressed as Hercules. He carried a club, and had the skin of a lion tied over his tunic. Four attendants followed him with torches. The crowd roared with expectation. Hercules stood stock still, perhaps stunned by the sudden light and noise. The attendants ringed him. As if awakened from a spell, Hercules swung his club at one of them. The blow was clumsy, easily avoided. Another attendant approached him from behind. Hercules twisted away, turning, looking for somewhere to run. There was no escape. As he tried to fend off one of the torches, another touched his costume. Hercules screamed as the pitch smeared on his tunic caught fire. Now they let him run. He dropped the club, tore at his clothes, beat at the flames. His hair and beard were burning. After a few staggering steps, he threw himself to the ground. Desperately he rolled on the sand. Liberally applied, the pitch could not be extinguished. His death throws did not last very long.

The peasant picked up a prawn wrapped in a fig-leaf. These elaborate executions at lunchtime did not interest him. Of course it was right that criminals – murderers, Christians, those guilty of other offenses against the gods – should be punished with exemplary cruelty. It was salutary for the public to see their suffering. But the point of such mythological charades often escaped him. Earlier, when a man with ineffectual wings strapped to his back had been dropped from a crane, he had had to ask a neighbour the character represented by the victim.

A slave proffered a fingerbowl, another dried his hands. Despite the costly perfumes which were sprinkled from the awnings, from the floor of the arena drifted up a smell unpleasantly like roast pork.

The morning's beast fights had been little more to the taste of the peasant. They had been lavish: leopards from Libya, panthers from Cilicia, a hundred lions from Africa. Even the meanest intelligence of a visiting barbarian would have appreciated the extent of the dominion of Rome, the wealth and power necessary to capture and transport such a number of dangerous animals. Yet the beasts had been killed almost as soon as they had emerged from the trapdoors. Some, mangy and enervated by captivity, had been unwilling to charge. They had been despatched with arrows. As for the herds of deer, ibexes, and ostriches, slaughtering them in the confines of the arena exhibited little expertise and no valour.

A slave proffered a tray of pastries. Biting into one, there was a taste of something like fennel with which the chicken had been flavoured. No doubt it was asafoetida from Persia. Asafoetida or Median silphium: such exotic delicacies had not appeared on the table at the Etruscan farm where the peasant had been born. In the Spring the year after a bad harvest, there had been next to nothing. The peasant had watched his mother grinding acorns to make bread. His father had got into debt. The farm had been sold. The family reduced to penury. The army had offered the young peasant a living, a means of escape.

Neither his brothers nor his sister had survived infancy. The peasant had been a strong child. His father had called him the bull. Both parents were long dead. Should his undertaking fail, they were beyond imperial retribution. He had a son of his own. The boy had been born into very different circumstances from the father. A couple of years before, Publius had been elected Quaestor. Now Publius was entitled to the broad purple stripe of a senator. Young Publius knew nothing of the plot. Yet he would suffer if it miscarried. Life was full of unforeseen risks. It was not ambition that had set the peasant on this path, but duty. It was for the good of Rome.

'Master.' The *silentarius* spoke quietly, as befitted his title. The peasant realised that he had not included the servants in his inventory of those in the imperial box. Not that they were of any account.

'The architect is outside with the new plans for your house.'

The peasant got up, and bowed to the emperor. Gallienus paid him no attention. Taking his leave, the peasant indicated Scarpio should accompany him. The merest nod told Cecropius to remain with Sempronius. The bald head of the senator was beaded with sweat. It was best not to leave him alone. His nerves were not strong. He needed constant reassurance.

Making his way to the steps, the peasant noticed that the crowd was silent, as if fifty thousand spectators were holding their breath in anticipation. He stopped. All that was left of Hercules was a black, oily stain on the sand, where his corpse had been dragged out. Slaves with rakes were removing the evidence of his passing.

Scarpio hovered impatiently at his elbow. The peasant ignored him. As a young soldier, when first seconded into the *frumentarii*, he had learned to pay attention to even the most trivial and inconsequential details.

Another fanfare, and a concealed lift brought to the floor of the arena an altar. A low fire burned on it. Next to the fire was a curved blade of obsidian. The peasant turned, and went down the steps. He had no desire to see a captured brigand sever his own genitals. Unlike several of those around him in the imperial box, he had not wagered on the chances of survival.

They walked down echoing staircases, along tall corridors, until they came out into the sunshine by the main eastern gate. The peasant looked up at the sky. Someone had told him the roaring of a pride of lions brought on thunder. The sky was clear.

The ferret was waiting by the sweating post. He was alone, dressed in nondescript civilian garb. The ferret was reliable. He was even carrying rolled papyri that an observer might conclude were designs for a building.

At the water feature, the peasant looked around to make sure that they could not be overheard.

A great shout from the amphitheatre indicated the bandit had mutilated himself.

'What news?'

'Ballista was in the Baths of Trajan. One of my men followed him down to the furnaces.' From the ferret's face it was obvious the report did not have a good ending.

'Your man was spotted.'

The ferret unrolled a papyrus, held it out so that the others could pretend to study it. 'Ballista beat him half to death. My man thinks that Ballista forced a bath attendant to guide him out through the service tunnels to the cisterns.'

'How long ago?'

'Less than an hour.'

'By now he could be anywhere. You are watching his house?'

'Yes.'

The Papyrus actually did have drawings of the elevation of a house. The peasant was impressed by this attention to detail. Another question occurred to him.

'Why did Ballista not kill your man?'

'He was disturbed.'

'Did Ballista discover anything on your man to give away his identity?'

'No.'

'Are you sure?'

'Certain. He had no time to search or question him.'

Scarpio butted in. 'He may not have found out anything that links the two of you to the conspiracy, but he knows that I am involved.'

'Then, if he reaches the imperial box, you had better forestall the tortoise.' The peasant kept his voice low and almost affable. 'Remember the wine on your carpet – once something is out of the jug, it cannot be poured back.'

The Prefect of the City Watch did not look comforted by the words or the memory.

'I have issued a new description,' the ferret said. 'Ballista has shaved his head, and was last seen wearing a blue tunic, and a Gallic hooded cloak in green. He is armed with a dagger.'

'Have him found,' the peasant said. 'Also detail some of your men to locate and follow Gallienus' half-brother and son. They need to be taken care of before tomorrow morning.'

'They are in the Palace. Both are already under observation.'

'Good.'

The ferret was pleased with the approbation. 'How is the tortoise?'

'Scared,' the peasant said. 'The senator is a coward, but the rider is with him.' Not, the peasant thought, that Cecropius's visit to Sempronius's house at dawn had put much heart in the timid senator.

'He had the courage to betray us,' Scarpio blurted out. 'The bastard tried to betray the very men who were risking everything to make him emperor.'

'Keep your voice down.' The peasant's finger traced the outline of an architrave. 'It was to be expected. His sort have no consideration for those they consider their inferiors. He does not approve of soldiers, let alone us *protectores*. It was fortunate that Acilius Glabrio thought the idea insane.' The peasant looked up at the ferret. 'If he had not written to inform you of the treachery, we might have been in a bad position.'

'A bad position? We would have been dead!' As ever Scarpio sounded weak and querulous. 'Anyway, Acilius Glabrio is another nobleman. Will he be any better as emperor?'

The peasant again peered at the papyrus, as if absorbed in the plans. 'Acilius Glabrio will not be implicated in the death of the emperor. He will be acceptable to the troops. Not having witnessed the depravity of Gallienus when away from the field army, many of them still favour him. And, as you say, he is a patrician, so the senators will be delighted to acclaim Acilius Glabrio Augustus.'

'He will not prove as malleable as Sempronius.' It was as if, once started, Scarpio could not control his litany of complaints. 'And who is to say that he will not turn on us?'

'Acilius is a different kettle of fish,' the peasant conceded. 'He led the cavalry charge that won the battle of Circesium, fought well at Milan. He sees himself as a general, and will seek glory against Postumus. But he is no more addicted to hard work than any other patrician. Vain and easily flattered, he will posture in gilded armour, and leave the tedious hard labour of governance to us *protectores*.'

Scarpio looked as if he wanted to say more, but did not. He stood, wringing his hands, the picture of abject fear. The peasant had been right not to tell him of Sempronius' attempted double-cross, or the decision to elevate Acilius Glabrio, until after they had both entered the imperial box this morning. Given time, the cravenness of Scarpio would have undone them all. The man was a mouse by name and by nature.

The ferret rolled up the papyrus. 'When the tortoise has struck down Gallienus, there is no doubt the praetorians in the corridor will kill the assassin?'

'Why would they not?' The peasant smiled. 'They know nothing. They will do their duty. Sempronius will earn the wages of his treachery.'

From the Colosseum came the brazen sound of trumpets, joined by the bass of a water organ.

'You keep searching for Ballista,' the peasant said to the ferret. 'We, however, should go back. If the mouse and I are not in our places for the start of the gladiatorial combat, our noble emperor might think that we were spurning his hospitality.'

We who are about to die, salute you.

Six hundred gladiators, among them four hundred Alamanni captured at the battle of Milan. The Alamanni would fight against each other in massed combat. The others would duel in pairs. Unlike the beasts and the executions, this was a proper spectacle. To fight man against man, blade in hand, demanded skill and bravery. It accustomed the people of Rome to the sight of blood. If even slaves and prisoners showed courage close to the steel, how much more should be expected of Roman citizens? The amphitheatre kept alive the spirit of the ancestors. Greek philosophers might whine that it was butchery, but what did they know of the *mos maiorum* that had given Rome her empire?

The peasant understood fighting. It had been his life. The empire was embattled, ringed around with enemies. Postumus had seized the West. Odenathus ruled as he pleased in the East, paid scant regard to Rome. Barbarians massed on every frontier. Deserters and brigands plundered the provinces. As never before, the empire needed a war leader on the throne. And Gallienus had lost his appetite for the fight. When every bronze coin was needed for the army, the emperor squandered incalculable sums on colossal statues, vast porticos and a city of philosophers in the Apennines. When the emperor should be marching with his troops, eating hardtack, living under canvas, Gallienus debated the tenets of Plato in the Palace, or dallied with whores in chambers decked with flowers.

To be sure, Gallienus could be roused to duty on occasion. Yet it had taken enormous effort, and endless patience, on the part of the peasant and others, such as his friends Tacitus and Aurelian, to finally persuade the emperor to issue the orders for the campaign across the Alps. Postumus had murdered Gallienus' favourite son, and still the emperor had been reluctant: endless specious talk of securing what they held, of not overstretching the resources of what remained of the empire, of attempting to suborn those around Postumus. It was not good enough. *To Hades with caution, and an indirect strategy.* What was needed was hard marching and hard fighting. After Postumus there would be Odenathus, and after him the Persian King of Kings.

Shapur the King of Kings was the heart of the matter. It was five years since he had captured the emperor Valerian. Five years in which Gallienus had made no attempt to rescue his father. Every day when the Persian wished to go riding, the aged emperor had to get on all fours in the dirt. As he mounted, Shapur would put his boot on the shoulders of Valerian, use the venerable Emperor of Rome as a mounting block. This is true, the Persian exulted, not the lies of the Romans.

Valerian had plucked the peasant from the obscurity of the ranks, had appointed him to command his horse guards. The peasant had given Valerian his oath, not with his lips alone, but with his heart. Valerian had raised the peasant high, and in every new office the peasant had served him loyally. If Valerian's son would not march to his rescue, the peasant would create an emperor who would undertake that sacred duty. The living symbol of the majesty of Rome could not be left in the dirt at the feet of a barbarian. The peasant would not break the word he had given to his emperor. He continued to serve Valerian.

Only those close to Gallienus realised the depths of his inertia. Even so, it had been necessary for the peasant to tread carefully. When approached, Tacitus had quoted some line from his ancestor the historian to the effect of praying for good emperors, but serving what you got. The peasant had pretended to be convinced, and Tacitus had gone to his distant estates. Learning from that rebuff, the peasant had recruited only an old companion, Heraclian, from the field army, and the three men in Rome. The mouse and the ferret commanded armed men in the city. The former was weak, and the latter untrustworthy by occupation. The troopers that Cecropius led were quartered in Milan, but the cavalry officer was on leave in Rome. Cecropius was another old tent-mate, a soldier to the core, a man the peasant could trust. The pseudonym of the rider suited him, as did those of the mouse and the ferret. They were as fitting as the peasant's own. When their allegiance had been secured, the peasant had held out the prospect of the throne to Sempronius. The senator reminded him of a tortoise. Just six men to overthrow an emperor. The smaller the conspiracy, the less danger of being betrayed. The conspiracy had not been small enough.

Despite his words earlier to Scarpio, the treachery of Sempronius had been completely unexpected. The peasant still found it hard to believe that a man he had chosen for his quiescence had possessed such guile and nerve. Ambition could drive the most unsuitable and unlikely men. Thank all the gods that Acilius Glabrio had revealed to the ferret the ambush set by Sempronius. Of course Acilius was not to be trusted either. Informing against Sempronius, the young patrician had expected the information to be passed to the emperor, and to be rewarded by Gallienus with a sizeable percentage of that senator's estate. Offered the purple instead, he had jumped at the chance. Acilius probably thought his birth entitled him to that eminence. Ambition had its spurs deep in him.

According to Acilius, another senator with the army in Milan had been amenable to overtures received from Sempronius. The peasant had had no contact with Nummius Faustinianus. That nobleman would be waiting for the news that the first act of Sempronius Augustus had been the execution of the peasant and his friends. When instead the laurel-wreathed dispatches arrived proclaiming the deaths of both Gallienus and Sempronius, and the accession of Acilius Glabrio, there would be little that Nummius could do. Still, he needed watching.

A huge cheer brought the peasant out of his reverie. The Alamanni were coming out onto the sand. Automatically the peasant checked that the net was stretched along the top of the arena wall, the rollers placed and the spikes on top to make it harder to climb, the archers stationed behind, arrows nocked, the praetorians in full armour backing them. He had faced these very barbarians at Milan. Years in captivity, and they still looked dangerous.

Would the Alamanni fight? When the emperor decided there had been enough killing, the survivors had been promised their lives. The barbarians would be split up, enrolled in military units across the empire. Would it be enough to make them kill their kinsmen?

A low *hooming* sound from the two groups of Germans answered the question. It was the *barritus*, the war cry of the North. The barbarians considered the volume of noise predicted the outcome of the battle. The warriors held their hands over their mouths. Usually they would use their shields to amplify the *barritus*. The peasant had advised they be given no defensive equipment. It would bring on the bloodshed with more speed, and, should there be a problem, make the combatants better targets for the bowmen. Some other courtier had suggested the sides be dressed in contrasting colours to make it easier for spectators to follow the contest.

The war cries rose to a crescendo, and both sides charged. The peasant watched with professional interest the hacking and stabbing, the gouts of blood and gaping wounds. This was the ultimate expression of the might of the empire. Rome's enemies compelled to fight to the death, while her unarmed citizenry enjoyed the sight. It had often occurred to the peasant that the amphitheatre was a model of the empire turned inside out. The savage barbarians placed at the centre, not the periphery, were still ringed by Roman troops, while the citizens, seated according to their place in Roman society, safely watched from the outside. In the Colosseum, civilization and humanity surrounded and triumphed over barbarity and chaos.

Not all the audience might be expected to be taking unalloyed pleasure from the combat. The peasant wondered what the emperor's German bodyguards would be making of the spectacle. Of course, most would not be from that tribe. But their commander, Freki, for all his years in the service of Rome, was by birth an Alamann. The peasant looked back at the big warrior. The German was impassive as ever. Whatever conflict of emotions he might be suffering, nothing showed.

If the peasant had been in Freki's position, he would have stared the problem in the face. He prided himself on a hard, clear-eyed pragmatism. It was a discipline never more needed than today. If the plot failed, if Ballista reached the emperor, or Sempronius failed to mortally wound Gallienus, what would be the consequences?

One myth the peasant knew was Pandora opening the jar. Embarking on a conspiracy was much the same, everything flew out beyond recall. Heraclian in Milan most likely could be trusted to keep his counsel. Yet if he were to fall in the coming war, it might be no bad thing. A dangerous mission, from which return was unlikely, could be arranged. The two senators with the army could not inform against their fellow conspirators without betraying themselves. The emperor did not care for senators. If they had any sense, Acilius Glabrio and Nummius Faustinianus should keep quiet. Likewise the ferret and the rider here in Rome, although the former was a concern. Perhaps a tragic accident could be arranged. Of course Sempronius would have to die. So too Scarpio; the mouse was weak, and sheer terror might make him talk. And there was Ballista. The peasant felt sorry for it, but Ballista had the ear of the emperor, and he might have uncovered too much. Ballista's eldest son must be of an age to take the toga of manhood. Familial loyalty would impel him to seek revenge. A feud was to be avoided. It was a shame, but both Ballista's sons must also die.

The peasant was encouraged by his ruminations. In politics, as in war, you needed more than one plan. You must always have a line of retreat. Giving his attention back to the arena, he remembered that one thing had remained in Pandora's jar, and that was hope.

CHAPTER 20

The Street of Lamentation

U NLIKE ORPHEUS ESCAPING FROM the underworld, Ballista had looked over his shoulder all the way through the tunnels which led out from under the Baths of Trajan. He had kept a firm grip on the slave that he had waylaid, let him see the blade in his other hand. By the guttering light of a lamp, the unlikely Charon had conducted him through the dark maze. Several times they had encountered other denizens of the subterranean world. They had stepped aside to let the working parties shuffle past. Ballista had hidden the knife. Although they had drawn the odd curious look, the slaves down here were pale and apathetic, ground down by unremitting labour in an unhealthy environment. No one had asked any questions. The unwilling guide had not spoken. Ballista had left him in no doubt of his fate should he attempt to raise the alarm.

At long last they had emerged by the cisterns. The light hurt Ballista's eyes. He had given the slave a small coin, told him that he should forget everything, as surely as if he had drunk the waters of Lethe.

Ballista stood for a moment, blinking in the sunshine. The slave had scurried back underground. If his absence had been noticed, he would get a beating. No doubt he would talk. Although Ballista thought it unlikely he would mention the coin.

He really should get moving. But it was pleasant with the sun on his face. And he was hurting. Back in the tunnels, before he had caught the slave, he had hacked rough bandages out of the hem of his cloak, and bound the wound he had taken. The cut was long, but not deep. It was on the left of his chest, the same side as the ribs he had damaged in the Tiber. Neither were too bad, and his ankle only felt stiff and ached. The most painful injury was the small cut on the palm of his right hand. When this was all over, he would lie for hours in the warm water of a *tepidarium*, then sleep for days. Of course, if it turned out badly, he would have an eternity of quiet and rest.

The camp of the *frumentarii* on the Caelian was not far. Ballista knew the general layout of this part of the city. The direct route was out of the question. Not only would it take him too close to the Colosseum, but he would have to pass by the quarters of the sailors from the fleet at Misenum, the armoury, and the various barracks of the gladiators. With the City Watch searching for him, such official buildings were best avoided. It was safer to walk east, through residential districts, then turn south, skirt the Mint, before circling back to approach the Caelian from the other direction.

Ballista strolled as if he did not have a care in the world. At least five hours remained until sunset. To hurry invited scrutiny. There was time to reach the Commander of the Strangers, divulge everything that he knew, and be escorted to the Colosseum. Once appraised of the threat, and ringed by the German guard, Gallienus would be safe.

Although not as opulent as the Carinae district at the western end of the Esquiline, this was an affluent area. There were spacious houses as well as tenements. Trees could be seen over garden walls. The streets were wide, but they were busy. There were shops set in the ground floor of the houses. Most were small cubicles with no access to the prosperous homes into whose structures they were built. Trying to convey an air of leisure, Ballista used their displays of merchandise as an excuse to stop, and check if he was being followed.

The third time he paused, there was something suspicious. A man in a dark tunic, unshaven, with a prominent nose. He was also looking into a shop about thirty paces away. The last time Ballista halted, the man had been engaged in the same activity outside another store about the same distance from Ballista.

It might be coincidence. There were a lot of people shopping. Taking no chances, Ballista cut down the next alley on the right, and came out on a street running roughly parallel. A market square opened off the street, and Ballista stood by the corner, looking back.

Sure enough, a few moments later, the man came out of the alleyway. The aquiline nose seemed almost to be searching for a scent, as the man looked first one way then the other up and down the street.

Before he was spotted, Ballista went into the market. It was obvious at a glance what was sold here. The high, blank walls on either side, the wooden block in front of the third wall with its solid gate and narrow barred windows. The main slave markets were in the Saepta Julia near the Pantheon in the Campus Martius, and behind the Temple of Castor off the Forum. You went to the former for exotic merchandise, the latter for a cheaper purchase. Yet there were smaller markets like this in every region of the city.

There was a reasonable crowd, with more people arriving. Dealers sold their less desirable slaves first. By now the slaves on the block should be starting to be of higher quality. Ballista worked his way into the cover of the throng. He took a place at the front. To disguise his height, he leant against the steps leading up to the raised platform. So far there was no sign of the man with the hooked nose.

'Clean and hard-working, honest and amiable, not given to gossip or drink; she is one in a thousand.'

The auctioneer was working hard.

'You could put her to any task: polishing furniture, folding clothes, weighing wool. Who will offer me eight hundred sesterces?'

The woman was not old, but servitude had aged her. She had been dressed in an incongruously bright and fine tunic, no doubt to distract potential purchasers away from her thin and puny limbs. Likewise, the cosmetics on her cheeks aimed to counterfeit youth and vivacity.

'Gentlemen, do you not recognise a bargain? I am giving her away at seven hundred.'

A portly man near Ballista called out two hundred.

'My dear sir,' the auctioneer recoiled in feigned horror, 'you would see me on the block myself. Such a pittance would not cover her transport from distant Lusitania.'

'Has she had children, any of them stillborn?' Most likely the man was a dealer. 'Do her menses come regularly?'

'Ah, a man with an eye to the future. Four children, all strong and healthy, the youngest just five. They were sold off this morning. Six hundred for this fine piece of breeding stock.'

'Three hundred, not a sesterce more.'

'Anyone with five hundred?'

'Looks melancholic,' a man said. 'Probably hang herself.'

'Five hundred?'

As a youth on the Palatine, Ballista had endured long afternoons with a philosophy tutor. To pass as a member of the upper orders in

Roman society, at least a certain acquaintance with its tenets were necessary. The influence of philosophy was pervasive. The morality of the plebs, who had never attended the schools, was largely shaped by its teaching. The major sects believed in a brotherhood of man. Everyone had a spark of the divine reason within them. Under the skin all mankind was the same. Given such thinking, Ballista had asked how slavery could exist. His classmates had sniggered. Evidently it was the sort of question only a barbarian would raise. The tutor had looked at him almost with pity at his ignorance. Ballista had completely misunderstood. What he took for slavery was nothing of the sort. Legal status only affected the outer man. It was an irrelevance to the moral purpose which defined a man. If the King of Kings of Persia, sat on his throne, master of all he surveyed, had a servile heart, then he was a slave. Conversely if the lowest slave, chained in the mines or about to be thrown into the arena, had a noble soul, then he was free. It was, Ballista thought, a belief most convenient for the Romans.

The woman had been taken back into the building unsold. Quite likely, when her finery was removed, she would get a thrashing for letting her owner down by not looking more cheerful on the block.

No one in the crowd seemed out of the ordinary. There was still no sight of the dark tunic and the distinctive nose. Best to wait a little, until he was sure to have moved on.

Next up was a strapping young man. Only a loincloth covered his nakedness. His feet were whitened with chalk. Opinion was divided. Some owners thought it not worth the trouble breaking in the newly enslaved like this youth. Others believed that they could be moulded like wet clay into whatever shape the master wished.

Around the neck of the boy was hung a placard. It gave his age as eighteen, and his place of birth as Cappadocia. In keeping with their view of the world, the Romans had fixed ideas about the potential of slaves from the many peoples within their empire and beyond: Greeks for secretaries and book-keeping, Egyptians and Syrians for pleasure, Gauls for labouring in the fields. No one would want a German as a personal servant. They were best employed as body-guards or as gladiators. As a hostage, Ballista had risen to high command in the Roman army, but in a sense it was nothing but a gilded servitude.

'Now, my friends, we come to the quality.' The auctioneer smiled, an insincere smile. 'A strong boy, like all Cappadocians, he would make an ideal litter-bearer. But with his looks, he would grace any table, or bedchamber. He would not look out of place in the Palace itself.'

'Let us see him then.'

At a nod from the auctioneer, the boy untied the loincloth. Reluctantly he let it drop.

'Get him moving,' one of the prospective buyers shouted.

'Do what the man says.'

The youth hesitated. When the auctioneer showed him the whip, he squatted down, then jumped into the air.

After all these years, Roman slavery still unsettled Ballista. It was not that they did not have slaves at home in Germany. There were unfree servants in the hall of Ballista's father. Old Calgacus had been a slave. But they were not a breed apart. Ballista had grown up with the children of the servants, had been treated no differently. There was not this cruel degradation. As adults, most of the slaves were set up on smallholdings in a dwelling of their own. They had to give a higher proportion of their produce to their master, and it was a hard fact that if times were difficult they could be sold, but otherwise there was little to distinguish them from peasants.

'Sound in his wind, graceful in his movements – what am I bid? Who will start me at two thousand?'

'One thousand.'

'With the man at back. One thousand, I am bid. Who will offer me twelve hundred?'

A couple of years before, out on the Steppe, Ballista had travelled with the nomadic Heruli. With their vivid tattoos, and elongated skulls from having them bound as infants, they were a strange race. Many of their customs were bizarre. But their attitudes to slavery were admirable. Their slaves rode with them to war. If any of them fought bravely, they were given their freedom. Several of the advisors to their king had begun as slaves.

Bidding for the youth was brisk. He was sold for two and a half thousand sesterces. It seemed a lot, but Ballista had not bought a new slave for years. People were always complaining of the inflation of prices. Successive regimes adulterating the precious metal in the coinage had not helped. The purchaser insisted on a detailed written contract: name, race, price, the full names of the vendor and his guarantor, date and place of sale, together with a certificate of health, and no record of running away or gambling. The crowd waited patiently enough while the formalities were concluded. Nothing looked out of place as Ballista surveyed the market.

'Gentlemen, for your delectation ...' The auctioneer paused theatrically.

His burly assistant led a girl out from the building and to the foot of the steps.

'Margarita! A pearl by name, a jewel in looks!'

A boisterous cheer from the assembled men.

'Come now, up you come, don't be shy.'

A gentle push from the assistant, and the girl scurried up the steps.

'Your wife won't like it when you take her home, but who could resist such a hot little number from Syria? We all know what they are like! More avid than sparrows, full of licentious oriental tricks.'

The girl was wearing a plain short tunic. There was no need for artifice to aid her looks. She stood, eyes cast down, hands clasped across herself.

'Show us what she's got,' a man called from the floor.

The auctioneer pulled her hands apart, then, with a practiced movement, tugged her tunic from her shoulders. The material pooled around her feet.

'Turn her round,' someone shouted, 'we want to get a good look at all of her.'

Naked, she shuffled around. Her reluctance seemed to fan the lust of the viewers.

Ballista glanced back at the throng. Everyone was studying the girl, every face captivated. Except right at the back, near the entrance, an unshaven man with a long nose was surveying the crowd. The two men with him also gave no attention to the girl.

Stooping, Ballista turned to where the assistant stood at the bottom of the steps. 'Do you have anything special kept back in the cells?'

The man looked at Ballista with contempt. With his ragged cloak, and the rent in his tunic, never mind the bruises and scratches, Ballista knew he cut a tatterdemalion figure. He opened his wallet. There were only two gold and half a dozen bronze coins left. He took out one of the gold.

'The Master always holds a few back for special customers.' The assistant's demeanour had changed. 'What are you looking for?'

'Something discreet.'

'Ah, one of those.' An unpleasant look of complicity appeared on the man's face. 'You want one that has been cut?' He whispered, as he took the coin. 'Come with me.'

Leaning forward, Ballista shuffled after him through the door.

Inside, metal cages opened off a central walkway. Wretched merchandise huddled inside most of them. From somewhere came the sound of sobbing. The assistant snapped at an underling to quiet that row.

'Here you are.' A young boy, perhaps no more than twelve, sat on the floor of one of the cages towards the rear. 'He was cut in Abasgia on the Black Sea; outside the empire, all perfectly legal.'

True or not, Ballista was sure that it was against the law to sell castrated slaves in Roman domains.

'Change of plan,' Ballista said.

'What is wrong with him? Good looking, perfectly healthy.'

'Nothing.' Ballista produced his last gold coin. 'Does the building have a back door?'

'Why?'

Sometimes it was best to tell the truth, or part of it. 'There are three men out front, I don't want them to see me.'

The assistant took the coin. 'Ask no questions, get no lies.'

There were two locks, three bolts and a bar on the door. Ballista forced himself not to fidget with impatience.

'It only leads into the alley.'

'That is fine.'

'Soon as you are through, it is shut and locked. Had people try to steal the goods before. You better not be thinking of any funny business.'

'No funny business.'

A mean alleyway. The door slammed shut behind him. A tall, unclimbable wall to the right, and a building site ahead. The alley was a dead end. The only way out, a corner which must lead back to the street by the entrance to the market. This was not good.

Labourers wheeled barrows of bricks down the passage, and unloaded them by ladders leading up to the half finished house. Other workers hauled the hods onto their backs, and carried them aloft.

Ballista walked behind a man returning with an empty barrow. Using the builder for cover, he peered around the corner. Two men were lounging by the entrance. Both wore cloaks too heavy for the weather. Under one could be seen the outline of a hilt. Ballista ducked back.

His last two gold coins had bought him entry into a trap. While there was life, there was hope. Ballista took off the cloak, screwed it up, and dropped it in the gutter. He pulled his tunic up through his belt, shortening it like a labourer. Hide in plain sight. If you act with confidence, you are seldom questioned.

Ballista strode to the foot of a ladder. He swung a basket full of bricks onto his shoulders. *Allfather, these things weigh a ton.* One hand holding the hod, the other grasping the rungs, he went up the ladder. Each time his boot came down, he thought the rung might snap under the weight. *There must be an art to this, or these labourers are as strong as oxen.*

At the top, he put the container down where others were stacked under the eye of a foreman. Without a word, he walked off along the planks on the scaffolding.

'Where the fuck are you going?'

Ballista stopped.

'And who the fuck are you?'

'New on site. The master told me to help out on the other side of the building.'

'Never told me about it. You got a trade?'

'Carpenter. Some of the timber over there needs looking at.'

'What's wrong with it?'

'Don't know until I look.' Adopting the air of a skilled man whose craft had been maligned, Ballista walked off.

One step, then another; waiting for a shout that never came. Clambering from one set of scaffolding to another, Ballista passed out of sight. Only then did he realise that the foreman had not noticed that he carried no tools. Probably the man was better with numbers on a papyrus than actually constructing anything.

There was less work going on away from the overseer. Wedged behind a partly tiled stretch of roof, two men were rolling dice. They looked up guiltily, but then grinned back at Ballista.

The other side of the building gave onto a patch of mud. One day it would be a garden, but for now was littered with building materials waiting to be lifted by a crane clamped to a platform at roof level. A low wall surrounded the yard. There was a gate. It was open, but a man stood there. Theft was as much a problem on building sites as in slave markets.

There was a drop of thirty feet or more from where Ballista stood to the ground. There were no ladders, and no scaffolding here. Looking at the ropes hanging from the crane, Ballista wished that he had been able to keep his cloak. Now there was nothing for it but to ruin his tunic or burn his hands. The cut on his right palm decided the issue. With the knife, he sawed strips from the bottom of the tunic. He wound them tightly around his hands.

Not for the first time today, he was glad that he had no fear of heights. Reaching out, he took a firm grip on one of the ropes. A deep breath, and he swung out. The muscles in his shoulders and arms strained – his hands slipped a little – and then he got his boots one above the other on the rope.

Even through the wadded cloth, he could feel the heat of the friction in his hands, as he slid fast to the ground.

'What the fuck are you doing?' The site watchman came over. Obviously it was an hour for people to ask questions laced with obscenities.

Ballista did not have time for this. With his wrapped right hand held rigid, he chopped the man in the throat.

Struggling to breath through his damaged windpipe, the man could neither shout nor scream as he fell.

There was no outcry. No one else appeared. So Ballista walked out of the gate.

CHAPTER 21

The Temple of Isis

'G ET YOUR COPPER READY AND you will hear a tale of gold.'
The cry was a traditional one, but the itinerant storyteller
obviously had a good reputation in the neighbourhood. At once a
crowd began to gather.

Ballista stood on the corner, from where he could see down both
streets. Time was pressing now, and he ought to keep moving. Yet
he was tired and famished. The audience would offer some cover
while he rested. On the other hand, if he found a cook shop, he
could get off the street and sit down. Perhaps he had enough coins
left for a mug of wine and a bowl of soup in comfort. It seemed an
age since he had eaten in the Street of the Sandal Makers. But then
again, if he was spotted, it might be more difficult to get away from
inside a tavern. He knew that he was dithering. It was hard to think
clearly through fatigue and hunger.

The decision was made for him when he caught a scent of
cooked meat. A vendor was weaving through the throng, a tray
of food suspended from straps around his neck. As if of their own
volition, Ballista's feet took him over to those gathering around the
storyteller.

The street trader was selling grilled pork wrapped in flatbread.
Ballista bought two of them with the last of his small coins. Wolf-
ing them down, he worked his way into the crowd; deep enough

hopefully to block him from the casual glances of those passing by, but not so far as to prevent him seeing out, or to hinder a quick escape.

'Who here believes in ghosts?'

Those assembled were of all walks and stations; free and slaves, men and women, gaggles of older children, others still with their nurses. They murmured with happy expectation, and smiled; one or two laughed. Some might prefer the mimes, but among most people the storytellers, along with singers and musicians, were as popular as jugglers and conjurers, entertainment as good as back-street boxing and animal fights.

'And when you are walking alone in the dead of night, down a deserted street, or out on a country lane? Do you then never look over your shoulder, never whistle or sing to keep away the spirits of the dead? Are you then so certain that the mere chink of metal, a shout, or the bark of a dog will send flitting away the vengeful shades of the murdered, the crucified, the hanged, of all those violently wrenched from life, of those denied burial, of all the dark multitude without a coin to buy passage across the Styx?'

The speaker was good. It was easy to overlook the teaming street, the safe afternoon sunshine, and the fact that he was perched on a crate that, by its smell, had recently contained dead fish. Ballista made sure that he kept an eye on those walking past. So far only one group had caught his attention; a party of off-duty escorts of a magistrate, standing out by their neat uniformity.

'Now I don't know about ghosts, but I can swear to the existence of other terrible creatures that stalk the night. What I am going to tell you is true. It happened to me, two winters past, not six miles from where we stand here.'

A frisson of pleasurable fear at the proximity of the supernatural ran through the crowd.

'When I was living around the corner – the lodging house that Gavilla owns now – I started seeing the wife of Terentius who kept an inn out on the Capua road. Late one afternoon she sent me word that old Terentius had gone off for the night drinking in the subura with some of his cronies. Let me tell you, I don't hold with philosophers, but those wise men who say that desire is a cruel tyrant know just what they are talking about. I decided it was too good an opportunity to miss, even if I had to walk half the night.'

An ex-soldier and his servant joined the edge of the listeners. Ballista tensed, ready to run or fight. The veteran was respectable looking. He did not wear a sword, and was nearing old age. The swordsmen at the Mausoleum, and the one in the baths, had been young, still of an age to be in service. They had been accompanied by no slaves. Ballista relaxed a little.

'There are a lot of thieves out in the country. So I talked another of the guests into walking with me as far as the fifth milestone. He was a soldier, sword on hip, brave as a lion. Fool that I am, I thought I was safe. Out of the city, where the tombs line the road, he goes off to one side. Thinking he needs to relieve himself, I wait, singing away, counting the stars. After a bit, I looked over, and do you know what I saw?'

The crowd, entering into the spirit of the thing, waited with baited breath. Ballista had a shrewd suspicion what was coming.

'The soldier had stripped off all his clothes. My heart was in my mouth. Naked as the day he was born, he pisses in a circle all around them. I stood there like a corpse. Then before my eyes, he throws back his head and howls. I was off, running down the road, like I was in the stadium. When I had gone a good way – the sweat pouring off me – I glance back. And there, in the pale moonlight, the biggest wolf you ever saw is loping off through the tombs.'

True or not, it had not happened to the storyteller two winters past, or any other time. Ballista had read the story in the *Satyricon* of Petronius when he was young. It was Maximus's favourite book. Ballista had used it to teach his bodyguard to read. *Werewolf, my arse, as the Hibernian might have said.*

Ballista's attention left the story, although he kept watch on the street. No distance now to the Camp of the Strangers. But, unable to convincingly affect the cowed bearing of a slave, his tattered and slashed tunic, let alone the bloodstain on the chest, drew attention. So far his attempts at disguise had been less than successful.

'She was awake all right. "If only you had got here earlier," she said. "A wolf got into the grounds, tore the livestock to pieces. But he didn't get away unscathed. One of the slaves got him in the neck with a spear." I could not close my eyes all night.'

An extraordinary figure was walking down the street. Tall with a shaven head, he was dressed in a long skirt of linen, hitched up high across his otherwise naked chest. Over his face he wore a mask fashioned like the face of a dog, one side painted black, the other gilded. Only his eyes could be seen. It was the priest of Isis from the street of the Sandal Makers, or at least one very like him.

Perhaps, Ballista thought, *the gods do care after all.* Sidestepping and twisting, insinuating himself into gaps, he worked his way out of the audience. He was not destined to hear the denouement of the story; the journey home, where the storyteller found the soldier, returned to human form, lying in bed, with a bandaged wound to the neck.

It took some time to get clear of the crowd – the storyteller was popular indeed – and the street itself was busy. For a moment, Ballista thought he had lost the priest of Isis. But then he caught sight of his bald cranium, some distance off. Most stepped aside from the priest, and he was walking steadily, making good progress. Ballista set off to follow. The jostling pedestrians did not get out of his way. The priest was drawing ahead. Soon he would be out of sight. Ballista could not risk causing a scene by elbowing and shoving. Then, a more religious man again might have seen the hand of a god. A train of three porters carrying heavy amphorae emerged from a side street. Their purposeful step, and the loads they bore, prompted bystanders to give them free passage. With just a few hefty pushes, which earned a couple of curses, Ballista reached their slipstream. Now, tucked in behind in their wake, if anything, he was gaining on his quarry.

Last night on the Campus Martius, Ballista had been economical with the truth talking to Diomedes and his gang of roughs. True he had never served in Egypt, but, thanks to a drunken night in a bar on the waterfront in Ostia, he was not entirely ignorant about the worship of the Isis. His informant had been an initiate who had become disillusioned. As far as Ballista could recall, the goddess had been incestuously married to her brother Osiris. Another god, possibly another brother called Seth, had killed Osiris, chopped him up, and scattered the chunks of flesh all over Egypt. Helped by Anubis – whose mask the priest was wearing – Isis had gathered up the body parts, and brought Osiris back to life.

It was regeneration, life after death, that the cult offered its adherents. To achieve it required much fasting, abstinence, and, after hefty payments to the priests, secret ceremonies of initiation with drugged wine, and much smoke and mirrors. Its exotic, foreign origins, its openness to women as well as men, combined with its wealth and mysterious rituals, made it an object of suspicion to the traditionally minded. They accused the cult of greed and sexual licence. There had been a notorious scandal in the reign of Tiberius. The priests here in Rome had persuaded a credulous devotee, a woman married to a senator, that Anubis would manifest himself to her if she spent a night in the temple. The dog-headed visitor had been vigorous, but no epiphany. Later, if he had resisted the urge to boast of his conquest, and how he had bribed the priests, her seducer would not have been unmasked.

The slaves with the amphorae turned left onto the Via Labicana. Ballista trailed the priest across the road. As they ascended the Caelian, there were fewer people on the streets. But they were not deserted. There could be no witnesses to what Ballista intended. Somehow he had to get the priest on his own.

Although it was still daylight, the priest held a lit lamp in one hand. In the other was a gilded rattle. The latter jingled as he walked. After a time the sound became maddening. It was no more than two hours until sunset. Ballista closed up behind the priest. Alleyways and courtyards opened off their path. Every time they passed one there were people in sight. Soon the priest would be safe inside the temple.

Assaulting a priest was frowned upon in most cultures. It invited eventual divine retribution, and much swifter human intervention. Having come so far, Ballista wondered whether to abandon the idea. But they were heading in roughly the right direction. He might yet get a chance, or something might occur to him.

On they tramped up the hill: two tall men with shaven heads, one in outlandish gleaming white linen, the other in a shabby and torn blue tunic.

The main Temple of Isis was down on the Campus Martius, but there had been another on the Caelian for generations. It stood opposite two groves of trees that flanked the home of the Tetricius family of senators. The head of the house was one of the main supporters of the pretender Postumus in Gaul. Perhaps it would be shuttered, the road outside deserted.

As the trees came into view, Ballista's hopes were dashed. The porter lounged outside, talking to no fewer than four litter-bearers.

Doubtless, like many of the noble families in times of civil war, the Tetricii hedged its bets, and maintained a relative in both camps.

Ballista quickened his pace. 'Excuse me, sir.'

The priest was on the threshold of the temple.

'My son.' Behind the canine visage, his eyes were shrewd, but not unfriendly.

It would have to be in the temple.

'Can I help you?'

'It is a delicate matter,' Ballista said.

The muzzle of the dog rose, as its owner looked at the top of Ballista's head. 'Have you cast off the man that you used to be?'

'I have.' Claiming to be an initiate was a risk. One drunken conversation had not produced all that much information that he could remember. Yet he needed to go with the priest into the temple, get him on his own.

'Follow me. We can talk inside.'

Beyond the gate was an open courtyard with buildings on two sides, and the temple in the middle. Other shaven priests strolled here and there, servants scurried about, and a few worshippers made their way to and from the temple. The priest led Ballista to the larger of the two ranges of buildings. Inside it was decked out as a communal dining hall. Servants were placing tables by just three of the many couches.

'It is a thing that calls for much discretion,' Ballista said.

The priest pinched out the lamp, and put it down, along with the irritating rattle. 'Do not be concerned about the slaves. They have served Queen Isis all their lives. They are house-born.'

A single witness would be too many. Ballista had to get the priest alone. Perhaps the events in the time of Tiberius suggested a stratagem.

'As you see, I am a poor man.' Ballista indicated his grubby and ripped tunic. 'But I am a freedman of a great house' – he paused for dramatic effect – 'that best remain nameless. My mistress has reached the boundary of death, and returned.'

The dog's snout rounded on him. Had he misused a half-remembered line of the cult? Before he could be questioned, he pressed on. 'Anubis appeared to my mistress in a dream. The god commanded her to make offerings of gold to the goddess, and to spend the night alone in the temple.'

'Impossible!' The priest had raised his voice. It sounded strange issuing from behind the mask, but clearly was intended to be heard by the servants. 'The rite of incubation has been denied to women since the time of the false priest Arbaces.' The priest continued to talk loudly. 'I am sorry that you must take that response to your mistress. But, as you are a worshipper of the queen of goddesses, before you go, let me offer you hospitality in my quarters.'

The priest's room was decorated with paintings and statuettes of strange Egyptian deities with animal heads. There were several large, inlaid pieces of furniture, and rich covers on the bed. The place smelt musky with old incense.

'A discreet visit may be possible, depending on the size of the offerings.' The priest turned his back, and undid the thongs that held the mask in place.

Ballista drew his knife, and put it to the priest's throat.

'What?' Freed from the mask, the priest's face was round. Sleek with good living, it exhibited no signs of fasting and abstinence.

'Do not make a sound. I have no wish to harm you.'

'You dare steal from the goddess herself?'

'Only a few trifles. She will not miss them.'

'It is sacrilege. You will be cursed. The goddess will hunt you to the ends of the earth.'

'I have been cursed before. As you can tell, I am still here, and I have a knife at your throat.'

'The goddess will pursue you beyond the grave.'

'Quite possibly. Enough talk now. Take off your clothes.'

'What?' The priest looked thoroughly alarmed.

'Don't worry, you can keep your loincloth on.'

'The temple servants will come at any moment. You will be caught. The authorities will torture you on the rack, nail you on the cross.'

'No they won't. You will not be missed until the ceremony of the closing of the temple at sunset.' *And before then*, Ballista thought, *I have to reach the Colosseum.* He prodded the priest with the knife. 'Stop talking, and remove your clothes.'

Once the priest was nearly naked, Ballista cut up the coverlets from the bed. With the strips, he tied the wrists and ankles of the priest, tethered him to a heavy piece of furniture, and gagged him securely.

Stripped to his own loincloth, Ballista fastened his belt around his bare waist. He slid the dagger in its sheath to the small of his back. It should not show there, but would be hard to get at. It was not easy fastening the strap which held the linen skirt in its unaccustomed place almost under his armpits, but eventually he got it right. As they looked more serviceable, he had kept on his own boots. The folds of the linen almost covered them. Finally, he put on the mask.

There was even a mirror. Ballista checked his reflection. It was not identical to the priest, but one tall man with a shaved head, and the face of a dog, looked much like another.

'Do not struggle,' he said. 'You will be free in an hour or two.'

Outside, as at the building site, Ballista walked purposefully, as if he had every right to be there. He strode across the courtyard towards the gate.

'Master!' A voice called behind him. Ballista marched on.

'Master!' The patter of running sandals.

Ballista stopped.

A servant ran up. 'Your lantern and rattle.'

Without a word, Ballista took them, and walked away.

Twenty paces to the gate. He could feel the eyes of the servant on his back. Ten paces, nine. Almost there.

Glancing back as he went out, through the eyeholes of the canine mask, Ballista saw the servant. The man was staring after him, but had not uttered a sound. Thank Isis herself that her servants knew their place, and were not encouraged to question the eccentric behaviour of her priests.

CHAPTER 22

The Camp of the Strangers

A PRIEST OF ISIS WAS NOT AN unfamiliar sight on the Caelian. Which was just as well, Ballista reflected, as a moment earlier he had walked past a squad of the City Watch. The headquarters of their fifth Cohort was just to the west of that of the *frumentarii*. Far too close for comfort, if he had not been hidden behind his canine face mask. It was a good job that the ridiculous linen skirt was girdled under his armpits, concealing the bandages wrapped around his chest. As it was, despite his outlandish appearance, the men of the Watch had not given him a second glance.

The Camp of the Strangers was set on the highest point of the hill. Although for the majority of the population it might be a place to be dreaded, its solid and distinctive, brick-built walls proclaimed it an army base. For Ballista, catching sight of it as he trudged up from the east, at this moment it represented safety at last, the final way station on his journey across the city to the Colosseum. The men inside were soldiers. They existed to protect the emperor. Should their prefect not be in the camp, once Ballista had told his story, any officer of the *frumentarii* would organise an escort to rush him to Gallienus. Once he had reached the emperor, everything would be alright.

'Halt.'

There were four *frumentarii* guarding the gate. They were armed, ready for trouble. The diversity of their armour and equipment pointed to the different regular units out of which they had been seconded. Like specially selected soldiers everywhere, they affected a certain slovenliness that would not have been acceptable in their original formation. Such chosen men always saw themselves above the petty regulations that bound lesser men serving under the standards.

'State your name and business.'

'Arbaces, priest of Isis.' Until he was off the street, Ballista had no intention of revealing himself. Or maybe lying became a habit. After ten years away, the home life of Odysseus must have been difficult.

'And your business?'

'I have information of a plot against the life of the emperor.'

'Centurion.' At the call of the guard, an officer emerged from the gatehouse. Another universal feature of elite units that were composed of disparate elements was their high number of officers compared with ordinary ranks.

'Another one who knows of a conspiracy.'

A resigned tilt of the head indicated Ballista should follow the centurion.

They walked between porticos which fronted two barracks. All the doors were closed. Normally, off-duty soldiers would be idling in the shade, playing dice, drinking and talking. Although there were never more than a couple of hundred *frumentarii* in the camp, today it was unusually quiet.

The centurion led Ballista to a small square. A dozen civilians sat or stood around under the bored gaze of four soldiers. Those waiting had nothing in common physically. One even wore the quilted jacket and trousers of a Sarmatian tribesman from the Steppes. They were not prisoners, but they all shared an air of furtive desperation. When a man was convicted of treason, the individual who had betrayed him to the authorities received a quarter of his confiscated property. In Rome some men made a living by denunciations. Informers like the men in this square were motivated as often by avarice or spite as concern for the welfare of the ruler. Under a suspicious or vengeful emperor there were fortunes to be made. Gallienus was neither as mistrustful or rancorous as some, but the trade remained lucrative, and it could never be stopped.

The centurion handed Ballista a small wooden tablet. On the tessera was scratched XIII. Even treachery had its bureaucracy.

'I need to see the prefect immediately,' Ballista said.

'Don't you all,' the centurion replied. 'Wait until your number is called.'

'I must see Rufinus now.'

'You can wait your turn.' The centurion looked around. 'Doubt he will get through this lot before dark. Best you come back tomorrow.'

Ballista began to untie his mask. It was time for crafty Odysseus to stand forth. He took off the canine face of Anubis.

'I am Marcus Clodius Ballista, and I have information that an attempt will be made on the life of the emperor as he leaves the Colosseum at sunset.'

The centurion looked startled. 'Ballista . . . *the* Marcus Clodius Ballista?'

'There is no time to waste,' Ballista said. 'Take me to Rufinus.'

The centurion jerked his head at two of the soldiers. 'You two, come with us.'

They halted at the steps outside the headquarters building. The centurion told Ballista and the soldiers to wait, and went inside.

He was back in moments, pushing a scrawny man in front of him. 'You get nothing.' He pushed the man down the steps. 'Clear off, or you will spend the night in the cells.'

Muttering at the injustice, glowering at Ballista and the soldiers, the gaunt figure shuffled away.

'Marcus Clodius Ballista, the prefect will see you now.'

They went up the stairs, and through the door, which shut behind them.

Rufinus was seated behind a desk. Two more soldiers, one with a nastily bruised face, stood on either side.

Ballista heard the blades slide from the scabbards before he felt their tips prod his back.

'Search him,' the prefect said. Given the nature of the work of the *frumentarii*, precautions were necessary.

Experienced hands patted Ballista down. Armpits, crotch, they missed nothing. A blade slit the back of the linen skirt, and the knife was removed from its place of concealment in the small of his back.

'On his knees, and bind his hands.' Precautions were one thing, but this was excessive.

Ballista did not resist. An unarmed man could not win against five soldiers with swords, six if their commander was counted.

When Ballista had been pushed roughly to the floor, his wrists tied behind his back, the prefect ordered all out except the two soldiers who had been with him at the start.

When the door was shut again, Ballista started to speak. The prefect told him to be silent, as if he already knew everything that Ballista might say. A feeling of dread sat like a stone in Ballista's chest.

Rufinus had a thin, pointed face. It reminded Ballista of a half-tamed polecat, a creature accustomed to sanguinary pursuits in dark places. Slowly a smile spread across the rodent-like features.

'The gods are good,' Rufinus said.

Both the soldiers laughed.

So this was the end. Ballista could not understand how he could have been such a fool. Despite their civilian dress, he had realised the swordsmen at the Mausoleum had served in the army. The terrible mistake had been to assume that their service was in the past. They had not deserted. They were still serving. They were *frumentarii*. And now here, standing above him, was the one he had battered unconscious in the tunnels under the Baths.

'Every man scouring the city for you, and you walk into the Camp of the Strangers. It is good of you, but, my dear sir, the trouble you have caused.' Rufinus spoke in a dispassionate voice, as if discussing the cost of a dinner party. 'Two warehousemen dead in a burned granary in Transtiberim. Four young equestrians assaulted in the subura. Two of the City Watch beaten to within an inch of their lives at the Bridge of Nero, another hurled to his death from a rooftop at the Markets of Trajan. No fewer than three of my men killed in the Mausoleum, and Labeo here pummelled near to death in the baths. The odd incident may have slipped my mind. Even so, it is quite a trail of destruction.'

Ballista said nothing. There was no point pleading.

'The Prefect of the City Watch is a fool,' Rufinus continued. 'The rest of us were against involving you, but Scarpio insisted. He does hate you so. A great, hulking barbarian favourite of our unworthy emperor, lolling in a seat of honour at the front of the imperial box, petted by Gallienus, while little mouse Scarpio has to keep out of sight at the back. It struck a chord in his soul. He does so want you dead, and, of course, he will get his wish.'

Death comes to cowards as well as the brave. 'I am sorry about the warehousemen, and the man who fell from the roof,' Ballista said.

The prefect gestured to Labeo. Throwing himself sideways, Ballista took the boot in the side of his head. With his hands bound behind his back, he could not stop his face hitting the floor. Labeo kicked him in the stomach. Ballista curled into a foetal position. Labeo walked around, and kicked him in the kidneys.

'Enough,' Rufinus said. 'I don't want bloodstains all over my floor. Get him upright.'

Ballista was yanked back onto his knees. The iron taste of blood was in his mouth. He spat on the floor.

Labeo went to hit him again, but Rufinus motioned him to stop.

'Are you a devotee of the schools of philosophy?' Rufinus was enjoying this. 'They argue that what does not affect the inner man is an irrelevance.'

'Fuck you,' Ballista said.

'Evidently you are some way off philosophical enlightenment. Even so, I would not want you to entertain any vain hopes as you make your way to the underworld.'

From the desk, Rufinus picked up a wooden writing block.

Ballista's heart sank.

Opening the block, Rufinus began to read. 'There is a plot to assassinate you . . . one is bald, another is said to look like a peasant . . . take all precautions . . . the bearer of this message knows nothing.'

Ballista could sense his self-control slipping.

'You write a good hand for a barbarian.'

'What have you done to him?' Ballista could not help blurting out the question.

'And every word you wrote was true. Even that the bearer of the message knew nothing. It only took a few touches of the hot irons to convince me of that. The little cousin of your wife was prepared to tell me anything.'

Ballista felt as if he was sinking into a well of despair.

'Little Decimus is here in one of the cells. As I am not an inhumane man, perhaps you might draw comfort from heading to Hades together.'

Rufinus tipped his head on one side, as if pondering deeply. 'Except, of course, without coins to pay the ferryman, neither of your shades will be able to cross the Styx. An interesting question – will you wander together or alone? Would an eternity of torment be improved by company?'

Ballista remained silent.

'And while we are on the subject of your family . . .'

Now Ballista knew he was nearing the depths of the well. Nothing left to do, but one last doomed struggle.

'They will have to die, but Scarpio is cruel, and, for one so mouse-like, extraordinarily lustful. He intends to enjoy your wife, before he strangles her. Well, she is a wanton-looking bitch.'

Gathering all his strength, Ballista prepared to hurl himself across the desk. Perhaps he could at least sink his teeth in his tormentor's face, before the swords cut him down.

The door swung open.

'We are not to be disturbed,' Rufinus snapped.

Two soldiers entered. They were clad in mail, but carried trays covered by cloths, like waiters. One had the end of his nose missing. The other was little more handsome.

'Oysters! The finest oysters from the Lucrine Lake,' No-nose said. 'Oysters for the prefect.'

'I did not order any oysters,' Rufinus said.

'Most probably not,' No-nose said. With a flick of his wrist, he tossed the tray, seafood and all, at the prefect.

'What?' Outraged, Rufinus surged to his feet, shellfish clattering onto his desk.

Open mouthed with surprise, the *frumentarius* on the right saw No-nose's blade flash out from under the cloth. A second later it punched into his stomach.

The *frumentarius* on the left got his sword up into a guard, but too slow to prevent the other man driving the point of his blade into his neck.

Neither had time to scream.

Rufinus went for his hilt.

'Do you think you can draw your sword before I bury mine in your guts?' No-nose said.

The commander of the *frumentarii* did not think so. No-nose went and disarmed him, pushed him back down into his seat.

'You took your time,' Ballista said to his bodyguards.

'Sure, it has been a trying few hours,' Maximus said. 'Been all over the city looking for you, since that magician turned up. The praetorians at the camp last night were most inhospitable.'

'Killing several fuck-mother-bastards,' Tarchon said as he cut the ropes that bound Ballista's wrists. 'Happy time.'

Maximus regarded Ballista. 'Why are you wearing a skirt, and where has your hair gone?'

'Long story. Did you bring me any clothes?'

'Do I look like a tailor?'

'Now kill this shit-arse-bugger, and off we go.' Tarchon had a way with compound obscenities. 'Everyone contented.'

'Wait!' Rufinus said.

'Kill quick, leave sooner.' Tarchon hefted his weapon.

'I am the head of the *frumentarii*.' Rufinus was pleading for his life. 'People tell me things. I know secrets, something you want.'

'Tarchon is right,' Maximus said. 'The soldiers out there will soon get suspicious. We had best be on our way.'

'No!' Rufinus held out his hands in supplication. 'I know who killed your friend Calgacus.'

Tarchon stopped, his blade poised.

'That is no secret,' Ballista said. 'It was Hippothous the Greek.'

'But I know where Hippothous is living.'

'Where?'

'Let me call for the guards, and I will tell you.'

'And then give us safe passage?'

'Of course, you have my word.'

'And watch us leave to tell Gallienus that you are plotting to kill him?'

Maximus looked at Ballista. 'Let me make him talk.'

'No time,' Ballista said. 'If he does not die now, the three of us will die in a few moments.'

Ballista walked behind the prefect's chair. He reached over, and took a metal disk that hung from a fine chain around Rufinus' neck. On the disk were inscribed the words MILES ARCANUS. It was the identity badge of a *frumentarius*; the words meant secret soldier.

Maximus passed Ballista a sword.

'Don't kill me, I beg you!'

Ballista pulled Rufinus' head back by the hair. Lining up the steel, Ballista thrust down into the prefect's throat.

CHAPTER 23

The Caelian Hill

THE TWO *FRUMENTARII* ESCORTED the strangely dressed prisoner down the steps from the headquarters. His face was
obscured by one of the dog masks that the priests of Isis wore, and
his hands were tied behind his back. It was not uncommon for a
man to enter the prefect's office as an informant, and leave as a prisoner. Nor was it unusual that they looked battered and dishevelled;
this one's linen robe was split down the back. What was strange
was the direction the group were taking. Normally they went to the
cells, not towards the main gate. The centurion strolled over.

'New orders.'

All *frumentarii* cultivated an offhand attitude. The centurion
did not recognise the one who spoke. Soldiers were always being
posted in and out of the camp, but this one had a striking white scar
where the end of his nose should be.

'Let me see,' the centurion said.

'Verbal, not in writing.'

The scar looked a bit like a cat's arse.

'Wait there,' the centurion said, turning away. 'I will speak to the
prefect.'

As soon as he had gone a few steps, the prisoner and escort set off
again between the barracks. They walked quickly, almost at a jog.

'Not too bright, arse-fucker-bastard.'

'Even a man of his limited intelligence might notice all the dead bodies and everything,' No-nose said.

At the gate one of the guards barred their way. 'Where are you taking him?'

Both the *frumentarii* fished out their identity disks: MILES ARCANUS.

'Rufinus wants him taken to the Palatine.' Again Maximus did the talking. 'Stubborn bastard, he is. The prefect thinks he needs the special expertise of the Palace cellars; the rack and the horse, all those cunning devices that loosen a man's tongue.'

'Well, that will be the last we see of him.' The guard stood aside. 'His Egyptian goddess can't help him now.'

As soon as they stepped through the gate, they heard the distant shout. 'Sound the alarm!'

'Could be time to start running,' Maximus said.

'Stop those men!'

Miraculously, the bonds fell away from the prisoner's wrists. Ballista tore off the face of Anubis, and pelted after the others. The long skirt tangled his legs, made it hard to run. Already he was falling behind.

'Not far,' Maximus called over his shoulder, as he vanished around a corner.

Stumbling after, Ballista saw one of the best things he had ever seen.

Across the street, blocking it from side to side, stood a wall of northern warriors. Shields, helmets, glittering coats of mail, fierce bearded faces; there must have been fifty or more of them.

'I stopped at the Gardens of Dolabella,' Maximus said. 'Thought we might be needing some help.'

The German Guard parted to admit the fugitives. Hands pounded Ballista on the back, strong arms embraced him. He recognised one of the warriors.

'Thorgrim, son of Svan, what are you doing here?' Ballista said.

'A man has to be somewhere,' the Heathobard replied.

'Sure, there was much debate in the Gardens,' Maximus said. 'Some of the men were for leaving you there. "Fuck him," they said. That was mainly the Goths, although the Franks agreed with them. And, now I think of it, most of the Marcomanni were of the same opinion. "Why should we be risking our lives for a cunt like him?" they said. It is extraordinary how many enemies you Angles make.'

Further discussion was curtailed by the arrival of the *frumentarii* around the corner. There were no more than a dozen of them. Seeing the northerners, they skidded to a halt, looked at each other anxiously.

Their centurion stepped forward. 'Marcus Clodius Ballista is wanted for treason, arson, assault, theft, and murder. Hand him over!'

'Is that all?' Thorgrim called back. 'Nothing serious then, nothing like fucking a Vestal Virgin?'

'Any man who gives aid to a traitor is guilty of treason himself.' The centurion was bristling with outrage. Outnumbered as they were, his men seemed less sure of their cause.

'Mind you,' Thorgrim said, 'he has fucked your wife. But we have all had her. Like throwing a sausage down the Via Sacra.'

'You barbarians had better give him up, or every one of you will be on a cross by tomorrow.'

'And will it be you driving the nails in, pretty boy?'

The centurion turned to his men. 'Seize him!'

The soldiers did not move.

'Obey the order! Get in there, and arrest the barbarian!'

From the ranks of the northerners came a low hooming sound.

The soldiers shifted uneasily.

The Germans took a step forward.

As one, the *frumentarii* turned and ran. Northern laughter and shouts of derision followed them.

The centurion was left standing on his own. He started to speak. Someone threw a stone. It missed. The centurion turned, and strutted off with a certain dignity.

'We had best get going,' Thorgrim said. 'Your Hibernian here said you had to get to the Games before the emperor leaves.'

It was a few hundred paces to the Colosseum. The route was straightforward. It should take no time. Turn right into the Street of the African Head, follow it down, the school for imperial slaves on the left, the gladiators' hospital and armoury to the right, past the fountain with the sculpture wearing elephant tusks that gave the road its name, and emerge between two gladiatorial barracks, the Dacicus and the Magnus, by the eastern frontage of the Colosseum.

The warriors shouldered their shields, and moved into a rough column. Ballista took his place at their head, feeling more than faintly ridiculous in his Egyptian linen.

As they rounded the corner onto the Vicus Capitis Africae, it became obvious that the journey would be neither quick nor easy. About a hundred paces ahead, under the arch where the Annian Aqueduct crossed, the street was filled with armed men. Bronze helmets, leather armour, swords and plain shields; it was the City Watch. Shoulder to shoulder, twenty men across, some five deep; about a hundred of them. Of course, the barracks of their fifth Cohort was just to the west. Even so, they had acted fast. Perhaps the centurion of the *frumentarii* had never expected the Germans to hand over Ballista, maybe he had just wanted to keep them talking, while a messenger turned out the City Watch.

The northerners halted out of the effective range of a javelin.

'What now?' Thorgrim said.

Before Ballista could answer, a groan came from the rear of the column. Rising on his toes, peering over the helmets of the men behind, Ballista saw its cause. The *frumentarii* had returned. Now there were about the same number of them as there were northerners. They spread out, in two rough ranks across the road. The way back was blocked. A blank wall on one side, high buildings with bolted doors on the other. The Germans were trapped.

'This is not getting better,' Maximus said.

Ballista looked at the sky. The sun was behind the buildings, but obviously getting low. Not more than an hour until sunset. The last hour of the day had begun.

'A thing of no consequence,' Thorgrim said. 'One charge will scatter the *frumentarii*. As for the others – the bucketmen aren't real soldiers. They will not be in a hurry to fight.' The Heathobard exuded confidence.

The same centurion of the *frumentarii* walked out from their line. He had no shield, and his sword was still in its scabbard. The officer had almost the assurance of Thorgrim the Heathobard.

'You are surrounded, outnumbered three to one.' Long years on parade grounds and battlefields had given the centurion a voice that carried. A man without experience did not end up as a centurion in the *frumentarii*. 'Lay down your arms, and hand over the wanted man.'

Ballista turned to a warrior whose arms were bright with gold torques. 'Now it is us that need to keep *him* talking.'

'Talking a waste of breath,' Thorgrim said. 'A thing for these southerners. Better we give them the song our swords sing.'

'The fighting will come.' Ballista spoke again to the warrior with the heavy gold bands encircling his arms. 'Tell him you will hand me over, if you can keep your weapons. Tell him you have sworn an oath never to be parted from your blades. Make up anything, just keep him busy for a few moments.'

The warrior walked out to the centurion.

Ballista turned back to Thorgrim. 'All you say is true, but then the City Watch will be between us and the emperor. Time is running out. I must get to Gallienus before he leaves the imperial box. Have enough men to hold the *frumentarii* from our backs. The rest form a swine's snout, and punch a hole through these bucketmen.'

The Heathobard grinned. 'You Himlings are leaders of men, deep thinkers. Not for nothing do the peoples of the Suebian Sea bend the knee to your dynasty.'

'How could it be otherwise, with the Heathobards as our allies.' Ballista tugged off the rent linen robe. 'I need some clothes. It might be difficult for a barbarian in a loin cloth to gain admittance to the imperial presence.'

The big Heathobard gestured another warrior to help him off with his armour. 'You take my mailcoat.'

'I will move faster, draw less attention, unarmoured.'

'You want my britches as well?'

'Just the tunic.'

'I am happy to fight these little firemen naked.'

'The tunic will do.'

By the time Ballista had pulled the tunic over his head, and someone had pressed a sword into his hand, the negotiations had ended.

'A very rude man, that centurion,' the returned warrior said in mock wonder. 'Told me to fuck myself. Said if I did not have my hairy-arsed tribesmen give you up, I would find myself eaten by a lion, or some such horrible beast.'

A few quietly spoken words from Thorgrim, and the northerners fell into place. Twenty shoulder to shoulder facing back towards the *frumentarii*, the other thirty or so in a compact wedge pointed at the City Watch.

'Much killing again,' Tarchon said with an unnerving glee. 'Suanians like me, having the great fondness for killing.'

Thorgrim had put his mail back on. Without a tunic under the armour as padding, it would be far from comfortable; dangerous too, if a blow snapped the rings, and drove them into his flesh. Notwithstanding, he had taken the position of honour at the tip of the swine's snout. Ballista tucked in behind him – Maximus on his left shoulder, Tarchon the right. Ballista was unarmoured. It would have insulted the honour of the other Germans if he had stood in the front rank.

A movement above made Ballista look up. The wall to the left was the outer wall of the camp of the City Watch. There were no battlements. No threat could come from there. But there were apartments on the right. The inhabitants of the upper floors had opened their windows, and were looking down. Those that had balconies were coming out for a better view. For a moment Ballista was worried that they might intervene. A tile or pot dropped from a height by an old woman or a child could kill as certainly as a sword cut from the strongest warrior. Then he remembered that the citizens of Rome feared and hated the *frumentarii* as much, if not more, than they did northern barbarians. The locals had no intention of becoming involved. For them this was like an impromptu gladiatorial contest. This was pure entertainment. They did not care who won. They loathed both sides. The more dead the better.

Swallows dived and hunted high above the roofs. It was a presage of good weather tomorrow, at least for those alive to enjoy it.

The voice of the centurion rang down the street. 'Are you ready for war?'

'Ready!' The *frumentarii* yelled back.

Three times the traditional call and response, then the soldiers charged.

They crashed into the Germans to the rear. The noise was deafening, like a mighty oak falling in a forest. The thin northern line gave a pace or two. Here and there a warrior went down. The *frumentarii* were real soldiers, men who had stared into the face of battle. But the tribesmen were also accustomed to stand close to the steel. Where their kinsmen had fallen, others stepped across into the space. The line held. Numbers would tell, and soon, but perhaps the Germans would buy Ballista enough time.

A low rumble came from Thorgrim the Heathobard. The rest of the warriors in the wedge facing the City Watch took it up. They held their shields over their mouths. The *barritus*, the war cry of the North, swelled like thunder.

Ballista was desperate for them to set off. They had to break through the men opposite before the *frumentarii* were on them, hacking at their undefended backs. Yet he knew that northern warriors needed to work themselves up into blood fury. For them the volume and confidence of the *barritus* foretold the outcome of a battle. Ballista realised that he was roaring with the others.

At last Thorgrim took the first step.

'Shields!' An officer of the City Watch was shouting. His voice was high, tinged with fear.

The northerners walked slowly forward in a wedge, shields locked, like one great armoured beast.

'Hold the line!' The Roman officer sounded as if he were pleading.

Twenty paces out, the shield wall opened a fraction, and the warriors from the North broke into a run. Boots pounding, armour and weapons jingling and rattling, the awful war cry on their lips, they swept down on the City Watch.

Over Thorgrim's shoulder, Ballista saw some of the firemen flinch, try and edge away from the impact. Gaps appeared in the centre of their line. But they did not run.

Like a wave into a headland, the northerners smashed into the City Watch. There was no noise like it on earth. The thud of shield into shield, the clatter and scrape of steel on steel, gasps and grunts of effort and pain.

The Roman front line staggered back. But the depth of their ranks slowed the momentum of the warriors. All too soon, they ground to a halt. The long swords of the northerner's slashed down at shoulders and heads. The City Watch crouched under their shields, occasionally thrusting underarm around the side. Such blows were the easiest to parry, but they exposed the least of the attacker. These firemen did not want to die. But they were brave. They were not running.

'Forward!' Thorgrim bellowed. Putting his shoulder to his shield, the Heathobard heaved the man facing him backwards. The watchman went barrelling into the next rank. Thorgrim moved into the space where he had stood. Knees bent, straining, the wedge of northerners shuffled after, deeper into the Roman formation.

An eddy in the scrum, and Ballista found himself in the front. One pace between him and a watchman. The flicker of a blade thrusting at his unprotected thighs. With no shield, Ballista blocked with his sword, forcing the man's blade wide. Recovering, Ballista aimed a backhanded chop down towards the fireman's right arm. The shield came up. Splinters of wood flew. Next a forehand cut to the left shoulder. Still high, the shield came across. Ballista pulled the blow, dropped to one knee, and lunged. His sword slid under the wooden boards, bit deep into flesh. The man screamed, and reeled away, clutching his crotch.

Just one rank to go. So nearly through. All Ballista could see of this final man were white eyes between the rim of his shield and the brim of his helmet. Ballista launched a series of attacks; low backhand cut, overhead slash, thrust to the face. The man was quick and agile. Every time the sword chopped into the leather and wood of the shield. Again Ballista tried the feint and underarm thrust. This time his enemy was equal to the stratagem. The man offered no offence, but there seemed no way through his dogged defence.

A terrible sound from behind. Ballista could not take his eyes off his opponent's blade. There was no need. It was cheering. It could only mean one thing. The *frumentarii* had finally broken through the rear-guard. Now they would be running towards the wedge of Germans fighting the City Watch. In a moment Ballista and those with him would be surrounded.

It could not end like this. Ballista had to get clear, had to reach the emperor. A desperate position demanded a desperate remedy.

He swung a mighty two handed blow down at the crown of the man's helmet. Sure enough, the shield snapped up. Ballista dropped his sword, and leapt. He landed half on the shield, his fingers like claws hooked around its edges. Using his weight, he drove them both to the ground. He landed on top of man and shield. Still gripping the shield, he scrabbled to one knee. The man started to rise. Wrenching the shield free, Ballista hit him in the face with the rim. The man slumped back, then began to lever himself up again. Three, four times, Ballista brought the rim of the shield down with all his force. Face a bloody mess, the man moaned, but did not move.

Some sense of danger warned Ballista. He rolled sideways, trying to haul the shield over him. Too late, and too slow. The blade was arcing down. The shield would not stop it. Ballista watched its descent, saw the bright decorations on the chest of the young officer wielding it. There was another flash of steel, even quicker.

The officer stared uncomprehending at his elbow. The blood was pumping from the stump. It splashed hot and repellent down onto Ballista.

'No good looking for arm,' Tarchon said. 'All gone, like you.'

There was a sickening sound, like breaking the carcass of a chicken, as Tarchon's blade sliced off the young man's helmet, and removed the top of his skull.

A man reached down. Maximus pulled Ballista to his feet.

The three stood alone, bizarrely overlooked in the chaos.

Behind them, the gap Ballista had forced had closed again. The northerners were ringed with steel. There were no more than a dozen on their feet. Thorgrim was one of them, but barely. He fought one handed. With the other he leant on his shield. His left leg was open, the white bone showing through the red of his lifeblood. As if he knew he was watched, the Heathobard looked at Ballista.

'Time to go, Dernhelm. Get to the emperor. I will see you in the Hall of the Allfather.'

Ballista scooped up a sword. There was nothing to say. He turned, and flanked by Maximus and Tarchon, he ran away down the street.

CHAPTER 24

The Colosseum

SENATOR SEMPRONIUS SAW the fear in the eyes of the gladiator. The gladiator was a myrmillo, helmet tucked under his arm, shield propped against his legs. He stood next to his opponent, a retiarius. They were on the sand in front of the imperial box, saluting the emperor. There was hatred as well as fear in the eyes of the myrmillo. Sempronius found himself quickly looking down to check the soldiers and the safety net. The rollers and the spikes on top would make it hard to climb. There would be ample time for the archers to shoot the myrmillo long before he made it over.

'That myrmillo has lost his nerve,' Cecropius said. 'I will wager you a thousand sesterces on the net fighter.'

Sempronius stared at Cecropius. How could the man appear so calm? These were veteran gladiators, one of the last pairs to fight. The clouds above were already marbled with the purple of sunset. No more than half an hour, and the games would be over. Half an hour, and the emperor would leave his seat. Gallienus would make his way out into the corridor. And then . . .

Of course Cecropius was calm. In half an hour, out in the corridor, it would not be Cecropius who would have to strike the first blow. Cecropius could stand back, anonymous in the entourage, and perhaps do nothing. Cecropius could watch Sempronius risk everything for freedom.

'Take the bet.' Cecropius had leant close, was whispering in Sempronius' ear. 'Everything must appear normal.'

Cecropius's breath reeked of garlic. A tyrant like Gallienus could take a goat-boy like Cecropius and give him high command, shower him with undeserved wealth, but he would still smell of his origins, still stink of the animal pens.

'A thousand on the myrmillo.' Perhaps Sempronius had spoken too loudly. One or two heads turned in his direction. 'Give me old-fashioned Roman sword and shield any day. Courage close to the steel, that is true virtue, not tridents and nets, feints and subterfuge.' The peasant was looking back from his seat behind the emperor. Sempronius stopped talking.

The musicians started to play. *Thank the gods, further conversation was unnecessary.*

The gladiators made their way to the centre of the arena. The music swirled around the stands; the high piping of flutes and the blare of trumpets, underneath the deep notes of the water organ rolling like thunder.

The gladiators were not alone. Each had their trainer standing a little behind him. Further off was a figure clad all in black, carrying a hammer. His face was obscured by a mask. Horns sprouted from his headgear. Charon the ferryman was ready to take the dead across the Styx to Hades. The hammer was to make sure they were dead.

The music stopped. Suddenly it was very quiet, as if fifty thousand spectators were holding their breath. Far above, Sempronius heard the snap of a loose awning. From somewhere deep below the arena came the muffled roar of a lion.

A lone trumpet blew one clear note.

The myrmillo rushed forward. The lighter net fighter gave ground, circling away.

Now the crowd came alive – a solid wall of sound made of tens of thousands of cheers, shouts and imprecations.

The myrmillo gathered himself, then launched into another ungainly charge. Again, the retiarius avoided the rush with ease.

Sempronius had done his military service as a junior officer in a legion before entering the senate. Later, as a magistrate, he had commanded another legion. Both had been on the Danube, but in both postings the frontier had been quiet; in neither had he seen action. After his time as consul, he had governed the unarmed province of Asia. Yet, although he had never fought himself, he was an habitué of the arena. He knew what was happening out on the sand. The furious attacks of the myrmillo were a sign of fear, not confidence. The gladiator just wanted to get it over with, one way or another.

Soon enough it was as good as finished. The myrmillo made another hectic onslaught. His opponent sidestepped. As the heavier fighter blundered past, the retiarius entangled his sword arm with his weighted net. A savage jerk of the net, and the sword was yanked out of the grip of the myrmillo.

The heavier fighter still had his shield. Its metal boss could be punched into the face of an enemy. The myrmillo did nothing of the sort. He backed away.

The crowd began to boo and whistle.

The retiarius had recovered his net. He advanced cautiously, brandishing the trident in his other hand. Obviously he suspected a trap. Was his opponent not a veteran of more than twenty fights? There was no trap. It was as Cecropius had said – twenty fights or not – the myrmillo had lost his nerve.

A swirl of the net, a sudden wrench, and the myrmillo had lost his shield. He turned and ran.

Here and there the myrmillo dashed around the elliptical expanse of sand. His pursuer was leaner, unburdened by an enclosing, weighty helmet. There could be only one outcome. Occasionally the myrmillo tried to dart back to where his sword lay. The retiarius headed him off, turning him like a greyhound working a hare.

Now the crowd was stamping its feet, screaming. *Coward! Kill him! Finish the coward!* Cushions and coins were being hurled down at the fleeing gladiator.

A graceful flourish, and the net encompassed the myrmillo. He went crashing to the sand. For a few futile moments, he struggled to free himself. When the retiarius loomed over him, he stopped, and tugged off his helmet. He gazed up at the imperial box, and pushed a hand through the net, first finger extended. His mouth was moving, but amid the din, no one could hear what he was shouting.

Jugula! Jugula! The crowd was baying for blood.

All eyes were on the imperial box. Gallienus got to his feet, a little unsteadily.

Jugula! Jugula! The sound rose to a crescendo.

Gallienus extended his arm, fist closed, thumb horizontal.

Jugula! Jugula!

The emperor made the gesture of death.

Sempronius closed his eyes. A thousand sesterces lost. Much worse, a bad omen.

A howl of outrage made him look back at the arena.

The games were a training in the endurance of pain and death. A gladiator should exhibit that virtue. When condemned, he should kneel, and accept his fate with dignity.

The myrmillo, trapped in the net, was trying to crawl. Like an animal, he was scratching in the dirt for some illusory safety. Disconcerted – this was not how it was meant to be – the retiarius hovered above the fallen man.

Kill him! Open him up!

The retiarius stabbed down with the trident. It was not a good blow. The myrmillo was still alive. As he tried to crawl, the trident protruding from his back wagged like some obscene appendage. The retiarius went to pull out the weapon. It was stuck. The retiarius put a boot on the wounded man's shoulder. He heaved, but the trident would not come free. The prongs must be caught in the ribcage. Charon walked over. The black clad figure swung his hammer. It took three blows to the head before the myrmillo stopped moving.

Sempronius took out a handkerchief, dabbed at his forehead. Of course it was not an omen. A gladiator that he had backed had abandoned himself to fear. It meant nothing. A gladiator might have a bestial ferocity, but he lacked the true courage of a free man. A gladiator was not a senator. Self-control and courage – these were the virtues that marked a senator out from the herd. They were qualities instilled by education. Sempronius searched for examples from the past with which to fortify himself.

Good riddance to bad shit! The crowd jeered as the slaves inserted the hooks, began to drag out the corpse. A smear of blood was left in the sand.

Cato of Utica was an example to all senators. He had been only a boy when taken to see the dictator, Sulla. Seeing the severed heads of Sulla's enemies exhibited in the house, Cato had asked why no man could be found to assassinate so ruthless a tyrant. His tutor had replied that it would be suicide, as Sulla was always surrounded by bodyguards. Cato had asked for a sword. From then the tutor had kept the child away from the dictator. Sempronius decided that was not the example he needed now.

Slaves were spreading fresh sand, raking it smooth. Soon all trace of the dead gladiator would be effaced.

A story from the war against Hannibal came to Sempronius. At the battle of Cannae, a mortally wounded Roman was being stripped of his armour. His hands mangled and useless, the Roman used his teeth to tear off his assailant's nose. At the last moment of life, it was a consolation to avenge himself. Again, this example from the past failed to encourage Sempronius.

A new pair of famous gladiators were in the arena. They were the last scheduled to fight. Infernal gods, time was running out.

In the back of Sempronius' mind was a story of a Greek philosopher. On the rack, whips and burning could not make the philosopher reveal the names of those who had conspired with him to kill the tyrant. Instead, with his dying breath, the indomitable sage whispered the name of the most loyal friend of the tyrant. The latter had his friend executed. Thus the philosopher managed to get revenge after his own death.

It was only when the crowd roared for the fight's end that Sempronius was aware it had even started. Another corpse was being dragged out through the Gate of Death. Now the emperor would distribute gifts, and then he would leave. Sempronius looked at the crumpled handkerchief. It was purple, genuine Tyrian dye, one of a batch he had bought from a Syrian merchant. His wife had complained of the extravagance. Another hour, Sempronius thought, and such trivial expense would not be an issue – one way or another.

Trumpets blared.

A hidden trapdoor opened in the middle of the arena. An unarmed man stumbled out into the light. The opening shut behind him.

This was not on the programme.

A herald went to the front of the imperial box. The crowd fell silent. What unexpected entertainment was about to be presented?

'Citizens of Rome!' The herald had a powerful voice. The acoustics made it carry even to the women and slaves in the uppermost tiers. 'This man has practised deceit upon the sacred imperial family. The jewels he sold our noble empress were made of glass. For such terrible impiety, it is just that he be condemned to the beasts.'

The crowd murmured. This was an awful penalty for such a minor crime.

The man – stunned either by the transition from a dark cell to the open expanse of the arena, or by the terrible fate awaiting him – stood immobile.

With a theatrical crack, a trapdoor opened in front of him. The man backed away. Another door yawned behind him. He shuffled towards the far side of the arena. Again the ground opened before his feet. The man fell to his knees, held out his arms in supplication towards where the emperor sat.

The late afternoon breeze raised little eddies of sand. The man knelt. Nothing emerged from the three black holes in the gleaming sand. The Colosseum was very quiet.

There was a clanking of chains, loud in the silence. The sand in front of the man sank. The sound of pulleys. An enclosed cage rose into view.

No one spoke. Sempronius could hear the thud of his own heart.

Suddenly the door of the cage sprang open.

The condemned man covered his eyes with his hands.

A burst of laughter, swelling and echoing around the amphitheatre.

The man lowered his hands, and saw the capon strutting out on the sand.

The herald raised his staff. 'He practised deceit, and then had it practised upon him. By order of our gracious emperor, he is free to return home.'

The plebs roared their amusement.

Typical of Gallienus – pandering to the plebs, a levity totally unfitting for an emperor. Everything was out of season with Gallienus.

New wine throughout the year, melons in the depth of winter, sleeping chambers built of roses, women invited into the imperial council, gems on the soles of his boots, gold dust in his hair, armies commanded by shepherds and barbarians, senators ordered to bathe with hideous old hags and forced to thank him for his generosity. A pollution on the throne of the Caesars. Sempronius knew Gallienus had to die.

Gallienus rose to his feet.

Sempronius was half out of his seat. Cecropius caught his arm. 'Sit down, you fool,' the protector hissed. 'The gifts!'

The gifts – Sempronius had forgotten – Gallienus was not leaving, not yet. First he would amuse himself throwing tokens to the crowd. Gallienus loved to see them scrabble and fight for the little wooden balls that might entitle them to claim a fortune in gold or something like a cabbage.

'Just a little longer,' Cecropius whispered.

Gods below. Sempronius hated Cecropius, hated all the *protectores.* This very evening, once he was clad in the purple, the German Guard would take care of Cecropius and the rest. The only thing that bound Sempronius to the *protectores* was mutual hatred of Gallienus. Once the tyrant was dead, the link would be severed. Sempronius was ready.

And if he should fail, Sempronius would make sure that he died in the attempt. Out in the corridor, if the swords of the praetorians did not kill him, there was the ring with the poison. The torturers in the Palace cellars would not practice their terrible skills on him. The pincers and the claws would not tear his flesh.

Should he fail, he had taken what measures he could for his family. His wife was not the partner he had hoped, and young Quintus was nothing compared with his dead elder brother, yet Sempronius had no wish to drag them with him to ruin. This morning, after he had sacrificed to his household gods, Sempronius had written the letter in his own hand. It was signed and sealed. His secretary had instructions to deliver it to the Palace in the second hour of the night. Either the servant would find his own master on the throne, or he would hand it to Gallienus. In the letter Sempronius exonerated his family from any involvement; neither his wife nor his surviving son knew anything of what he had planned.

That was not all the letter contained. Of course there was no mention of the senators that Sempronius had approached. Acilius Glabrio and Nummius Faustinus would be safe with the army in Milan. But the full treachery of the *protectores* was exposed. It was the peasant that had inveigled Sempronius into treason. There were dates and places, careful corroborating details. The peasant was named, so too the ferret, mouse, and rider. Outside of Rome, even though Sempronius remained unsure of their involvement, he had named Aurelian, Tacitus and Heraclian in the conspiracy. They might be innocent, and their executions unjust, but their inclusion would cast suspicion on all the *protectores*. With luck, a revengeful emperor might abolish the loathsome office of *protector*. Those jumped-up soldiers who Gallienus did not kill would be cast back onto the dung heap.

Like the Greek philosopher, Sempronius would have vengeance after his own death.

CHAPTER 25

The Temple of Claudius

AT STREET LEVEL, THE Vicus Capitis Africae was deserted. The inhabitants were watching the battle between the barbarians and the City Watch from a safe height. They crowded the windows and balconies of the upper floors. A few were even peering down from the rooftops.

Ahead, at the foot of the street, Ballista saw the massive bulk of the Colosseum. It was so close now. The noise of the crowd boomed through the surrounding streets. Running, they could cover the distance in no time. But to approach the amphitheatre by this route, they would have to pass by the armoury and the training school for imperial slaves. They would enter the open space around the Colosseum between two of the gladiatorial schools. There was no cover that way, and the public buildings that close to the amphitheatre must be under observation by both the *frumentarii* and the City Watch. Fifty armed warriors at their back would have ensured safe passage. The case was different with just the three of them.

'Follow me!'

Where the Street of the African Head diverged, Ballista turned left into Scaurus Street. Maximus and Tarchon followed, blowing hard under the weight of their mailcoats. Together they pounded under the Caelimontana Gate, the sound of their boots echoing back. Scaurus Street led down to the Great Market. Far better to work their way through its maze of arcades, and the alleys of the tenements that abutted the rear of the Temple of Claudius. They would get to the Colosseum from the west, by the Sweating Post fountain.

The street ran steeply downhill. The Colosseum disappeared behind the Temple, and that in turn vanished behind the tall apartment blocks. The sun was out of sight behind buildings, but it was getting very low. The sky was pink with its setting. Still, not long now – a quarter of an hour, no more. Get to the Gate of Life at the west of the Colosseum, walk through the numbered corridors, ascend the stairs that led to the imperial box. Gallienus trusted him. All Ballista had to do was speak to the emperor, and this nightmare would be ended. He could rest – go home, embrace his wife and children, a bath, have his injuries dressed, a meal and a drink, and then sleep. Rest for a few days, and then take a ship to Sicily, and the peace of the villa high above the Bay of Naxos.

There were still shoppers making their way home from the Great Market. They all stopped and stared. *Allfather, of course they gawp.* How could Ballista have been so stupid? Two armed men pelting down the quiet, residential street, chasing after a man with a drawn sword, his tunic soaked in blood – anyone would stop and stare.

Before Ballista had time to consider what to do about his alarming appearance, things got much worse. The gods were unkind. Just ahead, coming out of market, was a squad of the City Watch. Eight of them, axes one shoulder, clubs resting on the other, buckets in hand – a routine patrol that was about to turn into high drama. The watchmen saw the three men.

'After them!' The centurion commanding the patrol shouted.

The watchmen hesitated, evidently unsure what to do with all the equipment that encumbered them.

'Drop the fucking kit! Swords out!' Centurions of the City Watch were promoted out of the praetorians. They were more experienced soldiers than the firemen they commanded.

Axes and buckets and clubs clattered to the ground. The watchmen hauled the coiled ropes off their shoulders, dragged out their blades.

'Lucius, you stay with the stuff,' shouted the centurion.

The delay had bought a little time.

'In here!' Ballista dived into an opening between two buildings to the right.

Wedged between the street and the podium of the temple, the tenements here were packed very close together. The alleyway was narrow. The damp brick walls on either side almost rubbed Ballista's shoulders. It turned left, then right. Other passages opened on either side. Ballista turned into one at random. It was narrower still.

The sun never penetrated down here. The air stank of mould and piss. Ballista took another turning to the right. Unable to see the sun or the horizon, he was lost already, unsure in which direction he was heading.

Rounding a corner, he blundered into a man leading a donkey. *What the fuck was he doing with a donkey here?* Shoving the beast aside, Ballista grabbed the man by the front of his tunic.

'How do we get out of here?'

Terrified, the man goggled at him.

'Which way is west?'

Still the man did not speak.

From somewhere in the labyrinth came the sound of hobnailed boots.

'How do we get to the west gate of the Colosseum?' Ballista patted the man like he would a horse. 'Get to the Sweating Post?'

Still incapable of speech, the man pointed back the way Ballista had come.

'Fuck,' Maximus said.

Maximus was right, the thud of boots was coming from that direction.

'Come on,' Ballista said. 'We'll work our way around them.'

They moved more cautiously now. At every turning and junction, they stopped to listen. The noises of pursuit seemed to come from all directions. Had the patrol split up, or was it some trick of the sounds travelling down the walls? Worse, had they been reinforced? There were a lot of shouts and footfalls.

'Only eight fuckers,' Tarchon said. 'Walking out easy, killing them on way.'

'No,' Maximus said. 'Down here.'

A local shopkeeper was pulling down his shutters. Seeing the men, he quickly locked them and rushed for the door. Maximus was too quick for him. The Hibernian got his shoulder to the door before it could be shut. As Ballista and Tarchon bundled after them into the shop, a woman screamed.

'Quiet now, mother,' Maximus said.

'Take what you want,' the shopkeeper stammered. 'Don't hurt us.'

'We won't be hurting you, and we won't be taking anything,' Maximus said.

The woman was sobbing.

'Much hurting, if not quiet,' Tarchon said.

Huddled in the corner, the woman was silently shaking.

Maximus shut the door. 'Don't mind old Tarchon. We are just after a little sit down. We will be on our way before you know it.'

The shop was tiny, little bigger than a cell. A ladder went up to a miniscule sleeping platform. The whole was barely lit by a clay lamp. The oil it burned was cheap. Its rancid smell mingled with that of old vegetables.

From outside came the tread of military boots.

'Quiet as a mouse now, my darlings,' Maximus whispered.

The hobnails were getting closer.

Ballista indicated for Maximus to keep an eye on the woman. He put his arm around the shoulders of the man. Tarchon stood on the other side.

The soldiers were right outside.

A silence in the room so profound, it was almost tangible.

The footsteps stopped.

They all started as the door rattled against its hinges.

'Open up, Numerius.'

The City Watch had the right to enter any property.

'Come on, you old bastard, we know you're in there.'

Ballista put his lips right against the shopkeeper's ear. 'Tell him you are busy.'

The man looked at him as if he was insane. He had a point – what on earth could he be doing in this tiny cell?

'Say you attending to conjugal duties,' Tarchon whispered.

Somehow the shopkeeper managed to stammer out that he was with his wife.

The fireman outside laughed. 'We can wait, won't take you long.'

'Fuck off!' The shopkeeper managed to sound convincingly annoyed.

'Numerius, listen – someone down the alley said three men were heading this way. Did you see anything?'

'No.'

'If you do, stay inside. They are dangerous bastards. One of them has already killed a watchman and several civilians since last night.'

'I'm not going anywhere.'

Perhaps, Ballista thought, the moralists were right – being a trader accustomed a man to mendacity.

As the tread of the City Watch receded, everyone exhaled at once.

'Give them a chance to move away,' Ballista said quietly, as much to himself as anyone.

In the gathering hush, Ballista's thoughts wandered of their own accord. Scarpio, Prefect of the Watch, and Rufinus, leader of the *frumentarii* – both were equestrians, both held important posts. But they could not hope to overthrow an emperor, and survive the attempt. No one would accept either on the throne. There had to be more important figures behind them; senior commanders, senators or equestrians of higher rank. Neither Scarpio or Rufinus were bald, neither looked like a peasant.

'We should be going,' Maximus said.

The woman was sobbing again.

'There is something I must do first,' Ballista said. 'Take off your clothes.'

'Never!' The woman's voice was edged with hysteria. She was close to breaking point.

'Not you,' Ballista said, 'your husband.'

'Bastards!' The woman leapt up. There was a knife in her hand. She slashed at Maximus. The Hibernian stepped back, rising on his toes, letting the blade pass close across his stomach, like a beast fighter working a bull in the arena. He punched her once, hard in the face. She crumpled to the floor, hands to her face.

Tarchon seized the man.

'Sure, I would never hit a woman.' Maximus stooped, collected the blade. 'But a woman with a knife, now that is a deadly weapon.'

Blood seeped out between the woman's fingers.

'That was unfortunate,' Ballista said to the shopkeeper. 'All I want is to wear your clothes.'

Tarchon released his grip. The man tugged off his tunic.

'Tend to your wife.' Ballista pulled off his bloodstained tunic, wriggled into that of the shopkeeper. It was unpleasantly warm, with an odour of stale sweat, and it was too tight.

'Tie them up, and gag them.'

Maximus and Tarchon cut up strips of sacking, and went about the tasks with brisk efficiency.

Before the gag was inserted in the man's mouth, Ballista asked him directions to the Sweating Post. They sounded simple enough – second left, third right, right again by the sign of the Dolphin Inn, and you could see the fountain beyond the western side of the Temple – time would tell.

'I am sorry for the intrusion, and for your wife's pain. My name is Marcus Clodius Ballista. By tomorrow you will hear one of two stories. Either you will have helped me to save the life of the emperor, or you will have given unwilling aid to a traitor. It all depends what the Fates have spun. If the former, come forward, and you will be rewarded; if the latter, keep very quiet.'

The alleyway outside was empty. The gloom of evening had descended already down here. Time was running out. Even so, the three men went slowly, stopping to listen. In the distance, dogs barked, children squealed. High on the roofs, gulls screamed.

Second left. They passed a few people. Ballista had wrapped his sword in a rag. Despite the other two sheathing their weapons, their mail coats earned a few inquisitive looks. Third right. Almost out of this maze of miniscule alleys.

'There they are!'

Immortality must be dull. The gods sport with humanity to lighten the boredom.

A squad of the City Watch clattering single file down the narrow passage after them.

'You go,' Tarchon said.

Ballista and Maximus hesitated.

'Three years waiting to pay debt. All good now.' Tarchon turned his back, his mailed shoulders nearly filling the alleyway. With a flourish, he unsheathed his sword.

The leading man of the Watch slowed down.

Tarchon slid the tip of his blade down the brickwork, a rasping sound of infinite menace.

The watchman stopped. He was taking great gulps of air, working himself up to fight.

'Go now,' Tarchon said over his shoulder. The demented Suanian looked blissfully happy. 'Tarchon see you later. Maybe in another life.'

CHAPTER 26

The Sweating Post

THE COLOSSEUM, AT LAST. The sheer scale of the building was overpowering – three levels of arches piled on top of each other, above them the fourth, where windows replaced arches, and, at the very top, almost out of sight, the spars and rigging which supported the awnings. There were tiny figures up there, like black insects against the liquid gold and pink of the sky. The sailors from the fleets at Misenum and Ravenna were stationed in Rome for their expertise with ropes and pulleys, block and tackle, their skills at spreading and furling recalcitrant sails. Now the sun was low, and the spectators no longer needed shade, they would be hauling in the vast expanses of brightly coloured canvass.

Ballista had a good head for heights, but the idea of working up there, unharnessed, one false movement spelling disaster, was appalling. How long would it take to fall? His gaze travelled back down the edifice. There were gilded shields between each of the windows, but there were statues in only some of the endless arches. Almost two centuries had passed since the amphitheatre was opened. Emperor after emperor had poured boundless money into repairs and renovations. Yet still the Colosseum was unfinished. There was a Christian story about some people in the east who had tried to build a tower that would reach the heavens. Their solitary god had decreed that it would never be completed.

To punish humanity for its temerity, he had cursed the races of man with innumerable different languages. Seemingly it had not struck the Christians that their deity had given the lie to his supposed omnipotence by underestimating his own creations' ability as linguists.

The Colosseum dominated this low-lying area of Rome. The Sweating Post, the fountain by which Ballista stood, was dwarfed. Even the enormous statue of Helios, the sun god, was overhadowed. The bulk of the Temple of Venus and Rome was made to look stunted and squat. What sort of empire constructed as its central, most iconic edifice a monument to killing as entertainment?

'All done,' Maximus said. Wherever you went in Rome there were children on the streets, urchins living by their wits, always on the lookout for a few coins. The Hibernian had hired two of them to take his mail coat and their swords home to the House of Volcatius in the district of the Brazen Gate. It had seemed unnatural and foolish to disarm themselves, but there was no hope of gaining admittance to the imperial box openly carrying blades, and to be apprehended with concealed weapons would be worse.

'Will they not steal them?'

Maximus shrugged. 'If we are alive tomorrow, we can buy some more.'

Ballista felt a stab of regret for Battle-Sun, the sword he had left at the Mausoleum. A blade like Battle-Sun was not so easily replaced. Forged at the dawn of time by the dwarves, it had been brandished by Wade the sea-giant. The hero Hama had won it, and gifted it to Helm, the founder of the line of the Kings of the Harii. From Helm it had passed through the ages down the dynasty, until Heoden had entrusted it to his foster-son Ballista. A sword such as Battle-Sun was not inanimate. It had a history, and a personality. It might be lost to Ballista, but Battle-Sun would not serve a man without heart and courage. Should such a one wield the blade, it would turn in his hand.

'So how do we get in?'

Maximus brought Ballista back.

Even this late in the day, entrance to the Colosseum was tightly controlled. Around the amphitheatre was a ring of barriers, wooden rails fixed to stone posts. Imperial slaves were stationed at all the openings. They were backed by squads of praetorians. There would be more guardsmen inside. Admission was free, but only for those with valid tickets. Ballista had thought that they could find a couple of spectators who were leaving early; offer them money for their tickets, or take them by intimidation. There had been a flaw in his plan. These Games were the emperor's farewell, before he departed to the north on campaign. Whatever faults he had, Gallienus was generous. None of his subjects would leave until the open-handed emperor had finished distributing gifts.

'Now, if you had thought to pluck out the eye of one of the men you have killed on the way here – Rufinus would have been good – we could have bought a peony plant and a little oil of lily, and we would have been fine.'

Ballista did not stop scanning the barriers. 'What on earth are you talking about?'

'The eye of an ape would have worked just as well. I am assured it is an infallible spell for invisibility.'

There were stalls outside the barrier selling food and drink. They were quiet now, but would find trade as the crowds left. That would be too late.

'Or you can take the eye of a night owl and a ball of dung rolled by a beetle and the oil of an unripe olive, grind them together, and smear the paste all over your naked body. Once you have said "BORKE PHOIOUR", no bugger can see you at all.'

'Hmm,' Ballista murmured. 'Did you talk to that magician I sent?'

'Indeed I did, fascinating man. When Tarchon and I were setting off to look for you, he recommended both methods – said we could be sneaking across the city and up to the Praetorian Camp, and no one would be any the wiser.'

'I see.'

'Actually, it would have been quite good – if we happened to have the eyes of an ape and all the other stuff – because then Tarchon would not have had to kill those guardsmen. Very good for them, anyway.'

'We should be moving, before the news of the Germans fighting the *frumentarii* gets here.' Ballista fished out the MILES ARCANUS badge he had taken from Rufinus. 'This might get me in. I want you to cause a distraction at those food stalls.'

Maximus turned to Ballista. All air of banter was gone from him. 'This may be the end. It has been a long road. I don't regret any of it.'

'Nor me.'

The two men embraced.

'Snow blowing from one tree to another,' Ballista said. 'Nothing to choose between us.'

Maximus stepped back. 'When we were up north, didn't your half-brother say that to you?'

'Yes.'

'Just before you killed him.'

'Some things just happen.'

Ballista watched his friend walk to a stall. Maximus picked up a sausage, sniffed it, exclaimed in disgust, and threw it on the ground. The stallholder shouted. Maximus took another sausage, and did the same. The outraged vendor went to grab him. Maximus punched him. The man fell over. Four of the eight praetorians at the nearest entrance rushed out to restore order. Ballista started walking.

Sometimes walking casually could be one of the hardest things in the world. No one else was going to the opening. The square was almost empty. Ballista felt very exposed. At least the attention of the remaining praetorians was concentrated on their colleagues.

'Halt!' The guardsman's armour was silvered and chased, the plume on his helmet a flamboyant crimson. Praetorians looked impressive, and they were accustomed to ordering civilians around. Yet put them up against a frontier legion, and, for all their martial swagger, they would run like rabbits. Even so, four guardsmen with swords could still take down a lone unarmed man.

'Ticket?'

The other praetorians had reached Maximus. There was angry shouting.

'No one gets in without a ticket.' The guardsman was not looking at Ballista. His eyes were on the altercation breaking out at the stall.

'I need to speak to Lucius Petronius Taurus Volusianus,' Ballista said.

Maximus had thrown another punch. One of the praetorians was reeling backwards.

'What?' The guardsman dragged his gaze back to Ballista.

'I need you to take me to the Praetorian Prefect.'

A full-scale brawl had started at the food stall.

The praetorian facing Ballista laughed. 'Do you know, baldy, I thought you said you wanted me to take you to see the Bull.'

'That is what I said.'

The other three glanced back from viewing the altercation. They were smirking as well.

'And you are aware that Volusianus is in the imperial box?'

'Yes, and you are to escort me there without delay.'

A shout of pain. Maximus had floored another guardsman.

The praetorian speaking to Ballista was torn between dealing with this impudent idiot, or going to help his friends. 'You think the Master of Admissions will let anyone into the sacred presence, let alone a rough looking northerner like you?'

The two guardsmen still on their feet at the stall were drawing their swords. The distraction was almost over. *Allfather, let Maximus give himself up, just take a beating. Death-blinder, do not let them kill him.*

Ballista produced the MILES ARCANUS badge. 'Take me to Volusianus now!'

The praetorian was nonplussed. He studied the identification. 'What is your name?'

'ARCANUS means secret,' Ballista said. 'I don't have all day.'

'How do I know this is real? You could have stolen it.'

'You will answer to your prefect and the emperor, if I am not escorted to the imperial box now!' Ballista put all the authority he could into his tone.

The praetorian looked at the other three. One of them shrugged. 'Best do as he says.'

'Are you armed?'

'No,' Ballista said.

'You will have to be searched.'

'Be quick about it. There is no time to lose.'

Out beyond the barrier, Maximus stood with his hands down by his sides. A praetorian hit him on the side of his head with his sword. Maximus went down. There was no blood. Thank the gods, the guardsman had used the flat of the blade.

The praetorians patted Ballista down roughly, with a bad grace. One of the few things they shared with the plebs of Rome was a loathing of the *frumentarii*.

By the food stall the guardsmen were laying into Maximus with their boots.

'Follow me.' Reluctantly, the praetorian led Ballista towards the amphitheatre.

Maximus was on the ground, curled up, his arms protecting his head. One of the guardsmen was still down. The other three ringed the Hibernian. Their boots thudded into his exposed back and legs. They were exerting themselves. *Do not let them kill him*, Ballista prayed. *Not him as well as Tarchon.*

The praetorian ushered Ballista in by the west gate, the one that led out onto the arena by the Gate of Life. Triumphant gladiators left the sand by that route; maybe it was a good omen. Yet now the combats were concluded the Gate of Life was shut, so perhaps not.

'Get a move on,' Ballista snapped. 'I said there was no time to waste.'

They crossed three of the corridors that ran around the inside of the huge edifice. At the fourth, they turned right. There was a strange, subaqueous quality to the light down here. In the torchlit gloom, the paintings on the walls seemed to shift. Drinking fountains rilled and splashed. The distant rumble of the crowd filtered down through the unimaginable weight of concrete and brick.

'Step up the pace,' Ballista chivvied his unwilling guide. To have come so far, got so close, and fail at the last moment would be unendurable.

After they had gone past ten, twelve or more passageways opening off the corridor, at last the praetorian turned into one of them. A broad flight of stairs, and they emerged into the stands. After the darkness, both stood blinking in the early evening light. The roar of the crowd hit them with an almost physical force.

When his eyes adjusted, Ballista saw the vertiginous tiers of spectators, the great empty expanse of the sand. The arena was in deep shadow. Ballista looked up at the sky. It was the deep purple of an old bruise. The last hour was nearly ended.

But there – not twenty paces distant – was the imperial box. And there, standing at the front, perfectly untroubled, his golden hair gleaming, was the emperor. Gallienus was alive.

Ballista pushed past the guardsman.

A centurion of the praetorians blocked his way.

'That is as far as you go,' the officer said.

CHAPTER 27

The Colosseum

'No one goes into the imperial box.' The centurion was adamant. His bulk blocked the way. There were four praetorians at his back.

'Let me talk to Caecilius,' Ballista said.

'The Master of Admissions is not seeing anyone.'

Ballista flourished the MILES ARCANUS badge. 'You know what I am.'

'I know what you are,' the centurion said. 'Scum – the sort that invents stories against honest men, betrays their fellow soldiers.'

This was going nowhere. Like everyone else, praetorians mistrusted the imperial spies. It was natural. The *frumentarii* might be soldiers, but they existed to betray, inform, and execute. Ballista would have to take a risk. 'There is a plot against the emperor.'

'Isn't there always? Go back to the Caelian, and tell it to Rufinus.'

The centurion was unmoved. Yet nothing in his demeanour had changed at the revelation. At least he had not heard of the death of the commander of the *frumentarii*. More importantly, surely the centurion was not part of the conspiracy.

'Listen carefully,' Ballista said. 'There is no time to go to the Caelian. The emperor will be attacked as he leaves the Colosseum.'

The centurion shrugged. 'Gallienus has the German guard in there. He will leave by the private passageway back to the Palatine.

The praetorians will escort him. The emperor will be safe enough without your help.'

Ballista leant close, spoke softly. 'And if he is not? Do you want to be the man responsible?'

For the first time, there was a trace of doubt on the centurion's face.

'If he is attacked, it will be your fault. If he lives or dies, what will happen to the centurion who failed to stop the attempt?'

The centurion shifted uncertainly.

'Just fetch Caecilius.'

The centurion stared at the vine stick of his office in his hands, as if he might find the answer there. 'What name?'

That was a revelation too far. The centurion must know there was an order to arrest Ballista. 'That is for Caecilius to know.'

The centurion snorted. 'You expect me to say to Caecilius that there is a rough man outside, barbarian by the look of him, demands to talk to the Master of Admissions, claims to be a *frumentarius*, but refuses to give his name?'

Ballista racked his brains for something that would identify him to Caecilius, but not betray him to these praetorians.

'Why don't you just fuck off, and leave the emperor's security to those who know what they're doing?' The centurion started to turn away.

'Wait!' Ballista grabbed his arm. 'Tell the Master of Admissions that the former owner of Demetrius the imperial secretary is outside. Tell him that I have information vital to the safety of the emperor.'

The centurion brushed off Ballista's hand. He looked off into the distance, weighing up the best course of action.

'You have nothing to lose,' Ballista said. 'A few moments of Caecilius's time. If he thinks it is wasted, you can take me into custody, let your men give me a beating. Do what you like. You will have done your duty.'

'Alright. Stay there, and don't move.' Turning to go, the centurion spoke to his men. 'Keep an eye on him.'

A roar from the crowd drew Ballista's attention to the sweep of the encircling stands. Liveried imperial servants stood at the top of each block of seats. They had leather satchels. When the emperor threw a handful of tokens, the servants did the same. It was the only way the gifts could be scattered among fifty thousand spectators.

The crowd jostled and scrambled to catch the hail of little wooden balls. Men pushed and shoved. Here and there scuffles broke out. Elbows and fists were used to secure a prize. Some said Gallienus enjoyed watching his subjects fight. Senators thought his behaviour demeaned the imperial dignity.

A hush fell. All eyes were on the imperial box. Gallienus raised his arms. He swayed a little. Pippa, his Alamann mistress, steadied him. Gallienus just laughed.

'Two tokens to go.' The emperor's voice carried well. He had made himself heard on parade ground and battlefield. Here it was slightly slurred. 'From our boundless generosity, the holders of this one can claim' – Gallienus paused for effect – 'a dead dog!'

The crowd groaned and laughed. They pelted each other with the worthless tokens. Senators might frown, but the plebs adored this rough humour. A pound of lead or a pound of gold – you could never tell what you might get.

Gallienus raised a huge flagon of wine. Unsteadily, he whirled the pitcher, and sloshed out a libation. The wine went every-where, spattering the snowy-white togas of the good and the great seated around the emperor. The plebs howled their approval. There was nothing they liked better than seeing their betters humiliated. Nothing except, perhaps, gold – and that might still be coming.

The emperor drained the flagon in one. Again the crowd cheered. As he went to put it down, he almost overbalanced. The emperor was very drunk.

Was Gallienus worth saving? Ballista looked at the reeling figure, at the emperor's inebriated grin and dyed hair. *A king is a king because he has virtue. If he chooses vice, he becomes a tyrant.* Was Gallienus still fit to rule the empire? He had always been changeable. With him, everything was out of season: green figs in the depths of winter, gemstones on the soles of his boots, the senate treated like servants, buffoons and prostitutes as honoured companions. Now – while pretenders were dismembering the empire – he squandered money on colossal statues and porticos, founded cities of philosophers in remote mountain valleys. Was it true he reclined at banquets dressed as a woman?

True or not, none of it could make any difference to Ballista. He had sworn an oath to the emperor. Gallienus was his friend. Ballista owed Gallienus his life. More important – far more important – if Gallienus died, so did Ballista's family. To save his Julia and his sons, Gallienus must live.

'The one but last token,' Gallienus shouted.

Infernal gods, where were Caecilius and that centurion? One more gift, and Gallienus would leave. The last hour had almost run its course.

'Ten pounds of silver!'

The throng bellowed its delight. Gallienus was so close. Ballista could shout, but he would never make himself heard over the pandemonium. One last effort. Desperately, Ballista readied himself, measured the distances, planned his moves: rush the four praetorians, take them by surprise, knock them aside, then a few steps, ignore the door – there may be guards on the other side – leap for the railing, swing himself into the imperial box, and scramble over the seats, before the German guard at the rear could get to the emperor. All it would take was a few words.

'Is that you?' The Master of Admissions was peering at the battered, shaven-headed figure.

'Caecilius.'

'Ballista?' The functionary was puzzled. 'Have you shaved your head?'

'What?' The centurion started. 'Ballista, you say? Guards, arrest this man!'

'Not now!' Caecilius waved the centurion away. 'What has happened?'

Ballista knew this was the final roll of the dice. There was no more time for subterfuge. If the Master of Admissions had joined the conspirators, it was over.

'Gallienus will be assassinated as he leaves the Colosseum. Scarpio of the City Watch is part of the plot, so was Rufinus of the *frumentarii*. There are others, at least two. I don't know who they are.'

'You are certain?'

'I could not be more certain.'

'You had better come with me.' Caecilius gestured to the centurion. 'Bring your men.'

'No,' Ballista said. 'Trust no one but the German Guard. They will keep their sword-oath.'

The Master of Admissions hesitated, then made a decision. 'Centurion, stay here. Let no one else into the sacred presence. Gallienus departs after the final throw. We have only moments.'

'Marcus Clodius Ballista!'

As he was announced, Ballista saw every head turn towards him. The emperor looked over, eyes a trifle unfocused. Gallienus smiled.

'My old school friend, you have missed all the presents.' A look of utter bewilderment crossed the emperor's face. 'Your lovely hair!'

A senator jumped to his feet. He was portly, bald as a baby. He blundered towards the front of the box.

Ballista shoved Caecilius out of the way.

'Guards! Stop him! Guards!' No one was moving, but everyone was shouting at once.

Ballista pushed aside two seated senators.

The Germans were rushing down from the back of the box. 'Protect the emperor!' Ballista heard Freki, their commander, shouting.

Ballista hurdled a row of seats.

'Protect the emperor! Then capture them both alive!'

The senator had a blade.

Ballista dived, caught the senator around the thighs. Together they crashed onto the unforgiving marble floor. Entangled, they rolled against the side wall. Ballista cracked his head. His vision swam. The senator was on top of Ballista. His weight was crushing. One of Ballista's arms was trapped under his own body.

'Two bald men fighting.' Ballista heard Gallienus giggle. The deadly seriousness had not penetrated through the fog of drink.

A flash of steel. Someone was screaming. The knife jabbing down. With his free hand, Ballista caught the senator's wrist. The tip of the blade a handbreadth from his eye.

The sound of heavy footfalls. Two sets of boots at the edge of Ballista's vision. A voice of command ordering the Germans back.

The senator grunted, thrust down again, all his weight behind the blow. Ballista could not hold him. He twisted his head aside. The knife sliced past his ear, gouged into the marble.

Scarpio was standing over them. The point of his sword wavered as he sought an opening.

The senator reared up, ready to strike again. Ballista got his other arm free, grabbed his assailant's wrist with both hands.

Scarpio shifted his stance.

Ballista's arms were trembling with the effort. The knife was descending, inexorable. If that did not kill him, Scarpio would.

Scarpio was bundled to one side.

The thwack of a sword striking. Ballista felt the impact through the body pinioning him. The senator jerked back. The knife fell from his hand.

Out of sight, the sound of boots running.

Kneeling now, the senator was tugging at a ring on his finger.

'No need, Sempronius,' the Praetorian Prefect said.

'Don't kill him!' Ballista croaked.

Too late. Volusianus' blade took off the top of the senator's skull.

The dead weight toppled sideways.

The ruddy face of Volusianus loomed over Ballista. He reached down, gripped a hand, and helped Ballista to his feet. The floor was slick with blood. Gallienus was covered by a wall of overlapping German shields.

Ballista fought to get breath back into his crushed chest. 'Scarpio, where is he?'

'Hades!' The Praetorian Prefect looked around wildly. 'The little bastard must have scuttled off down the passage to the Palatine. No matter, I will get my men from outside. They will hunt him down soon enough.'

'No time.' Ballista staggered towards the curtain that screened the tunnel. 'Tell them to follow. We must take him alive.'

The passageway was broad, tall and vaulted. Its painted walls were lit by scented lamps. The gods forbid that an emperor should ever have to set foot anywhere squalid.

The weight of the senator had come down on Ballista's injured ribs. Each breath brought a white hot pain. Clutching his chest, Ballista ran as best he could.

It was said the tunnel had been built so the Emperor Commodus could walk untroubled from the Palace to the arena. Commodus had been obsessed by the Games.

From somewhere ahead echoed a shout, and the sound of something breaking. Ignoring the agony, Ballista ran faster.

Around a corner, two slaves were looking disconsolately at a broken jar of oil. A pool of liquid was spreading across the flagstones.

'He just came out of nowhere,' one said. 'It wasn't our fault.'

Ballista's ribs hurt too much to talk. Avoiding the oil, he ran past.

Another turning, and the tunnel branched in two. Of course, in his insanity, Commodus had fought as a gladiator. The narrower passage must run down to the cells under the floor of the arena. Which way would Scarpio have gone? The Palace offered a better hope of escape than the substructures of the Colosseum. By their nature – the need to contain wild beasts, and condemned criminals – the exits from the latter would be heavily guarded. Ballista staggered on. Now the ankle he had twisted was hurting. He was nearly finished, only willpower keeping him moving.

Yet another corner – this place was like something out of a myth – and the passage began to slope upwards. A slave was lighting the lamps, ready for the imperial party.

'Has a man been this way?'

The slave did not reply.

'Just now – a man running?'

The slave just stared at the blood-soaked apparition.

'Answer!'

'No, master.'

Through panic or cunning, Scarpio must have gone down under the Colosseum. Ballista turned back.

As he took the path that led down to the cells, Ballista heard the rattle of armed men coming down from the imperial box.

Pain was an irrelevance. So all the Stoics claimed. Each breath burning, Ballista disagreed. Pain had its own existence. Its insidious voice was in his head: just stop, let others catch him, Scarpio is nothing to you. Ballista knew that he had to go on. Only he could finish this.

Guttering torches lit the underworld. The black mouths of cages, iron-barred, were set in the outer wall. The air was thick with the odour of animal droppings, urine-soaked straw, the fetid stench of rotten meat. The roar of a lion made him start. It seemed to resound inside his chest.

Animal keepers were going about their tasks, putting things away, bedding everything down after the show. Ballista gazed up and down the curved corridor. There! Off to the right, four slaves not working, just standing, all looking at something. A glimpse of movement. A man dashing through one of the tall, thin openings into the next corridor.

Ballista ran through the nearest opening. There he was again. Scarpio vanished through an arch in the next wall. The corridors ran in concentric circles, arches opened in towards the centre. On every side were pulleys operating the lifts and ramps that brought men and beasts to the surface of the arena.

Three, perhaps four more corridors, and Ballista came out into the central aisle. Scarpio was nowhere in sight. At the eastern end was the tunnel that ran underground to the Great School of the gladiators. Its doors were bolted. Not that way. *Allfather, where had Scarpio gone?* Taking as deep a breath as he could, Ballista limped to the other side.

Scarpio was not in the next corridor. Some atavistic instinct, the feeling a hunter has for his prey, made Ballista stop. He knew Scarpio was behind him. Ballista retraced his steps.

Back in the central aisle, Ballista heard the praetorians who had followed him down. Only glimpses of them, but the sounds of their beating through the area were loud. The chink of metal armour. Staccato commands: *Keep the line! Don't let him slip through! He is armed, take no chances! Kill him on sight!*

Another sound. Discordant at this time. The clank-clank of a pulley being turned feverishly. Away to Ballista's left. The games were over. Nothing needed to go to the surface. Ballista started running. *Gods*, the pain in his chest.

A thump as a ramp came down. A waft of fresh air. Daylight around the next pillar.

The ramp stretched up to the sand. Boots thundered on the boards. Ballista saw the boots, the pounding legs. He ran up after them.

Ballista had never stood in the arena. For a moment he felt light headed. In the last light of the day, the smooth sand seemed almost infinite. Then he registered the great curve of the stands, wrapping around, drawing the eye. The sheer impossibility of escape.

A small, solitary figure was running towards the perimeter, black in the shadows, like a rodent seeking its hole. Ballista walked now. If he kept between Scarpio and the open ramp, there was nowhere the fugitive could go.

The fleeing man stopped. Ballista could see him looking up at the net. With its rollers and spikes, it could not be climbed.

A murmur, like surf on a shore. The spectators had not yet left. They gazed down in their thousands, wondering what last entertainment the day held.

'It is over,' Ballista said.

Scarpio turned.

'Give yourself up.'

'To the mercies of the pincers and the claws in the Palace cellars?'

'Name your accomplices, and you might be spared.'

Scarpio spat on the sand. 'You don't believe that any more than I do.'

'Gallienus is merciful.'

'To a barbarian like you, maybe. To honourable Romans he is nothing but a tyrant.'

Scarpio started to walk towards Ballista. The prefect still held the sword. Ballista stood still, and waited.

'I will fall on my sword. Death is nothing; a return to peace and sleep.' Scarpio swung the blade, as if trying it out for the first time, unaccustomed to its balance and weight. 'But I will have company as I go down into the darkness.'

'Why?' Ballista glanced over his shoulder.

The mouth of the ramp was empty. No sign of the praetorians.

'It is your fault.' Scarpio sounded insanely composed, as if discussing a point of logic in the philosophical schools. 'You corrupted Gallienus.'

'My fault? It must be ten years since I was last at court.'

Still no one on the ramp.

'Your sort.' Scarpio had stopped, Ballista almost within reach of his sword.

'My sort?'

How much longer could the praetorians take? Ballista had to keep him talking.

'Savage, irrational barbarians – beasts with voices. You should be on the slave blocks. Why else does Gallienus drink and whore, grovel to the applause of the plebs? You, that barbarian bitch defiling the imperial box. Gallienus panders to you, while honest

Romans are treated with contempt, reduced to waiting at the back, hoping for the leftover crumbs.'

The philosophic calm had gone. Scarpio was working himself into a fury of outrage. The attack would come at any moment.

'You, Gallienus praises; me – a loyal officer – he does not even notice.'

They were too close now for Ballista to look back. Still there was no sound from the ramp. What was keeping the praetorians?'

'I might have failed to kill Gallienus, but I will take you with me.'

Scarpio took a step, and slashed two handed with the sword. The initial movement gave Ballista warning. He leapt back, hollowing his body, letting the steel arc across in front of his belly. Scarpio cut backhanded. Again Ballista retreated, feet close together, balanced, ready to move in any direction.

Scarpio staggered a couple of paces forward, regaining his stability. *Not yet*, Ballista thought. *Watch the steel, wait for the opportunity, get in close, grapple him to the ground.* Watch the steel: all Ballista's being was concentrated on the sword.

'Aren't you going to beg, barbarian? *Please, master, don't hurt me.'*

Ballista said nothing. Scarpio talking was good. It ate up time.

'*A slave should not wait for his master's hand.* Get down on your knees and grovel.'

'Why?' Ballista spread his arms wide, inviting a blow. 'You haven't touched me yet.'

The provocation was too much. Scarpio lunged, the sword straight out. Ballista sidestepped. Blocking the blow forearm to forearm, he went forward, driving the heel of his hand into Scarpio's chin. His assailant's head snapped back, but he did not drop the sword. With his free arm, Scarpio grabbed Ballista around the neck. They grappled, staggering this way and that, like brawling drunkards.

A high pitched whine of ropes being run out too fast, and an echoing boom like a door opening in a cavernous building.

Ballista had both hands on Scarpio's sword arm. The fingers of Scarpio's other hand were scratching at his face, hooking towards his eyes.

A deep rumbling, like an avalanche; it reverberated deep inside Ballista's body. Both men stopped struggling. They stood, in an awkward embrace. Scarpio whimpered. Ballista turned his head, and saw why.

At the top of a second open ramp stood a lion. He was a male, big, heavy-shouldered. His great yellow eyes, blank yet cunning, regarded them. The lion was not young, perhaps past his prime. Most likely he was some old favourite of the crowd. That was bad. The beast was a man-killer, long versed in the ways of the arena.

Gently, Ballista disengaged himself from Scarpio.

The lion padded forward, then halted and roared again. The crowd roared back. The beast preened, as if accustomed to the applause.

'Dear gods, no!' Scarpio whispered.

The lion was to the left. The other ramp lay to the right. It was twenty or more paces – too far. Now a line of praetorians, armoured, shields locked, stood in its opening. They were not moving.

'Give me the sword,' Ballista said.

'No!' Scarpio was trembling like a leaf in a high wind.

The lion watched them, taking its time, confident in its prey. Ballista could smell its feral stench, the foulness of its breath.

'Don't move. Give me the sword!'

'No!' Scarpio screamed.

At the sound the lion tensed, its muscles twitching with pleasurable memory.

More praetorians had appeared, behind the lion, shoulder to shoulder across the entrance to the ramp through which it had emerged.

Without warning, Scarpio started to run. He careered off towards the right.

The lion gathered itself, then accelerated faster than seemed possible for such a hefty animal. Scarpio threw away the sword. His racing feet raised puffs of sand. The lion knocked him to the ground with its momentum. Scarpio went sprawling. In one fluid motion, the lion rolled back to its feet, spun around, and was on him. It pinned him with its weight and wide-spread, razor sharp claws.

Slowly, with no sudden movements, Ballista started to sidle away towards the left hand ramp.

Scarpio was thrashing and screaming, ineffectually trying to fend off the lion.

Eyes fixed on the horrible sight, Ballista edged around. Neither line of praetorians was venturing out onto the arena.

Delicately, almost tenderly, the lion sank its long, yellow teeth into the man's windpipe. Scrapio stopped screaming. His body arched, then lay still.

The lion looked up, its muzzle bloody. The yellow eyes studied the man still standing. Ballista stood stock still. What bestial calculations flickered inside that great skull? Heartbeat after heartbeat, Ballista stared back at the inhuman eyes.

An eternity of fear, and then the tongue lolled out, and lapped the warm blood. The lion settled to its feeding.

Softly, softly, Ballista walked backwards.

As the shields of the praetorians parted, all he could hear was the ghastly crunching of bones.

EPILOGUE

The Milvian Bridge
The Ides of April

When they reached the Milvian Bridge, Ballista pulled his horse out of the column, and looked back at the city. From here he could still see the Temple of Jupiter Optimus Maximus on the Capitoline, and the roofs of the imperial residences on the Palatine. Off to the right, its bulk diminished by the distance, stood the Mausoleum of Hadrian. It had all started there, at the last hour of light, fourteen days before.

Ballista had been feted. He was an acclaimed hero. The emperor had taken him out onto the balcony of the Palace, praised him to the assembled crowds. When Gallienus crossed the Alps, Ballista was commanded to be at his side, an honoured travelling companion. Henceforth Marcus Clodius Ballista would be numbered among the *protectores*. For the rest of his life it was his privilege to be armed in the imperial presence.

Ballista rested his hand on the hilt of Battle-Sun. The blade indeed had its own nature. It had remained hidden in the Mausoleum until Ballista had returned. Battle-Sun would not serve the unworthy. Almost as miraculous, despite vigorous questioning, the old Tiber fisherman had managed to keep the gold ring from the City Watch. Ballista had rewarded him well for its return, enduring another lengthy diatribe against immigrants, and their iniquitous influences.

Volusianus also had been celebrated as a hero by the emperor. Together, exhibiting no concern for their own safety, the Praetorian Prefect and Ballista had killed the assassins in the Colosseum. Volusianus had been given charge of the investigation to lay bare the ramifications of the conspiracy, and stamp out the embers of treason. The Praetorian Prefect personally had led the search of the mansion of Sempronius. His statement had told how the son and secretary of the senator had been apprehended destroying incriminating documents. Both men had been killed resisting arrest. Unfortunately the documents were so burnt that nothing of their content could be recovered. No other conspirators had been unearthed. The plotters were judged not to have spread their net far.

Ballista had his doubts. Sempronius and his son; Rufinus, Commander of the *frumentarii*; and Scarpio, Prefect of the City Watch. Just four men. Two senators and two equestrians, the latter not of the highest rank. It was not enough to hope to overthrow an emperor, and survive. The trade of Rufinus had been subterfuge and treachery. He had been meant to report to the Praetorian Prefect, but he would have been well versed in covering his tracks. But it was hard to believe that Scarpio could have remained undetected without his actions being shielded by more powerful figures.

And there were the words of the unknown conspirator to Sempronius reported by the dying man in the Mausoleum. *Strike quickly. Do not be afraid. The guards will not stop you. Remember we will all be there.* Apart from Sempronius, of the known plotters, only Scarpio had been in the imperial box. *All* implied more than one, *we* that the speaker would be present.

Then there were the descriptions that the mortally wounded man had given. Two men, both old, one bald, the other looking like a peasant. There was no doubting that the bald assassin had been

Sempronius. But the other man? Neither Rufinus or Scarpio in any way resembled a farm worker. Ballista had no idea what the son of Sempronius had looked like, but he had been in his twenties.

'Your hair is beginning to grow back.'

Ballista looked over at the speaker. Maximus was battered, but alive. That was all that mattered. Tarchon was in a worse state. He had lost two fingers from his right hand. Tarchon was tough. Already he was training himself to use a weapon with the other hand. Thank the gods, all Ballista's *familia* had survived.

The thought of his family caused a rush of mixed emotions. The reunion with his wife and sons had been blissful. Julia had been her old self. The distance between them had disappeared. His younger son had the uncomplicated happiness of the innocent. The older was of an age to comprehend the danger they had escaped. A few days of unalloyed happiness, and then the parting.

Ballista's eldest son, Isangrim, was to be educated at the imperial school on the Palatine. Ballista had requested the boy stay with him. Gallienus had been adamant. The order was framed as an honour, but Isangrim was as much a hostage as his father had been all those years before.

Ballista had sent his wife and younger son back to Sicily. It was a peaceful province, far from the borders, free from unrest. Grim the Lame, the Heathobard warrior, was with them. They would be safe. Decimus, Julia's cousin, had accompanied them to the villa to recuperate from his torture. He seemed not to blame Ballista for giving him the message that had caused his suffering at the hands of the *frumentarii*. The young man had a forgiving nature.

Ballista would have given anything to be travelling with them. That was the problem with being the hero that had saved the life of the emperor. You became a living symbol of loyalty, a man whose example was to be paraded. You were not allowed to retire into quiet obscurity. While the *familia* went by easy stages to Sicily, Ballista was bound for the war in the North.

'Someone coming,' Maximus said.

The long lines of infantry were shuffling to the side of the road, moving out of the way of a cavalcade headed by a man in resplendent armour.

'Hail, Marcus Clodius Ballista, *Protector!*'

Volusianus's voice boomed over the din, as it had all those years before on the battlefield at Spoletium. It was a voice of command, of a man risen from the ranks.

'Hail, Lucius Petronius Taurus Volusianus, *Protector!*'

The Praetorian Prefect reined in, every movement vigorous despite his age.

'Hail, Ballista *Protector!*' The voice was unchanged. Ballista had heard it recently, in very different circumstances – echoing up the corridor of an imperial sepulchre. Surely not, loyal Volusianus?

'A long march ahead, Ballista.' Volusianus smiled, his wide, bucolic face shining like the sun. 'There is a long way to go.'

THE LAST HOUR

Afterword

Playing with History

The Last Hour is a novel. While I have made every effort to make it true to history, on a few occasions I have altered the topography of Rome to fit the story.

Should someone have jumped from the **Mausoleum of Hadrian** in reality, the outcome would have been no better than it was for Tosca in Puccini's Opera.

The first Emperor Augustus laid out the **northern Campus Martius** as a stately pleasure park for the people of Rome. By the third century AD the area seems to have been built over, although in this novel it remains *rus in urbe*.

The **Via Fornicata** was somewhere in the Campus Martius, and not in the *subura*. We know the names of few streets in ancient Rome, and this one, with its agreeable potential for modern misreading, was too good not to use.

The Built Environment of Rome

Once in a while a book changes the way history is studied. Paul Zanker, *The Power of Images in the Age of Augustus* (Eng. tr., Ann Arbor, 1988), put the built environment at the heart of political, social and cultural history of ancient Rome.

Imagining the ancient city, while walking the modern, the best books to have in hand are F. Coarelli, *Rome and Environs: An Archaeological Guide* (Eng. Tr., Berkeley, Los Angeles, and London,

2007), and A. Claridge, *Rome: An Oxford Archaeological Guide* (2nd ed., 2010).

At home or in the library, L. Richardson, *A New Topographical Dictionary of Ancient Rome* (Baltimore, and London, 1992), is invaluable.

Literary sources are collected by D. R. Dudley, *URBS ROMA* (Aberdeen, 1967), and P. J. Aicher, *Rome Alive* (Mundelein, 2010).

An excellent overview is S. L. Dyson, *Rome: A Living Portrait of an Ancient City* (Baltimore, 2010).

The *Plebs Urbana*

The depiction of non-elite life is underpinned by three superb, and very different books: Z. Yavetz, *Plebs and Princeps* (2nd ed., New Brunswick, and Oxford, 1988); N. Horsfall, *The Culture of the Roman Plebs* (London, 2003); and J. Toner, *Popular Culture in Ancient Rome* (Cambridge, and Malden, MA, 2009).

The Background History

The most authoritative survey is Volume XII of *The Cambridge Ancient History: The Crisis of Empire, AD 193–337* (2nd ed., Cambridge, 2005), edited by A. K. Bowman, P. Garnsey, and A. Cameron. More accessible is D. S. Potter, *The Roman Empire at Bay AD 180–395* (London, and New York, 2004). Briefer, thematic overviews are provided by O. Hekster, *Rome and its Empire, AD 193–284* (Edinburgh, 2008), and C. Ando, *Imperial Rome AD 193 to 284* (Edinburgh, 2012).

The City Watch and Other Military Units in Rome

The standard work on the City Watch remains P. K. Baillie Reynolds, *The Vigiles of Imperial Rome* (Oxford, 1926). All military units quartered in the city are covered in J. Coulston, "'Armed and belted men": the soldiery in imperial Rome', in J. Coulston, and

H. Dodge (eds.), *Ancient Rome: The Archaeology of the Eternal City* (Oxford, 2000), pp. 76–118. In this novel the Urban Cohorts and the *Equites Singulares* are written out to avoid overburdening the reader with a confusion of military units.

The Colosseum and Gladiators

The best introduction, both wide ranging and exciting, is *The Colosseum* (London, 2005) by Keith Hopkins and Mary Beard.

Other interesting studies are T. Wiedemann, *Emperors and Gladiators* (London, and New York, 1992), and D. G. Kyle, *Spectacles of Death in Ancient Rome* (London, and New York, 1998).

The hideous theatrical executions in the arena are analysed by K. M. Coleman, 'Fatal Charades: Roman executions staged as mythological enactments', *Journal of Roman Studies* 80 (1990), pp. 44–73.

Slaves

In this novel, more than in any previous one, I have tried to explore Roman slavery.

The most imaginative way into the subject is *How to Manage your Slaves* by Jerry Toner (London, 2014); a work of profound scholarship lightly worn, as it straddles the line between fiction and history.

Much evidence is collected in T. E. J. Wiedemann, *Greek and Roman Slavery* (London, 1981).

Keith Hopkins, 'Novel evidence for Roman slavery', *Past & Present* 138 (1993), pp. 3–27, is a dazzling attempt to recover the thought world of ancient slaves.

Quotes and Sources

The prayers of the Pythagorean in Ch. 14 are taken from *The Life of Apollonius of Tyana* by Philostratus.

In Ch. 14 the interpretations of dreams of crucifixion can be found in Artemidorus, *Oneirocritica*, translated by R. J. White (1992).

Gnaeus' jokes in Ch. 16 are adapted from the translation of *Philogelos*, 'Laughter lover', by D. Crompton (London, 2010).

The debate on heterosexual versus homosexual love in Ch. 17 might strike a modern reader as artificial, or even unlikely, but it is abridged and only lightly altered from the *Erotes* of (Ps-)Lucian.

Unsurprisingly, Ballista's views in Ch. 18 on the symbolism of philosophical garb bear a close resemblance to the arguments of H. Sidebottom, 'Philostratus and the symbolic roles of the sophist and philosopher', in E. Bowie, and J. Elsner (eds.), *Philostratus* (Cambridge, 2009). The same is true of the political philosophy expounded in that chapter and analysed in H. Sidebottom, 'Dio Chrysostom and the development of *On Kingship* literature', in D. Spencer, and E. Theodorakopoulos (eds.), *Advice and its Rhetoric in Greece and Rome* (Bari, 2006).

Other Novels

All my novels include a couple of homages to other writers.

Setting out on a thriller, it seemed wise to learn from the best.

The classic *Rogue Male* (London, 1939), by Geoffrey Household, showed how to structure a chase, and provided an example of field craft.

Lee Child, *Personal* (London, 2014), was the inspiration for a specific fighting technique, and much more besides.

ACKNOWLEDGEMENTS

Writing a novel is often imagined as a solitary pursuit. For me it would never be managed without help and support.

I could not hope for more sympatico or critical readers than my new editor, Kate Parkin, or my literary agent, James Gill.

As ever, many thanks are due to various other friends: in Oxfordshire, Maria Stamatopoulou, Peter Cosgrove, Jeremy Tinton, and Kate and Jeremy Habberley; in Suffolk, Michael Dunne and Jack Ringer.

The greatest debt is to my family: my wife Lisa, my sons Tom and Jack, my mother Frances, and my aunt Terry. This novel is dedicated to the latter.

Dear Reader,

Thank you very much for reading *The Last Hour* – I hope you enjoyed it as much as I enjoyed writing it. Unusually for me, the opening came to me fully formed in one image: Ballista, the hero, standing alone on top of the Mausoleum of Hadrian, the sun setting behind him, the river Tiber far below his feet, the city spread out beyond the far bank and the bad guys coming up the stairs. And I suddenly saw what it was all about: Ballista has until the last hour of light the next day to get across Rome and save the Emperor and his own family. Jack Bauer in *24*, if you like, but set in ancient Rome.

The challenge I set myself was to write a thriller, a story with relentless menace, punctuated by bursts of violent action, a story that in modern-day terms would appeal to readers who love Lee Child or Michael Connolly. At the same time I wanted to paint an authentic and atmospheric portrait of the city of ancient Rome, taking in all its grandeur and squalor, summoning up its sights and sounds and smells, recreating the rhythm of its streets, and viewing its inhabitants from the grandest Senator to the lowest dweller in the slums of the Subura. If you've got this far, then I'm hoping I pulled it off!

The plot of *The Last Hour* with its tight twenty-four hour timeline, its focus on one main character, the relentless pace and the ticking clock (or hourglass . . .) instilled a new sort of discipline for me. Yet telling the story this way also comes with a responsibility. Historical novelists are the gatekeepers of history. We have a duty to get things right. And despite the 'modern' plot, as much research went into this novel as any of the historical works that I have published in the almost twenty years that I have taught at the University of Oxford.

If you enjoyed *The Last Hour*, please do look out for my next novel, which will be out in 2019. As yet untitled, it will follow a misaligned group of Roman cavalry who find themselves on what appears to be a suicide mission, cut off hundreds of miles behind enemy lines. There will be action, heroism, betrayal, twists and turns – in fact I'm thinking it will be *Bravo Two Zero* meets *Gladiator* . . .

If you would like to hear more from me about this and my other future books, you can get in touch with me at www.bit.ly/ HarrySidebottom where you can join the HARRY SIDEBOTTOM READERS' CLUB. It only takes a few minutes, there is no catch and new members will automatically receive an exclusive e-book short story. Your data is private and confidential and will never be passed on to a third party, and I promise that I will only be in touch now and again with book news. If you want to unsubscribe, you can of course do that at any time.

I'm always grateful, however, for readers who spread the word. If you have enjoyed *The Last Hour*, I would love you to leave a review on Amazon, on GoodReads, on any other e-store, on your own blogs and social media accounts – or even tell another human being directly! You'll help other readers if you share your thoughts, and you'll help me too: I love hearing what people think about my books – and I always read any comments.

But for now, thank you again for following Ballista on his mad dash across Rome in *The Last Hour* – I'm glad you came along for the ride.

Best wishes,

Harry